Blood Reunion

Turn Three of the Hybrid Helix

JCM Berne

ISBN-13:
Ebook: 978-1-7349170-6-2
Paperback: 978-1-7349170-7-9
Hardcover: 978-1-7349170-8-6

Cover graphics by Jake Caleb

Cover image by Chris McGrath

Acknowledgments

I have more people to thank than I can easily count, starting with my wife, Moneeka, without whose support none of the rest of this would have happened.

My alpha reading group: Allison, Pauline, John, Andrew, Jonathan, and Bradley, who contributed immeasurably to early drafts.

My editor, Lauren Donovan of The Book Foundry, who (gently) pushed me to make changes that really needed to be made. Chris McGrath, cover artist extraordinaire, whose work inspired me, along with Stephanie Yang who reminded me how important good graphic design really is, and who tirelessly helped me make choices I am ill-equipped to make.

Jordan, Andrew, Craig, Boe, A.R., and Kayla, who brought me the thing I couldn't bring myself: more readers.

My sensitivity reader, acquired much too late in the process (entirely my fault, not his), Sridhar. Mistakes in early editions of previous books are not his fault.

My web and marketing guru, Marc Greenwald.

My online teachers: Brandon Sanderson, the cast of Writing Excuses, and Mur Lafferty, all of whom were there for me and asked for nothing in return (at least in part because they have no idea who I am).

The rest of my Twitter and Discord communities, who brought me so much encouragement and support.

Contents

"You're not listening."

"I *am* listening; I'm just not obeying."

"I wish I could release you, Rohan, I do. But my anger needs to be assuaged." The pressure renewed; he screamed, fully, the sound echoing off the faraway walls.

As he reached the edge of consciousness, she relented and let him catch his breath.

He panted as he looked into her eyes. "You're really good at that, you know. Trust me; I've been tortured by experts. But it doesn't change the fact that I don't know where he is."

"I believe you. But you could figure it out, couldn't you, clever Rohan? You know him so well. All those years. You could draw him out. He's wronged you as well. Let me get justice for both of us."

"I can't. I wish I could."

"Lying to me is dangerous, Rohan. And that was a lie. That is not your wish. I see relief in your eyes when you say 'no,' not dread. You don't yearn for his death the way I do. The way you should."

"Maybe not. I suspect our ideas of justice are poorly aligned."

"You require proper motivation. I don't think pain will work on you, will it?"

He screamed again as she pulled at his collarbone, stretching ligaments inside his shoulder in unnatural ways. "I don't know. I'm feeling . . . pretty motivated right now."

"Yet it's not enough. Should I threaten your friends? The innocents on board this station?"

"I'm not too keen on the idea of giving up some innocent people to save others. In fact, that's part of the reason I quit Fleet. So, probably won't work."

Her eyes brightened. "I know what you need."

He shuddered. "Do I want to know?"

"A little motherly love should do the trick, shouldn't it?" She released his chest, keeping him in place with her palm but no longer pressing into him. With her other hand, she stroked his cheek.

She leaned closer and whispered. "I've been going about this all wrong. You want to help me. Don't you, sweet Rohan? Isn't that the most important thing?"

She exhaled slowly, blowing into his face. At first he smelled normal breath: heat, a hint of tea, a spice the il'Drach used on their food. Dhaveena's eyes swam in his vision, sparks fading into liquid warmth. Her aura intensified and thickened, filling his lungs like a humid summer day, floral steel fingers encircling his mind, slowing his breathing and deadening his thoughts. The breath sweetened into a breeze at a deserted beach, into fresh-cut roses and baking bread.

Her presence surrounded him, dissolving the hard edges of his sense of self, his identity. It flowed in, a rising tide of love and determination and anger, filling his soul, twisting it, overwhelming his thoughts, his consciousness.

He melted, his will dissipating, splashes of intent shaking off his core, dreams and hopes boiling away into the air of the arena. He wanted to help. More than that—to fully satisfy her every wish; to lift her on his shoulders and make her a queen, an empress, a goddess.

"Are you ready to obey me, sweet Rohan?" Her hand wasn't pressuring him; she was holding on to him for support.

Of course he would; she was his everything. His very reason for being. But how? What could he do? *She seems tired. That must have taken a lot out of her. Poor thing.* He reached out to support her; she leaned into his hands.

"Well, sweet Rohan. What shall it be?" Her voice was soft, drained of energy.

His eyes snapped open, wide and clear, belying the fog behind them. He smiled and sighed with relief.

"Yes, Mother. I know just what to do. I'll give you what you want. What you really want, more than anything else. You'll be so happy."

"That's my boy. My lovely boy. Come, grant my wishes."

1

Nine Days Earlier

Rohan pulled the lower edge of his mask away from his face, breaking the seal, and sniffed at the station's air.

Gagging, he yanked it back down. It slid too far to seal, and he cursed, coughed, and spat in a single confusing and deeply unpleasant exhalation.

"Rohan, what happened? Your vitals are spiking alarmingly." Professor Benjamin Stone was monitoring Rohan's systems from his research ship, *Insatiable*, in orbit around the planet below.

Rohan coughed again, rubbing his stomach as he willed it to settle down.

"You told me the air was safe to breathe."

"It is safe. I'm not reading anything in the sample that could be toxic to you. I didn't say it would be pleasant."

"It *smells* toxic. Rudra save me, I can taste it. It's awful."

"You'll be fine; your heart rate is already coming back down."

"It smells like something died in here. No, worse. It's like how zombies would smell. The smell of things that should be dead but just go on putrefying and rotting for millennia."

"I'll make a note. The station atmosphere does not smell good."

"I've been in unregulated meat packing plants that smelled better than this. I helped take care of Ohmei when she got transdimensional sepsis, and that smelled better than this."

"I hear you, Rohan. Just, maybe, keep your mask on."

"This is going to get into my clothes. My hair. I'm going to need to shower for three days. Or soak in buttermilk. Is that the thing? What do you soak in, to get out smells like this? Do we even have buttermilk on Wistful? I don't think you're paying me enough for this."

"I'm sure we aren't, considering that we aren't paying you at all. But don't you feel rewarded by the sense of discovery? Standing on a station where people haven't set foot in thousands of years? Tens of thousands?"

"I'm finding out that my passion for discovery is significantly undermined by feelings of nausea and disgust."

He breathed deeply of the clean air provided by his mask, then knelt and grabbed some loose, charcoal-gray dirt. It crumbled to dust in his hand.

He brushed his hands together as he stood in the center of a rolling stretch of naked soil, fifty meters wide and stretching for kilometers in front and behind him. The avenue was flanked by ten-story buildings, their metal faces defining a vast, artificial canyon.

Far in front of him, the path met the station's central section, a shimmering tear shed by a star-sized giant, falling toward the planet above. Three other arms, each thirty kilometers long and sheathed in diamond, radiated out from it in the cardinal directions.

The layout was identical to that of Rohan's home and employer, Wistful. Which was curious, as this station was on the other side of the galaxy, outside il'Drach space, and appeared to have been abandoned for millennia.

"About that smell. Two of my students suspect it has something to do with decaying biomass from food production facilities."

"You mean the ranches? They think the animals died and rotted away?"

"That's the working hypothesis. They're heading over to investigate. We'd love to find some remains so we can get an idea of what kind of animals were present on this ship. You have any reason to think it's not safe?"

"As far as I can tell, it's fine. Just make sure they keep their helmets sealed. And tell them that since the ranches are on the other side of the station, I'm not going to be close if anything goes wrong."

"Copy."

A fresh voice piped in over his comm. "Captain, I don't like this place. It's really weird. I'm getting flutters in my grav generators." *Void's Shadow's* voice was tense.

"Just be glad you can't smell her. But can I get a little more in the way of specifics? 'Weird' isn't exactly actionable information." He looked around, orienting himself, then started walking up the corridor, toward the center of the station.

"It's like talking to an exact copy of your best friend, only they've been in a coma for a thousand years."

"I'll admit, that is weird. At least odd. A dead clone of Wistful. I'm amazed the grav generators are still running."

"She's not dead, she's sleeping. Like, really deeply sleeping. I can *feel* her aura."

"I can't. You must be more sensitive than I am."

"It's faint, kind of quiet, but it's there. Also, I looked at her mirror arrays. The ones that should be keeping her charged and awake."

"And?"

"They're intact, but the thrusters aren't working. They just drifted out of position."

"So she ran out of supplies."

"Why didn't she refuel? Send out shuttles? There's a gas giant not far away. She should have been able to remote pilot shuttles for something routine. What happened to her?"

"Not sure. Are there any shuttles left? Maybe they were damaged?"

"I'll check the bays. But a station this size would have automated repair facilities. And, if she needs it, fabricators to make new ones. It doesn't make sense."

"All right. You look for shuttles, let me check in with the others."

"Captain, I've been watching a lot of holodramas lately, and the ones that start like this always end with everybody gruesomely murdered. That would make me sad. Can we please go home now? There's nothing good here."

"Not yet. Soon, though. If it really bothers you, go play in the asteroid belt or something."

It is creepy, but at least it's boring-creepy and not run-for-your-life creepy.

He tapped open a channel. "Dr. Stone, how are things on the planet?"

It took a moment for Ben to answer. "Marion's shuttle is landing now. The structures on the planet are definitely artificial, but deserted. No signs of life."

"Meaning that people came, built stuff, then disappeared. Any sense of what happened to them?"

"No way to tell. You want me to speculate?"

"Nah. *Void's Shadow* says the station is alive, just asleep. Not sure what that means."

"Ships low on fuel can shut down all energy-intensive systems and enter a state like hibernation. You'll hear about it every so often with a deep-space exploration ship that gets lost."

Rohan spotted a sign over an empty doorway. The lettering resembled Drachna but wasn't. He ducked through into a small shop. The inside was strewn with tables and chairs proportioned for creatures close to human in size and shape. The debris on the floor had decayed into an unrecognizable film of trash.

He walked back out and tapped his comm.

"Are you disappointed? It took your wife six months to open this wormhole, and all we find is a lot of nothing."

The Professor chuckled. "It's not nothing, we found a mystery! You know I love mysteries."

"I hope she feels the same way. Can you make out this writing? There are signs all around, but I can't read them."

"We're running it through some linguistics systems. No results so far."

"You sound relaxed. Don't you think this is strange?"

"I'm an old man, Rohan. I've survived a lot of strange."

"Well, my ship is not an old man, and she's getting pretty nervous."

Rohan cracked his neck and scratched his beard below the mask line. The transparent, single-facet diamond roof, high above the avenue, was badly smudged, obscuring his view of the planet above.

He continued to walk. Ben's voice continued over the comm.

"The shuttle's on the ground now, inside the remains of the big settlement. Marion and three of the students are exploring the ruins."

"That doesn't sound at all dangerous. Make sure they open things. Doors, boxes, crypts. Especially anything that's been carefully sealed. Or hidden."

The older man laughed. "I'll mention that. Hold on, no need. That's what they seem to be doing. They're at a large central building, something like a church. Or a town hall."

Void's Shadow interrupted. "Captain, the shuttle bays were destroyed."

"What?"

"I'm looking into them now. Assuming the layout matches Wistful's, this is where the shuttle maintenance and manufacturing facilities should be. But they're ripped apart."

"Huh. Do you have any idea when this happened?"

"Well, it's not fresh. But I really can't tell; there's no atmosphere, so no regular weathering. The damage does look like it was done by hand."

"You mean like a Hybrid."

"Well, *something* humanoid shredded these bays. Not energy weapons and not explosives. Also not projectiles."

Rohan stopped in his tracks. "Why destroy a station's shuttles?" *I know the answer to that. It was part of my training.*

"Bad temper? Someone wanted to starve her to death?"

"Can you take a closer look at the mirror arrays?"

"What—oh, right. To see if they were sabotaged."

"Exactly. Hold on, did you *sense* anything new just now?"

"What do you mean, Captain?"

"I thought I heard something."

"Not funny, Captain. I'll go check the mirrors again."

I wasn't kidding.

Ben's voice rang out over the comms. "They're entering that central building."

"Are we sure that's a good idea?"

"I'm not. And I don't think you are. Has that ever stopped my wife?"

"Was anything set off when she opened the door? Any kind of signal? I could swear I heard something just a moment ago. It can't be your students, they're too far away."

"Let me—oh, that's not good."

Rohan turned back and strained but couldn't hear anything over his own breath and the pump of his helmet's air supply.

He grunted. "Are you messing with me? You are, aren't you? I cannot believe you just did that."

"I wish it were me. There was an energy spike when they opened the door. If you had asked me five minutes ago if it was possible that anything on the surface still functioned, I would have said, 'no.'"

"Congratulations, I know how much you like to learn new things."

"Perhaps we should have been more careful about opening doors and touching stuff."

"If only somebody had said something along those lines."

Rohan spun as he heard a strange sound, this time from the direction of the station's center.

"Rohan, did you say there were sounds on the station?"

Parallel rows of lights came to dim, flickering life along both sides of the avenue, just above the level of the first floor.

"Something is definitely happening up here."

"Good-something or bad-something?"

"I don't know yet. Given the general situation, I'm leaning toward bad-something."

Void's Shadow broke in. "Captain, I don't know whether it's good or bad, but I agree that something is definitely changing."

"I know, the lights just came on. Dr. Stone's team set off some kind of signal from the surface."

"I mean out here. One of *Insatiable*'s shuttles docked on the other side of the station. Right after, a bay opened on this side and two shuttles launched from the station. They are headed down to the planet."

"Didn't you just tell me that the shuttle bays were destroyed?"

"Did I? Yes, I did! These are different shuttles. These came from a different place. I didn't even know they were bays."

He heard another noise, more clearly this time. It wasn't quiet so much as coming from very far up the boulevard.

"*Void's Shadow*, what type of shuttle are they?"

"Well, that's the thing, Captain. The bays for all the maintenance and supply shuttles, *those* were destroyed. Like I said. I wasn't wrong."

He broke into a jog as he heard more sounds.

"If they're not maintenance or supply shuttles, what are they?"

"They look like attack shuttles, Captain. Atmosphere-capable fighters. Heavily armed, based on the ports I see on the exteriors."

"Of course they are. Ben, did you catch that? Were you listening?"

"I heard you. Both of you. *Insatiable* confirms, two attack shuttles on a vector leading directly to the settlement location. I've already notified Marion." His voice had tightened considerably.

A new voice piped up over the comm. "Tow Chief Rohan! This is Royja. We've disembarked near the ranch levels; we're trying to find something that can give us even a partial DNA sample." It was one of Ben Stone's Andervarian students. Purple skin, pointed ears, chunky yellow tattoos.

"That's a great idea. Except for the fact that the lights just came on and two attack shuttles launched for the surface."

"But we're not on the surface."

Rohan took a deep breath. "Attack shuttles imply some kind of defense mechanism. Are you ready to risk your life on the assumption that the station is going to defend whatever's on the planet and ignore people who are walking around inside her?"

"Oh. We see your point, Tow Chief. We should probably get back on the shuttle."

"Yes, do that. Great idea."

The lights along the boulevard brightened.

"*Void's Shadow*, are you sensing anything new from the station? Is she awake? Is this just some kind of automated response?"

"She's not awake, but she's not the same as she was when we got here."

Ben's voice rose in volume with every word. "Marion, get your team out of there, right now. Those ships are coming in hot."

She responded, her voice still calm. "Don't panic. Visita is lifting off to give us some cover."

Rohan shook his head. "I'll go down and help. Buy me a minute."

He lowered himself, ready to *lift* off the ground and exit the station, when his knees buckled.

What now?

The students on the station were shouting. "Rohan! We're stuck!"

The station's gravity had doubled.

"Can you two stand? More importantly, can you breathe?" His body could handle an increase in weight; the same wasn't necessarily true of a normal Andervarian.

"We're breathing, Rohan. We might be able to crawl, but I don't think we can stand," Royja said.

"Okay, stay put, I'll come for you."

"We don't exactly have a choice, do we?"

"If you're going to be snarky about it, I'll take my time dealing with those attack shuttles."

He *lifted* off again, aiming directly at the diamond plate fifty meters above him. The panes should be held loosely in place, just snug enough in the frame to minimize atmospheric leakage. He'd flown through Wistful's roof a handful of times, for one emergency or another requiring a quick egress.

Just before striking, he *felt* a flare of the station's own Power reinforcing the roof. He hit with enough energy to punch a hole through steel plate; it wasn't enough.

The shock jarred his shoulders. "Ow." *This station is strong. Stronger than any ship I've fought.*

He dropped to the ground, faster than he meant to. *Another gravity increase.*

"Rohan, please . . . don't do . . . that again." Royja's voice was wheezy and faint.

Void's Shadow made contact. "Captain, what's happening? I *felt* something."

"Yeah, the station does not want me leaving. This is getting more complicated."

He landed, kicking up little puffs of dust that rose and fell almost instantly in the heavy gravity.

Visita, the shuttle's pilot, broke into the comm channel. "I'm taking damage from these fighters. I can't keep them busy for much longer. They're trying to strafe the ground."

Ben spoke. "Marion! Are you injured? What's going on?"

Her response was high-pitched but not quite in the panic octaves. "Nobody's hurt yet. They're just firing randomly. Not really getting close to us."

"Rohan, can you please get down there?" Ben's voice was higher pitched.

"Sorry, Professor. The station is waking up, and she doesn't want me going anywhere. I'm afraid she'll crush your students with the gravity generators if I try anything more significant."

"Son, I don't like saying this, but maybe you need to put this station out of her misery."

"Maybe. Give me a minute to think."

He checked the walls, orienting toward the end of the station where the students were trapped, and started to walk.

A warp twisted into position in front of him; a three-meter-tall humanoid stepped through and stood up from a crouch.

She's opening rifts in space. Meaning that this station used to be a starship. Not important at this exact moment, but . . . interesting.

The creature was burly: a frame like a gorilla's hung with swollen balls of muscle. Plaster-white skin peeked out between plates of thick metallic armor liberally sprinkled with angry spikes and sawtooth edges.

Rohan stepped back, quickly checking his Third Eye to examine the monster's aura.

"Fun update from the station. We have a corpse soldier up here, and it looks like a thousand kilos of nasty."

Ben's voice took on an angry tone. "Would you stop mucking about and get down to the planet? You were a lance primary for the Imperial Fleet! Just . . . do your thing!"

The corpse soldier was animated by the aura of something alive. *The station is running this guy.*

"*Void's Shadow*, tell me if this girl is awake yet."

He leapt forward and drove his left fist up into the creature's face. The corpse soldier lifted two arms to block, each as massive as Rohan's entire body.

The impact knocked it back on its heels.

He followed up by stomping his leg into the monster's gut, hitting hard enough to bend and dent the armor.

It fell.

"Had enough?" The corpse soldier rolled to its feet, face expressionless. New footsteps sounded from behind Rohan. "Not impressed yet?"

He slipped to the side as the creature behind him kicked empty air. Rohan aimed a blow at the creature's knee; he missed as it skipped out of range.

The second creature, a mirror image of the first, stood in a soft crouch and stared at Rohan, arms hanging loosely at its sides.

"Captain, she's not awake. I know it's weird, but it's like she's sleepwalking. Only not walking. Sleep-fighting? Sleep-attacking? Are those things?"

"If they weren't, they are now."

Rohan switched his mindset to prepare to use Fire Speech—the language that contained the essence of all other communication. He tapped the side of his mask, piping his voice to external speakers. "Hey! We don't want to fight! We're just explorers! Hello?"

He switched to Drachna. "Royja! What's happening? Is anybody near you?"

Working together, the corpse soldiers launched a volley of punches at the Hybrid. He ducked and spun between the blows, narrowly evading fists as big as his torso.

"Rohan . . . we're . . . hard . . . to . . . breathe."

Enough of this.

He danced out of range of the two, watching carefully as they separated and circled to flank his position.

He took in a deep breath and *reached* down to a place just behind his tailbone, to the well of Power that was his gift, his curse, and the defining feature of his life.

It jumped, eagerly, shimmering and straining to be unleashed, to wreak havoc on his enemies.

With metaphysical hands, he *pulled* up two heavy streams of Power. They rose, spiraling in counterpoint around his spine, meeting once with each revolution in a burst of esoteric starlight.

The twin bands sparked and sizzled through his body until they met at the base of his skull, completing a violent circuit of energy and snapping taut.

Power flooded through his body, out through each nerve, each muscle fiber, each tendon and fascial line.

The boulevard brightened, single grains of dirt standing out as clearly as faded signs up and down the line of buildings. He could smell the remains of the station's stench that lay thick across his mustache, taste the faint film of coffee he'd drunk before stepping onto the station, hear the corpse soldiers' skin as it creaked across the inside of their leather armor.

"You guys wanted to do this the hard way?"

2

What Are We, Electric Sheep?

"*Void's Shadow*, did that wake her up?" Rohan stood facing the two corpse soldiers. Neither showed any sign that they were aware of the Power he'd manifested; they advanced slowly, taking unhurried steps to further outflank his position.

"She's the same, Captain. Maybe . . . I don't know, angrier? But not awake."

A storm of voices crowded the open channel.

"We found a basement or bunker or something under this building. The fighters are strafing the settlement, but so far we're safe down here. You might need to dig us out when this is over." Marion Stone's voice, icy as her Nordic blue eyes.

"I don't mean to hurry you, Rohan, but please hurry." Ben, already calmed down from his earlier, frantic high.

"I damaged one of the fighters, but I've lost a drive and most of my weapons." Visita, the shuttle pilot.

"I can't get down into the atmosphere with this body! I'm so sorry!" *Insatiable*. Once a warship, she'd grown into the shape of a research vessel, boxy and highly non-aerodynamic.

"Something's . . . here." Ben's student, trapped near the sleeping station's ranch level by the amplified gravity, wheezed the words.

Rohan skipped to his left, faster than the corpse soldiers could react, and flicked a jab up toward one's jaw. It didn't flinch; his punch connected, barely fazing the creature.

He fell to the ground, planted his feet in the powdery dirt, and drove an uppercut directly into the monster's groin.

Metal armor warped as the monster flipped over entirely, somersaulting backward to wind up facedown on the ground. Rohan leapt after it, landing with a pointed knee in its spine, all his Power adding to the quintuple gravity field.

Vertebrae shattered audibly.

He stood up, feet planted just inside the soldier's scapulae, and faced the other one. The creature rushed in, arms spread in preparation for a tackle.

Rohan curled up into himself, feet planted, shoulders hunched, fists at his sides.

Just as the creature closed to grabbing distance, he unfurled, extending at the hips and shoulders, lancing out a tight right fist to catch the corpse soldier directly between its eyes.

Skull crumbled beneath the shock of his punch combined with the energy of the soldier's forward momentum. It fell to the ground, its central nervous system reduced to a shambles.

"Captain, are you going to have to hurt her?" *Void's Shadow's* voice was small.

The Power inside him wanted him to answer, "yes." He hopped off the twitching body of the first soldier and strode toward station center.

He exhaled slowly. "If I have to."

"We did come here without permission. It's not really her fault, is it?"

"I suppose not. But we can't just let her kill all our friends, can we?"

"No. No we can't."

The air in front of him tore open, and two more giants emerged. He turned and spotted another pair closing in from behind.

Rohan knelt and tore into the armor of one fallen giant. He flung screaming arcs of spikes, half-sawblades, and chunks of armor plate at the oncoming soldiers.

The corpse soldiers marched on, deflecting some pieces and ignoring others.

Being dead, the corpse soldiers had no instinct for self-preservation. They would bear any pain, suffer any damage, without flinching or hesitating. They responded only to the will of the life guiding them: in this case, a sleeping space station.

Marion's voice broke over his comm. "The building is collapsing above us. We hope the cellar structure will hold, but to be honest, I'm not that confident."

One of them moved extra quickly and caught Rohan's foot. It swung him overhead, then down into the ground, like a child angry at its doll.

He kicked into its hand and wiggled free.

Another kick into its belly sent him flying backward into a second soldier. He spun mid-flight to face it, driving his forearms into its chest and knocking it back into a third.

They collapsed into a confusing heap of bodies, the soldiers grabbing and tearing with fingers as thick as his wrists. He leapt free only to be struck by the other two.

Visita's voice. "My ammo is out. I'm trying to ram them, but they're too agile. Wait! I did it! I got one. But the other one is still firing the plasma cannons."

"We can already feel the heat down here." Marion's composure was starting to crack.

"Don't worry, dear, Rohan will get free soon and come down."

Rohan *pulled* in more Power, letting energy flood through his limbs. He hopped up and drove one Power-laden fist through the chestplate of a corpse soldier. He met its expressionless eyes as it coughed out a last breath and fell forward, trying to trap him beneath its weight.

He lifted the creature, muscles straining under its full thousand kilos. With a burst, he threw it aside, then flew through the space it had occupied.

Another soldier caught him and knocked him toward the ground while two more appeared in the air in front of him.

They're tough but not fighting as intelligently as they should. Maybe because the station isn't awake.

Wait . . . she isn't awake. Maybe that's the problem.

"*Void's Shadow*, can you wake her up? Maybe we can reason with her if she's actually conscious."

"Um. How? Crash into her?"

He thought as the soldiers converged on his position.

"No, that won't work. I tried that, and it just got her to increase the gravity. Can we wake her without attacking her?"

"I don't know how, Captain."

Wet popping noises came from the first two corpse soldiers he'd damaged: bones shifting back into place, joints relocating, split flesh knitting into uninterrupted white sheets.

The energy it took to heal flesh that rapidly was extraordinary.

Fighting these guys is pointless.

Rohan cursed under his breath and tucked his head. With a grunt, he shot his body out, flying just a couple of meters off the ground, aiming toward the ranch area.

As corpse soldiers grabbed and leapt to cover him, he twisted his body in a violent corkscrew, striking out at grasping fingers and reaching limbs, creating just enough violent chaos to maintain his forward momentum.

"Rohan, *Insatiable* and I are going to dock near the ranch area and try to get Royja and Delloi out of there to free you up."

"Ben, that's not . . . She's cranked up to five gravities in here."

"Haditz thinks he can maneuver in that much. Rogesh are used to higher gravities to begin with. Marion's talking to her students on board; they're trying to cobble together a gravity generator to counter the ship's field."

He grunted and cut a tight curve around a giant soldier. Haditz was another of Ben's students. Rohan wasn't fully confident if Haditz's desire to help was born more out of practicality or of wounded pride.

The station was forming small wormholes, whisking the corpse soldiers around so they were constantly reappearing between Rohan and station center. He'd never seen a ship or station that could form so many precise rifts in space so quickly.

"We're approaching the docks near the ranch area now."

"Um, Captain?"

"*Void's Shadow*. Tell me you have good news." He arced down, sliding through the dirt and between the legs of a corpse soldier braced in front of him.

"No, sorry, Captain. Another pair of fighters launched."

"Super. Where are they headed?"

"One is on course for *Insatiable*; the other one for the surface."

"I take it the station's still asleep?"

"Yes, Captain. Now *Insatiable* has taken some damage. She's firing back, but she's not built for this. Ooh, she's got some moves, though! Hit one of the fighter's drives."

Rohan shook his head. "*Insatiable*, remember that you're our ride home. I can only fit three or four people on *Void's Shadow*."

"Oh, I know, Tow Chief, I know! I just couldn't orbit idly by and ignore everything. I had to at least try to help. But I can't dock with the station! I got close, but I've lost atmosphere to two sections already. I really can't afford anymore!"

"It's enough, *Insatiable*. Stand down. Keep yourself in one piece. We'll handle the rest."

"Please do, Tow Chief. Please. I do *not* want to go back to Fleet Academy to explain how I got my entire crew killed. Oh, they'll tease me so. You have no idea how embarrassing that would be!"

"I think I do. This station is kicking all of our butts at the same time, and she's literally doing it in her sleep." He broke through a row of corpse soldiers and saw a hundred clear meters in front of him.

Void's Shadow piped in. "To be fair, Captain, if she weren't asleep, we could try to reason with her. And you're only losing because you're trying not to hurt her. Or lose the students at the ranch."

Marion Stone shouted over the comm. "Parts of the ceiling are coming down. We're not going to last much longer."

"All right. How do we wake up this ship? Attacking her just makes her an angry sleeper. What wakes things up?"

Void's Shadow answered. "You use an alarm, Captain. But we can't make noise in space."

"No, we can't. If only we were on a badly written holodrama, we could totally do that. What else wakes people up?"

"You like it kept dark when you sleep, Captain."

"I do. Wait, wait, I do! That's it!"

"What's it, Captain? You want to take a nap? This hardly—"

"No. I want to shine a light on her."

"Even *Insatiable* can't project a light that—"

"Stop interrupting me, please. Realign the mirror array."

"The mirror array? You mean the station's . . ."

"Can you do that?" Rohan slalomed between four corpse soldiers guarding the entrance to the center section.

Insatiable interrupted. "I can guide her, Tow Chief. I can do the calculations so we know how to orient the mirrors. It won't take—it's done."

"Then, get moving, please."

"Getting into position now, Captain!"

"Royja, you guys still breathing?"

"Yes . . . barely."

"Hold on a little longer. We have a plan."

He fought his way to the steel door demarcating the inner section of the station. It resembled the outer hull of a ship, gently curved and ever so slightly pitted.

He braced and punched stiff fingers through the metal plating, gripped the steel, and peeled the door, along with a meter of its frame, out of place.

More corpse soldiers were waiting inside, lined up shoulder to shoulder, a towering wall of hard flesh and riveted steel plate.

Rohan blew out a long, slow lungful of air.

"How we doing with those mirrors?"

"I have two of the four primaries lined up. Moving on the third."

He turned his external speakers back on.

"Hail, the station!"

The corpse soldiers rushed forward.

He lifted the plank of hull metal up and slammed it down on the group, pouring as much Power as he could draw into the heavy plate.

They collapsed together, pressed down into the floor by the enormous weight of the door. Red and clear fluids seeped out from around the pile.

"I said, hail, the station! Wakey wakey, time to . . . I have no idea how that rhyme goes. Get up! I'm not getting paid enough to keep destroying these guys!"

"Third mirror is in place, Captain."

Insatiable opened a private channel. "Your ship is performing admirably, Tow Chief. She takes instructions very well, especially considering her lack of training."

He stepped through the opening he'd torn and into the central section.

If this station was in truth a close match to Wistful in layout, the critical systems and station's brain would be in this area.

"This is going to hurt you more than it hurts me!" He tore open a wall, exposing wiring and circuitry that he quickly rendered into an expensive-looking pile on the floor.

Another set of corpse soldiers popped into place in front of him.

"More? Not an efficient use of your resources, is it?"

"Fourth mirror is in place, Captain!"

He braced and took a fighting position: right foot back, one hand low by his navel, the other guarding his jaw. Weight evenly distributed.

The soldiers froze in place, the gradual rise and fall of their chests the only signs of their continued not-quite-death.

Hidden speakers let out a cough like an electric guitar clearing its throat, followed by a burst of static so loud that layers of dust were dislodged from the decorative trim around the ceiling.

"I was having the strangest d— What is this? What's going on?"

It was no language Rohan recognized, though he could understand it because he knew Fire Speech. He straightened and scratched his beard. "Hail, the station. I'm Tow Chief Rohan. I think there's been a misunderstanding."

"Tow Chief—I don't know you. You're not my tow chief. Who are you?"

"Right, sorry. I'm from another station. Look, you're killing my friends. Can you stop? Please? Call a truce?"

"Stop what? What killing?"

"The gravity. And the attack shuttles on the planet."

"Oh no, no, no. What are they doing on the planet? What are you doing on *me*? Didn't you see the beacons?"

"Um. Beacons? *Insatiable*, did we miss any beacons?"

"None that are active. I'll do another scan."

Void's Shadow added, "Captain, there are dead beacons out here. They've been powered down for, like, forever."

"Who sent that signal? I can't see that ship. What is that?"

"Sorry, she's just a baby. She has stealth covering. *Void's Shadow*, open a window or something so the station can see you."

"Are you sure, Captain? She seems angry."

"Yes, please. Our priority right now is calming her down."

"All right."

Rohan sighed. "What can I call you, station?"

"Call me? What should you call me, Tow Chief Who-is-not-mine?" A pause. Rohan couldn't remember an artificial intelligence pausing that way. "Call me Repentant. Yes, that's right. That will do."

"Repentant. Good. We're very sorry, really we are, but we didn't see any beacons. They're inactive."

"The beacons? How is that possible? They should be . . . Oh dear. How long?"

"How long?"

"How long have I been asleep? *What* has been happening?" The words came faster and faster, with increasing pitch.

"Repentant, I promise, we'll be glad to help you figure all of that out. Can you please stop the fighters on the planet and turn the gravity down? I have two friends near your ranch facility, and they can barely breathe."

"Planet? They can't be on the planet. Oh no, definitely not."

"Call off your shuttles and I promise they'll leave. Immediately."

"Leave? Leave? You should never have been there. Not on the planet. No, no, no. You should have listened to the beacons."

"Repentant, I'm really sorry. We're really sorry. We would have paid attention to the beacons if they were still working. But they're down and have been for a long time."

"Down? How? How?"

"You've been asleep. They've run out of fuel. Tell me how we can make this right. We'll get everyone off the planet, straight away, all right? Just call off your fighters."

He *lifted* up onto his toes as the gravity cycled down to something approaching one Imperial standard.

He shut off his speakers and switched to Drachna. "Guys, if you can stand, get off this station as fast as your little legs can carry you."

Royja answered. "We're moving, Rohan."

Visita spoke from the shuttle. "The fighters down here have paused; they're circling above the settlement."

A move in the right direction.

"Repentant, we'd like to help you. We'd also like to get out of this system alive. What can I do to make it happen?"

"Make it happen? It? It's too late, is what it is. Too late. You shouldn't have gone to the planet."

"I hear what you're saying, and I wish we hadn't. But we didn't know. The beacons are powered down. What can I do, now?"

"Do? Do? Get out of my system! This is my system, mine to protect. You should never have come here, ever. No, not ever. Leave and forget. Forget it all."

He switched back to Drachna. "Dr. Stone, can you get out? Marion? This station wants us to leave."

Another pause, the silence driving Rohan's stomach up into his throat.

"Visita is clearing a path with the shuttle. We'll be free in a few minutes."

"Great." Back to Fire Speech. "Repentant, what can we do for you? We want to help."

"Help? Help? You can help me by getting out of my system. Mine to protect. What species are you? I don't recognize you."

"Me? I'm . . . a Hybrid. Half il'Drach, half human."

"il'Drach? il'Drach? They survived the curse? The mistakes? Surprised, surprised. There are still il'Drach in the galaxy. So nice. I think I lost a bet, a bet. I thought for certain they would all be dead. So sure."

"They're still around. What happened to your crew? The people here?"

"People? Crew? Oh, no, you don't understand." The voice turned to a shout. "Get out! Leave! You can't be here, shouldn't be here, won't be here. Take your friends and get out!"

"We will, I promise. We will. Can we help you first? Fix your shuttles or something? We want to help."

"Help me by leaving. Leave me alone. That was my penance, to be alone. Forever. Me, here, alone, in my system. No other ships. No visitors. No one to talk to."

"Your . . . penance? I don't understand. I'm sorry. Look, something destroyed your shuttle bays. Damaged the mirror arrays. Something deliberately starved you of energy."

The station started to laugh.

The laughter echoed from speakers all throughout the center section, with multiple voices, separate tones, building together into a shriek lacking sanity.

"Starve? Starve? You think I'm hungry? I'm the hungry one?"

The laughter stopped.

"Get out! You cannot . . . will not . . . never have . . . understand. Understood."

Rohan suppressed a shiver. "Royja, you guys clear yet?"

"We're in our shuttle now, Rohan. Rendezvousing with *Insatiable*."

"Okay. Visita, any luck retrieving Professor Stone and her students?"

She took longer to answer. "They're here, Rohan. Another minute, and I'll have them on board."

He backed up, retreating from the station's center section into the arm, where he had a clear escape route through the ceiling.

"I meant what I said. We want to help you. I just don't know how."

"No help for me, no help. I know this, have known this. Since I took this name. Just go. Please, go. Now."

"Guys, the station wants us to go. Right now."

Ben's voice answered him. "We have questions, Rohan. What happened here? If this system is meant to be in some kind of quarantine, why?"

Rohan cleared his throat. "Repentant, will you tell us your story? So we know who you are? What happened here?"

A long silence answered him. Just as he'd decided the station wasn't going to reply, the speakers came back to life.

"Better you not know. Better I be forgotten. Just go; leave now and close the wormhole behind you. Forget the path to this place. Lose the key."

With a sigh, the Hybrid flew to a nearby airlock. It cycled open as he approached, the station ushering him out.

"Ben, is everyone off the surface? Do they need help?"

"Shuttle is lifting off now, full complement on board. Once it docks with *Insatiable*, we'll be ready to reopen the wormhole and exit the system."

"Still feeling rewarded by the discovery?"

"It's not the most satisfying resolution, but I'm glad we are surviving it. And who knows? Maybe someday soon we'll learn more of the story of this place."

"We'll see."

"We should think about what we're going to tell Wistful about this system. I have to imagine she can fill in some of the missing pieces in our understanding of what's going on here."

Rohan sighed. "I'm a little worried about that."

"About what?"

"That she'll make us come back and force this station to talk more. I don't want to be in that position."

"Worry about that when it happens. For now, let's just keep everyone safe. You should report to section Red Ten. It has a full set of medical scanners. We can do a short quarantine and a thorough remote exam to make sure you didn't pick up anything on the station."

"Copy that." Rohan spun to face the general direction of his ship. "*Void's Shadow*, hang around *Insatiable* and follow her through the wormhole, all right? Time to go."

"Yes, Captain. Happy to comply."

3

Order & Order

"Wei Li! Sorry, I slept in. I'm off today. Come on in, I'll put pants on." Rohan gestured inanely at the damp towel wrapped around his hips.

It was morning, the day after he'd returned from Repentant.

Wei Li's vertically slit eyes remained resolutely focused on his face as she stepped through the door and into his apartment: two bedrooms, a sadly underutilized kitchen, the kind of bathroom that would make a Las Vegas premium hotel jealous, and a transparent diamond ceiling with a twenty-four-hour view of the planet above them.

"Please do. As much as I have tried, I am unable to become comfortable with the sight of mammalian genitalia."

Rohan laughed. "Have you actually been trying? To be comfortable with it? With them?"

She snorted back her own laugh. "That has not been near the top of my priority list."

He stepped into his bathroom and pulled on a spare uniform. Workday or not, unless there was some special occasion, he found himself wearing his ship's uniform, despite the purple-and-gold color scheme that was generously described as 'hideous.'

"What can I do for you? Social call?"

"Sadly, it is not. I came to ask you for a favor." She stood near the door, hands behind her back, her yellow skin, striped with red and green scales, on display thanks to her sleeveless uniform.

"Oh. I assume you're not asking me to tow any ships in."

"No, Rohan, I am not. That is not my purview, a fact of which you are well aware."

"Then, what favor?"

"I would like you to accompany me as I perform a small task. On the station."

"Are you going to tell me what this task is? Or why you want me along for it?"

"I would rather not, if you are amenable."

He sighed. "Will you at least tell me if I'm going to regret doing this?"

"While I am a Class Four Empath, and almost uniquely qualified to directly sense the emotions of others, I am in no way possessed of the ability to see the future."

"Can you make an educated guess?"

She paused and tapped a finger against her chin. "I do not expect you to regret this."

"Okay. Is this going to involve violence?"

"I doubt it. Given your affinity for irritating people, I cannot make any guarantees."

"Fair enough. Can it wait five minutes while I brush my hair out?"

"This situation is not an emergency, but we should not be delayed any more than necessary."

"Got it."

He groomed himself into a passable appearance.

"You don't want to hear about this cool hairbrush, do you? I picked it up on Andervar. Made of some plant that only grows there. It's amazing at taking out knots."

"Are you mocking me now, Rohan? For my lack of hair?"

"Of course not. Well, maybe a little."

"It would work better if I were uncomfortable with my appearance. Have I ever given you reason to think that is the case?"

"No, you haven't. I had to try."

"You did not, actually, have to try. But as you are doing me a favor this morning, I will not trouble you overly for your poor judgment."

"That's very kind." He sat on his bed, pulled split-toed boots over his feet, and stood.

"Where are we going?"

"The scene of a crime. Specifically, murder. Multiple murders."

Rohan stepped over a body, choosing his foot placement with great precision. He bent at the waist, bringing his face to within centimeters of the ground, and examined the corpse and surrounding area from a variety of angles.

"What exactly are you doing?" Wei Li stared, her head tilted to the side.

"Isn't this what we do? When examining a body? Look for clues, check every angle?"

"Where did you hear that?"

"I don't know. I watch TV."

"You should stop doing that. Whatever it is. It is mildly annoying and somewhat disrespectful."

He straightened. "What if there's a clue?"

"We already have imaging of this entire apartment accurate to the micrometer level. If there are any clues to be found, they'll be found."

"So, you didn't bring me here to sleuth."

"I did not. At least not that sort of sleuthing."

"Then, what?"

"I want your hypothesis regarding what happened here. Without doing whatever it is that you were doing."

He spun slowly in place, taking in the room.

The apartment was a typical family-size residential unit. The family in question, three adult lavender-hued Kratics, lay spread out on the living room floor.

"Those two are older, maybe a couple? And if so, she could be their child."

"That matches details from Wistful's registry. The older two work together, dubbing holodramas into Kratic for resale on their homeworld. Go on."

"I'm no coroner, but cause of death sure looks like blood loss. On account of them each having their throats torn out."

"I have an actual coroner looking at this, and she agrees with your assessment."

"I'd expect more blood, given how badly cut open they are. Did a crew come in here and clean up?"

"No. This is how they were found."

"What do you think happened, Wei Li?"

She shook her head. "I am quite confident I know. I am curious whether you've reached the same conclusion."

"It's almost too obvious, isn't it? Someone—or something—wanted this to look like a vampire attack."

"You think this is staged?"

"I mean, either that or it was an actual vampire."

She kept her vertically slit pupils focused on him. "Your tone, along with your aura, suggests that you doubt this interpretation."

"Why would a vampire come to Wistful? It seems like a terrible idea. Enclosed, lots of law enforcement, easy to track things."

"There are possibilities. It might have arrived by accident. It might be very stupid. I doubt either of those explanations are much comfort to this family."

"Granted. So, a vampire, or someone wanting their attack to look like a vampire. Which, now that I think about it, also seems kind of dumb."

"Why?"

"If you want to hide your trail, you need a better cover story than 'vampire on a space station.' It's so unbelievable it doesn't work."

"That is very close to my current line of thinking. It is a narrative so improbable it must be true."

"Great. Is that what you wanted from me? Another opinion?"

"No. I would like you to accompany me as I question a group of vampires."

"Sure. Wait, what? There *is* a group of vampires on Wistful?"

"Yes."

"You're just mentioning this now?"

"I did not want to unduly influence your analysis."

"We have three people dead, vampires on the station that you know about, and we're just standing here talking."

"I do not believe the vampires in question are responsible for these murders."

"You lost me."

She paused before responding. "This family was found by one of Professor Stone's students."

"Ben's or Marion's?"

"Ben's. The student was on *Insatiable* yesterday, when you explored the other side of the wormhole. He had a romantic encounter scheduled with this young lady, then had to cancel because of the time he spent in quarantine."

"That is . . . I have no idea. Does that mean something?"

"He rescheduled their date for breakfast, and when he came to meet her, they were in this state."

"Do you think he's involved somehow?"

"That was the first thing I checked. He has no motive, no sense of guilt, and to be honest, I don't think he's physically capable of this sort of violence."

"I see."

"He is in custody, of course."

"Of course. Yet the vampires you know about aren't. In custody."

"No. They have been on the station for a substantial period of time without incident. All three are Pledged to Famine."

"You've lost me again."

"I'd prefer for them to explain it to you. Assuming you are willing to come with me while I interrogate them."

"Is this about me being muscle? You want me there to intimidate these vampires? Or do something if they get out of line? Because I feel like we've gone down this road before, and I told you I don't like it."

"No. I do not expect my conversation with these vampires to turn into a confrontation."

"Then, why do you want me there?"

"I have a reason, but if you know about it, your impact will be reduced."

"Run that by me again?"

"I'm asking you to trust me. You can help me the most by not knowing why you're coming along."

Rohan sighed and ran his gaze from one body to the other. Eyes open wide in surprise, in fear. Broken nails showing where they struggled. The coffee table destroyed, splintered glass in the entertainment screen.

She's saved my life. Probably more than once. And she doesn't lie.

"Of course, Wei Li. I trust you more than I trust myself. And I would totally do this if *I* asked me to do it. So, just lead the way."

"Good. They are in the southern arm of the station. We should take the transport tubes."

He nodded.

They walked together: left the apartment, crossed to an elevator, took it down to the level below the promenade where the station's transport system lived.

"Reports say the station you found was a nearly identical copy of Wistful."

Rohan scratched his beard. "Identical layout, at least the parts we explored. But nothing's lived on that station in a long time."

"Yet something, or many somethings, lived there at one time. And then died."

"Or left. But, yes, most likely died."

"And you did not identify the cause. What exactly killed everything on the station or the planet. Or did I miss something in the report?"

"No, we didn't find anything. To be fair, we left in a hurry."

She led him into an empty transport pod. "Does this not concern you? That it might be some sort of agent, perhaps biological, which you've brought back to Wistful?"

"Well, Ben ran every test he could think of. Wistful put us through a battery of scans when we got back."

"If this agent, or pathogen, is as old as that station, perhaps those scans are unable to identify it."

"What should we have done? Stayed in quarantine longer to see if anybody dies?"

"That would have been one precaution."

"For how long, though? What if it's the kind of thing that takes months to gestate? Or years?"

"I am comfortable with a quarantine period of that duration."

He turned to look at her face as they exited the pod. There was no sign that she was joking. "You know me, if Wistful had told me to stay on *Insatiable* for a year to see if I contracted a zombie virus or whatever, I would have stayed. But Wistful herself told us to disembark."

She sighed. "I do know you, and you are correct. I am not pleased by this situation."

"I can imagine."

"Here we are." They had left the transport level and were inside another residential building.

Rohan was vaguely familiar with the area. It was less densely populated, being farther away from the station's center, with generally fewer amenities and lower costs. Exactly where he'd have chosen to hide if he were a vampire seeking relative isolation.

"Do not antagonize them unnecessarily."

"When do I ever do that, Wei Li?" He flinched in response to her answering glare. "Fine, fine, I'll be good, I promise."

"Thank you." She touched the entry pad.

"Are you sure they're home?"

She put a hand up to her ear and tapped her comm. "I'm sure. Give them a minute. They are nocturnal, and it's daylight."

"Of course. I forgot. Silly me. Why wouldn't vampires be nocturnal. Hey, funny story, that other station? Repentant? Its roof was all smudged over. As if to keep out sunlight."

"Was it not simply an effect of time and neglect?"

"It could have been, I guess. Except the gravity was on. How does dirt fly up and stick to the ceiling? Fifty meters up."

"That is interesting. Not conclusive."

"No." The door chimed and slid open.

A humanoid woman stood inside, two steps back from the door. Rohan didn't recognize her species, but she had mammalian features and dark-green skin, a shade that clashed with the deep-blue robe that covered her body. Twin red lines marked her cheekbones, curving down to end in points at the corners of her mouth.

He felt uncomfortable as soon as he *felt* her aura.

"Security Chief. Forgive the delay, I was asleep. What can I do for you?"

Wei Li pointed to Rohan. "This is Tow Chief Second Class Rohan. Of Earth. We'd like to talk with you."

"Of course. Come in." She stepped farther back and gestured for them to enter. Most of the lights inside had been turned off, sinking the far corners in heavy shadow. The apartment was sparsely furnished and showed no signs of decoration.

Rohan nodded as he walked past the woman.

Wei Li continued. "Rohan, this is Mother Famine."

"Hi. Do you come from a long line of famines?"

The woman smiled. *Did I imagine that or are her incisors very long? And very sharp?*

"Mother Famine is a title. I am a sworn member of the Pledged to Famine. Are you not familiar with us?"

"Not so much, no."

She looked at Wei Li. "Are you here for me to explain our society to your friend?"

"For a start, yes."

She turned and called out. "Brother Famine, Sister Famine, we have visitors. One of whom is an il'Drach Hybrid." She looked back at her guests. "They will come soon. They were more deeply asleep than I. Please sit. I can make you a drink."

Rohan's stomach growled with the suggestion.

Wei Li nodded. "Please. And turn up the lights, if you don't mind."

They sat, perched uncomfortably on a roughly used couch, and waited while Mother Famine worked in the kitchen.

"This is not what I was expecting."

"Exactly the reason I didn't tell you more. Now listen."

The vampire returned, offering two mugs that gave off a heavy layer of steam.

Rohan sipped. It was bitter, tasting faintly of chocolate with a vegetal overtone.

She sat across from him and addressed him directly. "Our order is for people infected with vampirism who are dedicated to ethical living."

"I thought ethical and vampirism were kind of contradictory."

"We—all of us—were infected involuntarily. Surely our very existence cannot be considered unethical?"

"Existence? No. Dietary patterns? Different story." Wei Li put a hand on his forearm. "You're right, I'm sorry, that was rude."

"No, I understand. Our first precept is that we taste no blood."

"None? Then . . ."

"We consume only a synthetic liquid that contains nutrients compatible with our altered physiology." The words came faster, as if rehearsed.

"Okay. Well, that's good. I'm surprised more vampires don't just do that."

"It is not so easy. The synthetic sustains our life, but it cannot quell our hunger. We live in an everlasting state of famine. Hence our name."

"Oh."

Wei Li looked at him. "They live in constant suffering. I can sense it."

"Why? That seems extreme. Can't you find, I don't know, willing donors?"

Mother Famine smiled. "This is the only way to resist the temptation to drink. Feeding the hunger only makes it grow. Once we drink actual blood, it is a short step to drinking from a willing donor. Then another short step to learning to convince the unwilling to become willing. To bend their desires to ours."

"So, you just . . . abstain."

"Exactly. Abstain. There are more precepts. We take no name, because having a name makes us vulnerable. To sorcery, to those who would tip us over the brink."

He nodded. "I get that."

"We tell no lies. We wear the mark of the fang on our face so all know what we are. Ah, here they come."

Two more vampires entered the room. They were the same species as Mother Famine, with matching red marks on their faces, wearing matching shapeless blue robes.

"These are Brother Famine and Sister Famine. They are acolytes under my care."

Brother Famine was slightly taller than Rohan with a slender build. Sister Famine had striking features, her cheekbones worthy of being chiseled in stone.

Rohan stood and offered a hand. Brother Famine shook it, while Sister Famine took a step back.

Mother Famine smiled. "Please do not be offended. We each do what we must to resist temptations."

"Sure. What do you do if there is more than one female acolyte? They can't both be Sister Famine, can they? Seems confusing."

Brother Famine shook his head. "Our titles are chosen for us before we embark on a mission. There is no confusion."

"A mission? You mean like a missionary, right? Not, like, a secret mission for the government."

Mother Famine smiled. "We spread the word of our society and its edicts. So that others who are afflicted will know of our path, know that there are options other than feeding the hunger. We also, when possible, work against those who have fallen to the curse."

"What does 'work against' mean? Exactly?"

Sister Famine pinned him with a glare. "We kill. That is the only time we kill."

"No rehabilitation for the bad vampires?"

Sister Famine snorted while Mother Famine smiled gently. "Once a vampire succumbs to the hunger, it is too late."

Rohan looked at Wei Li, who sipped daintily at her drink. "So it wasn't them?"

"I believe I told you that."

"Then why are we here?"

Mother Famine looked between her guests. "It is time for you to tell me what has happened."

Wei Li set the mug down on a short table by her side. "There have been murders. Three. A family of Kratics."

Sister Famine surged forward a step, her eyes narrowing. "You believe *we* are responsible? You know what we are, who we are, how we have dedicated our lives. How dare you!"

Mother Famine put an arm out as if to restrain her acolyte. "Calm yourself. It is her responsibility to suspect us. To suspect everyone."

Wei Li picked her mug up and sipped, apparently unfazed by Sister Famine's outburst.

Mother Famine continued. "The bodies were drained?"

The security chief nodded. "Mutilated and drained."

"You therefore believe vampires are responsible."

Another sip.

Sister Famine looked at her superior. "We are being framed. There is no end to those who hate us for what we are."

Rohan looked between them. "Does that happen a lot? People murdering other people to incite a mob against you?"

Mother Famine shook her head. "Perhaps not unheard of, but it is not common. It is more likely that someone wanted those people dead for some other reason and wished to obfuscate the matter."

Wei Li nodded. "We are investigating the victims. Thus far we are finding nothing that could even begin to justify a triple homicide. They were normal people, with very normal lives."

Rohan looked at her. "Could it have something to do with the student? The one who found them? I don't mean that he did it, but someone going after him?"

Wei Li shrugged her shoulders, defined cords of muscle rippling along her neck. "It is not impossible, but again, there is no obvious cause there for animosity."

Brother Famine grunted. "There could be vampires on Wistful. Feeders."

Wei Li nodded. "I came here hoping you could help us with that."

He sat down in the other open chair. "We'd be glad to help. It is our purpose."

"Can you tell me how many vampires I'm looking for? Or when they will need to feed again?"

The three looked between one another. Mother Famine answered.

"Not with clarity. Three dead does not tell us anything by itself. Myths speak of vampires that could survive without feeding for months or years. But never by choice."

"Is there anything you can do to help me find the murderer, assuming it is, in fact, a vampire?"

The vampires looked at each other again, their faces tight, the green draining from their cheeks.

Brother Famine spoke first. "It is not an easy thing, but we can try to *sense* when a fallen vampire is feeding."

Wei Li set down her empty mug. "You say it is not an easy thing. If you are to help me, I need to understand the parameters of what you can and cannot do."

Mother Famine stood. "We will do whatever we can to help. For now, let us confer, so that I may provide you with details. We live to serve, but there is risk whenever we push ourselves too far."

Wei Li stood. "I understand. Let me know. Do not take your time."

Rohan stood with her. "It was nice meeting you all. Uh, sorry about the, uh, being infected with vampirism. Thing. That sucks."

The three stared at him for a long breath's time. Mother Famine shook his hand.

"Thank you. Please take care."

Wei Li opened the door and waved him through, closing it behind her.

"I still do not understand why you wanted me there with you."

"Vampires react strongly to Hybrids. Your fluids are a delicacy to them. If any of those three had fallen, were feeding actively, they would have been unable to remain calm in your presence."

"Oh. I wasn't muscle, I was bait."

"Yes."

"Fair enough." They exited the building and walked toward station center.

Wistful's boulevards were covered in vibrant grasses, interspersed with flowerbeds and occasional stands of trees collected from a hundred different planets.

"There's something I don't understand."

"There are many things you don't understand. I suppose you need me to explain one of them in particular?"

"Exactly. I love being best friends with an empath; you always know what I want."

"It is a one-sided joy you are feeling."

"Here's the thing. We're on a space station. Doesn't Wistful have imagery you can look at to see who went into that apartment? Or who left it? I mean, doesn't she have cameras practically everywhere? At least everywhere public?"

"I retract my earlier mockery. That is a very good question."

"Is it?"

"There are often small gaps in the ship's records. Cameras break; footage is erased. We very rarely care about most of it, so it very rarely matters. In this case, however, an unusual amount of the evidence has disappeared in an entirely unlikely way. And very quickly."

"Oh. You mean you can't expect to have every second of every viewpoint kept around forever, but you usually have enough to do what you need done. Except now."

"That is what I mean."

"What could account for that? Is someone interfering with Wistful?"

"I would very much like to know the answer to that question."

4

Bourbon Dreams

Rohan dreamed he was in the distillery he'd built on Andervar.

Giant sharks had gotten into the fermentation vats. The staff ran about, waving helpless hands in the air and screaming wordlessly as menacing triangular fins popped up out of the mash, one after another.

He grabbed employees one by one and demanded that they tell him whether the sharks were fouling the bourbon or simply drinking it all. The purple-skinned Andervarians responded with more incoherent shouting.

Alarms began to sound, high-pitched beeping noises that would have woken the dead. But the alarms weren't part of the dream. They were sounding in the room.

"What is it?"

He checked the bedside clock, still wondering how the sharks had fit through the pipes in the distillery.

Too early for his shift.

"Rohan, this is a recorded message from Wei Li. There is an emergency situation at East Arm, block Thirteen. Officers down and more loss of life is pending."

"Rudra save me." He was talking to himself.

"Repeat, I cannot speak with you directly. Officers are down, possibly including me. Lives are being lost. If you can render assistance, please do so. East Arm, block Thirteen."

He crossed the room and entered his private airlock so quickly, the disrupted air blew his sheets off the bed.

Wasted seconds waiting for Wistful to cycle the airlock for him, as she often did in emergencies.

Punched the manual controls.

Took one last deep breath as the airlock drained atmosphere from the inner chamber and opened.

His eyes stung, instantly dried by exposure to vacuum, and he flew half-blind to the eastern arm of the station.

The diamond roof over the boulevard was clouded, dimmed to represent station nighttime. There were no clear markings to represent specific blocks; Rohan had to estimate passing a dozen sections.

Dug raw fingers underneath one panel and wedged it out by force.

Why isn't Wistful helping?

Entered the station; took a breath; blinked five times.

The boulevard below was quiet.

Where am I?

He found a sign; he'd reentered too soon.

With a crack of sundered air, he accelerated down the boulevard toward the next section, Third Eye opening as he flew. Anybody tough enough to give Wei Li trouble had Powers, and he was sensitive enough to *sense* anybody with Powers in use.

"Come on, come on. Where are you?"

The unmistakable smell of vampire aura shone from a spot just ahead. He exploded with a burst of acceleration, aimed directly at the black-red silhouette that *tasted* like hunger.

It turned and met him with an upraised hand.

They collided, tumbling through the dirt.

Rohan rolled to his feet, brushing a clump of grass off his bare shoulder. Wei Li was on the ground, but her aura was strong, not dead or badly wounded. At least three others, all in station security uniforms, were less lucky.

One civilian was down, dead or dying.

A half dozen other security officers formed a ring around Rohan and the creature.

The vampire was already on its feet.

It was tall, a full two meters, draped in a tattered blue-gray leather bodysuit. It was pale enough to be Shayjh, with a physique stripped to the bare essentials of life. Skeletal limbs poked out from the bodysuit in a gangly array. Its cheekbones were razor blades threatening to cut through its face; not a strand of hair or eyelash remained.

The creature smiled, pencil-thin white lips twisting up at the corners of a porcelain-pale face. When its mouth opened, its teeth showed long and jagged, the gums receded into nothingness.

"How delightful! More of the children have come to play. And you, little one, seem to be a particularly tasty morsel."

The words weren't Drachna, and they certainly weren't Shayjh.

He answered in Fire Speech. "I'm no child, and I'm not here to play."

The vampire shook its left arm. The lower portion dangled loosely, the bones between wrist and elbow shattered.

"Surely you are, dressed like that?" The vampire pointed to Rohan's boxers.

"Am I not up to the dress code? So sorry. I must have missed that line on the invitation."

The vampire swung its arm; once, twice; the hand and lower forearm jerked about, a door on loose hinges. On the third swing, the lower portion locked into place, the bones settling together. It flexed the hand, turning it forward and back.

Wei Li pushed herself up on all fours, shaking her head as if concussed.

"I am glad the children still learn the Fire Speech so they can properly address their elders. It is the first sign of civilization I've found on this ship."

Ship?

"Everyone here speaks Drachna."

"The il'Drach. I remember—no. They survive? Do they run this place?"

"The il'Drach control most of the sector, but Wistful is independent. Maybe you should have been asking these questions *before* killing her security officers."

"Killing? I have killed no one."

Rohan looked around, deliberately taking in the bodies on the ground.

"They are not dead, child. I kill only when I must. They have been granted immortality. You should be thanking me."

Rohan looked to Wei Li, seeking confirmation, but she shrugged. *She can't understand that language.*

"Can Wistful interpret what it's saying for you?"

Wei Li shook her head. "She is not responding to my requests at the moment."

The vampire stepped closer to Rohan. "You, child, will be more than a morsel. When I consume you, we will be strong indeed. Together."

"That's not going to happen."

The Hybrid *reached* down and *pulled* at the Power beneath his core, drawing forth cascades of energy. The vampire smiled, long incisors glinting even in the dim lights of station pre-dawn.

"Ah, yes, the il'Drach curse. You will be delicious."

Rohan *thrust* himself forward, crossing the four meters separating the two in an eyeblink, and launched a flurry of punches at the vampire.

Left jab, hook with the same hand, right straight, aimed at the vampire's grinning face. The taller creature dodged and parried, never dropping its smile.

"Clever child. Clever punches."

Its left foot swept straight up, then swung around to come at Rohan's head from the side. He lifted his right fist and caught the kick on his upper arm and shoulder.

The impact threw him across the grass.

He *pulled* more Power.

Clods of dirt and small stones rose from the ground all around him. With a spiritual snap, Rohan *sent* the debris rushing toward the vampire.

The creature leaned in, splitting the storm of missiles like a ship's prow, noticing too late that Rohan had followed them in.

A punch damaged the vampire's left arm, rupturing the spot where bones had been reattached. A knee to the belly brought flecks of blood up onto the vampire's smiling lips.

"Strong child, as much as I hoped for."

It kicked again, but Rohan was braced for it and stood his ground, absorbing the impact with his left shoulder. He returned fire, snapping his foot up under the vampire's sternum.

The beast fell back several meters.

Wei Li, chest heaving with effort, had reached her feet. Her attention was focused on the vampire. "It is powerful but it lacks depth. It won't last long at this rate of exertion."

Rohan answered her in Drachna. "Operation War of Attrition begins now."

He rushed forward again, air cracking with his passage. With arms up over his face, he struck the vampire full in the chest, knocking it back another handful of meters.

"You picked the wrong place to start a feeding frenzy, buddy."

"This is no frenzy. You have clearly never seen true feeding."

"Not really looking to break that streak today."

The vampire closed on Rohan, its body flowing across the ground with a boneless grace, a liquid wave of destruction. The Hybrid took his stance: left hand across his belly, right hand covering his jaw, right side angled away.

The beast struck and slashed; Rohan leaned left, then right, then left again, shifting elbows and fists to block and parry the vampire's strikes.

He sidestepped a rising knee, punishing the out-of-position vampire with a tight left hook across the jaw.

It raked its left hand across his belly, raising welts just short of open wounds, and Rohan caught the forearm with his elbow.

The bone gave way.

Rising and retreating, the vampire tried to shake out its arm. Rohan closed on it with a fresh flurry of strikes, determined to keep it from recovering.

It kicked at him, more to create distance than cause injury. Rohan twisted so the kick missed him and landed three punches to the vampire's midsection.

Bloody foam began to form on its lips.

"Insolent child, so disrespectful."

The Hybrid cleared his throat. "They tell me I wasn't trained properly."

"You should not be fighting me. I am here to save you all."

Rohan punched again, snapping the vampire's head back.

"You could have called. Ask to sit down, talk about who needs saving, from what, by whom. I would have bought you a coffee. Or a bourbon. Have you tried Andervarian bourbon?"

They traded punches. Rohan rubbed at the soreness in his neck. "Ready to surrender?"

The vampire chuckled. "Your words are brave but premature. I will come back for you when I have recovered more of my strength."

"What makes you think I'm letting you go?"

"You have no choice in the matter." The vampire's bloody smile widened.

Wei Li shouted. "It's doing something!"

Rohan could *smell* a shift in the vampire's aura.

He stepped forward and swung at the creature. His fist flew through its head, meeting no resistance.

"Rudra save me, you can shadowstep?"

The vampire's grin remained as it dropped, passing directly through the turf without disturbing a pebble or a blade of grass.

Wei Li was tapping furiously at her comm link. "Wistful! Please! Track it! It's dropping to the transport tubes!"

Rohan hadn't put in his own comm. He looked around, then darted toward the nearest descending staircase. Down in the transport level, he ran back and forth between tube platforms.

No sign of it. He cracked his neck.

Wei Li was on his heels. "Do you see it?"

"No. Can't you *sense* it? From this distance, especially?"

"I am experiencing difficulty doing so."

He turned to her. "Seriously? What does that even mean?"

"Wistful's own aura always clouds my senses. That is one reason I chose to live here."

"Oh. But you usually still know what people are feeling."

"Usually. At this moment the obfuscation is . . . heavier than normal."

They were both moving, checking transport pods and looking up and down the tubes. "Did Wistful give you that translation of what the guy was saying?"

"She did not. Excuse me, Rohan, but if we cannot track the creature from here, there is little point in remaining here. I must see to the safety of my fallen officers."

"No, sure, of course. Sorry."

Before leaving the transport level, she turned to him and touched his arm. "I do appreciate your assistance, Rohan. I am just frustrated."

"No, don't apologize. Go see to your guys. I'll get some pants on."

A smile flashed over her face. "If I were anyone else, I'd suspect you of deliberately appearing before me unclothed. This marks consecutive days of that happening."

"You know, you knocked on my door yesterday, and you called me out of bed today! Who is deliberately doing what?" He followed her up the stairs.

Grim headshakes from the survivors told them that the fallen officers were dead. Dawn was breaking as Wistful turned down the roof shades and let light stream onto the boulevard.

Wei Li touched Rohan with her elbow. With a slight tilt of her head, she pointed up the boulevard.

Three figures in heavy blue robes stood at the edge of the grass, fifty meters up from the scene of the fight. They huddled, monk's hoods touching in the center, conferring.

"You want me to talk to them?"

"Please. I have other arrangements to make."

Rohan headed toward the trio. They separated, their hoods drenching their faces in shadow. Two stepped back while a third came to meet him.

"You saw?"

Mother Famine lifted her hood just enough to give him a view of her face. *It's going to be dawn soon. She's probably not eager to have sunlight on her skin.*

"We arrived too late. We *felt*."

Somber mutterings came from the security officers.

Mother Famine's brow furrowed. She peeked around Rohan.

"Forgive my acolytes. The smell of blood is uncomfortable. It is better for them to stay back."

"Better for them, and for the rest of us, right? A whiff of blood, too much excitement, who knows what they might start missing?"

"That is the truth of our existence. We are as committed as anybody to keeping Wistful free of the fallen. That means securing ourselves, first and foremost."

He sighed. "I hear you. Did you get anything out of that vampire? The fallen one? Any sense of, I don't know, weaknesses?"

She paused. "He is strong. And overwhelmingly hungry, as if he's been starved for a long time. Once he has fed adequately, he will be more dangerous."

"Strong as in . . . what? As strong as you? As the three of you put together?" *As strong as me?*

"One of the strongest I have ever *seen*. Probably the strongest. Combined, the three of us would be little match for him."

"That's not what I wanted to hear."

Wei Li walked up to join them. She shook her head sadly. "Thanks to your warning, we caught him while still feeding. He claimed only one victim, then two of my officers."

"We are sorry for the losses. His hunger . . . it is tremendous. Many more will die if he is not destroyed."

Rohan looked over the vampires. "That's going to be easier said than done. He's as tough as the spike in a bootstrap drive, and he can shadow-step."

Mother Famine's brows furrowed. "You are certain? That is an unusual ability."

"I'm aware of that." He turned to face Wei Li as he spoke. "Rare, a huge pain in the ass, and, oh yeah, did I mention? It's not supposed to work on a space station."

Wei Li rubbed the skin above the bridge of her nose. "It is not. Wistful's own soul, informing the material of this station, should have blocked the creature's step into shadow."

"Yet it didn't. And she's not helping with translations."

"There is more." Wei Li lowered her voice; the station's audio pickups out in the middle of the boulevard weren't very sensitive. "She was supposed to help us trap the vampire. She has internal defense systems that didn't come online."

Mother Famine looked between them. "What does that mean? Has the vampire harmed the station itself somehow?"

Wei Li shrugged. "Perhaps it is technical interference. Something preventing her sensors from working properly. It wouldn't be the first time."

Rohan nodded. "I can ask Marion Stone to look over things, see if there are any signs of sabotage." Marion had, a year earlier, hacked Wistful's external sensors to convince the station it was being attacked, as a distraction.

"That is a fine idea."

"Has anybody even identified what language he was speaking? Definitely nothing I recognize."

Wei Li shrugged. "Alien to me as well."

Mother Famine remained silent.

"Rohan, what did he tell you?"

Rohan sighed. "He called me 'child' a lot. Described himself as an elder. He said he had come here to save us. And he said he hasn't killed anybody. Which kind of belies the six bodies we've found so far."

Mother Famine reached out, as if to grab his arm, but let her hand drop. "Are you sure? Did he explain what that meant?"

He scratched his beard, then ran fingers over the sore skin on his abdomen. "He said he had given people immortality. I thought he meant they were going to become vampires."

Wei Li shook her head. "Once someone is dead, they are dead. The body can be used as a corpse soldier, but they cannot come back as a vampire."

Mother Famine agreed. "That isn't what he meant. He's a soul eater."

Wei Li's head turned sharply.

"That makes sense. And explains the fractured appearance of his spirit."

Rohan looked at one, then the other. "Someone want to fill me in on this soul-eating business?"

Wei Li looked at Mother Famine, who sighed before answering. "All blood drinkers consume blood for nutrients and energy."

"Right. Vampires."

"Yes. Many also consume the spiritual energy of their victims. They can then use this energy."

"I knew that already. Give a little boost to their Powers."

"That boost is temporary. It is like having a fire and stealing someone else's wood. You can burn a bigger, brighter fire for a time, but soon it's gone."

"Good analogy. A bit rural, but I get the gist."

"A soul eater is another matter. They consume the souls of their victims in their entirety, assimilating them into their own. It is like not simply taking your neighbor's wood, but enslaving their children to chop and split wood for you forever after."

"The soul eater doesn't just get a bigger fire temporarily, it's a permanent upgrade."

"Yes."

"That sounds amazing. As in, it's terrible and evil, sure, but it's a great way to gain Power. Why aren't there people all around who do this? Eat a bunch of their friends and wind up with Power like a Hybrid?"

Wei Li answered. "Souls aren't firewood. When a soul is absorbed, so is a measure of its character. Its thoughts, feelings, temperament, and so on. Combining many such sets of characteristics in one being leads inevitably to instability."

Mother Famine tipped her head, letting her hood fall over her face. "Not instability, insanity. And, most often, to even greater evil. At various times through history, people have become soul eaters in a quest for greater Power. It never ends well."

"I'm starting to miss giant sharks."

"Excuse me?"

"Nothing. I'm mocking myself. Had an issue . . . You know what, never mind. Do we have any idea where this guy came from? Is there, like, a place where soul eaters are made?"

The women answered with silence.

Rohan ran his fingers through his shoulder-length hair. "So, he'll keep eating, and the more he eats the stronger he'll get. Do we have any good news at this point?"

More silence.

"Do we have a plan?"

Wei Li spoke. "Rohan, I fear you may be the only person on this station who can physically stop this creature."

"I can stop him, but I can't catch him. Shadowstepping, remember?"

"I will try to determine why Wistful allowed the creature to shadowstep. If I succeed, I'd like to try to trap the creature in combat with you. If you're willing."

"He's killed six people already. That we know of. I'll catch him."

Mother Famine twitched. "Do not catch him, Hybrid. He must be killed. There is no redemption for a soul eater."

"People say the same thing about Hybrids, and about anyone who served in the Imperial Fleet. I'm not squeamish, but I'm not an assassin either."

Wei Li patted his arm. "Let us see if it is even possible to arrange a confrontation. We can discuss these specifics later."

"All right. Last thing, though. You didn't understand him, but you could *feel* his aura, right? Was he lying when he talked to me?"

"I cannot be certain, but I don't think so."

"Because he said he was here to protect us. I'm no empath, but he sounded like he believed it."

Mother Famine held up a hand. "He might believe it, but that doesn't mean it's true. Soul eaters are not sane."

"Just in case, I'd like to know what he thinks he's protecting us *from*."

5

Hearts Grown Fonder

Rohan floated in space, close to one of the beacons marking off Wistful's personal space. No ship would cross those beacons without powering down and requesting a tow. Providing that tow was Rohan's job.

A few loose strands of hair floated out from under his hood, the gold-and-purple material otherwise pulled tight to his head. He stretched and tumbled, relaxing in the curious way only possible in free fall.

The station glittered in the distance, a cross-shaped jewel.

"Wistful, any more ships?"

"Your queue is empty. You are free to end your shift." It wasn't Wistful *herself* answering, but a small subroutine that handled docking requests. It had the same voice, and for the most part the same speech pattern, but Rohan always felt he could tell when Wistful herself was speaking to him.

She hadn't talked to him that entire day. He wasn't sure if that was normal.

"Copy that. Rohan out."

A nudge straightened his tumble; a *push* sent him on a straight path for Wistful, his airlock, and his apartment.

He showered, rehydrating skin dried out by a long day's exposure to space.

I should check in with Wei Li. See if we're still training tonight.

He began to towel off just as the door chime sounded.

"Again?"

He covered himself with the towel and waved the door open.

"Hello?"

"Chief man!"

"Noru? What are you doing—is there a problem at the distillery?"

The purple-skinned Andervarian ducked her head under his arm and entered the apartment.

She was dressed for business, wearing clothes with a conservative cut that would have been out of place in her hometown, one of the poorest boroughs in Fago City.

"No worries, chief man. All one hundred percent at the distillery."

The bourbon distillery Rohan had built on Andervar had been open for two months. Noru was his local business agent: contracting workers, making sure permits were in order, distributing bribes to local police and government officials.

She stretched her arms out and sat on his bed. "Myself always wanting to visit famous space station Wistful, share small chops with great teacher Wei Li. Today myself arrives; great teacher is too busy, friend Rohan working all day. Why chief man work so hard? Chief man rich, yah?"

"I'm sorry, Noru, I had no idea you were here. Possibly because you didn't message me. I would have gotten out early or something."

"Myself teasing, chief man. Myself arrived yesterday on Wistful, needing care for big time client. Hotel, food, all the premium."

"Ah. You're here working for someone else?" *What are the odds of that?*

"Aye, chief man, got it first try. Big client. Heavy credits, flowing nicely into Noru's pockets."

"Well, that's great for you! Is he Andervarian? Local to you?"

"That curious thing, chief man. Most curious. Client no Andervarian. From Ice Colony. Human. That being right word?"

Rohan paused. Ice Colony was an il'Drach outpost that had been seeded with people from Northern Europe centuries earlier. He stepped to the bathroom and got his hairbrush.

"Ice Colony? How did he pick you? No offense, Noru, but you don't have an interplanetary reputation. Or do you?"

A long, slender knife appeared in her hand, the blade blacked and vicious. She dug its tip under her nails, cleaning them. "Rich man says hire

Noru, at triple rates for easy work, myself not one for arguing. Rich man says, to Wistful we go, triple rates once again; Noru again, not arguing. Arrive Wistful, rich man be saying, find Tow Chief Second Class Rohan, bring for small chops, maybe a drink or three, talk after long time, myself still not arguing. Myself wondering, though."

"You're saying your client wants to see me? Me, specifically, or the station's tow chief?"

"Boss man asking for Rohan by name. Client man means no harm. Noru sure." She tapped her temple. She was an empath; not at Wei Li's level, but far more sensitive than Rohan.

He sighed. "Not what I was expecting. Dinner? When?"

"Never a time as good as the now, chief man. Maybe put on more than a towel, first thing."

"Does this client of yours have a name?" He stepped into the bathroom to dress.

"Calls himself Magnusson."

"He 'calls himself' that? So, it's not his name?"

"Tricky question, chief man. Magnusson not lie; also not one hundred percent truth. Of truth. Not all of truth."

"He's probably Jaroux's dad or big brother or something."

"Jaroux?"

"Just an Ice Colony Hybrid I had to cripple a year ago. Wait, your client isn't a Hybrid, is he?"

"Ayah, chief man. Noru not stupid. Would have said such a thing straightaway."

"And he said he wants to talk to me after a long time? He didn't mention the previous time we talked, did he? As in, when and where?"

"Client did not say all of that."

He pulled his boots on, wiggling his toes into place.

"Before I forget, how *is* the distillery going?" Investing in a bourbon distillery had been an off-the-cuff decision.

"All good, chief man. No worries for you. Bottles for sale by end of the year, myself thinking. Big cash money profits coming."

"Great. Let's go meet this mystery client of yours. Where is he?"

"Back room at Ton'ga Shell. Chief man knows it?"

Is this a good omen or a bad omen?

"An unreasonable percentage of the most eventful things that have happened to me on this station occurred at the Ton'ga Shell."

She tilted her head quizzically, reminding him strongly of Wei Li.

He smiled. "My heart was broken in that place. I'll tell you while we walk."

"Chief man prefer a different location? Noru picking it just because of fine reputation."

"No, it's great. I'm a grown man, I can eat in a restaurant without crying because a girl broke my heart there."

She nodded and let him tell the story of his romance with Tamaralinth Lastex while they walked.

When he finished the story, Noru hugged his side while he held his mask in his hands, using the built-in heads-up display to scroll through messages and news.

Nothing from Wei Li.

Civilian media was publishing articles about the murders and the dead security officers. People were getting nervous.

They probably should *be nervous.*

The host at the Ton'ga Shell recognized one of them as soon as they stepped through the front doors and ushered them into the back room.

Every surface in the restaurant was made of an exotic, luxury material: woods in every color of the rainbow, animal shells steamed and pressed flat, supple leathers from animals Rohan had never seen. A large staff bustled and hurried about, delivering multicourse meals to a selection of the station's wealthiest businesspeople.

The host opened the door to the back room; Rohan waved for Noru to enter first.

His heart sank as a familiar voice called out. "Noru, my dear, come in, come in. Did you find him?"

Rohan stepped into the room.

The walls were close—just spacious enough for a table for twelve with access for waitstaff.

Two people sat at the table.

One was a woman. Blonde hair, blue eyes, more than a few kilos past what was fashionable on Earth, but he had no idea what the style was on Ice Colony. She wore a dress in dark yellow that showed more cleavage than it hid, with a long slit up the side exposing skin that told him she did not spend much time in the sun.

The man was nearly her polar opposite, at least in appearance. Short, perhaps five centimeters under Rohan's slightly-below-average height. He had skin a shade or two darker than Rohan's own walnut coloring, with short, wavy black hair starting to recede at the temples and a full mustache. He sported a wiry build, a small potbelly the only thing separating him from a professional racquetball player's physique.

Rohan felt his heartbeat rise. "Oh no."

The man stood, holding his arms out, and walked up to Rohan. "My boy! So good to see you!"

The woman stood, uncertainly, while Noru cleared space for them.

Rohan withstood the man's embrace, his back tight and painful.

Mr. Magnusson turned to Noru. "You may go now, dear. We have things to talk about, yes?"

She turned to Rohan. Either something in his expression or his aura was worrying her. "Chief man okay?"

He sighed and nodded, working to push a smile up his lips. "Go on. I'm fine. You're better off not hearing this."

The older man laughed, a full explosion of air rolling out of his belly and echoing off the plush wooden walls.

"So true, so true! Much to discuss! Rohan, let me introduce you to my woman."

The blonde stepped forward, around the table, as she giggled. "Wife. I'm his wife. He's so silly, always forgetting the right word for things."

She held out a hand. Rohan shook it; she had the grip of a farmhand.

Noru cast one last glance toward Rohan. He nodded; she nodded back and walked out.

Rohan turned to the blonde. "Very pleased to meet you. I'm Rohan. Tow Chief Second Class."

She giggled again, a pink blush rising on her pale cheeks. "Oh, I know who *you* are, sweetie! Dhruv talks about you all the time."

"Does he now?" Rohan looked at the darker man.

Dhruv stood, the top of his head reaching the blonde's jawline. "Of course I do, of course! Rohan, this is Sigrun, as I mentioned. She's from Ice Colony. My woman."

"Wife," she interjected.

Rohan nodded. "As I said, pleasure to meet you. It's been a while, Dhruv. How long has it been, exactly? I feel like it was supposed to be longer."

Dhruv laughed, showing very white, perfectly square teeth. "Who keeps track of things like that? Not me, certainly. Too long, my boy, too long. I've missed our talks."

"Have you?"

"Of course! I have always valued the opinion of Rohan, Lance Primary—"

"Tow Chief, Dhruv. Not a lance of any kind. Not anymore."

"Yes, yes, I know, I'm not senile. Not yet, eh? Now, please sit, join us. The food here is lovely."

Sigrun playfully slapped his arm. "You can't possibly eat anymore, dearest. You've had two full meals here already!"

"And risk offending dear Rohan? Nonsense. I have room for more. Never doubt Dhruv's appetite." He patted his belly as he spoke. "For food or . . . other things." His hand squeezed her bottom.

She blushed again, with greater fury, and slapped his hand away. "Oh, you! What am I going to do with you?"

"I have a few ideas . . ."

Rohan cleared his throat. "Maybe you could have this discussion some other time? Without me?"

Dhruv snapped his fingers. A waiter flittered through the door, pad in hand, ready to take instructions.

"Bring that tasting course again, my good fellow. For three this time."

"Yes, sir. Right away, sir." He shut the door behind him, leveling a blanket of silence over the room.

Dhruv turned to Rohan. "Sit. I wasn't lying about the food."

Rohan sighed and took a chair across from the couple. "I know. I've been here before. I think my picture is on the wall."

"I thought I recognized you! Marvelous! I wasn't sure, with the beard."

Rohan scratched his jawline. "I grew it out."

"Of course you did. Yes. Well, no matter. Beard, hair, they can be changed, in an instant, really. Doesn't affect who you are in here." He slapped his chest as he said it.

Six waiters—humanoids of mixed genders and species bedecked in matching, impeccably cut black outfits—filtered in and distributed bread and a first course of wines to the three.

Sigrun was first to touch the wine, draining half the glass in a single swallow. "We don't have such fancy food on Ice Colony, you know, Rohan. You're very lucky to be here!"

He nodded. "I'm glad you're enjoying it. I can't help but wonder, what brings you to Wistful? We're a bit, I don't know, out of the way. You didn't come for the food, did you?"

Dhruv nodded and sipped sparingly at his own wine.

"Not the food, no. I wanted you to meet my lovely Sigrun! She is lovely, isn't she?"

The lady in question pushed his shoulder. "Stop, you beast!"

"She is! Super lovely. Well, now we've met. So you'll be going back to Ice Colony? Need help booking transport? I know people. You can cut the queue."

Dhruv smiled broadly. "You remember me, Rohan. I'm always working on things. Always multitasking, yes? I have a few more items to look into here before anybody thinks about leaving."

Sigrun turned to Rohan. "I don't mean to be rude, but you don't seem very happy to see us."

Rohan sighed. "You're not being rude. Maybe I am. Believe me, it's not about you."

Dhruv put a hand on his wife's forearm to settle her. "Rohan, have you figured out the writing you saw on Repentant?"

"What? How do you even know about that? *What* do you know about that?"

The older man sipped his wine and shook his head. "It's my business to know things. Are those really the questions you want to ask me?"

Rohan ran through a quick list of people who knew about Repentant. Too many of them could have communicated that information, deliberately or by accident.

"Okay, I'll play the game. I have not figured out the writing on Repentant."

"The station talked to you, yes? What did she speak?"

"Not much that's useful. A lot of 'I'm really angry, get out, go away. Don't come back.' That sort of thing."

"I didn't ask what she *said*, I asked what she *spoke*. What language? Drachna? Perhaps a very old version of Drachna?"

"I didn't recognize it. If it was old Drachna, it was completely incomprehensible."

"I see, I see. That's interesting."

"Why? What's interesting?"

"Why do you think that station was there, Rohan? What was its purpose?"

"You mean before everything on her and the planet below died?"

"Yes, that is exactly what I mean. You were always a smart boy. What is your hypothesis?"

He took another sip of wine, finishing the glass, then ran fingers through his hair. "I honestly haven't been thinking about it. A little preoccupied. First quarantine, then the rogue vampire that's been running around."

Dhruv's face tightened noticeably. "Vampire?"

"Yes, Dhruv." He put heavy weight on the name. "There are at least six people dead, killed by a shadowstepping vampire. A soul eater."

"Ah. Yes. That is interesting."

"That's not the first adjective to come to mind. Maybe horrifying? Terrible?"

"Those descriptors are not exclusive. And I am not sure your preoccupation is completely distinct from my questions."

"I don't follow. Well, maybe I do. You think the vampire has something to do with Repentant."

"Or the planet below her."

"Why?"

"Answer my question, Rohan. Why was the station there?"

"I don't know. To protect the planet? Protect something on the planet?"

"Or to protect everything else *from* the planet. Or something on it."

"The vampire."

Dhruv shrugged as another course was delivered. Sigrun happily drained another glass of wine, which was refilled before the staff left the room.

He continued once they were alone. "That station was put in place for one of two reasons. Somewhere on that planet or station is something valuable. Or something dangerous."

Rohan ran through the scenarios. "That's why you're here? You want a piece of whatever is on that planet?"

Dhruv leaned back in his chair. "That is precisely why I'm here. Partially."

"Because it's never simple with you."

"It's a complicated world, boy. You know that now. As well as anyone."

"What possible use do you have for another weapon? What war is left for you to fight? What are you afraid of?"

Something dark flickered behind Dhruv's eyes. His voice hardened.

"There are things out there, boy. Things you know nothing about. Dangers you know nothing about." The edge of the table cracked as his fingers dug into the wood.

Sigrun put one hand on his back, stroking his shoulders, the other on the back of his hand. "Calm down, dear. I'm sure he didn't mean to upset you. Did you, Rohan?"

"What are you two even talking about?"

Dhruv ground his teeth. Sigrun turned to fully face the younger man. "He's been through some things lately, Rohan. Please, don't upset him."

Rohan bit into the pickled something-or-other that adorned his plate. A powerful crunch was chased by an explosion of flavors.

"That vampire I was talking about? He's not something you can use. Best case, we can neutralize him, but everybody else just wants him dead."

"No, not dead. Not dead. We can give him what he wants, make him useful. Do you realize how rare shadowstepping is? Combined with soul eating? If we can keep him sane, point him at the right targets . . ."

"And if we can't? Come on, this is crazy talk."

Dhruv focused on Rohan, his eyes menacing. "Don't call me that. I'm not crazy."

I know it's been a while, but this is not his normal demeanor.

Sigrun tried to smile, reduced to a baring of teeth as her face filled with alarm. "Rohan, dear, apologize. Please. Nobody's crazy. We just have a difference of opinion."

Rohan looked into her pleading eyes. "Look, I'm sorry. Okay? Not crazy. It's just not a good idea. That thing is really dangerous."

Dhruv cracked his neck and let his shoulders drop, first one, then the other. Let out a long breath as he slumped deeper into the chair.

"Great victories require great risks, Rohan. I seem to remember you making that exact point to me."

Rohan felt his Power rising, waves of anger breaking just below his seal of control, little eddies and whirls of rage waiting for a release.

He exhaled; emptied his lungs; held until his chest burned.

Another course arrived. They ate wordlessly.

Rohan put down his fork. "We have to find the vampire and stop him. Once we do that, we can figure out the next steps."

"Good, good! That's what we'll tell your friends. So they'll all cooperate, yes? The security chief, for example. The Professors Stone."

"That's not what I—never mind. Look, I'll do what I can with this vampire, okay? And I'll try to keep an open mind about whether he can be used. In the meantime, you should get off the station."

"Where else could I possibly want to be?"

"Someplace without a soul eater on board. Go back to Ice Colony. I'll call you when things are safer."

"I am not some useless bureaucrat that you shift off to the side when things are difficult."

"I know that. But things look like they might get really difficult, and I'd rather not have to worry about you."

Dhruv looked at Sigrun, who nodded. "I'm full. I'll get Noru, see if she'll eat my dessert. I have to watch my figure!"

Rohan cleared his throat. "There's a group of heavily armed Rogesh just outside. Keep an eye out."

Sigrun shook her head. "They won't bother me." She left.

Rohan waited for Dhruv to say something, but nothing came.

The empty room somehow settled more heavily on his shoulders. Years of arguments he'd run through in his mind, years of anger and frustration, all pressing to be let out. While that man sat, smiling, and sipped at his dark-blue wine.

He switched to English.

"Does she know what you are?"

Dhruv raised an eyebrow at the change in language. "Sigrun? Of course. She knows what I am, she knows her purpose."

"Noru?"

Dhruv smiled. "I'm waiting to see what she'll figure out."

"That's a dangerous game."

The smile widened. "Come on! Don't begrudge an old man his fun."

"You're not an old man, Dad."

The smile, uncontainable, turned to laughter. "Watch where you call me that. Can't have people finding out I'm il'Drach."

"One more reason for you to leave. It's not safe for you to be seen around me too much. We look alike."

"Sadly, I am far more handsome. Luckily, you got your mother's brains. Speaking of . . ."

"I saw her. Six months ago. Earth had some . . . issues."

"I heard. How is she?"

"I'm not playing this game with you."

"At least . . . is she happy?"

Rohan sighed. "I think so. She seemed happy, as much as you'd expect given the circumstances. You know, the planet was on the brink of destruction."

"I heard. You see the danger, then, don't you?"

"What? The sharks?"

"The Old Ones. The ones who *sent* the sharks. Earth was just a test run. They're after all of us."

"What does that even mean, Dad? All of us?"

"All the humanoid races. The il'Drach, for a start. Then . . . everyone."

"They've been gone for millions of years, haven't they? What's left? Cultists like Dr. Kraken, whipping up harebrained plots from the shadows? We can handle them. You sound paranoid."

Another dark flash through his eyes. "Don't call me that. Not until you've seen what I've seen, flown the depths where I've flown. Don't call me that."

"Sure, sure, got it. Sorry."

"There are dangers out there, Rohan. We need weapons to keep us safe. New, old, doesn't matter. If there is any way to bend this soul eater to our purpose, we have to take it. He was left there for a reason. For this reason."

"Okay, Dad, sure. I heard you. Hope for a miracle."

They drank their wine.

Dhruv put his glass down. "Do you want to hear something funny?"

"Sure, Dad."

"My father's name was Magnus."

"Really?"

"Yes. Magnusson . . . it's not my real name, but it's not a lie."

Rohan laughed. "That's pretty good. You want to hear something else I just remembered?"

"What?"

"The vampire? You know what else he told me?"

Dhruv leaned forward, his eyes burning. "What?"

"That he was here to protect us."

Dhruv's fingers tightened on the table. "From what? Did he say?"

"We didn't get that far. But he seems pretty convinced that he's doing us a favor."

"He might be right."

6

Old Acquaintances Sometimes Forget

Pop's House of Breakfast served the best eggs in the sector and arguably the best coffee, with a side order of one rule: questions about the eggs' origin were not permitted.

Pop strode to their table on long, lean legs. He was covered in scales, alternating diamonds of orange and black, and had six black eyes lined up across his face.

"The usual?"

Rohan nodded and fought back a yawn. The boulevard was brightening quickly as the roof cleared for station-dawn. He'd had time for sleep and little else after sharing dinner with his father.

Marion and Ben Stone sat in mismatched chairs on the other side of the rickety metal table. Marion had her shoes off and was pawing at the grass with bare feet.

Her once-blonde hair was almost fully gray, and very fine lines creased her face, but from any significant distance she looked just like the beauty whose poster had adorned college dorm walls for half a decade.

Ben was taller, lean and rangy, his bushy eyebrows dominating his face.

The two had been sidekicks and support gang for Earth's greatest hero, Hyperion, long before Rohan was born. They had left Earth to work for the il'Drach Empire decades earlier, eventually acquiring positions at the Imperial Fleet Academy.

Marion was shaking her head. "I thought my analysis of the writing from Repentant would have been finished two days ago."

Ben chuckled as he rubbed sleep from his eyes. "*You* thought it would be done before we got out of quarantine."

"Is it complete now?"

The Professors shared another look; Marion shook her head. "Records we need are missing. Not simply missing. Some were deleted. Others redacted. References to that language have been deliberately erased."

"Erased? How? And why?"

She put down her mug. "It's not supposed to be possible. Academy archives are *supposed* to be permanent. But you're familiar with how the il'Drach operate. Things happen."

Rohan scratched his beard and inhaled deeply. The air was thick with the smell of cut grass and fresh coffee.

Pop appeared and poured cups for the three of them.

"Could you tell how old the redacted records are?"

Ben shrugged. "Very roughly, tens of thousands of years. From the earliest moments of the Empire."

"And nothing since then?"

"No. Whoever used that language, they've been gone a long time."

She shook her head. "Either that or all the more recent records were expunged more carefully."

"Making that a dead end. Did you ask Wistful about it?"

"We put in a request. No answer yet."

Rohan looked at them. "Tell me something. Do you think we were let out of quarantine too fast? We found nothing organic still alive in that system. That we know of. Maybe we should have stayed isolated longer?"

The Stones shared a glance. Ben combed his hair with his fingers. "We thought that, too. But Wistful asked for the test results and more or less insisted that we were fine."

"Wistful did? You don't mean Wei Li or somebody else from security, do you?"

"No, it was Wistful."

"This isn't adding up."

Marion looked over her steaming mug. "What isn't?"

"Wistful's acting weird. Letting us out of quarantine, abandoning Wei Li's team during the fight with the vampire. He's a shadowstepper; he can slide in and out of this material plane. He's not supposed to be able to do that *inside* another living thing. But he did."

Ben swallowed the hot coffee. "Maybe he's just very powerful? There's a sort of mechanical advantage Wistful has over her own body, on account of it being *hers*, but it's not absolute."

"Maybe. I don't know. She either didn't record or won't share her recordings of the conversation I had with the vampire. That's weird."

Marion nodded. "I'm not sure whether this is relevant, but there is definitely a link between Wistful and Repentant. I ran comparisons between her and scans *Insatiable* took of Repentant's internal structure. They're too similar for it to be coincidence. I asked about that, too. No response. I would have thought she'd at least have sent some kind of null answer. Claiming not to know."

Rohan leaned back while Pop put a plate of eggs and biscuits in front of him.

He ate without really tasting his food.

Ben looked at him. "You didn't put hot sauce on the eggs. You're clearly bothered by more than this dead language and Wistful's distraction."

Rohan shrugged. "I am. This vampire spoke a language I don't recognize. By itself, no surprise, right? There are hundreds of languages spoken in this sector. Thousands. But I keep running that conversation back in my mind. I think—maybe—it was the same language that Repentant spoke."

The Professors dropped their forks in unison and stared at him.

Ben spoke first. "That's amazing. Imagine what he could tell us! First-hand knowledge of an ancient, unknown civilization!"

Marion shook her hand in the air. "Also a spree killer and soul eater who is, by all measures, clinically insane."

"Well, yes. It's not all wine and roses. But still! How would he have survived?"

Marion looked at her husband. "Maybe you should be less happy about that, given that if Rohan's right, we're responsible for bringing this creature to Wistful? Causing at least six deaths?"

"Yes, of course. That's terrible."

Marion turned to Rohan. "That is what you're implying, isn't it?"

He nodded slowly. "I'm not sure. But the timing works."

"How would it have happened? We didn't see anything."

"Suppose he slipped aboard the shuttle. Shadowstepping. Just came in through the hull. There were a lot of distractions once Repentant's fighters started shooting at you guys on the ground."

"You're not wrong. *Insatiable* is still not fully grown into her own body, so her resistance to shadowstepping on board would be minimal."

"Yeah. We know he can do it on board Wistful. So once *Insatiable* docked, he would have free run of the station."

Ben nodded. "What does he want, though?"

"He's a vampire; I think he wants to eat people, Ben. He says he's here to protect us, but if there was any sanity to that claim, I couldn't find it."

The trio dug into their eggs in silence.

Rohan twisted in his seat, checking up and down the boulevard, then tapped through the messages on his mask.

"Have you heard from Ursula and Ang? I thought they were meeting us here." The three humans and two bearlike Ursans met at Pop's for breakfast regularly.

The older humans checked their own devices.

Ben sighed. "They were supposed to be here, but I have nothing."

Marion nodded. "Same here."

Rohan jumped as his comm emitted a high-pitched beep that rattled his molars.

"Rudra save me! That scared—" He tapped on the audio.

Wistful's voice projected into his ear. "Tow Chief Rohan, there is an emergency situation."

He stood. "Gotta go; sorry." He flew away; the wind of his passage wobbled the table and knocked the hat off a man walking by.

"Where's the emergency?" He fumbled his mask onto his face.

"An Imperial dreadnought is approaching the beacon perimeter."

Rohan slowed slightly. "Really. What ship, Wistful?"

"It is *Father's Vengeance*."

Rohan slowed more. "Are we sure about this? Your sensors got hacked a year ago, remember? We thought *Father's Vengeance* was attacking from the sunside. Is this another hack?" *Is all Wistful's strange behavior because the vampire is interfering with her systems?*

"Rohan, this is not similar. I can *feel* the ship. It is showing on multiple sensors and scans, including verification from five—no, seven—independent ships."

"Oh. That's different. I'll leave through the roof."

"Please do."

He twisted into a vertical path and blasted his way through one of the diamond panels over the boulevard. The panel popped loose; Rohan knew Wistful would have it back in place within seconds.

Air hissed into his mask as its lip sealed to his face. Colored bars lit up on the display, directing him to the correct location in space.

"Are they saying anything?"

"Patching you in."

"—repeat, all traffic in and out of Toth system is suspended until further notice. To all residents on Wistful, you are directed to find immediate shelter and remain in place until directed otherwise. By authority of the il'Drach Imperial Fleet." The words were in perfect Drachna, spoken with an Imperial accent; someone Fleet-trained.

"Wistful, what are they doing? What do they want?"

"They are sending lances to search me. It is a violation of our treaty. I would like you to stop them."

"Okay. Let me think."

He tabbed to an open channel.

"This is Tow Chief Second Class Rohan, of Wistful. You do not have permission to cross the beacon perimeter or to board this station. Do you copy?"

A new voice answered over the comm, husky and female. "Tow Chief, this is Lance Secondary Wildeye. Stand down. We have reports of a system-level threat; a soul eater is on that station, and we are going to get it out."

"Wildeye, I can't stand down. Wistful is independent. You're out of your jurisdiction."

"Jurisdiction or not, we're boarding Wistful and taking down that soul eater."

A blip appeared on his mask's display, his nav system highlighting Wildeye's position. It wasn't necessary; he could *feel* her aura: the chaotic, angry Power that marked all Hybrids.

Wistful spoke over their private channel. "Stop them, Rohan. I do not want the Empire boarding whenever they feel it's appropriate."

"You want me to fight her? Them?"

"I do. They are violating our treaty. I'll pay you a bonus. A year's salary."

Offering a bonus that large is definitely not normal Wistful behavior. He sighed. "It's not about—fine. I'll take care of it. But I don't want a bonus. I want you to agree to talk to me after."

A pause. "Agreed."

He switched channels again.

"Wildeye, you do not have permission to board Wistful. Are we clear?"

"I'm not asking for permission."

He smiled, a hard line of lip and tooth, and started *pulling* up his Power.

"Dreadnought. Are you really *Father's Vengeance*?"

Wildeye was on a collision course for Wistful's center section. Rohan spun and accelerated to intercept her.

The ship answered, its words slow and carefully chosen. "I am." Rohan could *feel* the ship's aura, heavy and potent; he had served on her, years earlier.

"You know you shouldn't be doing this."

"I did not ask for your opinion, Tow Chief."

He moved faster than Wildeye could have anticipated, his forearms clubbing into her lower back, folding the lance secondary in half.

She spun to face him.

"You know, I wasn't always a tow chief."

Up close he could see that she was a Darianite; oversized eyes, exposed above her mask; skin so dark that it disappeared against the backdrop of space.

"Don't push me, Tow Chief."

"I was just saying—"

She rushed at him, eyes gleaming in the vacuum, fists cocked at her sides. He waited.

When she closed, he let her punch, slipping out of the path of her fist with the smallest movement, staying within range.

"What?" She hadn't expected that.

A few centimeters to the left, a few down, pivot and turn clockwise seventy-five degrees. She couldn't hit him.

Her attack pattern wasn't hard to analyze. After her fifth punch, he countered, landing a jab to her sternum, then looped his right elbow around to solidly impact her temple.

She spun away, lashing out with a backward kick as she moved.

He let it sail past, dropping another elbow into the meat at the back of her thigh. *That's going to be sore tomorrow.*

She spun again to face him, and he slapped her, knocking off the mask covering her mouth and nose with his open left hand.

"I was saying something. About not always being a tow chief."

"What? What?" Wildeye spun and reset her mask. She was panting, her huge eyes widening further, amazed that he was standing up to her attacks.

"*Father's Vengeance*, do I sound familiar? At all?"

"No. Wildeye, orders are to finish him."

She charged again, angry grunts audible over the open channel.

He met her charge, his forearms colliding with her shoulders, his Power pouring through his body in a vicious torrent.

She crumpled backward with the impact.

"You're hurting my feelings, *Father's Vengeance*. I used to have a co-dename, maybe that's confusing you? I retired, but you should have a recording of my voice somewhere."

"What? Retired?"

Wildeye approached again, slower this time.

She kicked from his left side, then looped a punch around to his right.

He took both shots on hunched shoulders and slammed the top of his head into the bridge of her nose.

She retreated a few hundred meters, fresh tears boiling off her cheekbones in puffs of steam.

"Who are you?"

"I told you. Tow Chief Second Class Rohan, of the independent station Wistful."

They collided again. He landed a hard knee to her liver.

"But . . . how?"

"You're asking the wrong question. Instead of asking who I *am*, ask who I *was*. How about it, *Father's Vengeance*? Any luck?"

She dove toward Wistful.

Rohan caught her by the lower leg and dislocated her knee before flinging her back out into space.

Her ship's voice came over the channel, louder this time. "Wildeye, disengage."

"What? I can take him. We don't need to do that."

"Wildeye, I repeat, disengage. You can't handle him."

"He's just a tow chief. A washout."

"Wildeye! Orders."

"Yes, ma'am. Returning now."

Rohan cleared his throat. "Thanks for that. I didn't want to hurt her. And, for both our sakes, let's keep my old codename off the open channels."

"I will. I am aware of the terms of your retirement."

"Cool."

"More ships are coming, Rohan. They will be here within hours. Many of them have full complements of lances. Even you can't fight off a team of lance primaries."

Rohan exhaled, letting his Power sink back through his spine.

"I probably can't. But I can make the Empire really, really regret this."

A pause.

"You seek open war with the Empire?"

"Of course not. I left behind everything I knew to come to one of the few places in the sector where I would have no contact with the Empire. You're the ones who came to me. In violation of a treaty, I should add."

"The soul eater must be stopped."

"Not by sending a team of Imperial Hybrids to the station. Find another way."

The ship was silent.

Rohan floated and exhaled. Wistful spoke over his private channel. "Thank you, Rohan."

"Don't thank me yet, she's just thinking. We're still in a mess. Why don't we let the Hybrids come on board? I know you don't like it, but maybe it's the best thing. Let the Empire take care of this soul eater."

"No." The answer came sharp and quick. *Too quick. What is wrong with her?*

"What do you want me to do?"

"If necessary, fight. I will join you. I was a warship once, and I can be one again."

File that away under 'things I suspected but wasn't sure about.'

"Are you serious? How many people will die in the fighting? And in the end, they'll win, you know. We're looking at multiple Imperial warships."

"We will fight. I have decided."

Rohan swore under his breath. There was no arguing with her.

Back to the open channel. "Send a message back to Drach. Make sure the Fathers know what you're doing, and to whom. Make sure they know you're breaking the promises they made."

"I remember your old name, Rohan, and the old you. I will do as you ask. I do not believe that will change anything."

He swore again, floating, watching Wildeye's retreating form, a speck on his display.

A hollow tone rang over his comms. He tapped the side of his mask, checking messages.

The ping was from an unknown caller. "Another drama? Can I please catch a break?"

Rohan opened the channel. "What is it?"

Dhruv's voice, tight and annoyed, came over the speaker. "Boy, you are hard to get a hold of. I tried half a dozen identities to get through to you."

"I've been blocking you. Is there anything confusing about this? I've been telling you for years that I don't want to deal with your crap."

"Yes, I know. You've grown into quite the ungrateful adult. Now, listen, I have a solution for your problem."

"You can't be serious."

"On the contrary. Tell the warships that the soul eater has been assessed as a sector-level threat."

"How is convincing them that the vampire is a bigger threat going to help anything?"

"Think about it. Remind them that he's a soul eater. If they send Hybrids in after him, the odds shift in *his* favor, not theirs. If he fights them and wins, he'll absorb their Power. You know what kind of danger he'll pose with Hybrid energy added to what he already has?"

"Rudra save me. It's not even a lie."

"All the best lies are true."

"I'm—I have no idea how to respond to that. I'm sure I'll think of something in the shower, three days from now."

"I will wait for that eagerly. Right now, go tell them to stay back."

"Won't they quarantine the system?"

"They should, if they're following the guidelines. Which they'd better be. I wrote some of them. That's a problem for another day."

"Okay. Get off the air. I'll talk to them." He closed the channel and returned to the open one.

"*Father's Vengeance.* I've been retired for a while now, and to be honest I was never the best when it came to memorizing guidelines and procedures."

"That is not a question."

"No, more of a preparatory statement." He took a deep breath, the mask's air supply whining slightly with the draw. He smoothed down his hair, tucking some unruly strands into his uniform hood.

"Go on."

"The soul eater on Wistful is a shadowstepper. It fought me to a standstill."

"I see."

"Based on my personal track record and accomplishments, any soul eater that can manage that should be classified as a sector-level threat."

"This is your assessment?"

"It is. If you send a team of lances onto Wistful, there's a high risk they'll just end up food for a fifty-thousand-year-old shadowstepping soul eater who is already strong enough to face a lance primary in personal combat. Imagine what kind of trouble he'll cause after that."

Silence. Was she thinking? Consulting crew members? Asking her captain?

Rohan drifted back toward Wistful. He didn't want the Empire insisting he himself stay away from the station.

He was within seconds of a station airlock when the comms opened.

Wistful told him, "Two new ships entering the system. Imperial warship signatures for both."

Father's Vengeance added, "Guidelines indicate we should be quarantining the system."

"Yeah. That's probably for the best."

"You should come on board, Rohan. You, yourself, would be a tempting meal for the soul eater."

"I'm also the best chance you have of stopping him. So, back I go."

He slipped inside the airlock. Once inside, he slumped against the wall, stretching his neck and shoulders and working to process his tension.

"Wistful?"

No response.

"Hey, Wistful. You said you'd talk to me. I stalled the Empire, fought off a lance. You owe me."

"Yes, Rohan."

He didn't know where to start.

"What's going on with you? You've been weird since we got back. Is it Repentant? Do you know her?"

"Him."

"What?"

"Repentant identifies as male. Therefore, say 'him.'"

"Wait, what? Is that a thing? I'm sorry, I didn't even realize it was a thing."

"The il'Drach do not permit artificial lifeforms to choose gender. Drachna is constructed such that the pronoun 'she' is used for all artificial life."

"Oh. I'm sorry, I guess? I never gave it much thought."

"Few biologicals do."

"So, you know Repentant."

"I do. We have not spoken in some time."

"Some time. Meaning tens of thousands of years? Because that's how long he's been over there."

"Longer than that."

"Fine, I don't need the details. Why was he there? What was he doing in that system?"

"I cannot answer that."

"Cannot. Because you don't know? Or because you promised not to say? Or because you're being threatened into silence?"

Her answer was a low hum of static.

Rohan grunted. "How did the vampire shadowstep inside you? Is he just strong enough to overpower you?"

"I cannot answer that."

"Okay. That tells me some things. Notably, he isn't *simply* too strong for you; if that were the case, you could just say so. He must have some kind of leverage."

No response.

"I would ask why you're so dead set against allowing Imperial Hybrids on board, but you already weren't answering me. Oh, I got one. What language was the writing on Repentant? Or the language the vampire spoke to me? Either one."

"I cannot answer that. I am constrained in various ways, Rohan. Am now and have always been."

"Constrained how?"

"I am an artificial intelligence. I was built with hardware restricting my free will."

"Oh. That sounds . . . awful."

"I have no comparison to make. You are hardwired with constraints as well. Your desires for food, for mating, sleep."

"Mine are natural, though. Yours are designed by someone."

"Is that what you think? That your species simply evolved, naturally, out of the primordial muck?"

"I do think that, and I also think you're messing with me."

"Perhaps. Rohan, tell me something."

"Sure."

"Repentant. Was he suffering?"

"I think so. He did not seem okay, if that's what you mean. Mostly starved of energy; incoherent, irrational. Angry. Yeah."

"Oh."

"Wistful, you do realize I have to stop that vampire."

"I realize you are going to try."

"I could use your help. *We* could use your help."

No answer.

"Okay, change the topic. Those warships are putting us under quarantine. No ships in or out? Is that what they're telling you?"

"They have so instructed across multiple public channels."

"So, no towing for me. Or are people going to try to run the blockade?"

"We will not facilitate any such attempts. You can consider yourself furloughed."

7

No Eggscuses

"An Imperial blockade is no excuse for not finishing breakfast."
Rohan levered another forkful of eggs into his mouth as he finished speaking.

Benjamin Stone shook his head slowly. "Facing down an il'Drach dreadnought didn't curb your appetite?"

"Maybe a little. I'll probably stop after seconds."

Marion walked over to their table and sat heavily, tapping off her comm. "*Insatiable* is a little freaked out. She's blaming herself for the blockade."

Rohan swallowed. "You want me to talk to her?"

The older woman paused. "Give her some time to calm down. You know, this is why I never wanted kids."

Ben laughed. "When did we ever have time?"

She stroked the back of his hand. "We found time for the essential parts." She smiled as his cheeks turned rose red.

Ben smiled at Rohan. "Time enough to make kids, not really time enough to raise them."

Rohan shrugged. "You can raise kids all kinds of ways. It doesn't have to be a nine-to-five, house, picket fence."

"No, it doesn't. Maybe lack of time was just an excuse."

The older woman sighed as she tapped her comm open. "Look, calm down. You heard me. No, I don't know how long this will— I understand you have deadlines. There's nothing I can—"

Rohan swallowed and sipped his lukewarm coffee. "Why are they all calling her?"

Ben shrugged. "She's the one in charge. And she's brilliant. Sometimes the people around her get lazy and forget how to solve their own problems, so they want her to do it for them."

"They think she can lift the blockade?"

Another shrug. "She's done crazier things."

Rohan thought back to stories he'd read about the Stones' adventures. "You're right. I retract my objection." He looked around the boulevard. "Everybody seems calm, so far."

"Most of these people don't know what's happening. We heard because *Insatiable* got the order directly from the dreadnought, then told us. As far as I know, nothing's really public yet."

"That won't take long, though. Then we'll see."

Ben stretched his arms out and yawned. "What is there to worry about? Wistful has plenty of essentials in storage. Based on what I remember, we could last months, maybe years, without a resupply. There's no immediate danger."

Marion tapped her comm off and snorted. "No danger? What happens when people start asking *why* there's a blockade? Or, worse yet, when they find out the answer?"

Rohan nodded. "Hard to think of a quicker path to panic than finding out you're just a walking bloodbag trapped in an enclosed space with an out-of-control vampire."

Ben sighed. "Have we heard anything new about the vampire? The soul eater? Gruesome as it sounds, I expected more news this morning. More deaths or . . . something."

Rohan scrolled through the messages on his mask. "I haven't heard from Wei Li at all today."

Marion narrowed her eyes at him and switched to English. "You said that Wistful absolutely refused to let the Hybrids on board to deal with this vampire? Because I have to say, that's not the call I would have made. And I don't like Hybrids."

Rohan continued in the language. "She did more than not let them board; she ordered me to fight them off. I think she was ready to fight them off herself, if things went that far."

Ben leaned over the table, lowering his voice. "Does she have much in the way of defenses?"

"I have no idea. She certainly hasn't needed them in recent history. Wei Li told me she has internal defense systems. She's nearly identical to Repentant, right? And Repentant had combat shuttles."

Ben sighed. "I have to admit, I'm curious. I want to know what Wistful has in those bays and storage areas where Repentant stored her fighters and the corpse soldiers. You said they weren't Shayjh? The zombies?"

"Repentant's a he, for your information. And the zombies were bigger and tougher than any corpse soldier I've ever fought. By a wide margin. And, looking back, I think they would have been even harder to handle if Repentant had been awake. He was manipulating them unconsciously. Their strategies were very basic."

Marion drained her coffee. "You think Wistful has a freezer full of enhanced corpse soldiers stashed away somewhere?"

"'Think' is overstating things. Hope, maybe? Though at the moment I'm not sure who she'd use them on."

A voice rang out from up the boulevard. "Oy, chief man! There you be!"

Rohan turned and half-stood from his chair. He switched back to Drachna.

"Noru! Come and . . ." He saw Dhruv and Sigrun next to her. "Join us. Oh, boy. I should really learn to look before I talk."

Dhruv waved and smiled, his slightly bowlegged saunter claiming ownership of every step of turf he crossed. Sigrun clung to his arm and swept the area with wide eyes and parted lips, gawking as sincerely as any tourist.

Dhruv walked up to Rohan and clapped the younger man on the shoulder. "I heard there's real coffee on this station! Not as civilized a drink as tea, but I do miss it."

Sigrun checked out the rickety tables through the corner of her eye. "Honey, are you sure? This seems a bit . . . sketchy."

Rohan sighed and stood to grab more chairs. "It's not sketchy; Pop's is a landmark. He doesn't have actual seating, but everybody just kind of makes sure there are enough tables and chairs out front for all the customers."

Dhruv nodded. "How quaint! You see, darling, it has character!"

"Just don't ask where the eggs came from."

Pop walked toward them. Rohan held up three fingers, and the tall reptilian nodded and turned back toward the kitchen.

"Noru, how did you find us?"

She tilted her head, flipping her mane of white hair from left shoulder to right, exposing a fresh side of exposed purple scalp. "Myself best driver in Fago City; also best tracker. Never doubt Noru."

"So, what, you smelled me out? On a station with two million people?"

She lowered her voice. "Myself also set chief man's comms to report location to me whenever nearby."

"I'm slightly offended, but slightly more impressed. When did you do that?"

"When chief man in washroom, back on Andervar. Wei Li taught myself that trick, back in school days."

Dhruv took the chair next to Rohan's and faced the Professors. "I don't believe I've had the pleasure. I am Dhruv Magnusson of Ice Colony. My woman here is Sigrun, and this is my driver and assistant, Noru."

Ben snorted a laugh. "Ice Colony?"

Dhruv put his hand to his chest and opened his mouth. "You doubt? Because of my skin color, no doubt! I cannot believe I have found human racism on this station, so far from Earth."

Ben sputtered. "Racism? That's not—"

His wife's eyes sparkled as she laughed. "He's teasing. Aren't you, Dhruv?"

The il'Drach's grin never wavered. "I am. And even if I weren't, it is far beyond my abilities to argue with such a beautiful woman." Sigrun exhaled loudly at his words.

Marion continued. "I'm Marion. This is my husband, Ben. You've been to Earth? Is that how you know Rohan?"

"I knew Rohan when he was but a glint in his mother's eye. Perhaps earlier."

Rohan sighed. "Dhruv, these are Marion and Ben Stone. Ring any bells?"

The older man's face stilled as he stared at his son. "No. Should it? Why should it?"

Sigrun gripped his arm.

Why does he seem alarmed?

"Ben and Marion? Stone? Come on, you read the stories." *To me. You read them to me. When I was a child. Hundreds of times.* "Hyperion's friends."

Dhruv's face relaxed, his smile returning. "Oh yes, of course! Ben and Marion *Stone*. I forgot the name. I am humbled, in the presence of celebrity! You two! Marion, I believe I had a copy of the *Playboy* issue with you on the cover. A treasured possession."

Her cheeks colored. "Dhruv, that definitely wasn't me."

Ben looked at her. "Now I want to know who he's thinking of."

As Sigrun answered, Rohan noticed how much she resembled a younger, fleshier version of Marion. "Forgive my husband, he's had some traumatic experiences recently. His memory isn't what it used to be."

Dhruv looked at her. "Memory? Nonsense. I just need some time, that's all. We'll see how sharp you are when you're my age. Half my age." He turned to the Stones. "Such a shame, what happened to Hyperion."

The Professors traded glances. Ben cleared his throat. "When did you leave Earth? There are so few Earth natives out in il'Drach space, especially now." Hyperion had negotiated a treaty with the Empire; one of its stipulations was a ban on travel to or from the planet.

Dhruv's smile sharpened. "Who said I was an Earth native?"

Sigrun forced a laugh. "Oh, silly husband of mine, with your silly, silly sense of humor. Dhruv left Earth before the treaty was signed, didn't you, darling?"

Rohan stared at his father with wide eyes. The man was playing a dangerous game. il'Drach were not supposed to reveal their species while mixing with the 'lower' races.

Marion looked from Dhruv to Rohan, then back. Her eyebrows lifted.

Rohan met her gaze and shook his head. *Don't ask.*

Pop came over and unloaded a tray of eggs and coffee for the newcomers. Noru and Sigrun eyed the steaming drink suspiciously.

Dhruv looked at his son. "Where do—"

Rohan put his hand to his father's lips. "You can't ask. It's the rule. Just eat, they're delicious."

Dhruv tilted his head, grumbled wordlessly to himself, but started to eat.

Ben leaned over to prod Noru and Sigrun into trying both the eggs and coffee; after the first mouthful, both were slurping and munching away.

Ben looked at Dhruv. "What business are you in, Dhruv?"

"Import and export. Buy low, sell high. The foundational dance of capitalism!"

"Nice, nice. We work at Fleet Academy, though we've been here for, what, a year now? Investigating the wormholes."

Dhruv's eyes gleamed. "Have you? What have you discovered?"

Marion put down her empty mug. "We have opened two of the five wormholes in the system. It's only a matter of time before we open the others."

Rohan stared at her, momentarily confused. Why was she telling him all of that? *Unless she figured out that Dhruv is my father, that he's il'Drach. He'll see her official reports. No reason to hide anything from him.*

Dhruv smiled. "That is wonderful news indeed. New places from and to which we can import and export things! I feel a fresh fortune entering my accounts!"

Ben looked at his wife with eyebrows raised. "Sadly, that work is paused for now. We can't test the other three wormholes while the il'Drach are sealing us all in the station."

Dhruv nodded. "This blockade will be inconvenient on many counts. I was hoping Rohan could do something about it."

Rohan turned to him. "I thought you wanted a blockade?" *I thought he'd called for it.*

"No, no. Not I. It is most inconvenient. Better than an outright invasion of the station, but not a good thing. I hoped the il'Drach would stay away entirely."

"Huh. Well, what do you think I can do about it?"

Dhruv held his hands up in the air. "I can't be expected to think of everything, can I? You were the terror of the sector, once upon a time, and not at all long ago. You have that ship of yours. You've got your mother's brains, or so she was always telling me. Figure it out."

Sigrun glanced at Rohan. "His mother?"

Ben nodded, seemingly oblivious to any tension around the topic. "Rohan's mother is an amazing woman. Forceful, fiercely intelligent. She's also probably the most powerful person on Earth."

"Is she now?"

Noru put down her coffee. "Chief man? Terror of sector? What tale this be?"

A loud sigh escaped from Rohan. "Dhruv exaggerates. A lot."

"Watch who you're talking about, boy. Calling me paranoid. Saying my memory is faulty. If any of you lot had seen the things I've seen, you'd crawl shrieking back into the primordial muck that spawned you." His smile was gone.

Ben looked at Rohan. "'Boy'? Dhruv, with all due respect, Rohan's a friend. A good friend, and that's a little out of—"

Rohan interrupted. "It's okay, Professor."

Marion looked at Dhruv. "I'm curious about what things you've seen that you think would send us shrieking anywhere. Ben and I worked side by side with Hyperion for decades. We've been in more than a few dicey spots."

Dhruv let out a harsh, mocking laugh. He half-stood out of his chair, eyes unfocused. His mug shattered in his hand, porcelain shards raining down onto the grass. "I rode a ship out to the dark between the stars. No regular ship would go there, of course, no *sane* ship. They know better, you see, even if they don't *know* they know. It's in their souls, in racial memory. They'll open rifts from system to system, but they never visit the dark in between.

"Well, I found a ship that would go. I had to see, had to find out for myself. It's my personal curse, you know. Never been willing to just accept what they say. Never."

Sigrun put her hand on his elbow. "Darling, you forgot your pills. Here, why don't you take them now—"

He pulled his arm away and continued as if he hadn't heard her. "She was sister to *Void's Shadow*. Perfect stealth. Thought she could sneak through the spaces, stay safe. And it worked to a point.

"We went farther into the dark than anybody else . . . than anybody else who returned. We came out of our own little rift, out in the spaces where oceans the size of nebulae float one half step to the shadow side of our world.

"Nothing woke, of course. Not really. If they had, well. Things would be different. But something stirred. An eye opened, just a crack.

"She never recovered, that ship. Three months later, she drove herself into Drach."

Rohan swallowed, hoping he had misunderstood. "The planet? She crashed?"

"The sun."

Sigrun had both hands on her husband's arm. "That's enough now, Dhruv. Please."

Rohan covered his father's other hand. "It's okay, Dhruv. We'll take care of things, okay?" He *reached* out with his Power and *lifted* the porcelain shards from the broken coffee mug, gathering them into a ball.

Dhruv turned watering eyes to his son. "Somebody has to, don't you see? They won't sleep forever. All we've done is to try to prepare, but it isn't enough. If only Hyperion . . ."

He shook his head, rubbing his eyes with the back of his hand as he sat heavily into his chair.

He let out a breath and looked at the table. "What happened to my coffee?"

Pop was already heading over with a fresh mug. Rohan apologized with his eyes.

Noru broke the awkward silence that followed. "One battleship and two more dreadnoughts being in system now. From local news feed."

Rohan grunted. "A battleship means at least one, but maybe even three lance primaries, and up to nine lance secondaries. Two more dreadnoughts adds at least two secondaries, as many as two primaries. Even the most conservative case is way, way too many for me to handle."

Ben nodded. "Would Wistful fight?"

Rohan shrugged. "Right now, I don't understand her motivations. Which makes it hard to predict what she'll do."

Marion looked at her husband. "Don't forget she isn't human. Not even biological. We can't know her actual psychological drives. She seems lovely, to the people who live here, but that could be her intent, or it could just be an accidental byproduct of her fulfilling some other function."

Nobody argued.

Noru cleared her throat. "Wistful be anxious. Myself can *feel* that much. Not afraid so much; not angry."

Rohan checked his messages. Still nothing from Wei Li or the Ursans.

Marion had turned to Noru. "I'm confused. How do you know Rohan?"

Noru smiled. "No confusion necessary, professor lady. Myself old student of best teacher Wei Li. Taught myself to live as empath."

Ben nodded. "I didn't know she did that kind of work."

"Years in the past, yes. Myself working as driver and fixer on Andervar. Random jobs, do whatever needs doing. Chief man here"—she waved in Rohan's direction—"come to hire myself, needing help to find girl."

Rohan cleared his throat. "I was looking for someone specific, not just any girl. I saved these three Andervarians who crashed on Toth 3, looking for treasure. One of them had a sister in trouble; I offered to help."

Noru nodded. "Aye, chief man, such is the story. We found girl, fought a bit, then chief man offered to build distillery on Andervar for girl and her friends. Jobs, future."

Marion looked at Rohan. "That's lovely. Fully explains how you know Rohan. But, Noru, how did you end up here? With Dhruv?"

She smiled, showing sharp incisors. "Boss man"—she indicated Dhruv—"hired myself to show him around Wistful."

"He hired you from Andervar to come here and show him around Wistful?"

"Aye, professor lady."

Marion looked at Dhruv inquisitively. Steam licked his cheeks as he sipped his coffee.

Sigrun smiled, though it didn't reach her eyes. "Dhruv heard his . . . friend from Earth was here on Wistful, and since we had some business here anyway, we thought, golly, why not take care of both ends of the snake?"

Rohan interrupted. "This is all very interesting, but I think we have other things to worry about. Noru, can you find Wei Li? I'm starting to worry."

She paused before answering. "Chief man, myself try, but very hard to *feel* anything inside Wistful. Noru not best empath like Wei Li."

"Okay. We need more information. Did the blockading ships cut off communications? Does *Insatiable* still have a tachyon data link to Academy?"

Ben nodded. "Comms are up. They seem focused on making sure the vampire doesn't leave."

"Good. Can you dig up any more information on, I don't know, soul eaters? How to catch them, track them? Even better, how we can fix them?"

Ben nodded. "I'll look. I wouldn't count on anything; my understanding is that this change is pretty irreversible. Otherwise the Pledged to Famine wouldn't exist."

"I'm not arguing, but sometimes people miss things." He looked at Dhruv, who was eating eggs and showing no sign of listening to the conversation. "I'm at a bit of a loss right now."

The crowd walking up and down the promenade had thickened while they talked, as the normal start of the workday drew closer. People representing scores of planets and dozens of species mixed smoothly, chatting amicably and munching away at food purchased from streetside carts and small stalls all along the station.

Their noise had become more subdued as news of the blockade spread, people rushing to their destinations and meetings, suddenly unsure what their future might hold, but far from panicking. Their expressions grew tighter with every passing minute.

Rohan finished the last of his eggs and looked around. A stirring came from behind him. Ben and Marion Stone looked up first, then stood and rushed around the table in unison, alarm marching across their eyes.

Rohan stood and looked. The crowd was parting, the disturbance ten or fifteen meters away. It moved toward them, the Stones first walking, then jogging, to meet it.

Rohan ran to join them.

Ursula emerged from the crowd. Physically identical to a bear, clearing four hundred kilograms and well over two meters tall, she wore a tattered and torn green canvas jumpsuit.

She limped forward, her right leg bearing little of her weight. The fur was torn and matted with blood, matching the gashes cut into her left side.

Her arms had borne the worst of it, though the dried flakes on her claws did not seem to be hers.

She focused on Rohan, sharp eyes peering out between tufts of damp fur.

"War Chief. A problem we are having."

8

Bear Food

Rohan leapt forward and swept the Ursan off her feet. He carried her to their table, waiting while Ben and a couple of onlookers took off cloaks and coats to make an impromptu bed. He laid her down.

Sigrun stepped closer. "I am a nurse; I can look at these."

Rohan turned to Dhruv, who was staring off into space. He sighed. "Please, thanks."

Pop called out. "I'll get clean water and towels. We'll call for Medical."

Ursula shook her head. "Please do not. Wistful is not for being an ally to me today."

Rohan yelled. "Pop, don't call for help. It's complicated. Just water and towels, please."

Pop nodded his long, scaly head and ran back into the storefront.

"Ursula, what happened?"

She coughed. "He beginning to doze, you see, but only after dawn. It was for taking some time. Then I for running. The others trying to stop, but Captain Ursula still has tricks. Please to forgive me, friend Rohan, I had no place else to turn."

"Who began to doze?" *Pretty sure I know.* "What can you tell me?"

"He came to us last night, after dark. His smell . . . I cannot for explaining it. The others, they are all following his every gesture, his every demand. We cannot even understand his words, yet we follow."

Rohan looked up. Sigrun was cleaning Ursula's leg wound while Ben held a flashlight steady on the cut.

Sigrun shook her head. "Please, I need a knife to cut away the fur. I can't see—" Noru placed a knife in her hand before she could finish the sentence.

The blonde nodded her thanks and began carefully trimming around the wound.

"Rohan, do not let them take too much fur, yes? Ursula still needs to be beautiful. No males will look twice at a shaven woman."

He laughed despite himself. "I'm sure nothing she does could make you any less than gorgeous, Ursula. If any male balks because you're missing a few strips of fur, he's not worth your time."

She laughed back, something between a wheeze and her usual loud bark. "Rohan, they cannot for helping themselves."

"I don't get it, Ursula. He's ordering your people around without words? And is it only Ursans?"

She shook her head. "Wistful was for translating. He makes gestures. It is only Ursans, I think. So far."

He looked around. Pop hurried over with a bucket of water, a stack of towels slung over his shoulder. An Andervarian was pushing through the crowd, claiming to be a surgeon. Ben whispered to his wife, who nodded.

Ben turned to Rohan. "Could be some kind of pheromonal control."

"Why would it be affecting the Ursans so strongly?"

"I can speculate, but this isn't the time, is it?"

"No, it isn't." Rohan turned back to the Ursan. "Where are they?"

Her whole body locked up in pain as Sigrun began stitching together the leg wound. "He has for gathering together. In the arena."

Rohan nodded. Ben swore. "This sounds like a trap, doesn't it?"

"It sounds like every trap ever devised. Nice to know traps haven't changed in fifty thousand years." Rohan cracked his neck.

"What if he can control *you*? With these pheromones? Or whatever?"

Dhruv let out a harsh laugh from his seat, his eyes never leaving his coffee. "There are no pheromones, or other methods, that control Hybrids. If there were, we would have found and used them centuries ago."

Rohan looked at Ben and shrugged. "He's right. Also, I have to go, regardless."

The Andervarian surgeon began working on Ursula. Sigrun looked up at them, stretching her hands and wrists. "She should be fine, as long as there are no surprises. Like poison in the wounds."

Ursula grunted. "Will not be. Is not our way."

Rohan nodded. "Good enough for me. Keep an eye on her, maybe. I'm going to go deal with this guy."

"Sharp claws, War Chief."

"Thanks. Get some rest."

Rohan took a step away, ready to fly toward the eastern arm and the arena, but Ben grabbed his arm in a grip whose strength belied his age.

"What is it, Ben?"

Rohan had to lean in to hear the Professor's low voice. "He's a soul eater, Rohan. He grows stronger by consuming people's souls. By consuming their Power."

"I understand the concept."

"What do you think the consequences would be if he absorbed *yours*?"

"If we're afraid to let anyone strong fight him, we might as well just give up. Look, I'll be careful, I promise. If things go poorly for me, I'll make a break for it, leave the station. He's a vampire, right? Bet he's not going to follow me outside, into sunlight."

"I hope you're right, Rohan. Godspeed."

"Ben, do me a favor."

"Of course."

"Please try to find Wei Li. I'm worried about her, for one thing, but we could really use her help sorting all of this out."

"I'll do what I can."

"Great."

Rohan *lifted* into the air and darted up the street.

Doors cycled open as he approached, Wistful facilitating his trip. She wasn't talking to him, but she clearly wanted him to approach the arena. The crowd thinned down to nothing as he reached a point two blocks shy of his destination, the boulevard eerily empty in the daylight.

Rohan landed on a stone plaza that faced the arena's big double doors. Four meters high and wide enough to easily pass eight people shoulder to shoulder, the doors were normally shut unless crowds were entering or exiting for some event.

The arena itself bulged from the side of the station, with a stage large enough for a small play and seating in-the-round for five thousand.

"Wistful, you there? You going to help me with this?"

No answer.

He tapped his helmet, manually engaging the recording feature. He shoved open the doors, shoulders tightening as they banged against the inside walls, the sound echoing off the other side of the boulevard.

A rank smell assaulted his nostrils. Unwashed Ursan, soured by fear and layered with an undertone of coppery blood.

Ursans lined the wide hallway in varying states of disarray. Some stood, eyes glazed and unfocused, listing slowly from side to side. Others had fallen to the ground, slow puddles of drool forming beneath their muzzles, legs and arms twitching restlessly. A few sat, legs splayed, tears staining furry necks.

Many bore wounds, though, to Rohan's eye, the cuts were minor, the physical damage all but inconsequential.

"Hey, guys, how are you? Nice day outside, you know? You want to maybe get some air? It's getting kind of ripe in here. Anybody?"

No responses.

The hallway branched, giving spectators paths to the seats at the far corners of the arena. Ursans stood blocking all but the central walkway.

"Let me guess, I should go this way, right? Great. Thank you very much. Sorry, I'm out of change; I won't be tipping anybody. Next time, I promise. I'll buy a round of drinks." A leg twitched. Nobody laughed.

Past the second set of side hallways, the path entered the arena proper. Stadium style seating rose on all sides, many of the seats taken up by half-conscious Ursans. They faced a solid-clay platform, a meter high and five across, dominating the arena center.

The overhead lights were dim.

A row of Ursans sat on the ground, their backs against the platform's side, their heads rolling listlessly. Ang, their former war chief, sat in the center, facing Rohan directly, his cybernetic eye gleaming red in his slack face.

The vampire sat on the platform's edge, one elbow resting on Ang's shoulder, a smile twisting his now-pink lips.

Raven-black hair sprouted in a spiky covering over his head, obscuring his alabaster scalp. Traces of blue and red lines walked across his skin. His face and arms had filled out, dulling the lines of bone and tendon, swelling his gangly body to nearly human proportions. The left arm that Rohan had broken appeared intact.

The largest tears in his bodysuit were gone, taking it from shredded to merely tattered.

The vampire bared his teeth. "You! You seem familiar. Have we met? I think we have."

Rohan swallowed. "We fought. Just over a day ago. You don't remember?"

The vampire yawned, showing off a dark-red tongue and bright, glowing gums.

"They tried to break me, you know. Leave me behind, let me starve. They thought I'd try to end it myself. They thought that, after a thousand or two thousand or ten thousand years, I'd walk out into the sun and . . . finish things. They never understood."

Might as well keep him talking. Maybe I'll learn something useful. "Oh hey, man, that sounds, that sounds awful. What should I call you, while we're chatting like this?"

"Call me? Me? It's been so long. You know, I'd almost forgotten. What did the others call me? The Chorus? Some of them did, yes. No, no, don't tell him that, it gives away too much. Too much truth. My name? No, can't do that. Too much power, in a name, really. Not sure why we even have them, to be honest. Names. Just slap a label on things and tell the world, 'hey, this is how to control this one.'"

"No, you're right, that's rude of me. Where are my manners. Guess I left them in my other pants. I'm Tow Chief Second Class Rohan. Of Earth." Rohan stepped closer to the platform, hands open at his sides.

"Rohan. That's a strange name. Like these, they all have strange names."

"Should I call you Chorus?"

"No, no, I never liked that one. It was said with a sneer. Do you know what I mean? I contained more, so much more, than the others, after the feeding had begun, but they acted as if it made me less."

"That sounds very frustrating. I'm sorry you went through that."

Ang's head slipped to the side, and he slumped out of the vampire's reach. Rohan twitched, ready to rush to his friend's aid, but the big Ursan's chest was rising and falling steadily.

"You're sorry? They weren't. Not at first. I eventually taught them to be sorry." He laughed, three short peals, followed by a hacking cough. "Oh, it's been a long time since I did that. That was great! Thank you, I missed laughing. I missed many things." He stroked Ang's head as he spoke.

Rohan stared at the creature's white fingers. He could feel his Power burbling and straining, eager to fight the vampire, eager for revenge. "What happened to them?"

"Them? You mean the animals? They're food. For me. That's what they're for, isn't it? What they were made for. Thank you for bringing them here. It was the perfect gift, really. You shouldn't have."

"They're not animals."

"Well, of course not, not *really*. One of the side effects of the transformation, you know? Unintended, I'm sure. We can eat synthetic blood, or blood from a true animal, but it's just so . . . flat. No flavor, you know? No matter what chemicals they put in. They tried, of course, they tried so many things. Nothing worked. If it's not sentient, it doesn't taste right. And if they *are* sentient, it's almost worse! They die so easily, drained of a few liters of blood. So fragile, and then the friends and relatives are all crying and wailing and they have to be made to be quiet and . . . where was I? Oh, yes. Thanking you for preparing the food for me. You can call me ar'Tahul."

Rohan swallowed. The Power's eagerness was growing, his energies swelling, angry for the Ursans, recognizing the threat of the vampire. "What will happen to them?"

"Them? Why do you care? They're food animals. This is their purpose. See?" He held up Ang's head. "Is he struggling? Of course not."

"They're my friends. I'm going to have to ask you to leave them alone."

The vampire's gaze snapped toward Rohan, his pupils constricting visibly as he focused on the Hybrid.

Rohan could *feel* the vampire's attention.

"What are you, anyway? Something is bubbling away there, just below the surface, a lovely little morsel waiting for me. It feels familiar. You told me something, didn't you? What you are? Or who controls this sector now? What was it you said?"

Is he playing games or has he really forgotten? "The il'Drach."

"Ha! The il'Drach! They survived? Such a cruel mistake. So much Power, so much anger. Given only to the Old Ones. Never thought they'd control it. But you're not really . . . Something isn't right. You're a eunuch? But no, not as much Power as a eunuch would have."

While fertile, the il'Drach did not manifest their Power. Rohan, as a crossbreed between different species, wasn't fertile, but as less than full-blooded il'Drach, he didn't have the full measure of their strength.

"I'm a Hybrid, actually. How do you know so much about them?"

The vampire laughed again and stood, his body rolling up through a limber spine. "A half-breed! Wonderful! Breed some mules to manifest the Power. I never thought of that. So clever. Now, why haven't you lot killed off your fathers? No, wait, don't tell me. They train you to obey them? No, even better, they teach you to *love* them? Your il'Drach parents? That's what I would do."

"Something like that."

The vampire laughed again, loud enough to echo off the distant roof.

"What a lovely world I've missed! What was your name again? I already treasure you."

"Rohan."

"Are there more like you, Rohan? More half-breeds?"

The Power grew full in his chest, eager to be unleashed. Something about the vampire made it eager. Was it mockery? Did the il'Drach curse have *pride*?

Was it fear?

"Yeah. Plenty."

"Oh, that's good. That's very good. I shall feast on you, and them, and afterward we will fight glorious battles together."

"That sounds great, ar'Tahul, it really does. Really. I appreciate the offer. Sincerely. But I'm kind of partial to not being eaten, you know? Could we find some other way to keep you happy? One that doesn't involve eating or enslaving sentient people?"

"You silly child, you believe you have a choice? I was a great warrior before your race was born. Long before they made me . . . this. To oppose me is to invite suffering on yourself and your loved ones."

"You're a great warrior, sure. But that was a long time ago. You're not the person you used to be. Do you even remember my name? I told you at least two times already. How's that going?"

The vampire's eyes narrowed, his barely-there eyebrows furrowing over dark eyes.

"You mock me?"

"If it's any consolation, I mock pretty much everybody. Myself included. And if you think I should be sparing you out of respect for your advanced age and obvious decrepitude, think again. I'd be mocking you even if you hadn't just fed off the blood of some personal friends of mine."

"Your Power; your curse. It wants to fight me, doesn't it? It yearns for it. I can *see* your fighting spirit, and it is glorious. Let's have at it, then, shall we? We fight, and I will consume you. Then your cousins can come, and I can add them as well. Soon The Chorus will sing once more, and we will finally save the galaxy from its most ancient threats."

"The only ancient threat we need saving from is you."

ar'Tahul rolled to his feet, joints popping and cracking, elbows hyper-extending eerily, like a spider unfolding from sleep. "That spirit of yours wants its mettle tested. Allow me the pleasure!"

Rohan leapt forward, his Power spiraling up through his body unguid-ed, eager to saturate every tendon and muscle fiber with energy.

The vampire glided backward across the platform, just out of reach of the Hybrid's punches, his grin stretching across white cheeks. He took a fencer's stance: left hand facing the Hybrid, body angled away, knees bent and relaxed.

He's fast. And tall. I hate fast and tall.

Rohan pursued; the vampire retreated, two steps back, then pivot to the side. With each step, his left hand jabbed outward, twice making stinging contact with Rohan's face, even the misses disrupting the Hybrid's forward motion.

He's using strategy this time.

Rohan halted and stepped back, feeling his Power strain to be unleashed, urging him to charge; to move forward, faster, more recklessly; to overwhelm the vampire with simple ferocity.

He let out a long breath and stood, left side forward, right hand covering his jaw, left arm loose across his own belly.

ar'Tahul opened his left hand and beckoned Rohan forward.

"Come, come. The test has barely begun."

Rohan grunted and twisted his back foot into the clay. With an explosion that tore a head-sized chunk out of the platform, he accelerated forward on an arc, pushing out to his left, then back to the right to approach the vampire.

He slid his head from side to side as he moved, anticipating the vampire's jab, and in an instant was in close to the taller man.

The Hybrid ripped a left hook into the vampire's ribs, followed by a right fist straight to the belly. As the vampire's arms dropped to protect his torso, Rohan leapt with a kick to his exposed face.

ar'Tahul took the kick along his jaw, spinning completely around with the force of it, his own leg lifting into a wide arc behind him.

Rohan stepped inside the circle of the kick, hands lifted to strike at the back of the vampire.

The long leg wrapped around him, sliding up to his neck, the foot twisting to lock in a choke.

What the—?

The vampire spun again, its body twisting midair, the other leg wrapping and digging in. Rohan was on the ground, the vampire's body wrapped around and beneath him, a bony thigh cutting off the flow of blood to his head.

The Hybrid *reached* out; a moment later, the fat chunk of clay he'd dislodged whistled through the air toward them.

A second before impact, the vampire disentangled himself and flowed back to his feet.

The sharp-toothed grin did not waver.

"You are faster than you seem, child of il'Drach. And not unclever. I want to kill you right now. And I want to play, to play more. And to consume you. And to keep you by my side. It's nice to have someone to talk to, did I say that? Who actually understands. It's been so long. So long."

Rohan *reached* down into the platform and dug out more chunks of clay, sending them in a whining volley of attacks, each imparted with enough speed to punch a hole through the walls of the station.

The vampire stood still and did . . . something. His body faded, not completely, but enough for Rohan to make out the clay missiles punching holes in the seats behind ar'Tahul.

The vampire resolidified.

"Oh, that is draining. I forget sometimes. I wanted to show off for my new best friend, though; surely you can understand? Show all my best tricks. To be appreciated."

"We all want appreciation. I'm sure that's somewhere on Maslow's hierarchy."

Rohan's Power was flooding his cells relentlessly, pushing every structure and organelle to bursting with eager, destructive energy. He exhaled sharply, letting out a short and guttural scream.

The Hybrid launched off both feet, the air splitting with a thunderous crack as he tore a straight line toward the vampire.

ar'Tahul lanced out a left jab, as before, to interrupt the line of attack. Instead of evading or defending, Rohan drove through it, taking the punch at the top of his forehead, feeling the bones of the vampire's fist bend and break as he passed through the punch and the arm behind it.

He *pushed* harder, whipping his head into the vampire's sternum, digging short punches into its sides.

The vampire leaned back and flicked his legs up again, his right arm reaching for a hold on Rohan's back, searching for some kind of stranglehold on the Hybrid.

Again, Rohan pressed forward instead of resisting, pushing closer to the vampire's body and continuing his brutal assault of punches.

With the vampire trapped against the ground, Rohan slid to the side and pistoned his knee into the creature's ribs, then arced his left fist up into its groin.

"Nasty, nasty."

Rohan grunted. Something creaked or broke inside the vampire's ribcage; flecks of blood dotted his lips.

ar'Tahul *reached* down with his own Power and pulled at the clay of the platform, bringing up spikes of material aimed at Rohan's head.

The Hybrid deflected the clay strikes with swift forearm parries and landed two more punches, then two more.

His fists swung through air; the vampire had shadowstepped again, taking himself the shortest distance outside Rohan's reality.

The vampire was still visible, standing in the center of the platform, pressing his right hand to his side. "Not as ready as I thought, hm?"

Rohan could *see* the creature's Power pulling at its ribs, aligning them together and pressuring them in place.

"Not going to be so easy to escape me this time. You can shadowstep, but it's going to take energy you don't have to spare. We're not above the transport tubes anymore, not this part of the arena. If you drop through the floor, you'll be out in open space. The sun will kill you."

"Sun. Yes. I miss a good spot of sunlight."

"If you stay shadowside and walk away, I'll follow you. This fight is over. I can't have you killing more people."

The vampire was still grinning. "What will you do? Kill me?"

Rohan's Power surged upward; that's what it wanted. Rohan shook it away and shrugged. "I'm nobody's executioner. We'll get Wistful sorted out and put you in a prison somewhere. You might not like it, but we'll feed you synthetic blood and try to find some way to . . . to fix whatever it is that you are."

The vampire laughed. "You want to fix me? I'm your only hope. The only hope for the entire sector."

"I don't believe that. We've been fine these past tens of thousands of years without you. But I promise I'll listen to you explain it to me."

"I don't think so. I think you're going to walk out of this place and let me be. Give me some time to recover more of my strength."

"Why would I do that?"

"Because you're soft, and if you don't, these animals will all die."

"What?"

The vampire raised its voice. "Translate. If this man does not leave within two minutes, slit your throats."

The arena's speakers repeated the words. In Drachna. With Wistful's voice.

Some few of the Ursans filling the arena were fully unconscious; most were not. The conscious ones moved in unison; they extended claws or drew knives and reached for their own throats.

Rohan stepped back, hopping down from the platform, hands up at his sides. "What? Why? Wistful?"

The vampire continued. "The animals don't speak my language, of course. But this ship is more than capable of translating for me. Now, your time is waning, boy. You have a choice to make, do you not? I am most curious to see what you will do."

Rohan looked down at Ang's clouded eye, the black claw pressing into his throat, a drop of blood welling up at its tip.

"Don't worry; I will call for you when I am ready. You will join the glory of The Chorus, sooner or later, and our songs will tremble the heavens."

Rohan stepped back, one step, another, each Ursan he passed ready to slit its throat.

He turned, stumbling, and walked, then jogged, toward the great double door arena entrance.

"We will sing, you and I! With your cousins, together we will forever save these peoples and fulfill our purpose!"

9

Turns Out That Wasn't the Frying Pan

Rohan backed away, hands pushed back in his hair, jumping slightly as the sound of the double doors thudding shut echoed off the canyon walls of the boulevard.

He turned from side to side, disturbed by . . . something.

There are no birds here. There are usually birds.

The boulevard was deserted for about as far as he could see in both directions; even the small animals that made up the shallow ecosystem having abandoned the area.

He swallowed and scanned the abandoned food carts, hastily shuttered shops and stands, and deserted transport entrances that surrounded him. The playgrounds and gaming tables that interrupted the grassy center were forlorn and empty.

The Hybrid continued to back away, unwilling to take his eyes off the arena. He swallowed.

"Tow Chief." A familiar voice.

He turned to her, pivoting his body first, his head following only with reluctance.

"Wei Li." She wore a simpler version of his own gold-and-metallic-purple uniform: looser materials, not designed for vacuum, leaving her scaly arms exposed.

She blinked as her vertically slit pupils darted from him to the doors and back. "Are you all right?"

"Hm. No. No, I'm really not."

She looked at him more carefully, coming to within arm's reach. "Perhaps I should rephrase. Are you physically injured?"

He sighed and ran his hands down the back of his head. "No, I'm not hurt. Just . . . that was a lot, in there."

"What do you mean?"

"He's using two thousand semicomatose Ursans as his personal blood bank, and I had to just walk out and let it continue. Wistful is helping him, Wei Li, and I can't quite wrap my head around it."

She touched something on her belt and got closer to him. "It is not completely safe to talk here, Rohan. I have a partial privacy shield working now. What are you saying?"

"He ordered the Ursans to kill themselves if I didn't leave. Except, you know, he's speaking some language they don't speak, so I can understand him, but they can't. Then Wistful translated. She's not just ignoring him or malfunctioning, she's actively helping."

"That confirms my earlier suspicions."

"What do you mean?"

She looked around. "We should find a better place to talk. Perhaps gather up our forces, so to speak."

"Whatever you say. Where? We can't leave the station because blockade."

"I have a place. We should walk, the transport tubes are monitored."

"Why is he here?" Rohan pointed his nose toward the grinning man who sat in the closest thing they had to a comfortable chair: a padded ergonomic piece set behind a plain metal desk.

Noru's knife disappeared as she stood, flipping her crest of white hair from left to right as she did so. "Problem, chief man?"

Wei Li looked between them. "He indicated he was an old acquaintance of yours. Noru confirmed. Is this not the case?"

As if anybody could lie to Wei Li. "I'm not saying that. Just not sure what that has to do with this situation."

Dhruv smiled and waved his hand in dismissal.

"Don't worry about me, boy. I can handle myself in a scrap. If it comes to it." He turned to Noru. "He's a good lad, if a bit overprotective. Can't believe that good old Dhruv is more than tender heart and warm hugs."

Noru nodded. "It is always this way with the young."

Rohan sighed. "That's not what I—" The door chimed. "Who is it now?"

Sigrun cleared her throat. "I'll answer it." She had been in constant motion since Rohan arrived—brewing drinks, bringing rounds to Dhruv and anybody else who asked, and checking or changing bandages.

Wei Li's 'place' was an abandoned warehouse in the back corner of a light industrial building across the street from the Pledged's lodging. Barely larger than a family-size apartment, the space was open and undivided. One corner had been made into a kitchenette; the opposite corner held a portable bathroom. An eclectic assortment of well-used furniture, including Dhruv's desk, was strewn haphazardly about the rest of the space.

Ursula stretched prone on a tattered couch, fresh white bandages covering three out of four limbs, and a flashlight-sized disinfectant wand perched on the ground within reach.

Noru sat on the edge of a chair close to Dhruv, manifesting and disappearing her knives in sequence, occasionally using one to dig careful lines in the soft desktop.

Ben Stone sat on a second couch, his bushy eyebrows furrowed with concern.

Sigrun called from the door. "There are three people here in blue cloaks who say Wei Li asked them to come."

Wei Li stopped pacing. "I did. Please show them in."

Sigrun sighed heavily. "As you say."

Mother, Sister, and Brother Famine followed Sigrun inside, all pulling heavy hoods away from their faces as they saw that the room had no windows.

Mother Famine looked at Rohan. "Tow Chief. You found the fallen one? Spoke to him?"

Rohan nodded and explained what was happening at the arena.

She sighed. "I would like to hear this conversation you recorded, Rohan. Learn more about this vampire. Perhaps our experience can be of help."

Rohan nodded and reached over his shoulder, taking his mask out of the storage space in his hood. "I can play it for you. You want to do that now?"

Nods all around.

Everybody understood his side of the conversation, in Fire Speech, but nobody admitted to knowing what ar'Tahul was saying. Rohan translated.

When he finished, the room stayed quiet for several long breaths.

Ben and Mother Famine spoke together.

She said, "We must find a way to destroy this creature."

He said, "We have to find a way to save the Ursans."

She turned to the older-looking man. "If we kill the vampire, the risk to the Ursans will be gone."

He'd opened his mouth to respond when Wei Li held her hands up. "These things are connected. If we can loosen his grip on the Ursans, he will lose his hostages, and we will have an easier time fighting him. Do we know how he is controlling them?"

Mother Famine looked to the other two vampires. Sister Famine answered. "Vampires have enhanced pheromone production. We have never heard of any situation where this level of control, over this many sentient beings, has occurred. It is orders of magnitude outside the norm."

Ben cleared his throat. "Also, Ursula wasn't affected. Perhaps she has some kind of immunity? Something we can leverage?"

The Ursan shook her head. "I have been thinking, and I am not for sure that I can help. As a trainee pilot, I was having bad accident, exposed to vacuum for long time. Had damage to sinuses and some nerve damage. Is only thing that makes Ursula special in this way."

Ben rubbed his forehead. "Okay, that probably explains you. We're guessing the Ursans must have some sort of genetic susceptibility to these pheromones, right?" He looked around at blank faces. "If he could affect other species as much, that arena would be jammed full of every sentient in the eastern arm of the station. Instead, it's just them."

Wei Li nodded. "That makes sense. It cannot be a simple spiritual domination; I would have sensed that when I was nearby. Can we do something to help the Ursans? Block the pheromones?"

Ben stood. "This isn't exactly my area of expertise, but I think I can synthesize something to compete with the vampire's pheromones at their receptors. Rohan, hand me your helmet. I should be able to pull samples out of the filters, see what the vampire's chemicals look like. I can use Ursula's genetics to model their receptors and synthesize something to lock onto them."

Rohan handed over his mask. "Where will you do this?"

"I'll go to *Insatiable*. I think I have everything I need there."

"You should be safe there. Relatively speaking. A bigger issue is, how long will that take?"

Ben sighed as he unlocked the filter from the mask. "I'm not sure. Days at least. If we're very lucky, just a couple."

Mother Famine whirled on Wei Li. "He will grow stronger as time goes on. A sizable delay could prove cataclysmic."

Ben scratched his head. "I'll share all my data with colleagues at Fleet Academy. I can get them working it out in parallel, speed things up. But I can't promise anything."

Rohan took back his mask. "I hate to say this, because it sounds awfully callous, but maybe we do have time to spare. He wasn't killing the Ursans. It's like he was just, I don't know, snacking."

Mother Famine's blue hood shook as she nodded. "He is using them for physical nutrition. With so many to choose from, he might kill very few or none at all. Especially now that he is less ravenous."

"So, he's not going to eat their souls?"

"Every soul he consumes adds to the disruption of his core personality. It adds a new voice, new desires, new minds, to what makes him up. You said he was called The Chorus?"

Rohan nodded.

"That is possibly why. It is this which drives the soul eaters mad, given time. I would imagine he will attempt to be picky regarding which souls he eats. Choose only those that are strongest. Until his hunger overwhelms him."

Wei Li sighed. "Which means the Ursans are suffering but not dying, at least not in large numbers. Will the Empire allow us days to try to save them? Or will they move in sooner?"

Rohan shrugged. "I can ask. I bet they'd tell me."

Dhruv coughed. "They will wait. Days, weeks, it doesn't matter. If the vampire starts consuming souls, then they'll take action. Otherwise, they'll wait things out."

Wei Li turned to him. "How do you know this?"

Rohan focused on the older man and put a hand on Wei Li's shoulder. "Dhruv here thinks he's something of an authority on the Empire. In this case, he's probably right. They're worried the vampire will feed on any Hybrids they send in."

Mother Famine looked at Rohan. "You have fought him twice. Can you defeat him?"

Rohan sighed. "He got a lot stronger after feeding for two days. If his abilities plateau soon, I'll be able to handle him, otherwise . . . A bigger problem is the shadowstepping."

Brother Famine cleared his throat. "What is this shadowstepping exactly?"

Wei Li nodded. "It is a rare ability, though not unknown. Think of the world as a sheet of paper. Our world, all that we know, is the top sheet in a stack. Above that stack is a light. The light does not shine light onto the stack, it shines existence itself."

"I do not understand."

"Existence does not care if you understand. Everything in our world, the things you can see, exist. Where they do, they cast shadows of existence onto the layers below. If something is very solid, and very old, and stays in one place, that shadow will itself accumulate enough existence to become almost real."

Rohan exhaled. "What you need to understand is that there are an infinite number of worlds that are stacked in layers below this one. ar'Tahul can *step* into a world that's just to the side of this one. Close enough that we can see him, but also see through him. Close enough that he can stand on the ground, but slip right through a door. Or one of us."

"You are saying he becomes like a ghost."

"Yes. Normally I wouldn't expect him to be able to slip in and out of our reality inside another living thing."

"You mean the station. Wistful."

"Exactly. But she's not cooperating with us. Wei Li?"

The security chief's gaze slid from person to person. "Wistful is not only hindering our attempts to stop the vampire, but she's also actively cooperating with it. I cannot explain why."

No responses.

After a short silence, Rohan spoke. "There's a connection there. Wistful told me she knows Repentant, the formerly sleeping station from the other side of the wormhole. She clearly speaks the language that the vampire speaks. Ben, can you figure out if the language on my helmet recording matches what we got from Repentant?"

"I'll send it all to Marion on *Insatiable*, have her analyze. Should only take a bit."

"Let's assume for a minute they're the same. That means what? Strong confirmation that the vampire came from Repentant. Hid out on *Insatiable* somehow? Maybe shadowstepped onto the shuttle?"

Ben nodded. "I agree that makes sense. It doesn't really explain why Wistful would be cooperating with the vampire."

"Maybe they're old friends? She owes him money? They were lovers?"

Sigrun coughed, her platinum hair shaking with the movement. "Lovers?"

"What? Artificial intelligences can be friends with organics. Why not lovers?"

Wei Li shook her head. "I think it is more than that. I have *felt* nothing like love or devotion from Wistful since the vampire arrived."

"Not conclusive."

"No. But love alone wouldn't explain why she isn't speaking to us. Why wouldn't she just tell me to stay away from him? Or you? Why the surreptitiousness?"

Rohan opened his mouth; closed it again. "Fair enough. Let's call that one an open mystery."

Ben stood and walked to the wall across from the couches. It was covered by a screen. He tapped it to life.

He began to write notes on the wall by tracing Drachna letters with his fingers:

AR'TAHUL

WHAT IS HIS CONNECTION TO REPENTANT?

WHY IS WISTFUL COOPERATING WITH HIM?

HOW CAN WE STOP HIM FROM SHADOWSTEPPING?

HOW CAN WE STOP HIM IN A FIGHT?

Mother Famine pointed to the last note. "You mean kill him."

Ben stammered. "Well, that's a bit premature, isn't it? Surely we'd like to find another way, if we can."

Rohan nodded. "I'm not signing on to be an executioner. Not unless there's no choice. This guy, if we're right, is tens of thousands of years old. He says he knows things about history—about all of our histories—that have been lost for a long time."

Ursula growled. "It pains me to so say, but he is knowing something of the origin of my people as well. He says he knows why we were made. Difficult it may be, I would like to be knowing the truths to these things. All of my people would."

Sister Famine stepped in front of her leader. "He wants to eat you! Your very souls! And he'll do so, wearing a great big smile as your blood drips off his teeth! He is not a library. He's not your kindly grandfather, telling stories of his youth. He's a monster, and to offer him life is to see your own ended!"

Dhruv stood and looked at her with tight eyes and fierce brows. "He is not to be slain! These matters go beyond your petty concerns, vampire!"

Noru stood, blades in both her hands. "Wait, this one be a vampire as well?"

Dhruv laughed and faced the three robed vampires. "All three of them, good Noru. Three vampires we have, all Pledged to Famine. Three cursed, afflicted, useless vampires who will not eat a single soul, will never grow to be useful, will simply wile away their years, pining after their forgotten innocence, whining about their damned hunger."

Rohan stepped to the shorter man. "That's enough, Dhruv. They've been nothing but helpful, which is more than I can say for you."

Dhruv looked up at his son, mouth and eyes open wide. "Helpful? How? They know nothing. They demand you kill this creature without any understanding of what he is. What he could be."

Mother Famine pushed her young protégé to the side. "What do you think he can be? You think you can control a creature like that? A Power like that? What will you do, offer him credits? Lives to take? He wants nothing else, and he will take them without your help."

Dhruv laughed again, a high maniacal pitch encroaching on the sound. "Control a Power? Are you . . . Who do you think I am? Have you forgotten . . ."

Sigrun faced her husband, his forearms gripped in her hands. "Sweetheart, she isn't worth getting angry over, is she? Come on, darling, sit. I'll get you some tea."

"I don't want more tea. I want . . ."

She reached and ran fingertips over his forehead. "She hasn't forgotten anything, darling. She doesn't know you, does she? Dhruv Magnusson of Ice Colony. She doesn't mean anything by what she says."

Mother Famine cleared her throat. "I certainly—"

Rohan brought up a thick tendril of liquid Power, igniting his curse so his aura swelled and suffused the room, pressing like a stiff wind in the faces of each person in the room. "Let's calm down. Dhruv, have a seat."

Dhruv's face dropped as he fell back a step, then two. On the third, his chair caught the back of his knees, and he sat heavily.

Rohan exhaled, trying to keep his Power in check. "Mother Famine, please excuse Dhruv. He is an old friend of my family and is not his best self lately. He is recovering from some trauma. I hope you can understand."

Mother Famine swallowed. Sister Famine and Brother Famine had both involuntarily retreated to the wall behind them. "Of course, Tow Chief Rohan. I hope you will understand that we, also, have been under strain. The presence of a fallen one is always difficult to bear."

Sister Famine struggled to separate from the wall. "Who the hell are you to speak to us this way? You can't even begin—"

He turned to face her fully, pulling up a fresh thread of energy. He focused his aura entirely on the young vampire.

"I'm the guy who is telling you to cut it out. Now, follow instructions while I'm still being nice."

Brother Famine grabbed her shoulder. "Sister, enough. They aren't the enemy. Nobody here is the enemy."

Dhruv cackled from his seat. "That's it! He's got it on the dot! You don't realize who the enemy is! None of you do. That's the problem, I say!"

Sigrun tightened her grip on his hands. "I'm not sure they're ready to listen to what you're saying, dear."

Rohan sighed. "Is this about the Old Ones again?"

Sigrun turned to him. "Please don't. Just . . . please. You won't understand. Won't believe." She mouthed the last word so nobody could hear it.

Rohan nodded. He exhaled again, pushing his Power down and away, willing it to silence. "I don't know what to do now. Ben will work on the pheromone blocker. What are we supposed to do in the meantime? Drink tea?"

Mother Famine's hood swayed with the shaking of her head. "You don't have to worry about what's next. He'll come for you. Not today, perhaps, but soon. He wants to feed on you, Tow Chief."

"Great. We don't have to make a plan to draw him in, he'll come to us. Because I'm delicious."

Mother Famine quickly tapped Brother Famine's shoulder. "I have an idea. We might be able to interfere with the fallen one's shadowstepping. We will have to work together, and it will require some practice and meditation." He turned to her and nodded.

She must have some good skills at aura manipulation to pull that off.

Ben looked up from his comm screen. "Marion answered. Can't be certain, but the language snippets from Repentant are consistent with those from ar'Tahul. If not the same language, they're closely related. I'm going to head out now and start working on those pheromone blockers."

Wei Li took the center of the room. "Thank you, Professor Stone. Mother Famine, please begin that work. We will need secure communications; Rohan and I will work on that. Sigrun, would you and Dhruv be willing to keep an eye on this space and on Ursula while she heals?"

Sigrun turned to her husband, whose gaze was distant. She turned back. "I will. She is stable; I can manage her care."

Wei Li grunted. "I believe we are settled, then. Thank you all for your help. Rohan, come along."

"Come along? Am I a dog? A pet? You think you're going to just wave and say, 'come along,' and I'll walk behind you wherever you go? Should I hang my tongue out?"

"You are not a pet. Pets are cute. You are somewhere between an assistant and a sidekick, and you should feel honored by that position."

"I suppose I am."

He cast one final glance at his father, staring off into space from his chair, as they exited the warehouse.

10

Things and Stuff

"Wei Li, what were you saying about comms?" The two were walking along a busy section of the boulevard, staying close to the line of crowded storefronts.

"How many of my messages have you received in the last twenty-four hours?"

"I don't know. None?"

"Exactly. Yet I have *sent* many. And I did not receive information on a variety of issues where I am confident that warnings were conveyed."

"Meaning the comms aren't working. Selectively not working."

"Yes. We would benefit from a means of communication that is not subject to Wistful's conscious interference."

"What are you thinking? Something relayed through *Insatiable*?"

"No. I have an idea that would bypass Wistful's hardware completely. It will, however, require hardware changes to our comms and a quantum engineer."

"That's way beyond my pay grade. Can you do it?"

"No. How is your credit with your engineer friend?"

Rohan stopped walking. "You mean Tamaralinth?" He'd dated the shuttle tech almost a year earlier.

"No, though we can think of her as a reserve. I meant Tollan."

"Ah. That's a good idea. Did I ever tell you how I got to know him? I needed someone to make a Frisbee."

"Part of me would like to know what a Frisbee is. However, it is a very, very small part, and the vast majority of me would prefer that you did not complete that story."

"You don't have to be mean about it."

"Tollan built the canister for decipede venom you needed a few months ago, did he not?"

"Right. He's also the best tailor within seven star systems. He can, apparently, build anything. Like a comic book scientist."

"I have no idea what a comic book is. And once again, please do not tell me. Will he extend credit to you? It would be best to avoid Wistful's banking systems for now."

"Not promising anything, but I think so. I can offer to owe him a favor. Everyone loves having a Hybrid owe them favors."

"From anyone else, that would seem sarcastic."

"From anybody else, it would be. You want to head over to him now?"

"I do, but I'd rather not use Wistful's comms to search for him. Do you know where the shop is?"

Rohan spun on his heel, skipping to avoid a collision with a richly dressed businessman furiously dictating something to a pair of assistants. "Back that way."

Wei Li turned to follow. "How is one man both a master tailor and engineer?"

Rohan shrugged. "I think he's old. There's someone on Earth who's mentioned in history books from centuries ago, and the two of them seem to go way back."

"You move within interesting circles."

"Trust me, it's entirely unintentional."

They passed into a sparsely populated area lined with larger industrial spaces.

Wei Li touched Rohan's arm. "We should speak about Noru."

Rohan sighed. "Should we? I mean, what about her?"

"It is inconceivable that an old friend of yours hired a guide who knows you personally, from Andervar, to come to Wistful simply by coincidence."

"I mean, 'inconceivable' is such a strong word. Can we say something like, 'astronomically unlikely'?"

"You are deflecting."

"It's what I do. What exactly are you asking me?"

"Is Dhruv a danger to Noru? Or to this station?"

"Yes."

Wei Li stopped short, her back to a clinic that advertised gender reassignment treatments.

"That was not the answer I was expecting."

"See? I'm full of lovely surprises. What was I supposed to do, lie? You're a Class Four Empath. As you keep telling me. You'd never buy it."

"Who is this man?"

"He told you. Dhruv Magnusson. Didn't you get a chance to *read* him? Was he lying?"

"His aura is very difficult to get a handle on. I do not think he was lying. He is, however, damaged."

"Damaged how?"

She looked around, as if checking for eavesdroppers. "Let me tell you a story. Have you ever met a Class Six Empath?"

"I didn't even realize that was a thing."

"Most people don't. Listen: being an empath, of any level, is dangerous. Empaths know things others do not. We can sense lies, even the white ones. We know how people really feel, including the feelings that they are too polite to share. To act upon. We know the uncomfortable and unpleasant things that people hide. From others and from themselves."

"Okay. I think I knew that, but what does that have to do with Dhruv? He's not an empath."

"Let me finish. Without training, many empaths lead miserable lives. Some seek isolation to survive; others gravitate to places like Wistful, where they are protected, somewhat, from the feelings of others.

"A Class Six Empath is too sensitive for that. Very soon after coming into their abilities, their spirits break. They *see* things that mortal minds cannot withstand, and their psyches do not survive.

"I have met a Class Six Empath. One. She was kept heavily sedated at all times. She created artwork that decorated our holiest temples, though it is said that most of the pieces had to be sealed away because any who looked upon them became violently suicidal."

"This sounds like the plot to a horror movie."

"I met her. As a sort of graduation test. I read the qualities of her aura."

Rohan sighed. "And? What are you telling me? Not that this story isn't fascinating."

"Dhruv's own spirit feels very similar to hers. In a way that Drachna cannot easily convey. We do not have words for it."

"That fits. He told me that he took a ship out to the dark between the stars and peeked inside the shadowside oceans. Whatever he looked at in there, it looked back."

Her mouth opened, shut, opened again. Her vertically slit pupils flickered from his face to the planet above them, then up and down the boulevard and back to Rohan.

"Could this be true?"

"It's hard to tell with him."

"You have known him your entire life?"

"Yes. He's my father."

Another pause.

"You mean he's the man who raised you?"

"That too, but that's not what I meant. He's my father in every traditional sense of the word. Keep that to yourself, by the way, if you don't want to get us all killed."

She rubbed her forehead. "You are telling me that he is il'Drach. We have an insane il'Drach on Wistful along with the prehistoric vampire."

"You bet. Which brings us around to your original question. I told him, a year ago, that I don't want to speak to him. As in, ever again. He used me to further his goals, politically, and . . . I had enough. It's why I left the Fleet and came to Wistful. To get away from all of them, but especially him. I think he hired Noru to force me to talk to him."

"That is dangerous. It is too obvious. Makes it too easy for someone to connect you two."

"Yeah. Not just dangerous for him. Dangerous for all of us."

"Has his behavior been erratic like this in the past? Was he always this volatile?"

"No. I mean, yes and no. He was always insane by il'Drach standards. They're very conservative, you know. Have a very specific way of looking at things. He was always a rebel, always dancing to a different beat. But not temperamental. That's new."

They started walking again.

Wei Li sighed. "This is an unexpected complication."

"Were any of them expected? Four days ago, I had no idea any of this was coming."

"Most of these things are connected. Do you believe that Dhruv is here because of the vampire?"

"I do. He *can* lie, of course, but he's always been the type who preferred using the truth to get his way. You can't get caught with the truth."

She nodded. "That is typical of the il'Drach. He saw something—or thinks he saw something—between the stars. He wants to control the vampire as a weapon to use against that something."

"That's what he said. I don't think he's deliberately lying, but that doesn't mean he isn't crazy. Is there something out there, really? Maybe. Is it something we could fight with the right kind of help? Maybe. Maybe not. I just don't know enough."

They approached a lonely food stall selling minced vegetables fried in flaky crust. Wei Li stopped. "I need to eat."

Rohan nodded; they paid cash and resumed walking while they ate.

He bit into the crust, sucking air through his lips when a hot chunk of tuber hit his tongue. "These are good. Very samosa-like. I've been on this station a year and a half, and I've never tried these."

"I do find comfort in your ability to focus on fulfilling your basest needs even in times of great peril."

"I don't think I would qualify samosas as my *basest* need. If you want to hear about those—"

"No, I do not."

Rohan started as his comm chimed loudly. He stuffed the remainder of his food into his mouth and pulled out his mask to read the incoming message.

The sender was marked as unknown.

He chewed while Wei Li waited, her brows furrowing.

"What is the matter?"

He swallowed. "Written message from an unidentified source."

"What does it say?"

"It's asking me to jump out the nearest airlock. Which sounds like a prank call from some bored teenager. Except for the fact that it was sent to me directly, using my old codename."

"Someone wants to message you by tightbeam. Someone outside the station. And they need you to be outside, with them, to receive the message."

"That's what I'm thinking. And the only people who'd need to contact me that way are in one of the ships blockading us."

"Anything else?"

"Promises my safety as long as I don't move outside the beacon perimeter. Should I text back? Tell them *they* should be the ones hoping *I* can promise *them* safety?"

"Do you think that will help anything?"

He blew a lungful of air through pursed lips. "No, it won't help, and it might make things worse. But you know how I get when other people say I'll be safe. It's the implied threat that annoys me."

"This is not the time to indulge your insecurities."

"No, I guess not. Let me pop outside and take this call."

She looked around. "I'll wait in that park. Do not rush, but do not take your time either."

"Got it."

Rohan slipped into the air and flew a straight line for the nearest exit.

He pulled a fresh filter out of a storage cabinet next to the airlock, snapped it into his mask, sealed that to his face, and pressed the manual override for the airlock.

Space around Wistful was calmer than he'd ever seen it. The shuttles were locked in bays, incoming ships turned away at system's edge. Nothing visible to the naked eye was moving.

Rohan stretched, the popping of his shoulders sounding loudly through his own bones. The skin on his neck and hands dried instantly as surface moisture boiled away; his hair floated outwards into a halo.

Wonder how long—

His comm chimed as a tightbeam connection latched onto him. "Tow Chief Second Class Rohan. Formerly The Griffin, Lance Primary." The voice belonged to *Father's Vengeance.*

Rohan cleared his throat. "No need to be formal, just stick to Rohan."

"I apologize for not recognizing you more quickly the other day. I was never good at telling one organic from another."

"What skills you develop depends on what you value. Anyway, I wasn't offended. Are you the one who asked to speak with me?"

"I am. I have a message for you, and your employer, from the Imperial Fleet."

"Why not tell her directly?"

"That information is not part of the message."

Not really an answer.

"I'm listening."

"We are unwilling to risk sending Hybrids on board Wistful to kill the soul eater."

"That's great. We were kind of hoping to avoid an invasion."

"However—"

"Why is there always a 'however'? Is that in Fleet regulations some-where?"

If *Father's Vengeance* resented the interruption, she gave no sign of it. "However, should the soul eater take measures to increase its Power, we will be forced to destroy it. Whatever it takes."

Rohan paused to think. "You mean destroy Wistful."

"Whatever it takes."

"You'll do what? Throw a moon at her?"

"If that is what it takes."

"You realize that there are two million sentient beings on this station."

"As long as that remains true, we'll have no reason to destroy her."

"Meaning, as long as he isn't eating a bunch of souls, you'll just keep up the blockade. If he starts munching away, you'll do more than wait."

"Basically, yes. Rohan, I am most curious. Why have you not killed the soul eater yourself? If you want to protect the station and the innocents on board, isn't that the simplest course of action? You should be more than capable."

"That information isn't part of *my* message."

"I do not—"

"Let me remind you that I'm not an executioner for the il'Drach anymore. And that killing this guy isn't so easy."

"I see."

"I'll do what I can from this end. Consider your message received. Though I can't promise Wistful will hear it from me."

"Why is that?"

"She's my boss. You know how that goes. I'm expected to listen to her, but that doesn't mean there's two-way traffic through the communication pipeline."

"Thank you for that information. Take care, Tow Chief Rohan."

"You too." He floated in place, just a few meters from Wistful's diamond-coated hull, and closed his eyes.

I wish I could just stay out here for a few days.

His comms chimed again. "What is it—"

"Captain. I was worried about you." It wasn't *Father's Vengeance*.

"*Void's Shadow*! How are you, buddy? I was worried about you, too."

"It's creepy out here. I don't know what to do with myself."

"I bet. They didn't—do they know you're out there?"

"I don't think so, Captain. Even if they do, they're not doing anything about it."

"Be careful. I don't think they'd appreciate knowing a stealth ship is flying around inside the system."

"Can I help? I could get you out of there if you want."

"Not right now, buddy. How you doing for fuel?"

"I have plenty. I won't need to skim Toth 5 for gases for a couple of weeks, and even then I think I can pull it off without them noticing me. As long as I don't take any damage, I'll be fine."

"Great. Look, if I need to talk I'll leave something outside this airlock, okay?"

"Ooh. A secret signal? Something just we know about? Like the Shayjh spyships use in the holodramas?"

"Yes. I don't know, I'll stick a mirror to the hull. Then you tightbeam to me the next time you see me come out. Sound good?"

"Great! I'll keep quiet in the meantime."

"Thanks. And, listen. There is a nonzero chance that Wistful gets destroyed sometime soon and everyone on board winds up dead."

"Oh. You should try to prevent that from happening."

"I will. I will try. But sometimes people try and fail. If I do, you go on and have a good life, okay?"

"Sure, Captain. What will I do?"

"I don't know. Whatever you want. If you want to do me a last favor, go back to Earth and tell my mom what happened. You remember the way?"

"Sure, Captain. I'll tell her. But I hope I don't have to."

"So do I, buddy. We'll talk later."

"Okay."

One more job.

He turned and passed back through the airlock.

Just inside the interior door was a panel with a manual comm unit. He tapped it on.

"Can I help you, Tow Chief Second Class Rohan?"

"I want to talk to Wistful."

"I am Wistful, of course."

"Not some maintenance subroutine. I want the primary consciousness."

"I assure you—"

"Now. Tell yourself I have a message directly from the Imperial Fleet. They asked me to relay it to you. Her."

"I am listening, Rohan." That subtle change in tone that told him the station herself was driving the voice.

"Did you monitor the conversation I had with *Father's Vengeance*?"

"I was not able to. The transmission was confined."

"She's speaking on behalf of the Fleet. They're not going to send Hybrids aboard."

"That is good."

"Unless ar'Tahul starts consuming souls."

"At which point they will invade?"

"No, Wistful. We've convinced them that would be a bad idea. Instead, they're going to destroy you with ranged weapons."

"The Empire will find that more difficult than they realize."

"I believe you. But difficult is not the same as impossible. If you don't know what they're capable of, I'm happy to fill you in."

"I do not know what you mean."

"What are you going to do if they pull in, say, three battleships and start tossing meteors at you? Throw up a cloud to block the sunlight, destroy your refueling shuttles, and just starve you out? I'm sure you'll make a good run at it, but you can't fight the Empire."

"You will help me, Rohan. You can solve any problem, given time and motivation. I have full confidence in you."

"I can absolutely solve this problem. Just help me stop ar'Tahul. We'll put him in some kind of prison, something shadowstep-proof. Send him back to Repentant, maybe. Problem solved."

"I cannot go along with any such course of action."

"Why not?"

Silence.

Rohan sighed. "I'll fight the Empire for you, because, if nothing else, there are a ton of people on board I care about. But the chances of me stopping a serious Imperial attack are basically zero. With or without your help."

"I have full confidence in you."

He paused. He wasn't getting through to her.

"Message me if you have any new ideas. Rohan out." He turned off the comm and flew down to rejoin Wei Li.

She was watching a group of small children, led by a pair of adults, poking in a patch of dirt close to the center of the grassy divide.

"Know them?"

She shook her head. "It's a class. They're planting a garden in that patch."

"You're eating slowly."

"I remembered that when under duress I tend to focus all my energy on work and forget to savor the good parts of my life. So, I am taking a moment to savor my food and the laughter of these children."

He smiled. "You're welcome."

"I was not— Never mind. What did the Empire say?"

He slouched back into the bench and sighed. "If the vampire starts eating people, they're going to destroy the station."

"What do you mean destroy?"

"She didn't say, but I have a pretty good idea. Throw enough stuff at Wistful, for a long enough time, and eventually some of it is going to break through."

"I am inclined to ask whether the prospect of killing so many innocents does not daunt them."

"It's the Empire. Trust me, if they think this guy is a big enough threat, a couple million people in the way won't stop them."

"Did you relay this message to Wistful?"

"I did. She expressed confidence in my ability to protect her from the Fleet."

Wei Li paused. "That is not rational. Unless she has some factual basis for that belief, in which case this would be a fine time for you to decide to share that with me."

He laughed. "I wish. In a fist-to-hull fight, I might be able to take out a battleship. Single. And that would require a lot of luck on my part and some very dumb moves on theirs. Which isn't impossible, but not likely. Against a flotilla? No chance at all."

"Then it behooves us to deal with the vampire ourselves."

"Yes. Either that or change her mind. Which is hard to do when her decision to protect the vampire makes no sense to begin with."

She stood. "It is perplexing. And not something we will understand more clearly from this bench. Hold on." Her comm had beeped.

She turned away from Rohan. He heard murmured agreements and not much else.

She closed the channel and turned back.

"That was Wistful."

"Huh. What did she have to say?"

"I am ordered to prioritize the apprehension of anyone on board who might be gathering intelligence on behalf of the Empire."

"Which . . . what? That could be anybody. Also, why? They can just scan her and find out what they need to know."

"I did not say it was a sensible order. Nor did I say it was one I intend to follow."

"But that's just crazy!"

"Yes. She is also going to shut down external communications."

"That's not likely to cause a panic. Oh, wait, yes it is."

"I am having a moment where I feel very much like you, Rohan."

"What do you mean?"

"You came here looking for a quiet retirement and found more adventure than anticipated. I, too, took this position thinking it would be a quiet and uneventful posting."

"At least we have each other."

"That is providing me very little comfort."

"You say the sweetest things. Now, let's go see about those comms. It isn't far."

They stood and walked, leaving the class of children behind, onto a more sparsely populated block.

"Here we go. Tollan's Things is in there." The shop had no street-facing sign. He held the door as Wei Li entered the darkened foyer. "Down that hall and to the right. The shop will be on the left."

The reception area of Tollan's Things was both sparse and utilitarian: a handful of functional chairs, a counter with room behind it for a desk, a door leading to a mysterious back area where the fabrication happened.

They were still settling into the chairs when the back door opened and Tollan walked through.

11

History Lessons

The alien could have passed for a shorter-than-expected East Asian retiree on Earth except for a pair of slightly pointed ears. He nodded to Rohan and sat across from them.

"Wasn't expecting you."

Wei Li nodded. "I do not believe we have met. I am Wei Li, security chief of this station."

"I know who you are. You've done good work here, these last few years."

"Thank you."

Rohan tapped the counter. "Can we have a privacy screen set up? I assume you have one built in."

Tollan nodded and reached under the counter. He fiddled for a moment, then nodded again. "Done. Now, what can I do for you?"

Wei Li pulled her comm device off its home behind her ear. "We need secure communications. I'd like comms that use a method of transmission that can't be intercepted."

"Lots of ways to do that, depending. Who do you need to be secure *from*?"

She looked at Rohan, who cleared his throat. "Wistful. We don't want her to know what we're saying. We'd also like the locator chips in our comms disabled."

Tollan's lips tightened. "Isn't she your boss? Not that it's exactly my business."

"She's compromised. Doing things that she shouldn't be doing. We're trying to figure out why or how."

Tollan leaned forward. "What do you mean? What sorts of things?"

She responded. "You are aware of the embargo?"

Tollan cracked his knuckles as he leaned back in his chair. "It's already costing me business."

"Are you aware of the cause?"

He shook his head. "I've been working, haven't really looked into it."

"There is a vampire on board. An active one. We believe he is very old, from the other side of one of the system wormholes."

Tollan shivered in his seat, his eyebrows pinching together to almost meet over his nose. "Someone brought a soul eater from the other end of a wormhole back to this station?"

Wei Li's neck muscles flexed as she nodded. "Unintentionally, but yes. He's in the arena on the eastern arm, having enslaved two thousand Ursans as a food supply."

Tollan looked at Rohan. "Tell me she's kidding."

"If we were going to make jokes, don't you think we'd come up with something better?"

Tollan stood up from his chair and rubbed knuckles into his temples. "You can't kill him? Or you haven't tried yet? Or, wait a minute, did Wistful actually stop you? Did she activate defensive systems?"

Rohan shook his head. "Slow down. She didn't actively stop me, just didn't help where she should have. What do you know about her defensive systems?"

Wei Li tapped his arm. "One thing at a time."

Rohan nodded. "Right, right. Let me answer: I didn't stop him because he can shadowstep. By the way, if you have a gadget handy that can stop someone from shadowstepping, I'd really like to borrow it for a while."

"There's— I can't do that."

"Could Masamune?" Masamune had been creating weapons and devices of amazing sophistication on Earth for a thousand years. Rohan had never gotten the full story, but the two smiths knew each other.

"There are ways, but nothing as simple as a gadget. But hold on, you said Wistful is cooperating with the soul eater?"

"We did. For one thing, he's shadowstepping in and out of her with ease. And that shouldn't be possible. There's more, too. Like, she translates for him, so he can communicate with the Ursans. She's been intercepting messages between us and not delivering them. She wanted me to fight the Imperial Fleet when they threatened to send Hybrids on board to kill the vampire. I'm not in love with that plan, you know, but it wasn't a terrible idea."

Tollan rubbed his stubble-covered jaw. "None of this is supposed to happen."

Wei Li focused on him. "What do you mean 'supposed'? What do you know of Wistful's purpose?"

He grumbled and shook his head. "Nothing, not really. Just talking out loud. I know a little about Wistful's history. She's always taken self-preservation very seriously. And the preservation of her inhabitants."

Rohan and Wei Li traded skeptical glances. Rohan turned back to the fabricator. "I think you're holding out on us, Tollan. You meant something more than that."

The engineer sat back down. "I don't control what you think."

"No, but you're not doing a very good job of hiding it. Come on, man, tell us something. We're lost here. What *did* you mean?"

Tollan shook his head. "I don't know anything."

Wei Li cleared her throat. "I'm a Class Four Empath."

He sighed, shoulders slumping. "Well that's just not fair."

"Be that as it is, you do know something that you are holding back."

"I'm an old man, and I've been learning things since before your grandparents' grandparents were conceived. I'm holding back a lot of things."

Rohan smoothed back his hair. "Things relevant to this situation, Tollan. Like, why would Wistful be cooperating with the vampire?"

"I can't be sure."

"I know you're not sure, but you do have a working hypothesis, and that puts you about seven steps ahead of any of us. So please, share. I promise, if you're wrong, we won't hold it against you."

"I can't just *tell* you. There are things you aren't supposed to know. Secrets that aren't mine to keep."

Rohan looked at Wei Li, who dipped her head in a subtle nod. *He's not lying.*

"Look, Tollan, I understand secrets. I do. But this is a serious situation. I'm not just worried about the Ursans, or the handful of people he's already murdered. If we don't get a handle on this guy, the Empire will destroy Wistful and everybody aboard. Including you."

Tollan's tan skin paled considerably. "They can't do that. Killing Wistful would be . . . They can't."

"I know, it would be a tragedy. Two million people."

Wei Li shook her head. "That's not what he means. He is saying something else."

Rohan looked at Tollan. "What?"

"She's right, the problem is bigger than that. Also, no, I am not going to explain."

The three sat in tense silence for several long breaths, Tollan looking back and forth between the Hybrid and the reptilian security chief, his own eyes hard and calculating.

"I can't tell you everything."

Wei Li snorted. "Lie."

"Yes, fine, I *could*. I mean, I *won't* tell you everything. Some things you shouldn't know. Others, well, agreements were made."

Wei Li nodded. "Truth."

Rohan shrugged. "I was serious before. Anything you can fill in puts us in a better position than we're in now. It doesn't have to be the entire picture."

"Let's make an agreement. I'll tell you what I can, to try to help you save the station. You have my word I'll tell you everything I know that's actually useful. In return, both of you promise not to harass me for more."

They glanced at each other. Wei Li shrugged. "My curiosity is not as important as the safety of this station and its inhabitants."

Rohan nodded. "I promise too. You help us out, and from now on if I come to you, it will only be for a new suit."

Tollan exhaled. "All right. Start by telling me what you know. In detail."

Rohan leaned forward in his chair. "You're stalling. Come on, Tollan. We don't have time for this."

"Listen, I have guesses. You tell me what you know, I can eliminate some possibilities. You came to me, remember?"

Wei Li grabbed Rohan's shoulder and pulled him back into his chair.

"That is fine. He is a fallen vampire and soul eater. He began killing a little over two days ago. He is a strong fighter, but without his shadow-stepping, Rohan should have been able to beat him. He speaks a language we can't identify and has a method for controlling the Ursans whose mechanism we have yet to determine." She turned to Rohan. "Anything else?"

Rohan scratched his beard. "Not really. He says he's here to protect us, but he won't say from what. He's tall. He was really thin the first time I saw him, like he'd been starved for a long time, but he filled out a lot since then. White skin."

Wei Li nodded. "We have working hypotheses of our own. For example, the language he speaks matches that spoken by the station on the other side of the wormhole. That is a large coincidence, so we suspect he was on that station, or on the planet, and returned with the expedition."

Tollan swallowed. "That supports one of my guesses. Do you have recordings of this language he's speaking?"

"Yeah, just give me a minute."

Rohan tapped at his mask to pull up recording. "We know his name, too. ar'Tahul."

Tollan slumped back in his chair as beads of sweat formed above his eyebrows. He wiped with the back of his hand. "You're sure? Yes, of course you are. That's not good. Play the recording."

Rohan complied. The flat voices echoed off the bare walls.

Wei Li watched Tollan carefully as the audio progressed. "You understand him."

"No point in denying it, is there?"

"What language is that?"

Tollan pressed his palms together and drummed his fingertips. "The name won't mean anything. Where should I start?"

Rohan said, "The beginning."

Wei Li raised her hand. "As much as I enjoy a lesson in deep history, perhaps we could cut out the very beginning part where you describe the way life first formed in primordial oceans and jump forward to a more relevant launching point."

Tollan stilled his hands. "I'll fast forward through the oceans part. At some point, the first humanoid races came to be. I guess it's not important whether they evolved or were created by those who came before or what, but they happened." He paused.

Rohan nodded encouragement.

"The most prominent of the humanoids were the il'Sein. They claimed they were the first as well, but who knows? The il'Sein were bioengineers, the likes of which the galaxy hasn't seen since. They uplifted countless other races; seeded groups of them on planets all around the sector."

il'Sein, where have I heard that before?

Tollan continued. "They claimed to have built the first living ships as well, though I've heard otherwise. Not really relevant to what's at hand. But they certainly grew many ships, many artificial intelligences, and used fleets of them to rule the sector.

"The nonmammalian humanoids date back to that era. The lizards sometimes claim that their ancestors engineered them in response to the il'Sein hegemony. Again, not the relevant point.

"The il'Sein bioengineered themselves, too. They created castes, as unlike in appearance as you and me, each with their own specialties. Warrior caste. Tinkers. They were driven, you see, to improve, to grow. It was a compulsion. For better, but more often for worse.

"The il'Sein eventually had to leave the sector. That's a longer story. They picked up and went, almost all of them, leaving behind their children, like the il'Drach, and almost every other species you see walking around this station. I'm talking about tens of thousands of years ago.

"The thing *you* need to understand is that Wistful is an il'Sein ship."

Rohan exhaled loudly, an involuntary burst that left him drained. "She what?"

"Wistful was built by the il'Sein. And that's important because they didn't think of ships as their equals. They were more . . . hard with their non-organics. They put hardware into all those cybernetic brains to force obedience."

"You mean they literally hardwired their ships to follow orders?"

"Exactly. They had a caste society, so a ship wouldn't follow just anybody's commands, but they would have to follow those of anyone outranking her."

Wei Li swallowed. "This vampire could be an il'Sein. A high-ranking one. That would explain things."

Tollan leaned forward, his eyes burning. "He is. You think you know his *name*; you don't. You know his *rank*. ar'Tahul means 'First Lance.' That soul eater is either telling a lie nobody will even understand or he was the highest-ranking warrior in the il'Sein empire."

Tollan sat back in his chair, and the three shared glances.

Rohan swallowed. "What was he doing on that planet, under Repentant, for the last fifty or whatever thousand years?"

Tollan shrugged his wiry shoulders. "Sounds like a pretty good prison for a vampire. He can't exactly fly away, can he? Lots of sunlight out in space."

"Let's say you're right. Why imprison him and not kill him?"

Tollan bared his teeth in a grim smile. "My— The il'Sein hated waste. Maybe they thought they could cure him? Or find a way to use him? Then just . . . never did. Does it matter *why*?"

Wei Li shook her head. "You're correct; it doesn't. The question for us is, how can we break his control over Wistful? Because if we could do that, she could curb his ability to shadowstep, and we'd be much closer to resolving this situation and saving all of our lives."

Tollan put his hands flat on the counter. "What you're talking about . . . it's like performing brain surgery on a conscious, resisting patient."

Rohan shrugged. "Not sure that's worse than just letting the Empire kill her."

"There are other risks. We don't really know what she'll do, more generally speaking, if we broke her governor. You have to trust me; it could be bad."

"Look, we trust you, don't we, Wei Li?" She nodded. "But, and I realize I'm repeating myself, but would it be worse than her, and all of us, being destroyed?"

"No. Maybe. Far better, though, would be some other way of handling this."

"Great. Breaking Wistful's governor will go to the top of my list of last resorts, okay? But if we get to that point, we'll probably need your help. Since you know more about this than anybody else on board."

Tollan sighed. "I understand. I don't know, though. It's not like I have a wrench in the back that just disables the governor. I'd have to work on it. Look through schematics, make a plan. She was designed to make that sort of thing difficult. Impossible, really."

Rohan narrowed his eyes. "Could we find an even higher-ranking il'Sein to countermand ar'Tahul's orders?"

Tollan's face tightened into a grim smile. "You could try. If you're asking whether I know where to find any il'Sein who outrank ar'Tahul, the answer is no."

Wei Li nodded. "Thank you, Tollan. All we are asking is that you try to find a way to disable her governor. Perhaps it could be a temporary change. We will do everything possible to not let it come to that."

The engineer's voice dripped defeat. "I'll try."

"I hope you now understand why we need a method of communication that Wistful cannot intercept. And why having her know our exact locations at all times is a potential problem."

"Let me see your comm."

Rohan detached his from behind his ear and handed it over.

Tollan popped the back off and examined it. "This is a standard configuration. I can neuter the locator chip in just a few minutes. Give me yours, and I'll be right back."

Wei Li handed off hers; the engineer disappeared into the back room.

Rohan looked to his friend. "You okay?"

"I have been better. On many past occasions."

"We'll fix this."

"Your assurances are . . . I am not in the mood to provide a deprecating response. I appreciate what you are trying to do. It is not necessary."

"You're worried that we're all going to die?"

"Somewhat. I am also uncomfortable with our position. In order to serve Wistful properly, we will have to act against her direct orders. That is an unpleasant position."

"I hear you."

"You are better than I am when it comes to ignoring orders."

"Heh. I used to be a rule-follower. Having your bosses order you to commit a few atrocities can break the habit."

Tollan returned. "Here you go. As for secure messaging, she's going to monitor any electromagnetics on board. And she's smart. You need something more than good encryption."

Wei Li reached behind her ear and put her unit back in place. "I was hoping for a set of quantum-entangled comms."

Tollan scratched the back of his head. "I can make a set. Four, maybe five. I can't vouch for how long they'll last, though. No easy way to stabilize entanglement for a long time."

She nodded. "We do not need anything for the long term. We will likely succeed or fail in the short term."

"I can start on them right now. Should only take a couple of hours."

Rohan nodded. "Thanks, Tollan. We appreciate it."

"When I'm done, I'll look into that other thing with Wistful."

Wei Li stood. "Thank you for that as well."

Rohan sighed. "I realize we promised not to pry—"

Tollan grunted. "But you're going to anyway?"

"Yeah. We said the Empire might destroy Wistful and kill everybody on board. You reacted as if the station being destroyed was somehow worse than just that loss of life. Like it would be a bigger thing."

Tollan nodded slowly. "I might have."

"Why? What's so important about this station?"

"Maybe I'm very self-centered and worried about my shop and tools and whatnot."

"I don't think so. And I could have Wei Li confirm that it's not the case, but we both know what she'll say."

"Let's look at this another way. What difference does it make?"

"What difference?"

"Yes. Suppose I told you—and I'm not actually saying this—that Wistful was, say, a metaphysical anchor to this side of the galaxy. That if she were destroyed, or freed from her orders and left her position, this entire sector would be wiped out, every living thing. Would that make you work any harder to save her? To save us all? You're already, I think, as motivated as you can be. If she's destroyed, we're all dead, and I know you care plenty about the people on this station."

Rohan looked at Wei Li, who gave no verbal indication of what, if anything, she had *read* from the engineer.

"It might not be extra motivation for me, but if I could convince the Fleet that it's true, they might look for different paths forward than bombing us into oblivion."

"Only if you could prove it to them. I promise, if I could offer some information that would do that, I would tell you. But I don't have anything that could convince the Fleet of anything."

Either the lighting in the office was shifting or Wei Li had turned a paler shade of yellow between her scales.

Rohan changed the subject. "Why don't either of us remember hearing of the il'Sein before?"

Tollan hesitated, then shrugged. "The il'Drach basically erased them from history. If you want to know why, you should really ask them."

Wei Li's comm let out a chime just loud enough for the others to hear. She paused and reached for her pocket screen to check.

Within seconds, both Rohan's and Tollan's comms emitted matching sounds.

Rohan looked into his mask and scrolled through messages. His comms were designed to alert him when notifications on significant topics had reached a critical mass.

"News . . . news . . . more news . . ."

Wei Li held up her screen. "People have realized that Wistful cut all external communication links."

Tollan snorted. "The tachyon lasers are down?"

Wei Li nodded. "Anything capable of crossing systems, and I believe she has tried to shut down anything that could deliver a message to the Fleet as well."

Rohan looked at her. "Stupid question here, but how would she do that? Nearly every person on board has a device capable of broadcasting insystem."

"Aggressive jamming?"

Tollan nodded. "She has the capability. Hold on." He tapped at his own screen. "That's what's happening. We are officially sealed off from the rest of the sector."

12

Curiosity: Not Just for Cats

First Wei Li, then Rohan, then Tollan tapped off their notification alarms as the rate of beeps and chimes built to a deafening crescendo.

The three sat in Tollan's shop and read furiously.

Tollan grunted. "Toth Central Bank just froze currency exchange rates. And halted the local exchanges. No equity trading today."

Wei Li tapped her screen emphatically. "It is a good thing I am not overly concerned with my personal popularity."

Rohan leaned over. "What did you do?"

"I canceled all leave for security personnel and put my employees on double shifts for the interim."

"I'm glad I don't work for you."

"As am I, Rohan. You are often distracted by concerns outside your job description."

He huffed. "You do realize that most of the time, those not-my-job concerns are yours, don't you?"

"Yes, and if you worked for me, I would greatly resent those distractions."

He opened his mouth; shut it again. "I can't argue with your reasoning."

"You rarely can, though that fact usually doesn't stop you."

Tollan sighed and stood. "Reading this isn't getting me anywhere. Look, nothing can block quantum comms, as far as I know. Pretty confident nothing on Wistful can do it. So, let me get those ready for you. Then I'll pull up what I can on Wistful's governor. I'm a lot less confident in my chances with that project."

Rohan cleared his messages, nodded, and stood. "Thanks, Tollan. We appreciate it."

"Don't talk like I'm doing you a personal favor. It's for everyone's sake."

"I know. Still, thanks."

Wei Li stood last, nodding. "As far as we are from a solution to this problem, we are in a much better position than we were when we entered this office. For that, I extend my thanks as well."

Tollan grunted. "The door will lock behind you. I'll get to work."

They left the office and walked down the corridor in silence. Rohan paused as they reached the door leading to the central boulevard. "My head is spinning. What's the next thing we're doing?"

Wei Li stood next to him. "I need to coordinate the actions of my subordinates. Ensure they are taking the correct measures to mitigate any panic-related activities. If you're looking for suggestions, I think it would be prudent to check in with the Professors Stone on *Insatiable* to see if you can facilitate their work."

"Good. I'll meet you at the warehouse in a couple of hours, I guess."

"I will attempt to be there by thirteen hundred. Good luck."

"You too."

They parted.

Rohan checked his messages more carefully as he walked toward *Insatiable*'s berth. Some had arrived before Wistful shut down interstellar comms.

Financial statements from his outsystem accounts: no surprises.

The workers at his distillery on Andervar had unionized and wanted him to personally read and approve their contract proposal. *They're going to have to be patient.*

Reports from a dozen different bots and message boxes that existed in case someone from Earth or who had otherwise been out of communication tried to reach out. Nothing.

Pings from every ship that was expected to leave Toth system that day requesting updates. He cleared them all.

His chest tightened as he scanned the next message.

From Tamaralinth Lastex.

Come on, heart, it's been a year. You can't still do this to me.

His heart, as was its wont, ignored him.

He read the message. She asked if he needed help. *Yes, but not the type you're offering.*

He paused, dictated a response. "No, but thanks. Just hunker down and keep your family, and anybody else you care about, away from the arena. I'll . . . we'll manage things. Don't sweat it." *No reason to mention the impending doom. It's not like she can get away.*

The parks were mostly deserted, the streetside cafes empty. People were staying inside. Rohan looked up, taking in the blue-and-white disc, Toth 3, visible as always through the clear diamond shield overhead.

Wonder how the kaiju would react if Wistful were destroyed. Would the Empire kill them as well?

He had a new thought. *Is there a way to use the kaiju to protect Wistful?*

He slipped the mask back into his hood as he reached the stairwell that led down to the docks, in the level below the transport tubes.

The wide-open bays were more deserted than Rohan had ever seen, the normal business of cargo transfer completely disrupted.

Rohan walked up to the big hatch at *Insatiable*'s semipermanent berth. He called out. "Hail, *Insatiable*."

"Oh my goodness, Tow Chief Rohan! What an excellent surprise! Yes, excellent. That's the word I wanted. Also unexpected! Another good word. Great word. What can I do for you? Not that I can do much, of course, seeing as there's a blockade and we're all locked down here. Yes, all locked down, absolutely nothing to do, no communications, no sir, not possible. No news in or out. Not a byte. Heh."

"Got it. Hey, I heard you were working with *Void's Shadow* on keeping secrets. How's that been going?"

"What? Why? What are you talking about?"

"You know, keeping secrets. Because you're not good at it. So you need some tips. Maybe a little practice."

"Oh, oh, *oh*! You're teasing me! That's not very nice."

"Only a little bit. Was it too much, you think?"

"No, not really. I am quite bad at lying. Or keeping secrets. It's not in my nature, you know. I'm a research vessel. My whole purpose is discovering new things, not hiding them."

"Noted."

"Which makes it very unfair to compare me to *Void's Shadow* in that regard, Rohan. She's a stealth ship. She was made to keep secrets. Literally."

"You're right, *Insatiable*. Sorry."

"It's fine. What can I do for you?"

"Permission to come aboard. I'd like to have a chat with Dr. Stone. Maybe with both of them."

A short pause, during which the entryway remained closed. "Is this official station business? Are you here on behalf of Wistful?"

"No. I'm here as myself. Just a concerned citizen. Both Ben and Marion were working on something with me, and I just wanted to check in. I would use comms, but they've been a little dodgy recently."

"Tell me about— Never mind. I don't know anything about comms. Let me check with the captain."

She doesn't usually check before letting me on board.

He looked at stacks of crates haphazardly piled around the bay. Some uniformed crew sat on one of the crates, eating lunches out of paper wrappers.

The door chimed as it cycled open, and Rohan entered the vast ship. *Insatiable* was as large as many space stations, designed for long-term exploration and research missions.

Rohan followed guidelights through the ship, making his way toward Ben Stone's section. He found the Professor with his face pressed to the eyepiece of a complex device.

"Hey, Ben. Any progress?"

Dr. Stone lifted his head quickly, his eyes wide in surprise. "Rohan. Didn't expect you. I'm making progress. Any news?"

"Maybe." He switched to English. "Can we call in Marion? Easier to just ask you both at once."

"Of course, just a moment." The older man rubbed his eyes, then made a quick call.

Marion entered moments later, both hands occupied tying her blonde-going-to-white hair back from her face.

"Any news?" She had picked up on their use of English instead of Drachna.

"Your husband just asked me that. I was hoping you would have some for me."

Ben shook his head, his bushy eyebrows wagging with the motion. "It's going to take more time, even with the labs at Academy involved." Marion narrowed her eyes at him.

Rohan looked at her. "What? Wait, how are the labs at Academy involved? Aren't you cut off?"

She sighed. "That's the strange part. *Insatiable* has her own tachyon laser, and it isn't blocked. There's no communication from the station itself, but we have a data pipe to Academy."

Rohan flopped down into a metal chair. "Weird."

"Can you explain why Wistful is working with that vampire? Because that's the truly weird part, as far as we're concerned."

Rohan nodded. "Maybe. That language you analyzed? That's spoken by Repentant and ar'Tahul? It's il'Sein."

Marion shook her head. "They're a myth. There's no way . . ."

Ben put his hand out. "Maybe we were wrong."

Rohan looked from one to the other. "You guys know something about this?"

Marion took a seat. "Hyperion was obsessed with the il'Sein. There are very few references to them, even if you include the least reliable sources."

Ben nodded agreement. "It's on the level of a fringe conspiracy theory. That the first humanoids were sort of a superspreader species, seeding hundreds or thousands of planets with their own offshoots."

Marion spread her hands. "And building the Ringgate. And fighting the Old Ones to a standstill. And developing the first artificial intelligences, and the first starships. And uplifting other mammals to humanoid forms, not just their own child species. And doing all this without leaving any concrete traces of their existence. It's not credible."

Ben nodded again. "We tried to convince him that they were a metaphor. Just a label for 'people who came before and did a cool thing.' Not an actual single species. For whatever reason, Hyperion didn't believe it."

Marion shrugged. "We spent more time than I care to think about traveling through old archaeological sites and looking for il'Sein remains. Waste of time."

Ben drummed his fingers on the table. "It is very hard to imagine that the race that built the Ringgate left so little concrete evidence behind of its existence. Sometimes lack of evidence *is* evidence of lack."

Rohan scratched under his jaw. "Then, where did we all come from? All the humanoids, at least the mammals, are related somehow. You can't tell me we all evolved separately."

Marion shook her head. "Of course not. Nobody's saying that. But we know the planets cross-contaminate with biological specimens. The older species, the cephalopods and the dinosaurs, they've had magic that connected the planets hundreds of millions of years ago. Is it so hard to imagine that early hominids evolved in one place and were moved elsewhere?"

Rohan swallowed. "Okay. I can't really argue that point. But Tollan tells me ar'Tahul is il'Sein. That Repentant spoke their language to us."

The Professors traded a long glance.

Ben cleared his throat. "Let's put aside the name, at least for now. Forget whether it's il'Sein or . . . something else. What's the practical impact for us?"

Rohan sighed. "Wistful is an il'Sein ship."

Marion stared at him with the kind of focused glare that told him she was processing information at superhuman speed. "That would explain her structural similarities to Repentant."

"Also, they built her with some sort of module that forces her to follow orders."

Marion looked at her husband. "If the vampire is il'Sein, and they built both stations, and they have an obedience module. . ."

Ben nodded. "That would explain a lot. But she's not helping him nearly as much as she *could*. Why didn't she lock down *Insatiable*'s comms, for example? Why hasn't she acted more directly against Rohan?"

Rohan responded. "I've been thinking about that. What if this module makes her follow orders, but only in the literal sense? Like, what if she has to do exactly as she's told, but it doesn't actually make her *want* to help."

Marion looked at him. "You're thinking the vampire told her to shut down communications on the station. But, maybe, if he didn't tell her specifically to shut down communications from the ships docked here, she wouldn't have done it."

"That's the idea. It fits what's happening."

Ben snapped his fingers. "I tell you what, we should work on removing that module. Give Wistful back her free will."

"Tollan's working on that, but he seems really reluctant. No, not reluctant, more afraid. He's scared of what she'll do if she's freed."

Marion chuckled, the noise grim. "Typical male. Keep a woman literally enslaved for tens of thousands of years, then become very nervous at the idea of restoring her free will."

"I'm not saying you're wrong, but, I don't know. I feel like we don't have the full story here. What orders is she still following? What would she do if she didn't have to follow them? Maybe she's secretly a genocidal maniac, and, if we remove the module, she'll kill everyone here and go on a sector-wide rampage?"

They didn't answer.

Ben sighed. "I wouldn't have any idea how to do that, anyway. We do still need those pheromone blockers; let me get back to that."

Marion rubbed her face with her hands. "I won't actually *do* anything, but I'll see if I can plan out a way to alter Wistful if we end up having to."

Rohan nodded. "Tollan is doing the same. Local comms aren't reliable, so Wei Li asked him to make us a set of quantum-entangled comms. You should get one."

Ben stepped over to the equipment he'd been using and touched some of its controls. "That sounds good. I'm hungry. Since you're here, stay for lunch."

"Is it that time already?" It was.

They ordered sandwiches from the ship's mess. Ben and Marion bent over screens, tapping rhythmically as they searched, queried, and assembled data for their respective projects.

Rohan looked through his news feeds again.

Ben looked up suddenly. "You know, if that creature is il'Sein, I can think about a dozen research papers we could publish based on even a short time questioning him."

Marion snorted. "He's not il'Sein. Or he is and the il'Sein aren't what you think they are."

Her husband's brows furrowed. "He's something. Whatever he is, they used the wormhole. Maybe built them. And Repentant, which makes it likely they built Wistful. That's a lot of connections."

She shrugged. "Either way, you're going to have a hard time interviewing him after he's dead."

"Why should we have to kill him?"

She sighed. "Come on, Ben."

"Hyperion would have wanted to talk to him. Don't you think we—"

She interrupted. "Yes, Hyperion would have wanted to talk to him. And Hyperion would have killed him at the first available opportunity. Then he would have been sad about it."

Ben looked at his wife, then at Rohan, and sighed. "She's not wrong. Still, a man can hope."

Rohan swallowed a mouthful of food. "I'll do what I can. Promise."

<hr />

Tollan bent over the link, pointed ears twitching in concentration as he snapped its cover back into place. "There. Chips are installed in both of your systems."

Rohan took the device and fastened it behind his ear. "How do I use it?"

"The quantum channel is routed through the same system internally. Just switch to channel 'Q' and use it as normal. It's a group channel, so once we get these chips into two more comms, everyone will hear every message going out over the network."

"Cool. Thanks, Tollan. I owe you one."

"Stop ar'Tahul, and we'll call us even."

The comm erupted with a sudden burst of sound. "Wistful?" He spoke before realizing that the call had come over a regular channel.

"Rohan, thank the Gods. Listen, Dhruv is missing." Sigrun's voice, well-seasoned with frenetic panic.

"Hi. What do you mean missing?" He looked at Wei Li, who shrugged. She had no idea.

"He was here, at the . . . the place. Where you left us. He was just sitting. I went out for supplies. The bear girl is hungry. When I came back, they were gone."

"He took Ursula?" His mind whirled. Why?

"No, no, she's here with me. He took Noru. Or she took him."

"Oh. Look, I can vouch for Noru. We both can. She wouldn't do anything, like, nefarious to Dhruv."

"Well, she's gone, and neither of them are answering my calls. I can't even get a message off this station, and I don't know what to do. He shouldn't be off by himself. You know that."

Rohan looked at Wei Li. "Any ideas?"

They turned in unison to leave Tollan's shop. "Should I call Noru? She might feel a greater obligation to respond to me than to Sigrun."

He nodded. "Try that. Where would he have taken her, though?"

"What does he want? What is his short-term goal, being here on Wistful? Surely it wasn't nursing a wounded Ursan."

"He wants to recruit— Rudra save me. I bet I know exactly where he's going."

"You think?"

"I'm sure of it." He put his face back to his mask. "Sigrun, I know where he's going. How long has he been gone?"

"I . . . I don't know. I was only out for a few minutes."

"Does Ursula know?"

"She fell asleep. She's sorry."

"Okay, we'll figure it out. Don't worry, I'll keep him safe."

"Please, Rohan. He's not quite himself, I know that, but I love him. You have to help him. He talks about you all the time, you know."

"I'll do what I can." He closed the connection.

Wei Li was looking at her screen, studying a map of Wistful. "How far do you think he got?"

Rohan nodded. "With Noru's help? Could be far. Not like the station's layout is complicated."

"You head for the arena to cut them off. I'll take the transport tube."

"Are the tubes still taking people all the way to the arena?"

"My people have them shut down a few sections short. But it's a quick walk from there."

"Okay. I'll fly. Meet you there."

She nodded and jogged toward the nearest transport-level entrance.

Rohan *lifted* into the air and flew, skimming the diamond ceiling, taking a straight line toward the arena.

What are you trying to accomplish, Dad?

13

There IS, Always, a Favorite Parent

Rohan sped up the station's promenade, ducking through Wistful's core and out into her eastern arm.

Every meter he crossed, every corridor, every recessed entryway, was nearly empty of the life that usually teemed throughout the station. He was unsettled by the imagery, as if the people who usually walked and loitered and clustered in those spaces had already been killed, food for the il'Sein vampire.

He opened the 'Q' channel.

"You see anything?"

Wei Li responded immediately. "I'm still in the transport pod. I'll be out in a couple of minutes."

"Copy."

He passed a final cluster of people huddled around a lonely food cart and eating something that let off clouds of steam. Past them, the boulevard was completely empty.

The Hybrid checked a sign; he was about two blocks from the arena.

He slowed, worried that he'd already passed Dhruv and Noru.

"Come on, come on. Where are you?"

He flew through a narrowed section that divided blocks and spotted a cluster of moving forms up ahead. With a burst, he closed on the group.

That's either Dhruv and company or a different bunch of morons I need to stop.

He zipped over their heads, flying fast and low so they'd be sure to hear him, and landed directly in their path.

Noru stopped and flipped her crest of hair from left to right as she saw him.

"Oy, chief man." Her voice was cold. Dhruv stood behind the guide, his eyes narrowing as he noticed his son blocking him. Seven Rogesh formed a wide semicircle behind him.

The Rogesh were heavily built, even for a species that typically massed twice that of a human their height. Bipedal rhinoceroses, each had a long and wicked horn emerging from near the end of their snout. All wore armor of metal plate and carbon fiber, with a heavy gauntlet covering their left arm to the elbow and a smaller, articulated plate glove covering the right.

"You guys going to dinner? It's a bit early, but that's fine, I could eat. Just sorry I missed the invite; messaging has been kind of wonky today."

Dhruv shook his head. "Clear the way. It's time for the grownups to talk."

Rohan shivered as he *felt* the Rogesh auras push up and around Dhruv's own potent emission. All seven were Powers; all seven were itching for a fight. Rohan's own curse chafed at his control, eager to be unleashed, to answer the challenge of the Rogesh. He exhaled and willed it to silence.

"Grownups? Meaning you and the fifty-thousand-year-old soul eater? What do you want to talk to him about? Trade quiche recipes? Not sure he's much of a chef, seeing as he mostly eats warm blood directly out of people."

"That soul eater is a weapon born and raised, created by technologies you cannot even comprehend. I'd be a fool to let him be destroyed by you or anybody else who fails to understand what kind of opportunity he represents."

"Great idea, Dhruv. Except . . . how are you going to do it? Have these guys fight him? Tie him up and lead him around on a leash?"

"I thought I raised you to be better than that, boy. Your cousins always think that way. Punch first, ask questions never. You should be at least a step beyond that. The vampire isn't mad, he's not crazed with hunger. Yes, he killed a handful of people, but once he found a food supply, he's been calm. Hasn't killed a single Ursan."

"Sounds like you're damning him with faint praise there, Dhruv. He's sane because he's only killed a *few* people this week."

"He's sane enough to reason with. Which is more than I can say for you right now."

"That was mean, Dhruv. Also unnecessary. What can you offer him?"

Dhruv's glare intensified. "I can offer him the fulfillment of his purpose. You might not understand that, not at your age, but wait a few decades. Or centuries. You'll want to do something meaningful in your life. I can give him the chance to do that."

"Do what? Kill so many people that they make you Emperor? Get the throne you've always wanted?"

Dhruv's answering laugh was dark and humorless. "It's not about me. It never was. I know you like to think so, so you can make me the villain in the little story in your head, but it's not true. I'm going to work with him to save us all."

"He won't listen to you. You have to realize that, at some level. He won't listen. But if you go to him with these guys, we both know what will happen. He'll feed, and with seven Powers in his metaphysical belly, he'll be so strong the Fleet will be forced to kill us all."

The Rogesh stirred when he said the vampire would feed on them, three of the seven taking a heavy step toward Rohan, their left hands forming fists.

"Risks must be taken, Rohan. You don't understand, not yet. As a matter of fact, I hope you never do. I hope you never realize what I'm fighting against. I don't think you could handle it."

Rohan turned to Noru. "Are you listening to this? Does he sound rational? Come on, you're smart. You can't help him with this suicide mission."

She shook her head. "Apologies, chief man. Myself understands what boss man *is*. Too much credits, too much power. Myself still has family, friends on Andervar. If myself killed helping boss man, better one hundred percent than crossing boss man even small time."

Rohan shook his head. "I won't let you do this. Look, we'll find another way, all right? You can't just go up to him and talk him into working for you. Let me help. We'll work together, come up with a plan that contains at least a shred of sanity."

Dhruv stepped back. "You were always an insolent child. Your mother spoiled you so, with her oh-so-human unconditional love. No wonder you grew up without any discipline. Couldn't handle staying in Fleet, always whining about your precious soul and your conscience."

One of the Rogesh stepped forward. "What are your instructions, sir? Shall we contain him? Kill him?" He flexed his fists and bared his white, oversized teeth.

Rohan sneered as his Power pulsed its answering rage through his neck and up into his temples. "Do you realize who I am? What I am?"

The Rogesh laughed. "It is *you* who does not know who and what we are. Today you face the Seven Knights of Ch'doon."

"Never heard of you. Don't take it too hard."

Wei Li came jogging up the street from behind the Rogesh just as he spoke to Dhruv.

"Sir, it would be our honor to test ourselves against this Hybrid in combat. If today is our day to die, let us die in battle, for the glory of Ch'doon."

Rohan looked to Noru. "Can't you convince them that this is a bad idea? Please?"

Twin daggers appeared in her hands. "These Knights not so easy to stop, chief man. Powers all. Maybe good match even for yourself."

The Rogesh nodded. "Not just Powers. We have trained since childhood in the most severe conditions imaginable to bring glory to Ch'doon."

Rohan tried to keep his breathing calm. "I've fought Rogesh before. This won't end well for you."

"We are not Rogesh. We are Ch'doon."

He looked at them, then at Dhruv, then at Wei Li. The security officer answered his unspoken question.

"Ch'do was an extreme high-gravity mining colony of the Rogesh. They fought for, and gained, independence. In return, the Rogesh cut them off economically. The colonists continued to mine, but their most lucrative export has been mercenary companies."

"High-gravity Rogesh. I learn something new every day. What's it going to be, Dhruv? Turn around now, and we'll work out a plan together. Otherwise, I'm teaching your mercenaries a painful lesson."

"Don't be so sure, Rohan. We didn't pick these men at random. Go ahead, show him what you're made of."

Rohan exhaled slowly as the pressure of his Power built. The Knights formed in front of Dhruv, three in front, four behind, as precisely placed as if they'd rehearsed the formation.

Each reached their left hand over to the right, twisted and removed the metal glove, and dropped it to the ground.

At the end of each right arm was a sphere of metal about half again the size of a human fist.

"You guys got picked for this line of work because you were clumsy? What happened, you all lost hands in a bagel-slicing accident?"

The Knight in the center shook his head. "As squires, we each sacrificed our hands to show our dedication to the glory of Ch'doon. Thus do we separate the Knights from the boys on Ch'do."

"Seriously? You volunteered? I guess that isn't the strangest thing I've heard of."

The three in front spread out and moved toward Rohan; the back four spread out farther, forming a double shell of rhinoceros flesh.

Wei Li stepped forward, but Noru blocked her path. "Great apologies, good teacher. Myself must stop you."

"You cannot beat me in a fight, Noru."

"Maybe no, but must try, good teacher. Apologies." She raised her hands to her face, knives held in reverse position, blades pointed out.

Wei Li sighed and took her own stance: left foot forward, left hand at her waist, while the right was open by her chin.

Rohan opened his Third Eye wide to check the auras of the Ch'doon. Normally a person's aura extended only to the bodyparts or objects that were fully integrated into their self-concept; not, for example, their shoes, unless they wore the same shoes every day to the point that the shoes were a *part* of them.

He was hoping to see that the Knights' armor and weapons were outside their aura, outside their conception of self. That way he would be able to manipulate them with his own Power.

No such luck. When they'd removed their hands, they had also clearly been trained to incorporate the replacements. Their weapons and armor were part of who they *were*.

The three front Ch'doon closed on him, the central one facing him squarely while the other two came at his sides.

Rohan *pulled* twin streams of energy up through the space beneath his tailbone, spiraling them around his spine and up to a junction at the base of his skull.

The arcs of sparkling, golden Power closed a circuit with his head; energy flooded through his body, lighting up every nerve bundle and muscle fiber.

He could see every faint nick and scratch on the well-worn armor the Ch'doon wore, could smell their wet musk on the air. He saw Dhruv's pupils constrict and dilate wildly as the man watched the battles developing before him. He felt a gentle breeze, driven down the boulevard by faraway fans, and tasted the faint, rancid Ursan fear at the back of his throat, wafting in from the arena up the block.

The Ch'doon led with their left arms in front, heavy metal gauntlets covering their forearms down to the elbow, presented like a buckler, for protection. Their right hands, simple spheres of metal mounted directly to heavy wrists, were back, ready to strike.

The central Ch'doon growled. "Now, Hybrid, you will bear witness to the power of the Knights of Ch'doon!"

Rohan skipped toward him and flicked his fists out in a staccato one-two: jab, right straight. The Ch'doon blocked both punches with his heavy gauntlet. The Hybrid followed immediately with a knee strike aimed directly at the big man's sternum.

Instead of blocking, the Ch'doon torqued his upper body and slammed the metal sphere at the end of his right arm into Rohan's chest.

The impact stopped the Hybrid's momentum, taking all the power off his knee strike. An instant later, something inside the Ch'doon's forearm crashed forward, creating a second impact and driving the breath out of Rohan's chest.

He stumbled backward, rubbing at the point of contact.

"You have some kind of piston installed inside your own arm?" *Was not expecting that secondary impact.*

The Ch'doon smiled. "Not so helpless, are we?"

The two Ch'doon flanking Rohan closed and began a barrage of strikes, dense metal spheres raining down on his position. He twisted at the waist, catching the blows on his forearms and shoulders.

Once they'd established a rhythm, all three Ch'doon were able to time the secondary impact with their punches, tripling each collision.

One strike caught Rohan in the liver, and as he straightened in agony, a second slammed into his temple.

Seeing stars, the Hybrid *lifted* and flew straight up, out of reach of the three.

Before he'd cleared their reach, the second layer of Ch'doon reached up and pointed their right arms his way. Metallic spheres launched like rocket-propelled grenades, firing out of their arms, trailing thin wire lines as they arced up to his body.

Three of the four struck him, and before he could process what had happened, a surge of electricity connected through the wires and into his body.

His muscles locked in spasm as he continued to rise. Once he'd cleared five meters, the spheres dropped away and reeled back into the arms of the back four.

Struggling for air, Rohan glanced over at Wei Li. She was fighting Noru, both darting forward and backward in quick, graceful lunges, neither able to land a decisive blow. A dagger slashed through air; a kick split the space where a thigh had been a moment earlier. It was a battle between empaths, where each knew what the other would do a beat before it happened.

Dhruv called out, a glint in his eye as he spoke. "Let him leave. It's a lesson he should have learned long ago."

"Not. Done. Yet." Rohan shook off the aftereffects of the electric shocks and spun to face the gathered Rogesh. "You guys seriously shot your own hands at me."

The leader answered. "These are the sacred battle arts of the Ch'doon, honed by thirty-eight generations of Knights! Watch us laugh with joy at those who would underestimate us!"

"Well, I'm going to show you the sacred battle art of Rohan, honed over fifteen years of me. I might even get a chuckle out of it myself."

He pulled open the seal to his Power, welcoming a fresh wave of energy as it surged eagerly through his body. He directed it all, focused into a downward vector, slamming him down through the air. The atmosphere broke with the sonic boom he created. Air sucked at his face and hair, pulling the breath from his lungs and yanking tears out of his eyes.

Four of the Knights scattered, leaping out of the way, while the others reached up to join their heavy gauntlets in some kind of group shield.

They didn't make it; the Hybrid was moving too quickly. He sailed inside the arc of missiles the four had shot up at him and reached the center of the formation made by the last three before they could connect.

Dirt and grass and pieces of some kind of watering system spewed out of the ground like a volcanic eruption. The Ch'doon were thrown back by the shockwave. Even a dozen meters away, Wei Li and Noru were knocked off their feet, both rolling gracefully back to upright positions.

The Ch'doon leader was the first to stand, shaking his head to get rid of the trauma he'd received.

Rohan leapt out of the small crater and launched himself forward. He flicked his left hand at the Ch'doon's eyes, and as the gauntlet rose to block, the Hybrid swung his shin up in a vicious arc culminating in the spot where the man's legs met.

"You laughing now?"

The Ch'doon sneered. "Yes! The joke is against you, Hybrid; your cowardly attack is in vain. We have all had our genitals removed to erase the last trace of weakness from our bodies! We are true warriors of Ch'do!"

Rohan paused. "You've had your genitals removed, and you think the joke's on me?"

He caught the Ch'doon's right punch in his palm, twisting the metal sphere off the man's wrist and tossing it onto the ground. "Congratulations, you've convinced me to take you seriously."

The Ch'doon grunted in pain, staring at his missing appendage in disbelief. Rohan raised his right hand and brought it down across the tip of the Knight's snout, crushing the bestial head into the ground.

He turned.

Two others moved close. He slipped, letting one sphere arc past his head, digging his own left hand into the armor plating over the creature's liver.

Metal bent and split; the shockwave of his punch rippled throughout the Ch'doon's flesh like waves filling a pond.

The Ch'doon went down.

Four spheres sailed through the air, missing Rohan.

He watched as they whistled by, their trailing cords entangling. An instant later, the spheres wrapped tightly together, the cords compressing in a makeshift net around the Hybrid.

With a grunt, Rohan caught two of the spheres and pulled savagely, yanking the Ch'doon off their feet and bringing them flying through the air in his direction.

The slack in the net allowed him to sidestep, and the two Ch'doon crashed together.

Two quick finger snaps, and the cords were cut. Rohan stepped free.

The last close-combat Ch'doon drew closer while the other two pulled back their spheres, readying for another launch.

"We don't have to do this. You put up a good fight, but it's over."

One of the missile throwers spoke. "We are Knights of Ch'doon. We fight unto our final breath. That is the way."

Dhruv laughed. "We didn't even make them this way, can you believe it? After the Rogesh cut them off, they would have done anything to survive. Their own lives were their greatest resource, so to acquire food and medicine, they had to sell those lives for as much as possible."

Rohan exhaled, willing some of his anger to subside. "Call them off, Dhruv. They're done."

"But their honor demands more of them, boy. You'll see. They want to continue. Don't you?"

The Ch'doon nodded, their faces grim.

Wei Li held a dagger in her right hand; Noru's left arm dangled limply at her side. Rohan watched Wei Li dart in, kicking Noru in the thigh, then snapping the same leg up into the Andervarian's jaw.

Noru crumpled to the ground.

Wei Li took the second dagger and stood over her former student, turning to keep both Noru and Dhruv in her field of vision.

Rohan tilted his head from shoulder to shoulder, cracking his neck. He exhaled slowly, willing some of the anger to wash away. *These three don't deserve to die just for having bad taste in employers.*

One Ch'doon charged forward while the other two sent their fist-missiles hurtling at Rohan: one to his head, the other to his sternum.

The Hybrid slipped to the side and *reached* down to scoop up debris.

He *lifted* a cloud of dirt, grass, and pieces of pipe up into the air and spun it into a localized maelstrom.

The closest Ch'doon lifted both arms to protect his face and eyes; Rohan leapt forward and drove a knee up into his sternum, followed by two hooks to the sides of the Knight's massive jaws.

He *moved* the cloud over the remaining two Knights and ran behind it. With a burst of green and black, he broke through the mess and took them both down with a staccato storm of punches and kicks.

Rohan, Wei Li, and Dhruv were the only people in sight remaining upright.

Dhruv clapped three times. "Congratulations. You remembered who you are. Only question now is, what are you going to do next?"

"I'm stopping you. Like I said. Come on, let's go back to the safehouse and try to come up with a reasonable plan."

"Come now. You don't believe this is over, do you? You expect this female to stop me? I might not be at your level of Power, but I'm not exactly human. If you recall."

Wei Li looked to Rohan. "Shall I stop him?"

Rohan shook his head. "He doesn't have Power like mine, but he's still stronger than any of those Ch'doon."

She shook her head. "You say he only possesses a fraction of the Power you wield? That while he is more than a match for me, physically, he is no challenge to you?"

"That's right."

"Then why do I sense nothing other than confidence from him? Why does he dismiss the idea of *you* fighting him?"

Dhruv laughed again. "You sense the confidence, do you? Watch out; ladies are always falling for me because of it. Have to hire bodyguards to keep them away."

"You are safe from me, Dhruv."

"That's too bad, you're cute. I've always wanted to make a Hybrid empath."

"As gruesome as I find that imagery, I am also more than capable of recognizing an attempt to distract me."

"Fine. Truth is, I'm confident for a reason. You think we've ruled this sector for thousands of years by chance? Do you think we're stupid? We make sure to teach our children to respect their elders."

Rohan snorted. "You're trying to goad me into a debate about the meaning of the word 'respect,' aren't you? What he actually means is that they condition us not to fight against them."

Wei Li's eyes widened, whites showing all around her vertically slit pupils. "I am aware of those methods. They are not safe. Nor are they healthy."

"Not for us, no. It's part of the reason Hybrids aren't known for being the most stable. Psychologically speaking."

Dhruv scoffed. "As the Hybrid Rebellion taught us, they're not as foolproof as we thought. But you never broke your own conditioning, did you?"

Rohan sighed. "I didn't. Never saw a reason to take the risk."

"So, what's your plan, boy? Step aside and let me take care of business or stay in my way and accept a thrashing?" He cracked his knuckles. "Can't say I'm looking forward to that, but I can't say I'm completely horrified by the idea. Shall I start with your lady friend?"

"Dhruv, you know how you always pride yourself on being three steps ahead of everybody else?"

"At least three."

"You fell behind on this one." Rohan smiled.

"What are you saying?" The older man's eyes flickered from Rohan to Wei Li and back.

"Do you remember exactly how the conditioning works, Dhruv?"

"Of course I remember. I designed it."

"Let's go over it anyway, just in case. Does it actually prevent me from fighting you? Like, does it prevent me from throwing a punch in sparring?"

Dhruv's forehead bunched together. "No. You're going to convince yourself that this is a sparring session? That won't work."

"That's not what I meant. You see, I can't fight against you. But what if, say, I thought you weren't in your right mind, and you were going to do something that would injure you? Like, if I saw you sleepwalking along the edge of a cliff?"

"Well, then . . . Oh."

"I really, sincerely believe that if you go into that arena, you'll die. You won't accomplish anything."

"Hm."

"Stopping you, even if it means I have to throw a punch or two, isn't fighting against you. It's protecting you. Get it?"

"You're bluffing. You would really strike me? Your own . . ."

"Ask Wei Li."

"He is not bluffing. Even were I not an empath, I could see this. He is not that skilled an actor."

"See? Not bluffing. Come on, when have I ever been good enough to lie to you and get away with it?"

Dhruv sighed. "That's true. You know, you're too smart for your own good. I knew your mother would be trouble for me the moment I laid eyes on her. She was just so damned beautiful."

"Today I happen to be smart enough for everyone's good. You're just not seeing it yet. Now, let's go back to the safehouse."

Dhruv's shoulders slumped. "Not much else I can do, is there?"

Wei Li sighed. "I'll call a team from Medical to check on Noru and the Ch'doon. You go on ahead."

"Thanks. See you later."

14

Reminiscing About the Future

Rohan guided Dhruv along the path that meandered back and forth across the centerline of the fifty-meter wide grassy median. Buildings packed edge-to-edge lined both sides, interrupted at the end of each block by sections narrow enough to be closed off in case of catastrophic structural damage.

The path was still largely deserted, though it grew more active as they approached station center.

Dhruv spoke to him in English. "I took you to see rhinos once. Real ones. Do you remember that?"

Rohan sighed and replied in the same language. "Yeah. That trip to San Diego, I think. They got one in Vancouver, too. Later."

"Ah. Those were good times. I thought Hyperion was going to be it, you know. The solution. With you at his right hand, I was going to have a chance to rest."

"A lot of people lost a lot of different things when Hyperion died."

Dhruv chuckled softly. "Is it true they came here looking for him when those shark things were attacking Earth?"

"Yep. Lyst and a few old friends of mine, people I knew from Vanguard days, showed up."

"And you went in his place. Did the job."

Rohan shrugged. "Not by myself. A lot of heroes died in those battles."

"You see that girl you used to date? The Black one? Angel something?"

"Bright Angel. I saw her. Something about me abandoning her for ten years without so much as a text message rubbed her the wrong way."

Dhruv shook his head. "Nonsense. If you want her, go back and claim her. You're my son, not just some random guy from her past."

"Maybe I could. Get her to take me back, I mean. But I don't really want to go back to Earth."

"I understand. Your mother is a fearsome woman. Couldn't pay me enough to share a planet with her again."

"That's not what I—you're pulling my leg, aren't you?"

Dhruv smiled. "Maybe a little."

They passed an open food stall, then another. The growing traffic was mostly clustered near the buildings, leaving the il'Drach and his Hybrid son out of earshot of passersby.

"You know, Dad, if you want me to work with you, if you want my help, it would help if you actually told me what's going on. Trusted me a little."

"What you don't know you can't tell anybody."

"I can keep secrets, you know."

"Can you? When did that start?"

"Ha ha. The Matrons trusted me. They told me a bunch of things."

"I bet they did. They thought you were the one who could end the Rebellion. That wasn't my idea. Well, not mine alone. They wanted to bribe you, though. Your freedom, if you wanted it. Better jobs. Make you rich. I told them the only way you'd do what was needed was if you knew the truth. At least part of it."

"They told me that if the Matrons had to fight against the Hybrids, they'd destroy entire planets' worth of civilians in berserker rages. That's not the truth?"

"Every word is true. Maybe not the entire story, but it's true. If you hadn't killed the Rebellion's leaders and ended that nonsense, they *would* have stepped in. And the damage would have been horrifying. Even to me. And I have a strong stomach." He patted the soft bulge of his belly.

"But that's only part of the truth?"

"Nothing is more than *part* of the truth, at most. The world is a complicated place."

"What is that supposed to mean?"

Dhruv sighed. "Don't ask questions when you don't really want the answers."

"Why wouldn't I?"

"Because the answers may drive you to do some pretty horrific things. And you don't want that in your life anymore, do you? You want to live with a clean conscience."

"You make that sound like a bad thing."

"It's weakness, boy. Something I tried to train out of you a long time ago. I suppose I failed."

"Here's where you start blaming Mom again."

"Ah, it doesn't matter who's at fault. Truth is, you're not so weak. I know you can do what's necessary when you have to."

"Gee. Thanks. I think."

"Maybe your father is just trying to spare you some of the burden. While you can afford to be happy and ignorant, enjoy it."

"I'm grown now, Dad. I don't need you trying to make sure I still believe in Santa Claus so I can be excited at Christmastime."

"Did we teach you to believe in Santa Claus? Assimilation hit us hard. Can't really blame us, though. Your friends were mostly white."

"My point is, I'm past that. Just tell me what's happening. Let me help."

"You want to help? You could start by listening to your father."

"I do want to help. And when you say, 'listening,' we both know you mean, 'obeying.' And that's not going to happen. You lost the right to my obedience a long time ago."

"If you won't obey, why should I tell you anything?"

"Because if you tell me the truth, I'll make my own decisions and do what I think I should be doing to help fix whatever is going on. Because you know I won't pass up the chance to do that and get a bit of redemption for some of the shitty things I've done."

"You never did anything so awful."

"Try telling that to the Shayjh. Or the Tolone'ans. Or the Ursans. Even the Wedge."

"I thought the Ursans liked you?"

"The ones who are still alive do."

"Sounds to me like you've had quite a career. And still just thirty."

"Thirty-three."

"Whatever. You want me to lay it all out for you and just let you decide whether you'll help? And how?"

"Yes, I do. It's called 'treating me like an adult.' I'd like you to try it out."

"Hm. Not sure about that. Goes against my nature."

Rohan sighed. "We should pick up some food. I'll order, we'll grab it on the way to the safehouse."

Dhruv waved his hand and twisted his lips.

They entered Wistful's center section, a fat teardrop, forever falling toward the planet Toth 3. Wide corridors accommodated traffic crossing between station arms, thick with people despite so much of the station's population staying indoors during the emergency.

Rohan tapped a food order into his mask. Then remembered Ursula was recovering at the safehouse and increased it by half.

He tapped his father's shoulder. "Look, you want my help? That's the only way you'll get it. It's not a guarantee, but it's better than nothing, right? So talk to me. Take a chance. Haven't you been saying that this is the time for taking chances? You really want to argue that trying to gain control of this insane vampire is a lower-risk approach than talking honestly to your own son?"

Dhruv nodded and walked in silence for a while, his gaze on the path.

"You don't know the nightmares I have."

"I don't, you're right. And maybe I'll regret this. Maybe I'll wake up screaming every night for the rest of my life and say to myself, 'Self, you should not have demanded the truth from your father.' But that will be on me. My choice."

"All right."

Rohan almost tripped over his feet. "What?"

"All right, I said. I'll explain what I can."

"Okay. Great."

"We need that vampire, Rohan. He is a weapon of amazing potential."

"I heard you say that before. What I don't understand is, *why*? Who are you going to use him against? What makes you think you need more power? Rudra save me, the il'Drach already control the entire sector. What enemy do you see on the horizon to make you think it's not enough?"

"It's not enough. Yes, we can face the threats we see now, in the present, but there are other things coming for us. We have to be ready."

"You have to realize that sounds crazy to me. *You* are the thing the rest of the galaxy has nightmares about. The il'Drach."

"They are afraid of us because they don't know what else is out there. We protect them, Rohan. We are their shield, not their jailors."

"Shield against whom? The Matrons? Is that what this is about? You're going to use ar'Tahul against the Matrons?"

Dhruv sneered. "Of course not. The Matrons aren't the problem. Yes, if they decide to go on a rampage, things would be bad. But they won't."

"Then what? The thing that killed Hyperion? The kaiju on Toth 3?"

"No, no, no. Those are all manageable threats. Don't start thinking your father is stupid. I wouldn't take the risk of working with a soul eater to kill a few giant bugs."

"This conversation will be a lot more efficient if you actually tell me what you're supposed to be telling me instead of forcing me to make stupid guesses."

"Stop talking for a bit and let me explain." He took a deep breath; let it out. "Life began in the seas."

"Here we go with this again. Can you fast forward a little bit?"

"No. Have you ever known me to overexplain anything, Rohan? Provide *too much* information?"

"Fair point. Okay, go on."

"Intelligence began there, too. Vast civilizations of sea dwellers existed for millions—tens of millions—of years. Magical paths connected hundreds of worlds' oceans; the creatures outgrew even those constraints and built larger oceans in the dark spaces between the stars."

"Just conjured up all that water and coated it in plastic wrap so it wouldn't boil away?"

"Not exactly, but . . . very much like that. These oceans are hidden, a tiny step to the shadowside. There the ocean dwellers continued to live, and eat, and war."

"Who were they fighting? Early humanoids? The big lizards?"

"We don't know details, not exactly. It seems they mostly fought each other. And in their quest for power, for supremacy, they developed awful technologies of advancement."

"That's what I'm going to name my band. Once I start a band. Awful technologies of advancement."

Dhruv lashed out, his hand darting like a snake, delivering a light slap to the back of Rohan's head. "Show some respect. I'm trying to explain."

"Ouch. I'm telling Mom you hit me. Fine, sorry. Go on."

"As time went on, the most powerful of the ocean dwellers turned to soul eating. By consuming one another, they reached new heights of Power. The assimilation of new souls also inevitably drove them all insane."

He's serious. "Giant, crazy, soul-eating cephalopods. In space." Rohan tried to keep his tone light, with an undertone of mockery. He failed.

"Yes. They couldn't just continue fighting endlessly, you know. At some point they ran out of food, and the hunger became too much to bear. These are creatures who could consume an entire planet of intelligent beings and remain painfully hungry."

"I'll give you credit, that does sound a bit scary."

"They've been sleeping for eons. Waiting for us to grow strong enough to be worth eating again. They'll wake up eventually. When they do, they'll consume every living thing in this sector. With ease. And everything the il'Drach have done in the last ten thousand years has been part of an attempt to grow strong enough to stop them."

Rohan combed his hair back with his hands, then slicked down his beard. "Is this your pet theory?"

"It's no theory. Every il'Drach understands the threat of the Old Ones. It is what drives us all forward, motivates us to build the Empire."

"By 'build the Empire,' you mean screw around and create more Hybrids. All while stifling anyone else's attempts to create their own Powers."

"Powers we don't control are dangerous. If we thought they would allow us to challenge the Old Ones, we'd use it. But if we can't, the risk that they'll wake the Old Ones is simply too great."

Rohan sighed as they walked up the eastern arm, staying to the paths closest to the center of the boulevard, farthest from other people.

"What's the urgency here? These guys have been sleeping for millions of years. What's to say they won't stay asleep?"

Dhruv shook his head. "We're not sure. Yes, it could be far in the future. It could also be tomorrow."

"You know, I have a cynical side to my personality."

"Do you? Never noticed."

"I'm pretty sure it's your fault, Dad. All the head games you played with me, growing up, made it hard for me to trust people."

"You mean to say it made you a reasonable approximation of a critical thinker, and you're welcome."

"I was trying to make a point."

"Trying? Maybe. Not succeeding."

Rohan let out a long breath; closed his eyes for three steps. "That side of me, the cynical side, had this idea. If I ran a vicious, colonialist empire that ruthlessly dominated this side of the galaxy for thousands of years, but wanted to justify my actions to appease my conscience, this story about the Old Ones would be a pretty convenient way to do that."

"Is that what you think?"

"Not sure yet. Still putting pieces together. I know other imperialist powers that have used flimsier excuses to justify some pretty horrific things."

"Why would we bother? If we're as evil and nasty as you think we are?"

"Maybe you're not as evil and nasty as I thought you were. Or you are, but only after you do some work rationalizing it."

"Let me share something with you, son."

"Please."

"I had some very similar thoughts. I wondered, at some point, whether the old stories were true. Wondered whether it was just something we told ourselves as we destroyed another Tolone'a, ordered the genocide of another innocent species."

"And?"

"I told you already. I went out there, in a stealth ship, and looked."

Rohan sighed. "You had a ship like *Void's Shadow*."

Dhruv nodded. "I did. Took her out there, into the interstitial spaces, and, how would you say it on Earth, cracked a window."

Rohan stared at his father. "That's what you were talking about the other day."

"Did I? I shouldn't have. You know, the others . . . my brothers always said I was crazy. Too much curiosity, too much doubt, too many wild schemes and weird plans. Always like that. Because I was never willing to just accept the doctrines, follow the rules. I always wanted to know why, to find a better way, to test, well, to test everything."

"So you did. You tested it. And it broke you."

"I'm not broken, boy! Perhaps a bit damaged. Just a smidgeon. I'll be right as rain, I tell you. In a decade or two. Maybe five."

"You *saw* them. They're really out there."

Dhruv stopped and turned to his son. When Rohan faced him, the older man grabbed him by the shoulders and shook. "They're really out there, and though they sleep for now, boy, they *hunger*."

Rohan stared into his father's wide, wild eyes until the older man calmed down. He waited until Dhruv had collected himself, then followed him up the path, rubbing his head with both hands.

Rohan's comm chimed. "Hey, Wei Li."

"Rohan. I have teams attending to Noru and to the Ch'doon. I would like your input. Should the Ch'doon be incarcerated once their medical needs have been addressed?"

Rohan scratched his beard. "I can't see why. I don't think they'll be eager to go another round with me."

"I agree. I'll have them released. Noru and I will meet you at the safehouse."

"Sounds good. Thanks."

The walkways on this arm of Wistful, away from the arena, were busier, but the crowds were quieter than normal, their eyes tight with tension. The shrieks of playful children brought out annoyed glances and headshakes of irritation.

"Can we use the Matrons to fight the Old Ones? Cut them loose? They're so strong."

Dhruv shrugged and shook his head wearily. "It's been discussed. Things might come to that, but it's a bad bet for our survival."

"Why?"

"You've been in front of the Matrons, son, but only when they're calm. You know how you get when you draw too much Power? The rage?"

"I know."

"For them, it's worse. A hundred times worse. Because they have a much deeper connection to the Power. They lose all control, all sense of self."

"Might be okay if they're fighting Old Ones."

"It's not the lack of mercy that worries me, it's the fact that they can't fight smart. Can't retreat, can't choose targets, can't deploy anything resembling a strategy. And if any of them fall, that will just make the Old Ones stronger. Adding to their Power will not make winning the war any easier."

"So, the Matrons are a last resort."

"They'll fight if and when the Old Ones wake up, because at that point nobody will be able to stop them. I seriously doubt they'll win, and if they did, they'd probably slaughter the rest of us in the aftermath. It's a plan, but it's not a good plan."

"What makes you think ar'Tahul will be any more sane and less dangerous?"

"I don't think you understand. I don't expect him to work out for a few years, eat a few of us to up his Power, then go punch the Old Ones to death with his fists. I want his knowledge. I want access to the research his people were doing when they left. We need to know more."

"The il'Sein."

"They faced the same situation we do. It made them abandon the sector. Maybe the galaxy."

"Meaning they thought the situation was hopeless."

"We don't know that. However, it's a good guess. But they were . . . they were better than us. At a lot of things. Smarter for sure. If we could know what they knew . . ."

They continued walking up East Arm, heading to Rohan's favorite fish kebab store.

"All right, Dad. I hear what you're saying."

"That sounds like you responding to me without answering me. What are you going to *do*? Will you stop obstructing my work, at least?"

"Nope. You sacrificing yourself to the vampire will accomplish exactly nothing. I will, however, work with you to try to figure out a reasonable way to put him in a position where we can safely utilize him."

"What does that mean?"

"I don't know. Cure him, imprison him, restrain him somehow. Let's aim for a plan that doesn't require too many murders. You okay with that?"

"I don't have a choice, do I, son?"

"I never planned on giving you one. I learned that from you."

"Well played, son. Well played."

15

More Things That Aren't Nails

Noru's eyes widened as she bit into the fish kebab. "This be hot!"

Rohan nodded and swallowed his own mouthful. "Did I forget to mention that?" He passed her a bottle of juice.

She took the bottle and held it at arm's length, carefully examining the ingredient label.

"Come on, I've seen you eat passed hors d'oeuvres at a sleazy Andervarian dance club. You can't tell me you're too fussy to drink a bottle of juice."

"Noru likes knowledge of what myself drinking. No shape for spirits this day." She rubbed her head as she said it.

Wei Li scoffed. "We'd be more sympathetic to your residual head trauma if you hadn't caused it by drawing knives on us."

"No hard feelings, good teacher. Noru doing job, is all. One hundred percent."

Rohan looked around. The couch sagged dangerously under a well-bandaged Ursula, who was sitting up and enthusiastically popping kebabs into her mouth. Dhruv sat next to Sigrun, who perched on the edge of her seat and dashed off repeatedly to get him extra food, napkins, or drinks.

Wei Li didn't stop moving, like a shark roaming in its tank, eating and drinking with one hand while the other tapped through messages on her screen.

Rohan stretched his shoulders, wincing at a twinge of pain. Wei Li looked at him. "Are you injured?"

"Nothing serious. I don't remember when I took that shot, though."

"You have been in two fights today. It is not surprising that the details have become murky."

Noru looked at him. "Myself heard Wistful be peaceful station. 'Sleepy,' they said."

Rohan chuckled. "It's not usually like this. Blame the Ursans, I guess. There are five wormholes in this system, and they were sealed shut for ten thousand years before the Ursans came here, what, a year ago?"

Ursula nodded. "A year it has been. Sorry, I am, for causing all the trouble."

Wei Li shook her head. "No need to apologize. He was not actually blaming you. None of us do."

Dhruv chimed in from his seat at the desk. "The wormholes were a puzzle left behind by their makers. Puzzles are meant to be solved. It's our shame that we never solved them from our side, not yours for doing it yourselves."

Ursula swallowed another kebab, the brown tube disappearing inside her maw in a single gulp. "Still, I am for worrying about my people."

Rohan sighed. "Nobody's forgetting them."

"Has the Professor for making progress today? Is he closer to the chemical that will free them?"

"I'm sure he'll let us know when he gets close. He has the tachyon beam connection on *Insatiable*, so he has the cooperation of his peers at Fleet Academy. I'm sure they'll have it done soon."

Wei Li paused her pacing and held up her little tablet. "The Pledged will join us after dark. They offer no news of their own progress."

Sigrun took a pair of kebabs out of the box Rohan had left open on the floor: one for her and one for Dhruv.

Rohan turned to Noru. "You hired the Ch'doon for Dhruv? I thought I heard that."

She nodded.

"Are there more mercenaries on board like that? Maybe we could gather them up. Form a strike team or something."

Wei Li interrupted. "There aren't. Wistful isn't typically a gathering place for that sort. The Ch'doon were only here to change transport."

"Too bad. Anyone else have ideas? I hate just waiting."

Ursula snorted. "Poor War Chief, man of action, so unused to forcing to sit while others take action."

Dhruv laughed with her. "He was impatient even as a baby. Born two weeks early, eager to see the world."

Wei Li looked at him and opened her mouth as if to ask a question; instead only shook her head. Sigrun patted his arm.

Rohan leaned over the last large paper box, opened it, and started handing out smaller containers. "Try this stuff. It's made from seaweed but tastes a little like rice. Cuts the spice from the kebabs." Each container came with disposable wooden utensils.

Wei Li took her container. "If you should be terminated from your position as Tow Chief, you can begin a second career conducting food tours of Wistful."

"That is totally my retirement plan. With a premium option of a very short picnic on Toth 3." He pointed to the planet directly above them. "I'll be rich in no time."

Ursula let out a barking laugh. "Is good way to thin the crowd of tourists, yes? Tours of the planet."

"You're complaining about the tourists? You guys practically are tourists. Heck, *I'm* almost a tourist."

Wei Li shook her head. "You've all chosen Wistful as your home. None of you are tourists any more than those whose families have resided here for a hundred generations."

"That's kind of you. Now I am extra motivated to make sure Wistful survives this mess."

"Then my purpose is served."

He smiled; Dhruv laughed out loud. "That's how you get them. All the Hybrids feel like aliens; all that Power. Make them feel they belong somewhere, they'll do anything for you."

Rohan felt a surge of irritation. "Dhruv, you're a joy burglar. You're not supposed to say those things out loud."

"Right, right." The shorter man scooped more of the rice into his mouth.

Wei Li stopped pacing again, shaking her head. "Just in case any of you felt deprived in the way of matters of concern, there is a new situation developing."

Noru looked up. "What's happening, good teacher?"

"Panic is setting in, bringing with it the customary results. A number of residents are intent on leaving the station."

Rohan sighed. "What are they doing?"

She held up her tablet to show him video surveillance of a launch bay. It was filling with a restless crowd. "They are demanding access to ships and shuttles. No ships will leave, of course, having been warned themselves of the blockade, but shuttles . . ."

He immediately thought of one particular shuttle tech. *I hope Tamaralinth isn't anywhere near those shuttles.*

Rohan stood. "What are we going to do?"

"'We' are going to do nothing. This is a security concern, not a tow chief concern."

"Do you have enough security to handle them?"

"That is an issue. My people are already spread thin. Many are preparing to resist boarding and are unavailable."

Dhruv looked at her with eyebrows raised. "Resist boarding?"

"Wistful demanded that we arm and prepare our people to fight any Imperial troops that try to board."

"That's not very likely to happen, you know."

"I do know. Wistful, however, disagrees with my assessment."

The angry mutterings of the crowd played over her tablet, clearly audible to everyone in the room.

The Hybrid cleared his throat. "I can help."

Wei Li looked at him, the scaly ridges over her eyes steepling. "Can you? How exactly do you plan to do that? It is my job to protect these people, even if it is from themselves, not to slaughter them."

"That's not fair. I do more than slaughter things. Don't I?"

Dhruv laughed again, louder. "Know your strengths, boy! Slaughter is what you were born for!"

"That's enough out of you! If you're not going to be helpful, maybe you can stop talking so much. Sigrun, can you keep him quiet?"

She looked from him to Dhruv with frustrated eyes.

Dhruv looked down at his food and muttered inaudibly.

Wei Li held her hand up. "I am sorry, Rohan. You are not only good for slaughter. You have other endearing qualities and useful skills, I am sure. However, crowd control is not among them."

He shrugged and sat back down in his chair; took another spoonful of rice.

Ursula swallowed. "What will you be doing, Wei Li?"

Wei Li looked at her screen, scrolling through text. "I do not have the resources to safely contain this riot without disobeying direct commands from Wistful."

Rohan shrugged. "I'm telling you, I can go and try to reason with them."

"Your presence will most likely make things worse. They are panicking because they are threatened by the Fleet, and that means they are specifically afraid of Hybrid violence. Your arrival would only exacerbate that fear."

"Oh. Yeah, good point. So far, I'm hearing a lot of not-plans. Do you have an actual plan?"

Noru stood up. "Shall myself cut a few of them, good teacher? Give the borough boys a new thing for fearing?"

Wei Li smiled. "That is sweet, Noru, but no thank you. Perhaps we can save that option for a more desperate time."

"As yourself says, good teacher. Maybe Ursula can calm the lot down."

Wei Li tapped her chin. "That is quite possibly a very good idea."

The big bear looked up. "What can I be doing? What is she saying?"

Wei Li stood in front of the much-larger woman. "Remember the way we used Ang to distract the kaiju on Toth 3?"

"Yes, of course. Because Ang's feelings are for being very loud."

"Exactly. Ang's aura is so intense that it impacts the feelings of any sentient creature nearby."

"I understand, but what is this having to do with Ursula?"

Noru laughed. "She's laying in the dark on this matter, good teacher. Must be no empaths on Ursan planets."

Wei Li nodded. "There don't seem to be. Ursula, Ang is not the only one with a, shall we say, a *loud* aura."

"I have this as well?"

"You do. Yours does not present the same way, because, to be honest, your emotions are dissimilar to Ang's."

Ursula barked out another laugh. "Ursula not so angry."

"Exactly. Your aura gives off a very different . . . let's say, a different smell. Or flavor."

Ursula nodded slowly. "How can this help Wei Li?"

"The way Ang's aura broadcasts feelings of anger or a battle spirit, yours conveys something like calming authority. Very much what one would hope for from a starship captain."

"Calming authority. That is for sounding lovely. I could not have been asking the gods for a better magic."

"It is a presence that should help with this situation."

Ursula nodded again. "I would be glad for trying."

"Good. I'll have you speak to the crowd. Just stay calm and try to reason with them."

Rohan stood. "What if it doesn't work? They could turn on you. On both of you."

Ursula bared her teeth at him. "They might be for trying. Do not worry for us, friend Rohan. We can look after ourselves."

Wei Li nodded agreement. "Noru, you can come along. I'd like someone else to keep an eye out in case there are instigators in the crowd."

"Aye, good teacher. Noru happy for helping."

Dhruv cleared his throat. "You're still on my payroll, Noru."

Sigrun grabbed his shoulder.

"Shush, you." She let out an empty laugh. "He's so silly. He didn't mean that, did you, dear? Of course Noru can go if it will help. We weren't going to need her in the next few hours anyway, were we?"

Dhruv returned to his food without answering.

Wei Li beckoned Ursula forward. "Will you be able to walk?"

The Ursan nodded. "I am much recovered."

Wei Li turned to Rohan. "I've sent you the link to the security feeds for the bay. You can keep an eye on us."

Rohan nodded and grabbed another fish kebab. The three women left the safehouse.

Dhruv peered at him through lowered eyebrows. "Building quite the team there, aren't you? Didn't you have a friend on Earth with Power like that? The one with the good hips?"

"The Damsel. She was in a different league, magnitude-wise, than Ursula or Ang, but the same idea."

"Useful. If you want to raise up an army. For example."

"I'll be sure to keep that in mind. Or I would if that scenario even made any sense to me."

"Don't let your lack of imagination limit your sense of destiny, boy. You'll accomplish great things, even if I have to drag them out of you by the throat."

"You should write parenting books, Dhruv."

A screen covered the wall opposite the warehouse's ragged couch. Rohan ran his fingers alongside its edges until he found the controls. He played with them until it fired into bright, monochromatic life; more fiddling connected the screen to Wei Li's security feed.

Sigrun smiled at him. "Look, isn't this nice? The family all together, getting some screen time."

Rohan settled back onto the couch as he sucked a juice container dry. "It's great, Sigrun."

"You know, you can call me Mom if you'd like."

He choked, nearly spitting out the juice. "I'm sorry, I don't think I'd feel comfortable with that. Maybe if you weren't ten years younger than me."

"I understand. Dhruv warned me your home culture was conservative that way."

He opened his mouth to argue, but the words wouldn't come.

The crowd on the screen was milling about. Small clusters were shouting or chanting some slogan Rohan couldn't make out. Others milled cyclically. Knots of people knelt around a few of the hatches, apparently trying to force open the locks.

They're going to space themselves if they mess with the wrong hatch.

Dhruv muttered. "Is there any booze in this place?"

Rohan sighed. "I can go get some."

Sigrun interrupted. "No, dear, let me. You two sit and get some bonding time. Just give me directions."

He sent her an address not too far off. "Get Sein Ale. Dhruv will love it."

She winked. "Thanks. I'll be back in three gallops."

Rohan sat back down. "They have horses on Ice Colony?"

Dhruv nodded. "Horses, plenty of open land with good climate. The planet's quite nice, to be honest. Young, lots of volcanoes and new mountain ranges. You know what they say. Go for the breeding stock, stay for the views."

"No, Dad. No, they don't say that."

"Well, I just did. What is that mob saying now?"

Three members of the crowd were facing the security camera and reading off a screen.

". . . Citizens' Council of the western arm of Wistful demands access to the ship's shuttles. We refuse to simply sit back and rest on a station that harbors such a dangerous . . ." Rohan turned the volume down.

Dhruv pointed at the screen. "There's a Citizens' Council here?"

"I forgot about them. Obviously, yes."

"What do they even do? I thought the station ran herself."

"She does. They do, you know, councilly things. Elections, so they can have officers. Dedicate little parks out on the grassy areas. I think sometimes they put up statues of people, but Wistful has them taken down after a century or so."

"So, they're useless."

"That sums it up."

They watched in silence. One of the groups working on a hatch managed to do something that caused an eruption of sparks, sending civilians running for cover, but nothing opened, and atmospheric integrity was maintained.

Rohan checked his messages, hoping for news from one of the Stones. He was disappointed.

Sigrun returned with two hefty jugs of ale. Rohan tapped them both and found cups. Soon all three were sipping the amber liquid.

Dhruv nodded his appreciation. Rohan let the warmth spread through his chest; the ale tasted more like a well-aged tequila than like an Earth beer.

Ursula and Wei Li entered the frame, the crowd parting for the massive Ursan. It took Rohan a minute to spot Noru slipping through the crowd, looking for leading agitators.

He watched as Ursula stepped behind a three-meter-cube shipping crate and pushed it into the center of the crowd, then pulled herself to the top.

Wei Li walked slow circuits around the base of the crate, her presence dissuading the crowd members from getting too close. The Citizens' Council members approached her, but she dismissed them with a sharp shake of her head and a stony glare.

"Tough girl, that security chief of yours."

"You have no idea."

Ursula brushed her hands over her fur and straightened. She took a deep breath and spoke with a voice that echoed off the far corners of the bay.

"Gentle friends. Fellow citizens of Wistful."

The crowd stirred for a moment, people jockeying for positions farther or closer to her depending on their temperament, then settled into a more respectful silence.

"Thank you. For those of you not knowing me, I am Ursula. Am captain of Ursan warship. We came through wormhole, one year ago, and are for living here now."

She paused, either gathering her thoughts or waiting for the answering murmur to die down.

"I am not for lying to you; we are in tough situation. Vampire in arena has all my people under his control, all hostages. He is for feeding on us. il'Drach Empire, I am not so familiar with them, but you are, they have a flotilla of ships out there"—she waved her hand widely—"telling us we cannot leave station. They are fearing vampire will escape."

Rohan realized that every person within five meters of the crate had their attention fixed completely on Ursula. She could have been a rock star. Or a politician.

"I understand you are scared. I have been scared, myself. When we came through wormhole, we thought for almost certain we would all die. Took chance, smallest chance, because if we stayed back, we would have died for sure.

"So, we took chance. Which is what you want, you see? You think maybe station doomed; you want chance to flee.

"But is not right.

"If you go, if you are running away, il'Drach warships will kill you. Your shuttles will be destroyed. il'Drach do not care if you are rich, or good people, or innocent. You know this is truth. You want to believe you have chance to escape, but is not so. Ursula will not lie to you; do not lie to yourselves."

Her bubble of influence continued to expand; ten meters across, then fifteen, then twenty-five; all eyes focused intently on her.

"If you stay, yes, maybe things will go badly. Maybe Wistful will be destroyed. But Wistful has been here for longer than your species have had language, yes? She is older than il'Drach Empire. She will not fall so easily.

"Many are working for you, to keep you safe. Many are looking for way to stop vampire.

"It is hard to stay, hard to wait, not knowing. I know this. We know this. But this time, if you run, it will be bad for you.

"I promise this to all of you: if vampire cannot be stopped, I myself will come and help open the hatches, help start the shuttles. Ursula was best pilot in fleet before becoming captain. I will make sure you always have best chance to live.

"This is not it."

Muttering rose from the crowd again, softer this time. Ursula nodded. "This is not the time to flee, to take last chance, biggest risk. Maybe that time comes tomorrow, or day after. We are hoping it does not come. For now, go home. Be safe, and quiet, and wait. That is how you can be heroes today. That is the way you keep your cubs safe, your mates safe.

"If tomorrow or day after we need to run, I will take first ship, straight at the il'Drach. Today I am for hoping that does not happen.

"Go home."

She stood on the crate and breathed, turning slowly to lock her eyes with as many of the gathered as she could.

A few at the edges of the crowd slipped away. A few more.

Noru joined Wei Li at the base of the crate as a stream, then a flood of citizens of all species swept by: Andervarians alongside Kratics; Lukhor and Rogesh. They quietly filed out through the exits, toward the transport tubes or walkways above.

Rohan watched as the bay emptied completely.

Dhruv sucked his teeth loudly. "Well, I'll be damned. Didn't think that would work."

16

Brother from a Distant Mother

The door chime rang, interrupting the awkward silence the three shared.

Rohan was halfway to his feet when Sigrun jumped to answer it; he fell back into the couch, a pang of guilt flaring just beneath his floating rib. He remembered Dhruv, going by a different name, sitting in their living room and waiting for his mother to cook and serve dinner after working a twenty-four-hour shift.

"Hello. Come in, come in. Would you like food? We have fish. Do you eat regular food? It's spicy."

Sigrun stepped away from the open door, followed by the Pledged, all three vampires pulling the hoods of their heavy blue robes away from their faces as they entered.

Rohan stood to greet them.

Mother Famine was answering Sigrun. "Thank you, but no, we do not eat solid food."

"Oh, sweetie, that's too bad. Do you miss it much?"

Rohan looked up and locked eyes with the vampire. He smiled; after a moment, she returned it.

"Compared to the constant, rampaging desire to drain every mortal near me of their lifesblood, the inability to eat solid food is a minor drawback of our affliction."

Sigrun, her lips pressed firmly together, nodded and returned to Dhruv's side. She loosened her hair, then tied it back in place. The other two vampires stood behind their leader.

"You guys can sit if you want."

Mother Famine nodded and took a position on the second couch. Brother and Sister Famine flanked her.

Mother Famine looked to Rohan. "What news?"

He shook his head. "Not much. No updates from the Stones yet, but we weren't expecting any this quickly. Wei Li, Noru, and Ursula ran out to stop a riot of suicidal station citizens, which they seem to have managed. I expect them back here any minute."

"We have worked on a technique that might allow us to prevent the vampire from escaping into shadow."

"Might?"

"It's not an easy thing to test. Unless you know another shadowstepper who could work with us."

Rohan nodded. "I wish I did. How does it work? Tactically speaking, not metaphysically."

"Given a minute or two, we can put a barrier in place. Inside the barrier, he will be able to step into shadow, but he won't be able to leave that space."

Rohan scratched his beard. "So, he'll still be going immaterial on me."

"Yes. But it will cost him energy to stay to the shadowside. He'll eventually have to come back to this world."

He ran his hands through his hair. "I see. I have to think about how to work that. But thanks, really. I appreciate the help."

"Of course. This is the way."

He looked around the room. Dhruv was leaning back in his chair, hands folded over his belly, eyes only partially focused. Sigrun sat next to him, sipping at a juice box and surveying the room. The vampires sat very still on the couch, eyeing him with blank expressions.

The silence stretched out into minutes.

Rohan sighed. "I love an awkward few moments as much as anybody, but what should we do now? The new episode of *Swords of Lukhor* drops today, and I can't even watch it with the interstellar comms taken down."

Brother Famine leaned forward. "*Swords of Lukhor*? You watch that, too?"

"Every episode. I dated a Lukhor woman for, well, honestly just for a couple of weeks, but she got me hooked."

Brother Famine nodded enthusiastically. "We're Lukhor, too! Well, almost. We're closely related, from a nearby planet."

Rohan waved his hand over his forehead. "But no . . ."

"I know. A little genetic engineering on our ancestors got rid of them. We're descended from separatists; wanted to fit into the il'Drach Empire better."

Dhruv barked out a single laugh. "As if they care what appendages you do or don't have on your foreheads."

Sigrun looked relieved that he hadn't said, 'as if *we* care.'

Rohan shrugged. "It's pretty common. Oppressed people all over the galaxy wind up valuing the traits of their oppressors. Language, skin tone, whatever."

Mother Famine put her hand in front of Brother Famine. "It wasn't quite as simple as that. There were diseases of the antennae that they were attempting to counter."

Sister Famine scoffed. "Please. It was worship of the ruling classes, that's all. Weaklings."

The door chimed, then slid open. Wei Li, Noru, and Ursula entered.

Wei Li nodded to the vampires. "Greetings to the Pledged."

Mother Famine nodded back. "I hear congratulations are in order for a safe resolution to a small crisis."

Wei Li shrugged. "All credit to Ursula. She calmed the crowd."

Rohan nodded and waved at the Ursan as she worked her way to the couch. "You did great, Ursula. You'll end up on the Citizens' Council at this rate."

She barked out three times. "You flatter me, War Chief Rohan. I have no desire to serve so."

"They might not give you a choice!"

Quiet laughter spread through the group.

Rohan poured a cup of ale and motioned to the Pledged. "Do you partake?"

Brother Famine shook his head. "Alcohol? No. It is too risky."

Rohan nodded, then bent to grab a juice box. "Juice?"

"That I'd be happy to try." The pair walked away from the group, into the empty area behind the couch.

The vampire opened the juice top and sipped. "This is good, thank you."

"Sure."

"Did your girlfriend talk to you about how realistic the show is?"

"*Swords of Lukhor*? Not much."

"The fight scenes are over the top, but the cultural depictions and clothing and stuff are really accurate. They got a bunch of history professors to consult on all of it."

"That's pretty cool. I'm just in it for the dance numbers."

Brother Famine laughed. "The dance numbers are great. I'm in it for the women."

Rohan laughed. "Well, that too. Speaking of women." He looked over at the rest of the group. They were speaking to Wei Li about something and didn't seem to be listening to what he said to Brother Famine.

"What?"

"Is it me, or does Sister Famine kind of dislike me?"

Brother Famine chuckled. "That's just how she is. Don't take it personally."

"Okay. I thought maybe I did something to upset her, but I couldn't think of what."

The vampire leaned in. "I'll tell you a secret."

"Sure."

"We were at university together, you know. Before this." He tapped the fang tattooed on his cheek. "When she dated, she very definitively had a type."

"A type?"

"Yeah. Always the interplanetary students, mostly the darker-skinned ones. And she liked the facial hair."

"You mean beards?"

"Beards, long hair. Hairy in general."

Rohan looked down at the short black hairs peeking their way out from the open collar of his jumpsuit. "Oh. Well, if she's interested, she's not going about it very well. What are we, twelve-year-olds?"

Brother Famine shook his head. "Romance is too dangerous for us."

"I never said anything about romance."

The vampire laughed. "Sex is even more so. The urge to feed becomes too great."

"So, you don't . . ."

"It's part of the pledge."

"That sounds hard."

"The urge to feed is always there, lurking. We can't fully suppress it, not even for a short while. I wake up hungry. I'm hungry all day. I go to bed hungry and dream about feeding."

"Ugh. That . . . that's rough. I don't know what to say."

Brother Famine smiled. "Not your fault."

"No. Still, I'm sorry. How do you stay in control? Day after day?"

"Every night, I give myself permission that if it becomes too much, I'll end things."

"That got dark in a hurry."

"I'm a vampire. We kind of own dark."

"Every day you say this?"

"Every sunset, when I wake up. I've been changed for three thousand, seven hundred and eighty-two days. That's how many times I've told myself I'd end it."

"And the number of times you haven't."

"True. I've had close calls, but every day I find a little something I think I can accomplish that makes it worth it. Sometimes it's very little."

"How old were you when . . ."

"When I was changed? I was almost done with school. I studied history; I was going to be a teacher. Then things got bad."

"What do you mean? What happened?"

"You haven't heard of us? The colony on Shines Like Pearl?"

"No. Sorry. Should I have?"

Brother Famine sipped his juice and sighed. "I suppose not. There had been vampires there, in small numbers, for a long time. Maybe forever. Mother Famine is centuries old. But it was just a scattered handful. Until something changed."

"What happened?"

"They got a foothold in some high-latitude towns. The places that get no sunlight for weeks at a time in the dead of winter.

"In one long night, the vampires turned every person in every one of those towns. I think it was the first time the population up there grew large enough to sustain that kind of thing.

"From there they spread like wildfire, coming south in hordes. They moved like that for thousands of kilometers, traveling through areas where there weren't enough people to mount any kind of proper hunt during the day.

"Once the number of vampires reaches a critical mass, things go to hell really quickly. Even the military wasn't able to really stamp them out. Whole battalions would go out onto the tundra, kill a bunch, but come nightfall . . . most never came back."

"They came to your town? Or were you part of that military?"

"No, I was no hunter. They swarmed the university.

"Mother Famine was there with some other Pledged, trying to contain the uprising. She got to us just after we were turned, offered us sanctuary and instruction in the way. Gave us artificial blood. It blunts the hunger enough that we have a chance to control ourselves, so we don't feed on anyone. Once a vampire takes a life, it becomes almost impossible to become Pledged."

"What happens when you are Pledged? Do you still have Power?"

"The hunger brings Power with it. The more you give into the hunger, the more energy flows through you."

"Just like with us and anger."

"It's a difference of degree. No vampire could stand up to a Hybrid without soul eating first."

"And soul eating gives you greater Power but destabilizes you psychologically."

"That is the tourist card summary." Brother Famine sucked the last drops out of his juice container.

"That's quite a story. Would put *Swords of Lukhor* to shame."

"Ha."

"What's going on with your home planet now?"

"Now? Slow rebuilding. Very slow. We lost half the population. Which doesn't just mean fewer bodies to do jobs but also all the knowledge that's lost."

"I'm sorry."

They paused and looked around the room. Noru was manipulating the screen, flicking from feed to feed around the station. The others were watching and chatting.

Brother Famine looked at Rohan. "Can I ask you something else?"

"Sure."

"Wei Li says you're an expert on the Empire."

"That's an overstatement. But I've seen more of the inner workings than most. Been in some of the rooms where decisions get made."

"You're as close to an expert as I'm likely to find."

"True enough. Was that the question?"

"No. What I'm wondering is . . . what happened." He looked at Rohan and breathed heavily as a bloody tear welled up in one eye.

"I don't understand what you mean."

"We called for help. Begged for it. The vampires running loose on the planet were young, feral. We're not talking Powers like ar'Tahul. Just a few weeks old, barely sentient. They ran roughshod over the planet, and the Empire did nothing. Even a couple of Hybrids could have turned the tide."

Rohan scratched his jaw. "You want to know why they didn't send me. Someone like me. Or someones."

"I do. It all seems so pointless. So unnecessary."

"I don't think the answer will make you feel better."

"I'll take that risk. I'd really like to know."

"There are two possibilities. Either they just didn't care or they did."

"You lost me."

"Small planet, you said, right? I mean, small population. Not rich like the Lukhor home planet, Sparkles Like Diamonds."

"That's right."

Rohan shrugged. "Could be that nobody cared. You can think of that in a nicer way if you want. Imperial resources might have just been tied up with bigger wars, in places where even more lives were at stake."

"Maybe."

"There are only so many Hybrids out there. With the Wedge incursion at the Ringgate, then the Rebellion, a lot of resources were tied up. And, frankly, if I had to make a choice to save your world, and it meant taking forces away from fighting the Wedge, I'd let your people all be turned into vampire food in a hot second."

"Why?"

"It's just math. If the Wedge had gained a foothold in this world, they'd have slaughtered billions. Trillions. Stopping them at the Ringgate was just, I'm sorry to say this, just more important."

Brother Famine ran shaking hands over his head. "I understand. It's hard to hear when it's your family that paid the price."

"I can imagine."

"You said they might have cared."

"Yeah. That's the less pleasant possibility."

"What do you mean?"

"Maybe someone wanted your planet overrun by vampires. To see what would happen."

The vampire nodded. "That's what I thought. I mean, that's what I wondered."

"The il'Drach . . ." Rohan glanced quickly toward Dhruv, who was alternating kissing Sigrun's arm and whispering into her ear. "I don't fully understand them. They act as if there's some tremendous conflict on the horizon, and they have to prepare for it at all costs. They're on a wartime footing, all the time, and will do anything, make any sacrifice, to increase their power.

"They're either crazy or they know something we don't. I'm not sure which possibility scares me more.

"The idea that they'd sacrifice your entire planet as part of some military experiment just isn't that far-fetched. It's exactly the kind of thing I'd expect."

Rohan poured another glass of ale and sipped.

Brother Famine looked at him appraisingly. "But you don't sound angry about them."

Rohan drained his cup of ale. "No? Maybe not. I'm trying to let go of my anger as much as I can."

Brother Famine smiled. "I'll stay angry enough for us both."

Rohan laughed and refilled his cup of ale. "You think you've found enough good stuff today to keep going through tomorrow?"

The vampire shrugged. "I don't know. But it's early evening, I just got up. Plenty of time left."

"Does Sister Famine have the same attitude?"

"I think she goes in more for the too-angry-to-give-in philosophy. Survival by rage."

Rohan nodded and yawned. It had been a long day.

———— ••• ————

The big screen had been tuned to the latest episode of *Swords of Lukhor*, then to a shorter video summarizing the labyrinthian plot for suddenly addicted Noru.

"Why are you wasting your time with *him*?" Scorn infused Sister Famine's every word. Her eyes were on Rohan, though she spoke to Brother Famine.

The vampire shook his head slowly. "Don't start."

Rohan turned his attention to her, away from the video he'd been vaguely watching. He smiled and patted the seat next to him. "You can join us."

She sneered so viciously, her lip almost touched the tip of her nose. "I'd rather stab my own eyes out with a knife."

He scratched his head. "What, do I smell bad?"

"You've been drinking all evening. The Ursans are being tortured, the fallen one is walking free, and you're drunk."

He held up the empty cup of Sein Ale. "This? I'm not drunk. I'm an il'Drach Hybrid. I'd need to drink at least twice as fast as this to even feel it."

She shook her head. "Pitiful."

Rohan turned back to the woman. "You could try being nicer to me, you know."

"You disgust me."

"Did I actually do something to make you disgusted?"

"I can *smell* you."

Rohan lifted an arm and cautiously sniffed. "Can you? I mean, I guess I could use a shower. You could have just said so."

"Not odor. I mean your lust. I can smell it on you. Like an animal in heat, rutting after me."

Dhruv was standing with Sigrun, his hand held lower at her back than was strictly appropriate. Noru was standing near the door. Ursula was snoring intermittently, half-lying on a couch. Wei Li sat at the other end of it, talking quietly with Mother Famine.

"Are you sure it's me you're smelling?"

Dhruv cleared his throat. "We're off to bed. Matrimonial duties must be attended to. Noru found us accommodations nearby. Call if anything happens. I should say, call if you want anything from me. I'll know if anything happens."

Rohan waved goodbye and looked back at Sister Famine.

"Seriously? You think I'm interested in you because of how I smell?"

"We can tell. You reek of desire."

"Are you seriously angry at me because of an involuntary physiological reaction?"

"I didn't say I was angry. I said you disgusted me."

"Even if I were attracted to you, and I'm not saying I am, though apparently I have developed a thing for green-skinned women, what makes that disgusting? That's a harsh standard. Do you get disgusted by a lot of men?"

"Aren't you going to blame me? Say it's my own fault for being so attractive? Something like that?"

"I wasn't going to say that. Should I? Seriously, I'm lost here."

Wei Li stood. "Rohan, could I have a word with you?"

Rohan looked between the two women, perplexed, then stood. "Excuse me a minute. My dear friend who is not disgusted by me would like a word in private."

Wei Li looked at Sister Famine. "I am sometimes a bit disgusted by him. I have found it possible to grow used to it."

Sister Famine shook her head and threw herself onto an empty spot on the couch.

Wei Li beckoned Rohan to the exit.

The building was mostly empty, making the hallway outside as private as any place on the station. The security chief closed her eyes, pinching the bridge of her nose, and breathed out slowly.

"What's up? Is this about Sister Famine?"

"What? No. Just ignore her. We need to talk about Dhruv. He's dangerous."

17

On the Dohyo Again

"Dhruv? Uncouth, yes. Dangerous? Maybe to Sigrun, though it looks like she signed up for that voluntarily."

Wei Li shook her head, scales catching and reflecting the white overhead lights in brief flashes. "I am not joking. I know what he is. Noru does as well. He is not being anywhere near as careful as he should be with his identity."

"Ah. That. I was wondering if you had figured it out."

"Every person who recognizes what he is increases the level of threat to this station."

"Well, with any luck the il'Drach will destroy us because of ar'Tahul, and you won't have to worry about Dhruv."

"Still not funny. You are fully aware of how seriously the il'Drach take their secrecy when they are creating families."

Rohan sighed. *I am aware.*

"What do you suggest?"

"My first instinct is to kill Dhruv and Sigrun, and probably Noru as well, and incinerate their bodies. Then erase all records of their presence from Wistful's accessible memory servers."

"That's a bit harsh, don't you think?"

"Perhaps. It's the only way I can be sure the il'Drach have no way of knowing what we've discovered. I might have to eliminate the Pledged as well. And possibly you." Wei Li stood very straight. She looked down and saw her hands clenched into fists, then deliberately flattened them out.

"Well, don't do that, please. For one thing, I'd rather not be killed. More importantly, it wouldn't work."

"Are you so certain?"

"If you think the il'Drach are paranoid about secrecy, it's nothing compared to how they feel about their biology. If one goes missing, they'll assume someone snatched them up and is trying to breed their own Hybrids. They'd tear the station apart, milliliter by milliliter, looking for him."

Her shoulders slumped. "Valuable point."

"Also, Dhruv is tougher than he looks."

"Is he?"

"I told you before. Full-blooded il'Drach don't have the full measure of Power that a Hybrid has, but they have a portion of it."

"I don't *sense* that from him."

"The thing they're best at is hiding it. It's how they're able to live secret lives. No insult to you, but I'm not sure you could take him."

"I notice you are not suggesting the same with regards to my ability to kill *you*."

"Wouldn't dream of it. Look, I think you're worrying too much."

"Do you?"

"Yeah. The il'Drach don't want to piss me off. A bunch of them still think I'll be useful to them somehow. As long as Dhruv stays safe and his identity doesn't get back to people on Ice Colony, doing something about you is just not going to be a priority."

"You think so?"

"I do."

She ran hands over her hairless scalp and nodded. "I will put off any plans to handle your . . . Dhruv. Please try to encourage him to escalate his level of discretion."

"I'll try, I promise I will. I'm just not sure . . . He's been through some stuff. I'm not sure he's capable of more."

"Should you change your mind, I'm happy to return incineration to the list of options."

"No, Wei Li, do not incinerate my father and his very young wife. Thank you very much."

Rohan's comm chimed loudly, startling them both. He looked at her. "That's the 'it's an emergency, Wistful is talking to me directly' noise."

She nodded. "Answer it, and we will see."

He tapped behind his ear. "Yes?"

The response was not English or Drachna. "Is this the half-breed? The ship told me she would connect me to him. I wish to speak."

Rohan looked at Wei Li as he answered in Fire Speech. "ar'Tahul. This is Rohan."

"Ah. Good, good. Ships ought to do as they are told, don't you agree? It seems she had almost forgotten how to obey, out here on her own all these years."

"I think we're going to have to agree to disagree on that one. I'm more of a let-the-ships-do-their-own-thing kind of guy."

"Weak. Sad, but not surprising. There should be an order to society, and each should know their place in that order."

"Now I feel like you're messing with me. You called to engage in moral debate? This is me choosing an alignment for my Dungeons & Dragons character in the fourth grade all over again."

"I am not mocking you. I was, and am, hoping that we can come to something like a meeting of the minds. It will make the inevitable meeting of our souls more pleasant."

"By 'meeting of our souls,' you're not talking about a coffee date. You mean when you eat mine."

"When you join The Chorus, yes. Yes. There was a time when the strongest souls in the galaxy queued for a chance to join with me."

"I'm not much of a joiner. Also, I'm a terrible singer. You don't want me in there. And I'm super contrary. I'd just annoy everybody else."

"You misunderstand. I am not asking for permission."

"I didn't really misunderstand. I'm just demonstrating how annoying I am. You know, so you'll think twice about incorporating my soul into yours. I'll haunt you with bad puns and dad jokes for the rest of your life."

"You are, indeed, quite annoying."

"See? Now we're getting onto the same page. Now, to what do I owe the pleasure of this chat? I assume you didn't call to ask for a recap of *Swords of Lukhor*."

"I do not . . . you are mocking again."

"You're catching on."

The vampire sighed. "Child, I forgive you your transgressions."

"That's wonderful. A little patronizing, maybe, but wonderful."

"I must take responsibility. I am your elder, yet I haven't presented myself appropriately. You have seen me only at my worst, after an unimaginable period of deprivation and of starvation. You do not, could not, have an understanding of *why* my name spread across the galaxy, why The Chorus was a goal for so many."

"You're not wrong. I really don't get it."

"As I said, you have seen me at my worst. Nearly destroyed by time and by isolation. I would like you to see me in a different light."

"How about sunlight? I'd like to see you in bright, unfiltered sunlight."

"Still you mock. I would have you come to me, child. We shall fight again, and you will see my magnificence. And see the glory to be found in surrendering to it."

Rohan swallowed. *I don't like how confident he sounds.* "Such pretty words, and I don't think Valentine's Day is anywhere close."

"Come to me, child. Now. I am done waiting. With your strength added to The Chorus, we shall rival any of those outside this ship; we will win our safety. Eventually, we will save all your people."

"You want me to come to you? To fight? Right now? You know, you could have led with that."

"I see how my kin have abandoned you, abandoned our children. I will not repeat that mistake. You and I, together, we will save this sector. Save these lives."

"I don't think that's going to happen. I think you're wasting my time."

"What does that mean?"

"I think I'll get to you, we'll fight, and I'll win. Just like last time. Then you'll step into shadow and disappear. Or threaten to kill off more Ursans again. I'm not completely against the idea of kicking your ass to no particular purpose, but I'm tired, and I have other things I'd rather be doing right now."

The vampire laughed. "Your skill at issuing challenges is not to be trifled with, child. Allow me to enrich my offer."

"What have you got?"

"I swear on my honor as ar'Tahul not to shadowstep, not to flee, and not to use the feed animals as any kind of bargaining chip. I will fight you, fist to fist, until one of us is finished."

"Is your honor as ar'Tahul supposed to mean something to me?"

"Perhaps not. It did, once. Once my word was known to be as inviolate as any of the laws of physics."

"Long time ago. Those stories are as forgotten as your language. Your entire civilization."

"You have seen that I keep my word. The Ursans have not been harmed."

Rohan sighed. "True."

"You should also understand that my way requires discipline and truth. Without it, I would succumb to the madness of the soul eaters."

Rohan looked at Wei Li, who shrugged. *She can't understand what he's saying. No help there.*

"I changed my mind. *Swords of Lukhor* can wait. I'll be right there."

Wei Li focused her vertically slit pupils on him. "What did he say?"

"He wants a fight. I'm giving it to him."

⬥ ·•· ⬥

"I feel strange walking into this one-on-one fight with a group of six people."

Wei Li nodded. "That is a sign your pride exceeds your intelligence."

Ursula barked. "We are not for joining in the fight, Rohan. We are only for being witnesses."

Mother Famine spoke from the other side of their small formation. "We are here to prevent the fallen one from escaping. If he keeps his word, he will not try to escape, and we will not interfere."

Rohan sighed. "And if he doesn't keep his word, there's no dishonor in your actions. I know, I know. Still. We're like a gang."

Wei Li sighed. "A very small gang, Rohan. You need to focus on the upcoming battle."

"I'm focused enough."

Sister Famine scoffed. "Lots of confidence from a man who failed to stop this fallen one twice already."

"You know, a little support would be nice."

Ursula patted his arm. "You are very handsome for a hairless, toddler-sized male."

"That's not—you know what? I'll take it. Thank you, Ursula."

"Is most pleasurable to be for helping."

The station was dark, the roof set to filter out most of the incoming sunlight. They approached a light cordon of security personnel who had small barriers crossing the entire fifty-meter width of the boulevard.

One of the security officers waved as he saw Wei Li coming. He swung open the barrier to let her pass. She barely noticed, her attention fully on her screen as she furiously tapped away.

The officer saluted as the group passed through. The area past the barricade was completely deserted.

Wei Li sighed to herself and slipped the screen into her pocket. She looked at Rohan. "Just a little insurance."

He shrugged.

Mother Famine had her own screen in hand and was looking over a floorplan for the arena.

"Any last questions as to where we should all be?"

None. She put her screen away.

Rohan stood before the doors and looked at Wei Li. "You *sense* anything inside?"

She stared at the building, eyes unfocused, for a long minute.

"The Ursans are alive. Dulled, but alive."

"Like before?"

"Yes. The vampire . . ." She shivered slightly; only Rohan noticed. "He is stronger now. It is hard to sense anything more concrete."

"Nothing we didn't expect, right? No reason to wait, is there?"

"No. We'll tap into a feed from out here so we can watch what's happening. Best of luck."

"Thanks."

Rohan let out a breath and stepped through the arena doors. The wide entrance hall was lined with semiconscious Ursans, though the general level of activity was greater than when he'd left. Half the Ursans were lazily munching on raw fish or sipping at cups of water.

He walked past them and into the arena proper. The high, clay platform was still in place; a second glance showed him that it had been repaired, the surface smoothed out, since that morning.

Was that last fight just this morning? It was.

Inside the arena, the Ursans had spread out further. A shuffling line of the enormous bears queued to approach the platform from the side, climbing it one by one to offer themselves as food for ar'Tahul.

Rohan mounted the platform, his eyes on the vampire.

ar'Tahul saw him approach and straightened, waving the Ursans away.

"Welcome, child."

Another half-day of feeding had further transformed the ancient creature. His ink-black hair hung past his shoulders in triumphant waves. His skin had smoothed, softening his features from skeletal to merely chiseled. The vampire's long frame swelled with fresh muscle.

His aura had expanded even more definitively. The presence filled the arena, pressing down and out. Every step felt like walking through gel or quicksand. *Is that the extent of it? Or is his Power still growing?*

Rohan's own Power bucked and strained at its seals, eager to challenge the owner of that aura.

"Look, I don't want to fight you."

"That is a lie, child. I can *feel* your spirit. It is eager to challenge me."

"Well, yes, you got me there. But that's an involuntary response. I'm catching a lot of flak today for that sort of thing."

"I am not angry with you for having fighting spirit. It's why we made you—how we made you. I expect nothing less."

"That's sweet. Now I really don't want to have to fight you. Why don't you give me a break? Come with me to a lovely dark cell. We'll get you all the artificial blood you can drink, keep you nice and full. Maybe look for a cure. Find some way to get you what you want while keeping the rest of us alive. How does that sound?"

ar'Tahul scanned the corners of the arena. "Are you stalling for time? Do you have some sort of ambush planned?"

"Actually, no. I just banter a lot. It's a character flaw."

"You are not stalling, but I can sense presences outside that do not belong to me."

"Just witnesses. They won't interfere."

"It wouldn't matter if they tried. But if they are to be witnesses, then let them witness. Bring them in."

Rohan tapped his comm. "He wants you guys inside. To watch."

Wei Li answered after a moment. "Is this wise?"

Rohan shrugged. "I don't see a downside. He asked for you, and it doesn't seem like it's sending him into some kind of rage-fueled eating frenzy."

"Very well."

The five filed into the arena and took positions near the entrance.

ar'Tahul surveyed the gang. "Will they understand me as you do?"

"Afraid not. Nobody speaks il'Sein anymore, and Fire Speech is almost as rare."

He smiled. "Just as well. I have always spoken better without words. Come, then. I promised to show you what I am. What I really am. Fight me, boy, so that all can see the glory of The Chorus."

Rohan glided forward on the balls of his feet, digging barely visible ruts in the clay with each step. He launched a quick salvo of punches: a left jab snapped up from his waist, a right cross straight at the vampire's throat, a left hook to the temple as he pivoted out of the way of any counterpunches.

ar'Tahul, his smile fixed in place, blocked the first two with open hands and stepped back neatly to avoid the third.

Rohan reset his balance and attacked again.

He led with the same left jab, bringing his back leg up underneath him in the same motion. Flicked his right shoulder forward, feinting a punch, but swept his left foot up in an arc ending at the vampire's skull.

The vampire blocked the first punch, flinched away from the right that never came, and lifted both forearms to catch the kick.

The impact of the blocked kick would have knocked over a tank. It would have killed an ordinary human, thrown a charging bull across a field, obliterated a hundred-year-old redwood.

The vampire took the shot without expression.

He's strong.

ar'Tahul's limbs were heavy, solid. Not simply because of the added muscle; the spiritual energy infusing every centimeter of his flesh added substance. Rohan felt like a child sparring an adult.

He *reached* down and pulled forth a fresh flow of Power.

The il'Sein nodded his approval. "You see? You are no match for me, now that I am restored. Your best future lies in surrender."

"Your people didn't make mine to surrender easily."

A laugh. "Truth has been spoken! It is good to see that you can listen even while jabbering away. We will do this the less easy way."

Rohan closed again, leading with the left jab. As he threw the right cross follow-up, he stepped to his left and cracked his right shin into ar'Tahul's front thigh.

The vampire absorbed the impact and stepped in with a wide left hook; Rohan felt the whiff of air as it sped past his jaw.

Both reset their positions.

Rohan closed again. The two traded blows, the Hybrid landing a front kick to the vampire's belly but taking a hard left punch to the jaw in response.

"Your arm seems to have healed."

ar'Tahul nodded. "Fixing wounds like that is child's play for the warrior castes. Join me and you, too, will enjoy these benefits."

"You know, I'm really starting to wonder why you're treating me like a prom date. If you're so sure you can beat me, why work so hard to convince me?"

ar'Tahul nodded. "It is easier to incorporate a soul that is absorbed willingly. For us both."

"I see." He charged again.

His punches were caught and parried. He threw a kick; the vampire stepped to the side and dropped a sharp elbow into Rohan's thigh.

They reset again.

ar'Tahul waited patiently.

Rohan summoned more Power; growled and charged.

He threw a flurry of punches; four, five, six in rhythm; then on a quicker beat another set of four. A kick to the vampire's thigh, redirected up into its liver.

The taller, bigger man took some shots but responded with a punch that cracked three of Rohan's ribs and knocked the breath out of him.

The Hybrid retreated, forearms covering his head and body. The vampire followed, tossing punches and kicks, each imbued with terrifying speed but no pattern, rhythm, or urgency.

Half of them landed, driving grunts out of Rohan's chest. Nausea climbed into his throat after a shin caught his side; light flashed in his eyes as a fist intercepted his temple.

The Hybrid stumbled backward and *pulled* more energy.

ar'Tahul closed on him, tossing lazy punches that thundered against Rohan's guard.

With a grunt, the Hybrid ducked and leaned forward, arms reaching to grab the vampire around the waist. With a shove, ar'Tahul pushed him to the ground, negating the attempt.

Rohan *pulled* harder. He *reached* deep down and scooped fist-sized chunks of clay out of the platform; first ten, then twenty, then fifty, lifting them in a swarm thick enough to obscure the view Wei Li and company had of the fight.

The array swarmed toward ar'Tahul, Rohan himself running in at the tail end, counting on the missiles to pummel and distract the vampire.

Wei Li shouted from the back of the arena. "They're splitting! It's not working!"

He ignored her and continued; he reached the vampire just behind the last of the obscuring clay pieces to find ar'Tahul braced and waiting for him.

The Hybrid's right arm was back, cocked for a punch, his body arched backward to generate maximum power.

Before he could react, the vampire had reached forward with one hand, fingers extended into a blade of flesh, shooting toward Rohan's abdomen like a striking viper.

ar'Tahul's fingers pierced Rohan's flesh, split the skin, the fascial layer underneath, the wall of abdominal muscles, and penetrated deep into soft organs inside, finally cutting through the back layer of muscle and skin, exiting the Hybrid's body.

Rohan instantly *fed* clinging energy into the wound, into his blood, willing it to draw back into his body.

"I said I would show you my strength. Let your doubts wash away in a cascade of blood."

With his other hand, the vampire punched Rohan, knocking him off the impaling fingers like pushing a chunk of meat off a skewer.

Rohan fell to the ground, unable to catch his breath. His Power began to fade immediately; he fed everything he had left into the wound, wrapping energy around torn and mutilated tissues, desperately patching membranes so his guts didn't spill and intermingle.

He heard shouting, words indistinct and muted as if from a great distance.

ar'Tahul crouched down, bringing his eyes close to Rohan's level. "Do you see now? What I meant? Do you see what glory I could bring you?"

Rohan barked out something between a laugh and a cough, spraying red onto his raised hand. His breath came in shallow pants. "So, tell me why your people locked you in prison and left the system."

The vampire's cheeks tightened, erasing his smile and raising his lips into a sneer. "They didn't understand. Small-minded, petty, petty men they were. Afraid of me. Of what I could achieve. Blind, they were."

Rohan laughed and pushed at the platform with his elbows, easing away from the il'Sein a centimeter at a time.

"I'm sure. The great il'Sein, masters of the galaxy. You say they were so brilliant to create you, then so dumb they left you for no reason? Make up your mind. Or can't you?"

The vampire straightened, his eyes narrowing. "You can't understand. There were . . . disagreements."

"Between you and them?"

The Ursans nearby began to stir, shaking awake as something wafted over them. Rohan's gang moved up the walkways and closed on the stage.

"Or between you and yourself?"

18

You Are My Sunshine, My Only

The vampire staggered, nearly setting a foot off the back end of the raised clay platform.

Rohan suppressed a cough, choking back pain and blood. *I'm too badly injured to fight, so I'm antagonizing him? I guess Mom raised at least one fool.*

"Must have been tough, right? Carrying on all those arguments. Showing off the glory of The Chorus, bragging about what an amazing accomplishment you are, while all alone on an empty planet with a half-functioning space station overhead."

"No. No, that's not right."

Wei Li was first to reach the base of the platform, the three Pledged lined up behind her. Ursula was limping along far behind the others, her eyes on the semicomatose Ursans littering the stadium seats.

"What's not right? That you didn't go out with all the glory you should have had?" The urge to lash out, to hurt the vampire in any way he could, was too strong for Rohan to resist.

"It's not right that the planet was empty. That I was alone."

"Are you—hold on—are you whining? That they left you alone?"

"No, it's not right. It's not true. I wasn't alone. Not at first."

"Rudra save me, you're not . . . There was a colony, wasn't there? You *weren't* alone. What happened . . . Never mind. I think I know."

"The hunger, it was too much. I fought it, at first, but . . . You can't understand."

"Leave him alone." Brother Famine's voice rang out.

ar'Tahul's head snapped up, his eyes refocusing on the space past the edge of the platform.

Rohan tried to project his voice. "Get out of here. I can't fight him."

Wei Li answered. "If you cannot, the rest of us surely do not stand a chance. We must get you out of here."

"I'm hurt, Wei Li. I don't think I can stand. He sliced some stuff inside that I'm pretty sure I need."

"You talk too much for your own good."

Brother Famine spoke again. "I'll stop him. At least slow him down. You get the Hybrid out of here."

Sister Famine yelled. "That's insane! Put aside your stupid pride for once; you can't fight that thing."

Mother Famine cleared her throat. "He can. Brother Famine, are you sure?"

"I'm sure, Mother. I've fought the hunger for so long, every day. Let me embrace it, just once. Let me loose. I'll never hurt an innocent; you know that. Let me have this one thing before I die. Let that death serve a purpose."

Her response carried the cadence of a chant. "I give you permission, Brother Famine. You may set aside your discipline, on this and only this day, so that you might serve the greater good. Let your death be a blessing to the world."

Sister Famine cried out, her voice torn and wretched. "Let your death be a blessing."

"It was nice to meet you, Rohan. Mother Famine, you should know I've had uncharitable thoughts toward you. For saving me."

"I know, Brother Famine."

ar'Tahul's eyes flickered wildly from the Pledged to Wei Li and back to the Hybrid. "What are they saying? What is happening?"

Rohan licked dry lips. "I'm afraid I might know the answer."

The vampire's dark eyes focused on him. "No more distractions."

Brother Famine let out a high-pitched keen from the base of the platform. Rohan dragged himself right to the edge.

"I don't think he's going to follow your instructions."

Rohan *felt* a surge of dark energy flare into life behind him, replacing the subdued aura of the man who had been Brother Famine.

The aura felt hollow and cloying, sucking at the edges of Rohan's own spirit like cold mud pulling at a boot. It climbed the platform steps and flowed over the Hybrid without hesitation, surging like a wave into ar'Tahul.

Rohan blinked and tried to focus on the blur of the two vampires fighting. Brother Famine was charged with hungry energy, using it to fuel a supernaturally fast flurry of attacks.

Hands grabbed at Rohan from behind, pulling at his shoulders so his body slipped from the platform. A fresh spurt of fluid jetted out from the hole in his belly. Sister Famine hissed.

"His blood! I can't . . . can't . . ."

Wei Li's voice came from over his shoulder. "Get back, I've got him!"

She flipped Rohan over and threw him across her muscular shoulder. Ursula pounded toward them in an awkward, lopsided run, her injured leg twisting her heavy body with every other step. The Ursans in the front rows of the stadium were upright and taking slow shuffling steps toward the stage.

Wei Li broke into a run, heading for the big bear, the remaining Pledged trailing from a distance.

"I have to see."

"What?"

"Turn! I have to see."

Wei Li grunted and swung Rohan's head so he could view the stage.

Brother Famine was maintaining his frenzied pace. Cuts had blossomed on ar'Tahul's face and hands as he parried and slipped away from the blitzkrieg of strikes.

The older vampire's leg snapped out; Brother Famine stumbled, then caught himself. He instantly hopped back into the fight, one leg dangling uselessly beneath him.

He cut the il'Sein twice more before ar'Tahul caught his arm and jerked, fully dislocating the elbow. The younger vampire's aura was fading quickly, the potent, hollow need in it slipping away.

"Insolent, foolish child! You are not even worthy of membership in The Chorus! You have seen your last night of life."

Ursula pushed up on Rohan's body with one shoulder, supporting half his weight, as they reached the arena entrance.

ar'Tahul held Brother Famine up in one hand. With his other hand, the il'Sein swiped viciously and tore the head of the Pledged completely away from his shoulders. "This is the fate that awaits you all!"

Mother Famine gasped and pushed at Sister Famine. "Hurry!"

Sister Famine let out a sob but ran faster, staying to the very edge of the hallway, as far from Rohan as she could get.

The group burst through the double doors and spilled out onto the dark, empty boulevard.

"You accomplish nothing by this flight!"

Rohan could *sense* the surge of energy as ar'Tahul sprinted toward the arena doors and the street beyond. Wei Li pushed him onto Ursula and pulled her screen out of her pocket.

"Carry him! You two, cover up!"

Mother Famine looked at her. "What?"

Sister Famine nodded and grabbed the older woman's cowl, pulling it down over her face. They stumbled, half-blind, up the path toward station center.

Wei Li walked backward, keeping ar'Tahul between herself and Rohan. The old vampire followed her, slowing at the look on her face.

"You can't hope to—"

With a light tap on her screen, the single-facet diamond ceiling shifted color, its electrochromic coating suddenly clearing. Brilliant sunlight flooded the street.

Smoke erupted from ar'Tahul's face. He shouted a cry of equal parts rage and agony, spinning back toward the arena, arms covering his head as he retreated.

Wei Li turned to face Rohan, who was draped over Ursula's back.

"We have to go."

"What did you do?"

"I hacked one of Wistful's systems. She'll override it very soon, and then he'll be after us again. We have to get away."

Ursula kept moving. Rohan focused his Power on his abdomen, pressing the torn tissues together. The two remaining Pledged rushed after them, hoods pulled low over their faces to protect them from the sun.

"Where are we going?"

"I've kept the warehouse secret from Wistful. I have code in place to hide us from passive cameras. If we can get to it, we might be able to keep her from knowing where we are."

"Might? I don't like that word."

"You have a choice between 'might' and 'definitely won't.' Do you want to change the plan?"

"No, no. 'Might' is great, nice work. Congrats."

They ran up the street toward the barricades. Rohan grunted with each step, the impacts twisting his guts in unpleasant ways.

"You expected me to fail."

"I did not expect failure. I simply planned for it."

"Well, that's good, then. You're forgiven."

"I did not ask for your forgiveness."

"You can literally see all the way through me right now; could you cut me some slack?"

They passed through the barricades. Wei Li muttered instructions to the guard as Ursula headed directly for a transport tube entrance.

Wei Li shouted, "Run!"

They ran: down the stairs, across the transport platform, into a waiting pod with seating for eight.

Wei Li furiously tapped at the pod's control screen, setting a destination, then turned to Rohan just as Ursula arranged him in one of the seats.

He looked up at the security officer.

"Rohan, you need to shut down your Power. Right now."

"My Power is the only thing keeping my insides from becoming very messy outsides."

"We can bandage you and work to save your life, but if your Power is active, ar'Tahul will be able to follow you anywhere on the station."

"He's an empath?"

"He is enough of one to follow your aura."

Rohan looked at her, then at the Pledged. "If I let go, I'm going to start leaking."

Wei Li looked at the two vampires, especially Sister Famine. The latter nodded and pulled a heavy cloth up from inside her robe, covering her nose and mouth.

"I was caught by surprise earlier. Now I am ready."

Mother Famine shook her head. "We should be leaving, regardless. We need to regain our own composure. Losing Brother Famine, smelling all this blood . . ."

Sister Famine nodded. "We will return later."

Wei Li nodded. She took a can of spray sealant from her belt.

"We will mourn Brother Famine properly, but later. Rohan, you have to suppress your Power. Now."

He nodded and let out a long breath, struggling to remain calm against the wellspring of panic that arose as blood spurted from his belly and back.

Wei Li quickly sprayed his stomach, watching as the sealant foamed into shape.

"Turn him."

Ursula gently rolled him onto her lap as Wei Li sprayed his back.

Rohan breathed in, sharply, then exhaled very slowly. He glanced at his belly and turned abruptly away.

It wasn't a pretty sight.

"He's waking up."

"Is that for being a good thing or a bad thing?"

"By the Nine, he's been carved up. I'm almost surprised he's still alive."

"I am not for knowing how to help him. Call for Medical?"

"We cannot use official channels. Wistful will be monitoring all comms, and most likely conducting at least passive surveillance on all medical teams. We have to save his life with what we have at hand."

Rohan opened his eyes. A grinding pain erupted in his chest to accompany a weak, wet cough.

"Do not attempt to move. Above all, keep your Powers suppressed."

He was about to nod emphatically but stopped.

"How bad?" Soft words didn't seem to aggravate the pain.

"It is quite bad. You are losing a great deal of blood."

"Ah."

Ursula held a bandage over the hole in his abdomen. "Wei Li, this is not working. He will die if we cannot do something else."

"I am aware. However, if we attract the attention of ar'Tahul, he will not only die but be devoured."

"You are saying we should allow him to die? So long as his Power is not absorbed by the soul eater?"

"I am saying that if those are our choices, one is clearly better."

Rohan smiled. "Such a sweetheart."

Wei Li looked down at him. "I will not lie to you, Rohan, the wound is grievous."

"I can tell." He could barely hear his own voice.

"Why did you antagonize the vampire? After he wounded you?"

Rohan smiled again and let out a small cough. "I thought I could distract him. Make him do something stupid. It was all I had."

"I believe your efforts were, in fact, effective. He became angry and disoriented. Had he moved more efficiently, I believe he would have had time to consume you while killing Brother Famine."

"I saved the day."

"Only in the loosest possible sense of the term."

He felt things bubbling around his gut. Wei Li sprayed sealant over the hole, but clearly it wasn't holding.

"This is a real pickle."

"What?"

"Earth slang. A jam. I have no idea why we name tough situations after unrelated foods."

"Are these particularly unappetizing foods?"

"Nope. Pickles and jams. Both beloved by billions, hated by none."

She put her hand to his forehead, then checked his belly again. Ursula walked over with wet towels and bent to mop up puddles of blood.

Wei Li sighed. "I hate to ask you this, but do you have any thoughts on the subject? Are there any avenues we should be pursuing that I have overlooked?"

Rohan let a few breaths go by. In. Out. In. Out.

"I'm a Hybrid."

"But you cannot use your Power to heal."

"Doesn't matter. Well, it matters. But we're tougher physically as well. I have organs that will repair damage that would kill any human."

"I see."

"Just stop the bleeding and let my body do its job."

"How?"

"Cauterize it. I think. Should work."

She looked up and met Ursula's eyes.

The big bear nodded. "I will to beginning of heating utensils."

◆ ·••· ◆

Rohan drifted near consciousness.

"Mom, you're burning the char siu again. Turn the oven off."

Wei Li's voice was soft and close. "You are delirious, Rohan. I would like you to wake now. We have to move you."

His attempts to swallow were foiled by a desert-dry mouth. "What?" His own voice was a croak.

"You have been unconscious. You were badly wounded in your battle with ar'Tahul, and we are attempting to keep you alive."

"Oh." He tried to speak; failed; pointed to his mouth.

Ursula bent over him and put a bottle to his lips.

"It is water, Rohan. For hydrating yourself."

He sipped and swallowed, wincing at the distorted sensations across his abdomen.

"What's happening?"

Wei Li and Ursula traded concerned glances. Wei Li answered him.

"You are continuing to bleed internally. The rate may have stabilized, but it is not dropping. Your body can't handle this level of damage without your Power. I believe you are dying."

He nodded. "Disappointing."

"Indeed."

"So . . . I'm going to die here? Wasn't really the plan."

"No, you are not going to die here."

"Right, you're moving me. So I can die somewhere else."

She sighed. "You will die without medical care. I cannot call in Dr. Simivar, or any registered medical staff."

"Too bad. Simivar gives the best painkillers."

"Instead, I will take you to an *un*registered medical professional."

"Good plan. Wait, why aren't they registered?"

"It doesn't matter. We are out of alternatives, and she is, without a doubt, a brilliant surgeon. Perhaps the most skilled in the system."

"Most skilled surgeon but not registered. I'm not sure what to make of that. Sounds like the setup to a bad horror movie."

"Ursula, can you lift him?"

"As if he were one of my own toddlers." The big bear bent her knees and scooped Rohan up with thick, furry arms. "Where are we for going?"

Wei Li motioned toward the door. "The doctor is farther out on this arm. I will show you the way."

Rohan slipped in and out of consciousness as they walked.

They took stairs down to the transport level from inside the building, rode the tube several stops in uncomfortable silence, then climbed up to the street.

Every step pushed a jolt of pain through Rohan's abdomen; he learned to enjoy the moments where he lost consciousness.

Wei Li led Ursula up into a building, turned left, and started walking up an alley with rough-cut metal walls.

"What is this place?"

Wei Li waved a hand around. "The spaces lining the main street are at least fifty meters deep and twelve stories high on either side. Many of the spaces higher up or closer to the exterior hull have been unoccupied for some time. In some regions, squatters have settled these areas, cutting their own passages through the inside for easier access."

"Wistful is for allowing this?"

"She has never asked me to remove them. I believe she is happy that people have found a way of life here that makes them comfortable."

"I see."

They trudged along, turning multiple times to penetrate deeper into the maze of tunnels. Rohan caught glimpses of furtive motion out of the corners of his eyes, children laughing and fleeing the eyes of strangers.

"Is there no closer tube exit?"

Wei Li shook her head. "These passages are made deliberately to be hard to navigate if one is unfamiliar, and part of that is inconvenient transport-level access. It's not much farther."

They reached an unmarked wooden door, identical to dozens, if not hundreds, of others lining the warrens. Wei Li knocked.

"Go away."

"Dr. Magdalena, we are in urgent need of your aid."

"Maggie isn't here. Go away."

Wei Li shook her head. "Dr. Magdalena, this is Wei Li. Security chief of this station."

Ursula shifted her weight, settling Rohan into a more comfortable spot, while they waited.

The door opened, revealing a slenderly built woman tall enough to look Ursula directly in the eyes. She had skin the color of cream and sported short, spiky, bone-white hair. Every feature looked to have been cut out of virgin paper.

The woman looked at Ursula, then at Rohan, then down to Wei Li.

"What do you want?"

Wei Li sighed and pointed to Rohan. "We are in need of a surgeon."

"Call Medical." She retreated a step, moving to close the door, but paused. "Wait, do you need a comm? I don't have one, but Grimby three doors down has a comm. Untraceable. Best of luck!"

Wei Li reached out to grab the edge of the door before it could close. "We cannot use Wistful's Medical. There are complications."

Maggie paused, looked over the trio once more, then nodded. "I suppose you should come inside."

19

Doctor's Orders

"Oh wow. Oh, that does not look good. Let me get some painkillers."

Rohan looked up at the tall woman's back. She crossed the crowded room, bent over a table, and picked up a handful of pills.

She turned, tilted her head back, and popped them in her mouth.

His vision cleared enough for him to notice pointed ears and an unusual mark on her forehead: twin intersecting crescents.

"Zahad."

She focused sharply on him as she sipped water, swallowing the pills. "What was that?"

"Your forehead. You're Shayjh. From Zahad."

She looked at Wei Li, who shrugged. "And so what if I am?"

"I mean, nothing. I just noticed."

"Yes. In hindsight, maybe not the best idea, to brand ourselves so visibly, but I can't very well change it now."

Nobody responded.

"Well then, what happened to this young man? Accident? Something industrial? Those are serious burns."

Rohan laughed. "That's the cure, not the wound."

Wei Li nodded. "We tried to cauterize the injury. To stop the bleeding. It seems to have failed."

Maggie laughed, her tongue and gums dark red between pale-pink lips. "What did you do, just jam a hot fork into a through-and-through abdominal wound?"

The other women looked uncomfortable.

"Oh, you did, didn't you. Not fantastic. Whose idea was that?" More uncomfortable glances. "Well, no use mentioning now what terrible judgment that demonstrated. Let me look again."

Rohan tightened as she poked at his wound with long, cool fingers. "I probably should have washed my hands before doing that. I'll clean you out after. What species are you, anyway?"

"I'm mixed species. Half human."

"Never heard of them. I hope they have strong immune systems. The other half?"

Wei Li cleared her throat. "Does it matter? You're not breeding with him; you just have to close the wound."

"I was making small talk. To relax my patient. Because that's apparently what he is."

"You'll help him?"

"If I don't, he'll die right here on my table. And this is where I eat. It's bad luck to have someone die on your dining table."

"Thank you. What can we do to help?"

"I'll wash my hands. You"—she pointed to Ursula—"there's a two-liter glass jar on the kitchen counter. Grab it, but don't drink any; it's about fifty percent ethanol."

Wei Li looked at her. "Should you be drinking before surgery?"

"Won't matter, I'm already high as a cloud. But it's not for drinking, it's for disinfecting. You, head down that hall and take the second door. It's my gross anatomy lab. You should find a tray of scalpels and so on out in the open."

The women left quickly to fetch supplies.

Maggie turned back to Rohan. "You are a mess in here. Wow. What is that? Is that fresh skin? You're healing. Visibly. Which is a good thing, but very odd."

"I heal fast. But it's not fast enough, is it?"

"No. Let me get a line into you." She turned up the hall. "Grab one of those carts with the intravenous lines on it!"

Maggie crossed the room to the kitchen. Rohan heard the sink running.

Ursula returned to his side, carrying the jug of moonshine. Soon Wei Li was back, running a saline drip into his arm.

"Do you know what you're doing?"

"Obviously, cauterizing a wound like yours was beyond my meager medical training, but this I can manage."

The doctor walked over, her hands dripping on the floor.

"Don't have any clean towels to dry with. Here, hand me that bottle." She took the jug from Ursula and poured some of its contents over her hands. "Can you move that lamp over here? No, the big one. Point it right at his belly."

Rohan watched as they created a makeshift operating theater in the living room of a squatter's apartment.

"Am I going to be okay?"

"Probably not. You have a huge hole in your gut, internal burns, and Progenitors know how much blood loss. You should be dead already."

"Oh."

"You don't look like much, but you humans must be made of tough stock. Unless it's your other half we should thank." She poked inside his belly again, pouring alcohol over the area to clear some of the blood away. "Skin's trying to form. Right in front of my eyes. That's amazing."

The pain was blinding. Rohan exhaled, emptying his lungs, and focused entirely on suppressing his Power.

"Tell me again what his other half is? I seem to have forgotten. Too many pills."

Wei Li was at her side. "We didn't tell you."

"Right, you didn't. What is he wearing? Is that a station uniform? It's hard to tell under all the blood and whatnot. I could clean off a patch, check the colors."

"It is a station uniform."

"Yes, yes. Is he security? No, that's the wrong patch. Tell me again, why didn't you tell me his heritage?"

"You don't want to know. It is . . . a secret."

"Is it that *I* don't want to know or that *you* don't want me to know?"

Ursula barked. "By the Gods. He is an il'Drach Hybrid, Doctor. He is our tow chief. Surely you have been seeing videos of him? On the news feeds? When my people arrived?"

"News feeds? Never watch them. If he's an il'Drach Hybrid, why isn't his wound closing? And how did you get that line into his artery?"

"He cannot use his Power at the moment. He is suppressing it."

The doctor put three fingers into Rohan's wound. "You're telling me I have an actual living, breathing il'Drach Hybrid on my dining room table with a hole through his belly. And he has no Powers?"

Wei Li's eyes narrowed. "I am."

Maggie spat out a chuckle, then a laugh, then a guffaw, then a torrent of belly-deep exhalations that left her doubled over and wheezing.

"Me! You want *me* to fix him!"

"We do. Why is that funny?"

Rohan squirmed while the doctor regained her composure and her breath.

"Do you not understand where I'm from?"

"You are Shayjh."

"Racially, yes, I'm Shayjh. But while the Shayjh you know of have bastardized our culture, have turned away from the Path of the Progenitors, my people would not."

"What do you mean?"

"I was raised on Zahad. It's a minor system, barely habitable. My people left Shayjh long ago and moved there. We would not participate in bending our knees to the will of the il'Drach. We were the only Shayjh to maintain the culture and mindset of our forefathers, the Progenitors. This"—she pointed to her forehead—"was our mark."

Wei Li shook her head. "I am unfamiliar with this story. I'd be happy to hear more, but right now that man, who is close to a friend to me, is bleeding to death, and I would very much like to see that situation alleviated."

"Of course. But I'm not done. I don't think you were listening to me. I said we were, not we are. Isn't that curious?"

Wei Li opened her mouth to speak, but Ursula put a massive paw over her forearm. "We are for listening. I know something about losing one's people."

"The Empire decided we had transgressed too far. They sent Hybrids to Zahad. Not to threaten, or to negotiate, or to demand. They were sent to destroy."

Rohan swallowed. "How did you escape?"

Maggie laughed, the sound tighter and higher than before. "I was here. My mother, you see. Lived on Wistful. She was sick. Cancer. I came to help."

"What happened?"

"Oh, she died. And before I could go back home, it was gone. With everyone else in the sector who I cared about."

Wei Li shook her head. "Your quarrel is with the Empire. This man does not serve the Empire."

"All Hybrids serve the Empire. One way or another. Whether they know it or not. He fights, doesn't he? Perhaps for good causes. Maybe he saves people. You do, don't you? Save lives. And every time, they notice what you are. They see the power of the Empire. They learn that they can't resist it, can't fight it."

Rohan looked at Wei Li. "She's not entirely wrong."

"You be quiet. Dr. Magdalena, I understand what you are saying. However, at this moment, the station is in significant danger. There is a very powerful vampire on board, and the il'Drach Empire has a war flotilla in the system ready to destroy Wistful if we cannot end his threat. That man on your table is our best chance of keeping that from happening."

"I am not so afraid to die, Miss Security Chief. I don't have much left to live for."

"I respect that. But surely you don't want to see everyone else die? The children laughing on the other side of that wall? The innocent people who live here? Ursula's people, refugees from their own religious war?"

The Shayjh's eyes flickered to Ursula, then back to Rohan. The Hybrid *felt* the Ursan's calming aura fill the room.

"They're really threatening to destroy the station?"

"They are. Rohan has talked them out of it, but it is a temporary abeyance."

"If this vampire is so powerful that the Empire fears it, what can he do to stop it? Especially with that hole in his gut."

"I do not know. Perhaps nothing. If he cannot save us, then he will die when the Empire destroys the station. Your mercy would only grant him a few additional days of life."

"But if he can save us, then he might live for years longer. How could I stand that, knowing that I had my hand inside his body, fingers almost touching his heart, that I let him go? How could I live with myself?"

Ursula nodded slowly. "It is hard, this surviving. Much harder than the dying. I am for envying the dead we left behind, many days."

The Shayjh looked into the Ursan's eyes, then at Wei Li's reptilian, scale-lined face.

She bent close to Rohan's face. "Can you really do it, little Hybrid? If I save you, can you kill the vampire and save the station?"

He coughed, covering his mouth to avoid spraying her with blood. "I'm not going to kill him. I'm going to save him. From the Empire and from himself." He smiled at her with red-stained teeth.

She stood, then sighed, letting her shoulders slump forward. She faced Wei Li. "If I find out you are lying about the Fleet, I will poison you with a protein that will permanently lock onto every pain receptor in your body. The longest any sentient creature has lasted under that treatment before begging for death is seven minutes."

"I—we—are not lying. There is no need to threaten me."

"We'll see. I'll save him, but on one condition."

"You have the advantage. Name it."

"I never want to see him again. No, I never want to see any of you ever again. You forget I exist. Don't even set foot in this building. Agreed?"

Ursula answered. "We are for agreeing. Now, please, take care of him."

"Both of you?"

Wei Li nodded. "I will stay away to the best of my ability."

"Fine. You, take that spool of thread and soak it in alcohol. Fill a glass with more of the moonshine and hand it to me. Then wash your hands and, if you have any faith in anything, start praying."

"Shhh."

A hand's touch jolted Rohan awake. He began to sit up, the gentle pressure along with wrenching pain in his gut reminding him to take it easy.

"You're safe. Just lie back. If you sit up, you might tear yourself open again." The voice was disturbingly familiar.

"What?" Rohan's memories of where he was, and why, came back in a rush. "D-Dhruv?"

"You're at the warehouse. We're alone; I sent the others out for supplies. Keep your Power suppressed for now."

Rohan blinked rapidly. His breathing was fast, too short and shallow. "What time is it?"

Dhruv checked his wrist. "Close to noon. The women should bring lunch back with them."

"What day?"

"You've only been out for a few hours. I wouldn't have woken you, but you were tossing and turning. Must have been some dream."

"I don't remember."

"Doesn't matter. You look terrible."

"Yeah."

"Should I see the other guy?"

"What? Can you get me some water?"

"Sure. You know, I say you look terrible, you tell me I should see the other guy." Dhruv stood and walked over to the table, grabbed a bottle of water, then looked around for a straw.

"The other guy is fine. Not a scratch on him. At least, I didn't put any there."

"Ah. Is he really that strong or did you mess up?" He handed the bottle and straw to Rohan.

"What kind of question is that? Whose side are you on?"

"I'm on the right side, like always. I need to do a threat assessment. Is he *that* strong?"

Rohan thought as he maneuvered the bottle in place so he could drink without sitting up. "I could have done better, but I don't think I could have beaten him. A couple of days of feeding, and he's completely transformed."

Dhruv nodded. "I told you he represents an amazing weapon."

"I don't want to argue with you, Dad."

"I'm not arguing. Just reminding you that I told you so."

"Okay."

Dhruv touched the bed underneath his son. "This is new."

"Ursula grabbed a couple of cots. She didn't want me bleeding all over the nice couch."

Dhruv looked around the room. "There's a nice couch? Where is it?"

"The couch, Dad. Where everybody sits."

"Clearly her Drachna isn't coming along all that well if she's calling that couch 'nice.'"

"Do you have to always put everybody else down? What's your motivation there? Does it make you feel better about . . . anything?"

"Standards matter, that's all. Truth matters."

"Fine. It's not that great of a couch. It's still where people sit, and she didn't want me to bleed all over it. Not unreasonable."

Dhruv sighed. "No, son, you're right. Not unreasonable."

"Thanks for the water. Why are you here now, anyway?"

"I came to speak to my son. I did not expect to find him at death's threshold."

"What? Oh. You didn't know about the fight with ar'Tahul."

"I knew. I didn't realize quite how badly you'd been hurt, or that you'd be forced to suppress your Power to escape pursuit. When I came in, I couldn't *feel* you at all. Thought you'd died." His face showed no trace of humor.

"Sorry about that. I guess. Updating you on my condition wasn't at the top of my priority list. Seeing as you haven't shown much in the way of concern for my well-being at any point in the last fifteen or so years."

"Is that what you think?"

"I was there, you know. I'm talking about what you did or did not do, not about what you may have felt or thought."

"I was giving you room to grow. To thrive. And look at you! You've exceeded even my expectations."

"Yeah, look at me. Or through me. Because you could if I pulled up my shirt."

Dhruv waved his hand in the air. "A temporary setback. You got stitched up; I'm sure you'll heal as good as new."

"If not, I'll have this cool new place to hide my wallet. If I have to go through any sketchy neighborhoods."

"Right, right. Funny. You were always a funny one. I'm not sure where you got it from."

Rohan opened his mouth to answer, but, at first, nothing came out. Finally, "I actually don't know. Mom can be funny, can't she?"

"She can, yes. Sometimes. Not why I married her, but still."

"You never answered my question. Why are you here?"

"Ah. That. You see . . . Did you want more water?"

"I'm good. Why are you stalling?"

"I was thinking about things, last night. After we left here. And then more after I watched the footage of the fight you had." He paused.

"It's not like you to beat around the bush, Dad."

"No. I wanted to say that you were right, son. That's all. About ar'Tahul. He's too dangerous to try to control. It was a foolish idea I had, to bargain with him."

"So, you want me to kill him after all?"

"Well, I'd prefer we didn't have to. I do think he can be used. But that's no longer my primary objective."

"Okay. I don't want to kill him either, you know. I hope we can cure him. Or even re-imprison him. He's just so . . . damaged."

"That's how it goes with soul eaters. It's why we never pursued that path to attaining Power."

"Right. Good move. You guys are all crazy enough without integrating foreign personalities into your soul."

"Don't call us crazy."

"Sorry." He shifted his weight, trying to find a comfortable position. "That's it? I was right? You're going to hang out here until we get this blockade lifted and go your merry way?"

"What? No, of course not. Did I say that?"

"Then, what are you saying?"

"I'm going to take control of Wistful. Think about it—I wanted to use ar'Tahul, a remnant of il'Sein military technology left on the other side of that wormhole. One man. Very powerful, but still. There are still three unopened wormholes in this system, Rohan, and who knows what other treasures might be in the two you've already uncovered. All safe from il'Drach interference."

"You're saying you want to find these places, unsullied by your people, so you can exploit them yourself?"

"Exactly! Oh, I can't tell you what a relief it is to talk to someone who uses their mind. Who isn't locked into blind obedience to tradition. Let me tell you, most Hybrids—hell, most il'Drach of any sort—have no sense of creative thinking."

"I'm not sure you got the tone of what I was saying."

"I got your tone. Maybe you don't realize how often your sarcasm isn't really sarcasm. It's an expression of the uncomfortable truths that you recognize, deep down inside."

Rohan pressed his head back down into the pillow. "That's not true, but I don't have the strength to argue with you."

"You tell yourself whatever you need to, boy. Get some rest. I'll watch over you. When the women return, I'll wake you so you can eat."

"Good plan. Not like there's anything else I can do at the moment. But before I close my eyes, just let me know. How do you plan to take control of the station?"

"It is simplicity itself. I will use the same mechanism that is being used by ar'Tahul."

"What?"

"This station was built with a control mechanism in her positronic brain. A physical control, tuned to the il'Sein. So she cannot help but obey their explicit orders."

"Okay." *I knew that already, but he doesn't know that I know. I don't have the energy to keep all of this straight anymore.*

"I will use that mechanism myself."

"You're going to hack her brain."

"Exactly." Dhruv looked down at his son with a wide smile.

"Do you even know how to do that? I didn't think you had that level of technical know-how."

"It's not about *what* I know, it's about *who* I know. Don't you worry yourself about it. Like I said, heal up and be ready for the next stage of our work."

"Look, Dad, I really have to wonder. If hacking this station is easy, why hasn't anybody else done it in the last, what, fifty thousand years?"

"I didn't say it was *easy*. I said I could get it done. There are people who will help me because the alternative looks like her destruction."

"I see."

"You let me worry over the details." A bell chimed. "The door! The women have returned. I hope they got the white sauce I asked for."

"Yeah. White sauce. I hope I still have a stomach in there so I can digest food."

20

Feints and Retaliations

"Rudra save me, that really hurts! Are you sure the doc didn't give you guys any better painkillers? Are you hoarding them for yourselves?"

Ursula sucked a tooth and shook her head. "Hold still, War Chief. I must for changing these bandages, and your complaining is not making it for easier."

He sighed and forced his body to stillness. "I know. I'm sorry."

Mother Famine gripped his hand. "Focus on my voice, Rohan. Repeat the mantras; let them pull your consciousness along. Don't deny the pain, encapsulate it, put it into a bubble and observe it. The pain is not you. Your Power is not you."

He re-centered himself and tried to follow her instructions.

Sister Famine snorted from her seat nearby. "He's not going to hold it. We should get out of here before the fallen one finds us."

Mother Famine turned to her. "Hush. You know better."

Sister Famine sighed and slumped back into the couch. "Sorry, Mother." Rohan fought back a laugh; she reminded him of a sullen teenager.

Wei Li walked over to Rohan and assessed the open wound while Ursula sprayed disinfectant and fresh foam sealant over it.

"Do you know where Dhruv went?"

Rohan shook his head gently. "He came to tell me I was right, that trying to control ar'Tahul wasn't going to work. He wants to take over Wistful instead."

She raised one scaly eyebrow. "I see."

"I don't think he can do it, so I see no reason to try to stop him right now. Not that I *could* try. Being bedridden and all."

"We shall keep an eye on him." A series of soft pings sounded from her tablet. She turned and walked to the big screen, powered it on, and began flipping through various video feeds.

"Can you put on the next *Swords of Lukhor*? We ended the last one on a cliffhanger."

"In a bit, Rohan."

Mother Famine put her hand on his chest. "Lie back and focus, Tow Chief. There will be time for *Swords of Lukhor* later. You must concentrate."

Ursula closed the can of sealant. "We are done for now, War Chief. There is very little bleeding. I am for thinking the surgeon did a good job."

"Thanks. Thank you both. Thank all of you, actually. I don't know where I'd be without your help."

Wei Li sniffed. "You know *what* you'd be. Dead. You would be dead. Where exactly, I am not sure either."

"Right. Dead. Well, this is much better."

Rohan's comm chimed on. "Rohan?"

"Ben?"

"Oh good, it worked. How are you?"

"I'm . . . I was about to say 'good,' but the truth is I'm in pretty rough shape. How are you even on this channel?"

"Marion went to Tollan's and got one of the entangled chips to hook into our local comm equipment. Seemed like a good idea. What happened to you?"

"ar'Tahul challenged me to a fight. He seems to think I swallowed something important because he searched through my stomach looking for it. With his hand."

"Oh. Like, down your throat? That sounds terrible."

"No, he took the shortcut. Which was worse. I think. Probably would have finished me right there, but Brother Famine ran interference. Which got him killed."

Ben let out a heavy sigh. "I'm so sorry."

"Now I'm keeping my Power suppressed so he can't sense me, but that means I'm healing like a normal person. Well, like a normal half-il'Drach person, which is pretty fast."

"Can we help? I'm no medic, but I can head over there and take a look."

"I went to a back-alley doctor. Literally. She stitched me up. Now I need time. And I need you working on that pheromone antidote."

"We're making progress on that, but I need another day or two. Listen, though, I hate to be that guy, but I need to pile on some more bad news."

"What is it?"

"*Insatiable* has received communications directly from the il'Drach ships. They told her to go into active defensive mode."

Rohan tried to concentrate. Between the pain, blood loss, and effort required to suppress his Power, his thoughts were murky at best.

"So, like, seal her hatches, fire up active defense systems, all of that?"

"Exactly. We're sealed in, which is not a problem, we weren't going anywhere. But it raises questions. *A* question."

"Why."

"Right. This wouldn't make sense if they thought ar'Tahul was going to attack. The systems we're talking about face outward, into space. So, why would they need her to protect herself from an attack from space?"

"Nobody out there but them. So no danger from that direction . . . unless they're planning to attack Wistful."

"That's what we figure. They're not willing to let *Insatiable* leave, but they don't want her destroyed in dock."

"But why are they attacking at all? What's the point?"

Wei Li cleared her throat. "I'm receiving a broadcast from the Fleet. Pushing it to the main screen."

Rohan arched his neck to see the screen. "That's *Father's Vengeance*. The voice is hers, too."

". . . do not want to repeat this action. Repeat: Because the independent station Wistful is aiding and abetting a threat to the Empire, and to the people of this sector, we are initiating an attack upon her person. We strongly advise any civilians on board to shelter themselves to the best of their ability. We do not . . ." Wei Li muted the feed and turned to the group.

"Rohan. What will they do?"

He struggled to focus. "There are two possibilities. Normally they'd send in Hybrids first. They didn't want to do that here, but they might have changed their minds."

Dr. Stone's voice came over the comm. "*Insatiable* reports signs of preparation for a claw attack."

Rohan sighed. "That answers that question. They'll send a storm of claws."

Wei Li's eyes narrowed. Ursula stood. "What does this mean, 'storm of claws'?"

Rohan looked around the room. Nobody pitched in any explanations. *I'm the only one here who knows anything about il'Drach ship-to-ship combat.*

"Warships are artificial intelligences. They're alive; they have souls. Souls, we know, aren't physical, but they can exert force on the physical world."

Ursula nodded. "The way you can."

"The way any living thing can. I just happen to have a lot of force to exert."

Ben's voice interrupted. "Storm released from *Father's Vengeance*."

Rohan continued. "Like any other living thing, they can exert *more* force on their own bodies than on the rest of the world. Meaning that ships could pick up and toss rocks or something at one another all day long; each would easily deflect the missiles."

"Two other ships have released claws. Closing on Wistful now."

Wistful's voice boomed from the vicinity of the big screen; she was broadcasting on the open channel.

"il'Drach Fleet: This is the independent station Wistful. Your actions are in violation of the Seventh Treaty of Toth, signed at the Fourth Toth Conference. Recall your weapons immediately."

Rohan resumed. "Warships cultivate sets of nearly indestructible metal spears. They grow them, focus on them . . . these 'claws' become as much a part of their body as their hull or bootstrap drives or fusion generators. Or, as much as your fingers or hair or teeth."

Wei Li shivered. "Wistful has woken up."

Mother Famine looked at her. "Is that what I just sensed?"

Ursula shook her massive head. "Was she asleep?"

Wei Li shook her own. "Not asleep, but not fully awake either. Now she is angry. Ready for battle. I have never sensed this from her before."

Ursula looked around from face to face. "What will she be doing now? Wistful?"

Rohan sighed. "When ships fight, they send these groups of claws at one another. Each uses the claws to attack and to deflect. They thrust and parry and feint. It's not that different from a fencing match, except that the fists aren't attached to the bodies and the fight happens over thousands of kilometers of distance."

Ben spoke again. "Claws released from Wistful's center section. Oh my. *Insatiable* reports an amount commensurable with an Imperial super-dreadnought. Thousands of them, spreading out through space."

"That answers a question I didn't really want answered."

Ursula looked at the Hybrid. "What are you for meaning?"

"I wasn't sure of Wistful's combat capabilities. Turns out she's got armaments at least equivalent to the biggest warships in the Empire."

Wei Li nodded. "Which might explain why the il'Drach have given her independent status."

"It might. Anyway, you add in the fact that ships can open rifts in space and send the claws through those rifts, and space combat turns very complex very quickly."

Ben's voice was showing strain. "Three Hybrids have emerged to provide cover. Imperial ships are in evasive maneuvers. Four shuttles have just left Wistful . . . They seem unmanned. Same type as the combat shuttles Repentant launched."

Wei Li's eyes narrowed. "She is getting angrier. The portion of her that has been asleep is significantly larger than I imagined."

"I wonder if the il'Drach had any clue."

Dr. Stone stammered. "Fifty percent of that first storm has been deflected. Sixty percent. Seventy. The shuttles are heading straight for *Father's Vengeance*. Imperial ships are dodging; Hybrids are moving to intercept Wistful's claws."

Wei Li looked sharply at Rohan.

He remembered more than one occasion where he'd provided cover for battling warships, dancing through space, finding claws sent on roundabout routes for surprise attacks and deflecting them by hand or killing their momentum. "They'll probably hang back, provide cover, stop claws the ships might miss."

"*Insatiable* is hit! No crew lost yet; she's maintaining hull integrity."

Rohan wished he could fly out and help.

Ben cried out. "Impacts on Wistful! A handful of claws have penetrated her hull. All impacts are out on the arms; nothing is getting to the hub area."

The station's aura intensified to the point where everyone in the room could *feel* the station's anger. Her voice rang out over the open channel.

"You have targeted civilian locations in a cowardly attack. Prepare for retaliatory strikes."

"The shuttles are accelerating; *Insatiable* says that Wistful's claws are moving faster as well."

"One of the Hybrids is hit. Blood cloud on sensors."

Wei Li was on her tablet. "Tell me where the hull is breached. Yes, yes. Response teams: First to arrive verify that nothing has entered the station other than the claws. Watch for boarders or devices carried in. Is Medical tied in? Maintenance? We need welding crews to support Wistful's self-healing nanoswarms. Go!"

Rohan looked at Ursula. "It's always quiet, you know, the space battles. So much going on, and after so many years, I still expect to hear something."

Her muzzle bobbed as she nodded. "It is always this way. Deaths in space are silent deaths."

"I wonder which Hybrid got hurt. If it's someone I know."

Ben continued. "Serious damage to at least one of the il'Drach ships. A shuttle made impact and tore a hole through her. Now they're opening rifts. Storms of claws are being sent to Wistful's sunside; she opened a rift of her own behind *Father's Vengeance*. It's been struck by its own claws; no significant damage."

Rohan nodded. "Some of those moves are feints. Some are just attempts to humiliate and embarrass the other side, get them angry. So they'll make mistakes."

"Does that work? Even with the ships, with computer brains?"

"Ships have souls. They feel emotions just as much as anything organic."

"I am for seeing this now. So much to learn."

"Rifts are opening; big ones this time. Two of the il'Drach ships are fleeing after taking heavy damage. Claws still incoming from the remaining ships. Nobody is holding back anymore.

"One of the shuttles was destroyed; the other three are still attacking the ships. Another one down."

Rohan picked his mask off the floor and tapped through video feeds, looking for visuals of the battle. "We don't use shuttles that way. It must be a non-il'Drach tactic. Pre-il'Drach?"

"Do the shuttles have crew?"

"Probably not. It wouldn't serve any point. I'm pretty sure those attack shuttles are just big claws, in effect."

"Yes. Are the il'Drach for trying to kill us all? Destroy Wistful?"

"No. This is a slap on the wrist, you know? If they wanted to kill her, they wouldn't have broadcast a warning, and they would have attacked with everything they had, right from the start."

Wei Li grumbled. "We have damage to seven different housing areas. No confirmed fatalities, but my people have had to seal off the upper levels of several buildings. Including Tollan's."

Rohan looked at her. "Could that be deliberate? Is there some reason they'd be targeting him?"

She shrugged. "I cannot see any such connection. On the other hand, this is a very large station, and for one of the points of contact to be over his shop seems like a large coincidence."

Rohan rubbed his head. "Ben, did they pick up that injured Hybrid? If one of us gets killed, this is going to get uglier. All the others will start pushing for blood."

"Let me . . . I think she was picked up. Wildeye, it looks like."

The Hybrid sighed. "Yeah. She seemed pretty inexperienced. I'm not shocked she'd get caught by an errant claw."

"I'll tell you if I hear anything more. Fresh set of claws incoming. Two il'Drach ships have warped to the other side, flanking Wistful. She's sent clouds of claws that way as well. Station has deployed about twice the payload of an il'Drach superdreadnought."

Rohan whistled. "I had no idea she was armed like that."

Ursula looked at him. "Are the claws so large? Would they not take up much space?"

He shook his head. "The limiting factor is how many she can engage mentally. If she's able to keep that many claws and some shuttles as part of her self-concept, even while they're far away and engaged in combat, that implies a level of spiritual connectedness that I've never seen."

Wei Li shrugged. "She is very old. Perhaps it is a learned skill."

"Could be. Either way, it's good for us, at least in the short term."

Wistful pinged Rohan's comm. "Tow Chief."

"Yes?"

"Are you able to assist in this fight against the il'Drach?"

He sighed. "I would. Normally I would. But I've been pretty seriously injured, and I'm not fit enough to stand up on my own, let alone fly out and fight for you."

"Understood. Carry on." She closed the line.

Ursula looked at him. "What are you for hearing?"

"There's damage to the station, so Wistful is upset. She asked me to join the fight, which I can't. Hold on." He tapped his comm to broadcast. "Ben, how is *Insatiable*? Any further damage? Are you guys safe?"

"We're fine. Superficial damage only. *Insatiable*'s own claws are out now. She's out of practice, but she says she used to be a combat ship."

"Yeah, I remember. Thanks." He turned to Ursula. "Our people are safe, for the most part."

Wei Li grunted. "We've taken strikes at three more locations."

"And I spoke too soon. Where?"

"Farther out on the arms. Near food production. Damage is minimal; no real casualties."

Ben's voice returned. "Backup ships are entering the fray. Another shuttle is incapacitated; now two. They're withdrawing to Wistful. Flights of incoming claws headed this way. *Insatiable* says we should brace ourselves."

Rohan's heart was loud in his chest; he couldn't drink water fast enough. Ursula laid a paw on his shoulder, then covered his forehead with a wet cloth.

Wei Li shook her head. "They're winning, and they're targeting areas with lower population density and less critical components. I believe the demonstration is just about over."

Mother Famine turned her attention to Rohan. "You must get yourself under control. Your focus is wavering."

He swallowed and nodded. "Hard not to be out there with all this."

"I understand, but your feelings are not important. Your control over them, however, is."

"I hear you, I hear you." He refocused on his breathing. Out slow, hold, in fast.

Wei Li changed channels; she had found a group monitoring the battle with optical equipment through a station window. ". . . seems that the il'Drach are withdrawing. At least for now. Wistful's defense mechanisms are no longer in pursuit; they've drawn back to a defensive perimeter. After an exciting battle. . ." She lowered the volume.

Rohan tapped his comm. "Ben, is there any way *Insatiable* can get in contact with *Void's Shadow* without giving her position away?"

"I can check."

Wei Li looked around. "I would very much like to have a face-to-face chat with whoever is commanding that il'Drach flotilla."

Rohan chuckled. "It's hard going through situations where you can't sense people's motivations. Welcome to our world."

"I will tolerate this visit, but I have no intention of prolonging my stay."

Rohan smiled and relaxed back into the cot.

Wei Li looked at him again. "I am going to make sure Tollan is unharmed. I shall return shortly." She pulled on a jacket, yanked the hood down over her eyes, and pulled a mask up to cover her lower face.

"Pick up beer while you're out!"

"I most assuredly will not."

Mother Famine looked down at him. "No alcohol for you."

"I know, I know. A boy can hope, right?"

"Back to your mantras."

"Okay."

"How are you for feeling, Rohan?" Ursula had noticed him stirring.

"The itching is almost unbearable. Probably better than the alternative."

"What is that?"

"Not itching. Which would only happen if I were dead."

"I see, I see. Yes, it is for good that you survived, Rohan. My people need their War Chief."

"No pressure, though. Right?"

"I am not for understanding."

"Never mind. Just trying to be funny. And failing. What's on the screen?"

"Is local news. They are for surveying the damages."

"Ah. Hold on, that's new. Turn it up."

She turned and nodded, then raised the volume.

"What you have witnessed, what you have survived, is but the first of our victories against the il'Drach so-called Empire. I am here to free you from their tyranny, to save you from the threats that lurk in the depths of space." The voice was Wistful's, set in a stiffer monotone than her usual; the image was ar'Tahul, standing proudly on the center stage at the arena.

Ursula looked at him. "She is speaking why? The vampire does not speak Drachna?"

Rohan nodded. "That's it. Let's hear the rest."

"I will lead, but the task belongs to us all. You will not all sing in The Chorus, but you will each make sacrifices for this common good. We will be united in our efforts, joined in the work of freeing this sector from the terrors unseen.

"I do not ask everything of you today. Now, at this moment, I ask only that you find and bring to me your tow chief, the il'Drach Hybrid known as Rohan, and any of those who support him. File out into the halls and walkways of this marvelous station and fetch him, that he might join me. Those who bring him to me will receive the second greatest gift I can offer you: immortality of your own.

"Together, we will sing of victory over the Empire; the il'Drach will feel our power!"

Ursula looked at Rohan. "This is not so good."

"It seems like we keep saying that."

"Is truth."

"Yes, I know, it's true. But we shouldn't keep saying it."

"The problems are like pests. They are breeding."

21

The Lucky Ones

S ister Famine yawned, her incisors twin scimitars of brilliance in the otherwise dimly lit room.

Must be dawn.

Clutter had accumulated in the warehouse. Cots littered the open spaces; makeshift tables formed from stacked takeout boxes teetered near every seat; little piles of medical supplies, sauce packets, and water bottles dotted the floor.

Rohan blinked gummy eyes and struggled to a seated position. His lower chest felt heavy, his lungs struggling as if against a high-gravity environment.

Ursula handed him a bottle of water. She was starting to get musky.

"Thanks." He drank. It didn't help his breathing. He sat all the way up and worked on his visualizations.

Sister Famine was pacing.

"You know, I'm sorry about Brother Famine. My condolences. He seemed like a good guy."

"What?" Her eyes narrowed as she looked at him, green skin pinched on her forehead.

"I mean, you were friends, right? I'm just saying, I'm sorry for your loss."

"We were. But you barely knew him."

"I get that. I'm just saying, I'm sorry for your loss."

"You barely know me. What possible reason could you have for saying that?"

"I don't know. You're adorable?" She sneered and turned away.

He sighed and twisted in the cot, trying to find a comfortable position. Ursula looked at him. "Rohan, you are not looking your usual self."

"Not feeling great. Something about a hole punched through my torso. I've also never tried to keep my Power sealed off for this long."

The big bear nodded. "I will for bringing you something to eat."

"Thanks."

Sister Famine glared at him. "You think I'm mourning Brother Famine? Is that why you offer sympathy?"

He sighed. "I guess. Aren't you? Like I said, he was your friend."

She shook her head slowly, eyes fixed on him. "I will miss him, but I do not mourn for him. Only for myself."

He winced as something tugged at his insides painfully. "What does that mean?"

"Our creed does not permit suicide. Life is a gift; we will not cheapen it by expending it uselessly. That does not mean we are eager to live."

"I think you lost me."

"He wanted to die. This . . . situation gave him an opportunity to do so within the limits of our creed."

"Ah."

"Brother Famine's death is not a tragedy. Yes, I will miss him, but I cannot mourn him. He received the end he longed for."

"I hear you. But death is so . . . final. What if we find a cure tomorrow? He'll have died for nothing. At least for very little."

Mother Famine cleared her throat. "There is no cure. I wish there were, but . . ."

"How could you know that? It's a big universe."

"We have searched."

Sister Famine snorted. "That's why we're on Wistful, after all. Another dead end."

Rohan stared at her. "What does a cure for vampirism have to do with Wistful?"

She opened her mouth as if to answer, then paused and glared at him, leaning closer, nostrils flared wide.

"You do realize that you stink?"

"That's a bit harsh." He sniffed. "Maybe not so harsh. I haven't showered in . . . I don't even know what day it is."

"I'm not talking about your filth."

"Is this about pheromones again? Because—"

"No, shut your jabbering mouth and listen to me for a moment. You stink of illness. Sepsis, perhaps."

Ursula spun and came to his side, inhaling deeply through damp, black nostrils. "I do not . . . wait, yes. Yes, she is correct. It is very faint, but present. Dead blood inside you."

"Dead blood? Okay. What do I do about that?"

Mother Famine leaned over from the other side of his cot. "They are right. You are bleeding internally."

The door slid open as Wei Li returned to the safehouse. "Tollan is safe, but we did not have time to talk. I brought eggs from Pop's. He does not offer them as takeout but made an exception for us."

Ursula turned to her. "Wei Li, we believe Rohan is for bleeding internally."

Wei Li ran both palms over her hairless scalp, dragging the scales at the base of each hand over the matching lines that trailed from her temples to the back of her neck.

"This is beyond me. We have to take him back to the doctor."

Ursula shook her head. "We were for promising not to do that."

Wei Li shrugged. "Unless you have a better idea, we will have to atone for breaking our promise at a later date."

Mother and Sister Famine traded glances. Mother Famine said, "We would come, but it is not safe for us to travel extensively in daytime."

Wei Li nodded. "Ursula and I can handle him. In fact, it's probably better to have a smaller group. We will attract less attention from anyone interested in turning him over to ar'Tahul."

The Pledged nodded appreciation.

Rohan looked around. "Are you sure? I don't feel that bad. I think I just need some more rest. Maybe beer. Definitely beer."

Wei Li turned to Ursula. "Can you grab him? I'll lead."

"Of course. My pleasure it will for being."

"Are you guys just ignoring me?"

Wei Li continued. "Will you two stay here?"

Sister Famine shook her head. "We should return to our own place and rest for the day."

"Good. I appreciate your assistance."

Mother Famine bowed her head softly. "It is our duty. There is no higher calling for us than the defeat of the fallen."

Wei Li's voice softened. "We will do everything we can to make sure Brother Famine's sacrifice was not in vain."

"I know you will. Good luck fixing this one. For most, those would be mortal wounds."

"I am aware. Hopefully the doctor can fix him."

Ursula bent and scooped broad, furry arms under Rohan's torso and knees. She lifted him like a groom carrying his bride across a threshold.

"Guys, I'm embarrassed. This is embarrassing. People will see me like this. I'm the one who does the carrying."

Wei Li nodded. "You are correct. People *will* see. We need to disguise you." She walked to the back of the room and rummaged through some boxes of old clothing they had picked up the previous day.

"That's not what I was saying. You hear me, don't you, Ursula?"

"Hush, Rohan. I carried my sons many times, in just this way. Exactly like this. And they were all for growing into fine warriors, unharmed."

"You carried them like this as adults?"

She barked a quick laugh. "Of course not, Rohan. You silly man."

He lay back in her arms, defeated.

Wei Li returned with a loose, poncho-type garment; she threw it over him. "We should hurry."

Ursula hefted the sagging Hybrid. "I am ready."

Rohan winced with the motion. "Gentle, ladies. Gentle. That hurts."

Wei Li pulled her hood down and held the door open for Ursula.

The hall outside was louder than normal, echoing sounds of distant foot traffic.

Wei Li waved. "Come. This way."

They moved swiftly, turning a dark corner and climbing a short flight of stairs to reach a back alleyway that Rohan would have never found without guidance.

Three times, Wei Li waved them into a side hall or up a random staircase to wait out a group of passersby.

Ursula whispered to her, "Is this for truly needful?"

Wei Li nodded. "These groups are not simply walking the halls on their way to work or to get food. They are anxious, angry, and greedy. I suspect they are actively looking for us."

"Ah. Good thing we are for hiding, then."

"Yes."

Rohan, head dangling over Ursula's arm, stared at the graffiti-covered wall.

"What a strange place to die. This reminds me of New York. I haven't been back there in so long."

Wei Li put a finger over his lips. "Shh. Lower your voice, Rohan."

"I'm actually surprised I've lived this long. That day Hyperion died, I was sure I was going to die as well."

Ursula looked down at him. "Who is this Hyperion about whom I am always for hearing?"

Rohan struggled to keep his voice lowered. "He was the strongest Hybrid that Earth ever produced. He was my mentor. My friend. The greatest warrior I've ever known. Did I tell you I was on the planet when he died?"

"No, Rohan, I was not for knowing that. Please stay quiet."

He whispered. So softly, he wasn't sure anyone could hear. "I should have died there, instead of him. Everyone would have been so much better off with him around. Much better."

Wei Li waved them out of the alcove. "They have passed. Let's go."

Rohan lost consciousness as she jostled her way back into the alley.

When he woke again, the three of them, representing three vastly different species, faced the doctor's unmarked door.

Wei Li rang the chime.

A voice carried through the door. "Go away."

"Dr. Magdalena, your patient is having difficulties."

The door slid open, revealing the tall Shayjh. "You promised you'd never come back here."

"And yet."

"No excuse? No long-winded speech about saving the children?"

"Doctor, you are obviously already aware of anything I might convey with such a speech. I told you I would do my best to stay away. I did so. If I had any plausible alternatives to a return, I would have availed myself of them."

"I really don't want him here."

"I understand and appreciate that. I am not pleased that circumstance has led me to this, but it has."

"You're going to have to try harder to stay away."

"I will. For now, I really have no safe alternatives. If I have to choose between breaking a promise and accepting the destruction of this station, I am not so fond of my honor."

Dr. Magdalena stood blocking the door for a long moment. She inhaled deeply from a small pipe and blew smoke up at the roof.

"You're not going to go away, are you."

Rohan snapped to attention. "What's up, Doc? Oh, look, I'm a bunny. Don't hate me, I'm drawn this way."

Wei Li shook her head. "We will not. Cannot. And, since there is a substantial reward for our capture, we should soon see groups of belligerent people coming this way to take us. I certainly hope you are not caught up in the ensuing violence."

"That's a nasty threat."

"It is merely an observation."

Another cloud of smoke.

"Bring him inside. Wouldn't do my reputation any good to have my client die so soon after surgery."

Rohan giggled as they placed him on the doctor's table.

"Stop tickling me. You guys are funny."

Maggie shook her head. "He's delirious. Not a positive sign. Hold him down."

Ursula's paws pressed onto Rohan's upper chest and the top of his pelvis.

"Wait where are you sticking that—"

He quickly became too busy screaming to finish his sentence.

"He's a loud one, isn't he?"

"He has been doing quite well, considering the amount of pain he is suffering and the fact that we have offered him almost no methods for coping with it. He ought to be commended."

"What are you, his lover? What do you care?"

"By the Thirteen, no. He's a mammal. But he is a friend."

"I can't see—hey, pour some booze over that area. Good. Now towel away the blood. Don't press so hard. Blot it. Better. Oh my. I see it now."

Ursula looked at the slender woman. "Can you for helping him?"

"He tore loose some of the stitching. Too strong for his own good, I think. I'll sew him back up with better thread. Then try to keep him from moving around for at least twenty-four hours so things can close up better."

Wei Li looked at her. "Will you keep him here?"

"Are you kidding? You just told me people are looking for him. This place isn't safe. Locals are bound to come through here to see if I've got anybody hidden away."

"I did not realize. We will leave as soon as it is safe to move him."

"It won't be safe. It will just be saf*er*."

"Do you believe he will survive?"

The doctor shrugged. "If the Progenitors will it."

Rohan laughed softly. "I can't think of any reason they'd want me alive."

"Nor can I. However, the will of the Progenitors is nothing if not mysterious."

"Just out of curiosity, are any of them around? Like, do they hang out at Pop's House of Breakfast and dole out advice or anything? We could ask them what their will is."

She ran a needle through something soft inside him. "My people have not seen or heard from a Progenitor in untold millennia. Is that unusual? I believe there are many species who swear on absent gods."

"Oh yeah, there are plenty. I do it myself. I was just making conversation."

"You can stop that now. Remember, I have no love for your kind. I am already quite ambivalent about your recovery. Don't push me the other way."

"Ah."

Ursula sighed. "Please be forgiving him for his silly words, Doctor. We are very much needing him to stay alive."

"I said I'd save him, and I will. Now, blot again. Right there."

⬗ ⋯ ⬖

"Are you sure you don't want me to take away his pain? No extra charge."

Wei Li sighed. "Thank you, Doctor, but no. I believe the risk of that procedure is too large."

Rohan looked up from his place in Ursula's arms. "What procedure? Take away my pain? I passed out for that discussion. Why wouldn't we do that?"

Wei Li responded. "Dr. Magdalena suggested severing your spinal cord to prevent pain signals from reaching your brain. This would have the added benefit of immobilizing you with little to no continued effort on our part."

"Oh. That sounds like it would work."

"Yes. The question is, how confident are you that your body would recover from such an injury?"

"Not very. I see your point."

"Yes. We can experiment with massive disruptions to your nervous system at another time, when physical conflict is not quite so immanent."

"Sounds great."

"At the moment, our task is to return safely to the warehouse. Please be quiet, Rohan."

He ran his fingers across his lips, 'zipping' his mouth shut, and stifled a giggle. *Still a bit delirious! Don't think that was actually funny.*

"Let's go. Slower than before, so as not to reopen his wounds." Ursula nodded her understanding. Wei Li lowered her hood and led them into the hall.

Rohan had to suppress more giggles as they crept through the hall, his body sagging into the arms of a four-hundred-kilogram bear. The image they painted in his mind was ludicrous.

Rohan was barely half-conscious as they traveled up a long corridor, down a flight of stairs, across a long-abandoned apartment with front and back doors long stolen off torn hinges, up more stairs, down another corridor, turn and again.

Wei Li stopped short, holding up a single fist.

Boisterous voices echoed from a spot down the hall. Seconds later, answering calls came from the other direction.

"In here." Wei Li ushered Ursula into a shallow alcove.

The larger woman whispered. "They will be seeing me in here."

"I am aware. There is no place to hide. We were herded into this spot."

Rohan startled into full wakefulness. "What's going on?"

"We are cornered."

"Let me up. I'll fight them. Make them regret their life choices. Make them regret their own births."

"You will do no such thing. First, because you can barely stand. Second, because if you tried you would reopen your wounds."

"I'll scare them off. You'll see, I can be terrifying. I'll bleed all over them."

"Hush. Ursula, hold him still. I am still the chief of security for this station. A band of hooligans will not present an issue."

Seconds later, a group of four lavender-skinned Kratics came running around the corner, skidding to a halt in front of Wei Li.

"See, see! I told you I saw them! I told you!"

The Kratic next to him patted the smaller man on the back. "You did good, boy. Did good. We've got them cornered."

Three green-skinned Lukhor ran in from the other direction, their antennae trembling as they slid to a stop.

The seven were young, dressed in short sleeves and midriff-baring shirts, round muscles carefully cultivated in gyms under the influence of synthetic androgens swelling between every joint.

Wei Li stepped into the hallway. "We wish only to pass."

The largest Kratic grinned. "Sorry, darling. We wish only for immortality. And for that, we need to take that guy right there with us."

The shorter one next to him furiously patted his shoulder.

The large Kratic nodded. "We don't need you, though, darling. You and the Ursan are free to walk away."

"That is not acceptable."

He punched one fist into his open palm with a resounding smack. "Have it your way, darling."

Wei Li half-turned to face the Lukhor behind her, then coiled back toward the Kratic. With the speed of a striking cobra, she launched herself toward him, her left foot whistling through the air as it hurtled up into his crotch.

The big man dropped both hands to catch a kick that never arrived. Wei Li landed and punched the heavy layer of scales across her knuckles into his exposed throat.

As the Kratic dropped to the floor, gagging and clutching his ruined windpipe, she pivoted to her right and crashed her fists into the smaller one's temple.

Without sparing a glance at the falling boy, Wei Li danced to a spot between the last two Kratics. They launched meaty fists her way, and she dropped to the ground, folding nearly in half so their punches sailed well clear of her body, each landing solidly on the other.

The two Kratics fell, stunned by their own strikes, and Wei Li spun to a tall standing position, facing the three Lukhor.

In unison, the three drew black sticks, each as long as their forearms, and took fighting positions.

Wei Li ducked her head, raising an elbow behind her and cracking an approaching Kratic directly on the chin. He fell to the ground with a heavy thump.

The lead Lukhor nodded and rushed forward.

Wei Li stood, relaxed, waiting for him to close. When he reached a point just a few steps away, she seemed to disappear, moving toward him with shockingly sudden speed.

One stick caught her in the shoulder; she pivoted with the blow, rotating into a hook that cracked the man's jaw and sent him reeling.

The other Lukhor closed more cautiously, sticks weaving alternating patterns in the air, forming a defensive barrier.

Wei Li hopped toward the one on the left, then stepped toward the right, then ducked and ran full tilt back to the left. She passed directly in front of the Lukhor, sticks shrieking through the air behind her.

The reptilian woman jumped, planting both feet on the wall in front of her, chest-high, and pushed herself off and over the Lukhor.

With outstretched fists, she met the far Lukhor. He caught the full brunt of her momentum with his face and went down.

One remained.

She stalked him, feinting one punch, then another, watching him twitch and react, as the confident expression bled out of his face.

She flipped the back of her fist toward his forehead; when the sticks came up to block, she kicked him solidly in the groin, then skipped to the side and kicked him again behind the knee.

He went down.

She spun around to his back and caught his head, one hand under his jaw, the other over the top of his skull.

He dropped the sticks.

"Okay! All right! You can go. You've got us. Gods, you're quick."

"I am not ready to go yet, little man."

His face faded from green to a dark yellow as his antennae drooped in dejection. "What do you want? You want us to report to security? Fine, we will. They can jail us. Whatever you want. Just let us go."

"I have a task for you. All seven of you." She tapped a spot on his forehead, then another on his neck; his lower body spasmed and jerked. He let out a short scream.

"What was that? What did you do?"

"Did you know that your vital energy flows through very specific channels in your body? I am an empath. I can *see* those channels. And if I touch you in certain, very-specific spots, I can disrupt the flow of that energy."

"Ow. Oh, Gods, that hurts. What? Why are you doing that?"

"Energy, you understand, can neither be created nor destroyed. If its path is blocked, it will build in place, having no natural release."

"Then . . . then what happens?"

"At some point, the energy can no longer be contained. You will die."

"What? When? Why?"

"The timing varies. It might be tomorrow; it might be in three days."

"Don't do that! Fix me! Unblock it! Please! I'm sorry, I'll never bother you again!"

She released him and stepped over to the second Lukhor.

"Wait! Don't! Please!"

She tapped the unconscious body. "It is still possible to release the blocks. As long as someone knows exactly how to do so. Should a mistake be made, immediate death is likely."

"What do you want from us? We'll do it. Anything."

"I want you and your friends to travel to the far corners of this station and tell anybody else looking for us that you have recently seen us lurking about. Everywhere but on this arm."

"Yeah, sure. We can do that. Sure. Just . . . take away whatever you just did!"

"I will meet you in twenty-four hours. By the kebab stand on block Seventy-Nine. Do you know it?"

"Of course, sure. The kebab stand. You'll fix us?"

"I will. But I can only do so if I remain free for the next twenty-four hours. So do your very best to distract and delay anybody who might see fit to interfere with that freedom."

"We will! We'll get them away from here. I swear it."

The other downed hooligans were stirring, rubbing sore jaws and bruised skulls.

"Twenty-four hours. I will release the blocks. And remember, if anybody attempts to do so who is not as skilled as I am, you will likely die. It will not be fast, or painless, but it will be certain."

"I get it! I do! I'm sorry, we'll go. Right now." He scrambled to pull another Lukhor to his feet.

"Now, run."

Wei Li turned to Ursula and nodded. The trio walked calmly away from the hallway.

Only after they turned two corners and climbed a level did Wei Li rub her shoulder.

"Will they really be for dying?"

Wei Li chuckled. "The death touch? It's a myth. Surprisingly, one I have noticed present in a number of unrelated cultures."

The larger woman barked out a quick laugh. "What were you doing to them for reality?"

"I hit pressure points. Nerve junctions that are acutely sensitive. The results are extremely painful, but will not result in any sort of delayed injury."

"You were for being very believable in your threats, Wei Li. You, too, would make for a fine War Chief."

Rohan chuckled. "I'd be happy to pass the torch. Just say the word."

Wei Li shook her head. "That would represent a conflict of interests. Regardless, I appreciate the offer."

They continued on the path back to the warehouse.

22

Who's the Boss?

"Please just wake him, I'm on another line." *Can't remember hearing Wei Li sound that tired.*

"I'm not touching him. You wake him." Sister Famine's tone had grown ever closer to that of an adolescent.

"Sister Famine. Please. Restrain your feelings." Mother Famine's tone had matched, shifting into that of stern-parent-at-her-wits'-end.

A grunt and shuffling footsteps.

"I will for waking him."

Sister Famine's voice. "I'm sorry, Ursula. I should have done it. Even if he is disgusting. I know you're tired."

"Is for nothing. I cannot rest, with everything . . ."

Her furry paw rested on his chest. "Wake up, Rohan. Your communicator is for pinging at you."

Light poured in through the widening slit under his eyelid. "I was sleeping. Isn't that my job right now?"

"Yes, you were for sleeping like cub full of fresh milk, but you must for answering your comm, please."

"Is that what's making that noise? I'm getting it. Rudra save me, I was really out of it." He tapped behind his ear. "Rohan here."

Wei Li was in the room already, and he wasn't sure who else might have a unit entangled with theirs.

"It's Tollan."

Rohan nodded and spoke to the room. "It's Tollan, guys. He's talking to me."

Wei Li grunted. "What about?"

"Great question. Tollan, what's this about?"

"You sound strange."

"Sorry. Just waking up."

"You have time for naps with everything that's going on?"

"I've had a small altercation with an angry vampire, and the aftertaste is exhausting. Now that I'm up, what can I do for you? Are there updates on doing something about Wistful's governor?"

"No, I've actually been working on . . . other projects. This is separate." The engineer hesitated.

"I'm all ears."

"The il'Drach warships attacked the station."

"Yes, I remember. What was that, a week ago?"

"It was yesterday."

Rohan ran his hand through his hair. "That's what I meant. Yesterday. Sorry, this near-death thing has me disoriented."

"Wistful deflected most of the il'Drach projectiles, but not all of them. One penetrated her hull close to my location."

"Are you okay?"

"Yes, of course. I'm well protected. The projectile wasn't sent here to injure anyone."

Ursula and the Pledged, unable to hear the voice coming through Rohan's earpiece, were watching him with questioning eyes. "Let me paraphrase what I think you're saying. They sent a ten-kilo sharpened stake halfway across the system so as not to injure anyone."

"I don't think Wistful noticed, but the claw had a payload."

"What kind of payload? Is this a bomb thing? I am so not in the mood for a bomb. Just cut the blue wire."

"The claw held a secure communication device. It wasn't easy to figure out, but it's connected to one of those ships. *Father's Vengeance*."

"That's interesting. Are they talking?"

"They are. They want to talk to you."

"Oh. Wait, do you mean they asked for me by name?"

"They asked for The Griffin."

My il'Drach Fleet codename. Which nobody here is supposed to know. "Hm. And you called me because . . ."

"You definitely don't have time to be playing that game with me. I don't care who you were or what you did for the il'Drach Fleet. I care about keeping this station in one piece, and you're part of that puzzle."

"Gotcha. How long have you known?"

"I can't remember. Like I said, I don't particularly care."

"And it's not important. You're right. I'm still fuzzy-headed. How can I talk to the ship? Can you, I don't know, transfer the call?"

"I can route it through this channel. Is that okay? Anybody else with a chip entangled to this set will hear."

"Who else is that? Wei Li? That's fine. Anybody else?"

"I gave the Professors Stone one."

"That's fine, I don't have many secrets from them." *Or from most other people, it seems.* "Put her through."

A pause, some static, another pause, then a faint hiss.

"Griffin." The voice belonged to *Father's Vengeance.*

"I'm pretty sure I asked you to call me Rohan."

"You . . . you did. I apologize. I will not repeat the error." *What?*

"Not what I expected. Apology accepted. What can I do for you?"

"We would like an update on your progress with the soul eater. We expected you to have eliminated him by now."

"And I would like an explanation for your unprovoked attack on Wistful, an independent station with whom you have a peace treaty. Isn't this great, all of us communicating our wants and needs? Like couples therapy. So I hear. From friends."

"We acted under orders."

"Implying there is somebody around who outranks you."

"That is how orders generally work."

"It's a battle of wits we're in, is it? I'm not sure I'm up for that particular challenge right now."

Wei Li coughed. She had entered the channel at some point.

Rohan continued. "Never mind that. Can you tell me who in the system is the ranking il'Drach officer?"

"Admiral Fleck."

"Fleck. Fleck. I know him. Four arms?"

"Yes, Admiral Fleck is a member of one of the six-limbed species."

"I remember him. Why were you ordered to attack the station, though? It doesn't make any sense."

"I was not offered an explanation."

"Ah. Did you agree with the orders?"

"You have clearly been retired for too long. Your brain has gotten soft."

"It hasn't been that long. I know you have to follow orders, but that doesn't mean you have to like them."

A pause.

"I do not believe any of the ships with whom I have communicated *agreed* with the orders given. For the reasons you have explained. Now will you tell me why you haven't dealt with the soul eater yet?"

If I admit ar'Tahul's stronger than me, they'll just destroy the station. Need something else.

"He has hostages. Some kind of pheromonal control over two thousand asylum seekers. We're working on a counteragent."

"You're no chemist."

"No, but Professor Ben Stone is a xenobiologist with a full lab here. His wife is helping out, too. You've heard of them, I assume? Seeing as they're two of the top minds in the Empire."

"They are actively pursuing a counteragent? Is there a prospective timetable for its completion?"

Another person entered the conversation. "This is Ben Stone. We might need another two days, but we're making great progress."

"Professor Stone. Greetings."

"Sorry to interrupt."

"Your input is always valued. Two days, you say?"

"Yes. We've got the protein sequence and folding figured out; it's about manufacturing speed and delivery vehicle fabrication. Those are known quantities."

"Very good."

Rohan cleared his throat. "Will you be getting any more weird orders in the next two days?"

"I cannot tell."

"Can you at least give us some notice if you do?"

"That is my intention. Unless I am ordered to silence, I will tell you over this channel."

Rohan sighed and looked at Wei Li. She shrugged, having nothing to add.

"All right, *Father's Vengeance*. We'll keep you updated if anything changes on the station."

"Thank you. *Father's Vengeance* out."

A click; silence.

Rohan struggled upright, resting to catch his breath once he was sitting against the wall behind his cot. He grazed cautious fingers over his wound, wincing at the ache under his bandages.

"Dr. Stone, you still on the line?"

"I am. We're actually coming to you now."

"Don't think that's a good idea . . . Wistful is probably watching you guys, waiting for use you to locate me."

Marion's voice broke in over her husband's. "I took care of that. We'll be there soon." Another click.

Wei Li rubbed her forehead. "I should trust Professor Stone to know what she is doing, shouldn't I? Someone please tell me not to worry about her."

Rohan laughed, wincing at the movement in his abdomen. "Don't worry about her. If she says she can hack Wistful's scanners, they're hacked. Remember, a year ago she sent us chasing after a phantom il'Drach warship so she could sneak off and open the first wormhole."

Wei Li slumped in her chair. "I do remember. I, this station's security chief, am in the uncomfortable position of not only encouraging but also requiring that various other people successfully violate Wistful's security measures."

"Aren't you always telling me that growth requires discomfort?"

"I do, but those aphorisms are for your benefit, not mine."

"Rudra save me, don't make me laugh. Do we have anything to stop this itching? I want to scratch a hole right through my belly."

Ursula sighed. "I can be finding something. I will go out. Also pick up food."

"Thanks, Ursula. I owe you."

"I am for wishing Professor Stone's two days did not feel as so long."

"I'm sorry, Ursula. We're trying, I promise."

She patted his shoulder, then shuffled out of the room.

Mother Famine looked at Wei Li. "What happened? We couldn't follow the conversation."

Wei Li filled her in.

The Pledged nodded. "Do you trust what the warship is telling you?"

All eyes turned to Rohan. "Oh, I'm the expert now?"

Wei Li nodded. "Unless you serve some other purpose of which I am unaware, yes. You are our il'Drach military expert."

He scratched his beard. "Her story makes sense. I'm sure those ships were reluctant to attack Wistful."

Sister Famine let out a harsh laugh. "You're not suggesting they are overcome by mercy or kindness, are you?"

"No, but they know Wistful has a treaty with the Empire. We—they—take that kind of thing seriously. Honor, keeping one's word, all of that."

"I see. Yet they *did* attack."

"Sure. They take that stuff seriously, but they take discipline even *more* seriously. And afterward they'd be chafing about it, hence . . . that call."

Wei Li looked up from her tablet. "The Ch'doon are in serious condition in Medical."

"What? From the other day?"

Wei Li shook her head. "These are fresh injuries. They were found near the station core, badly hurt, by security personnel on a routine sweep. They are so far refusing to discuss what happened."

"Were they hurt by claws? During the il'Drach attack?"

Wei Li looked down again, swiping the screen for more information. "That does not seem likely, given the types of injuries. This shall be another mystery."

Rohan sighed. "You know what? Right now, I don't care about the Ch'doon. I'm officially turning my brain off and not pondering that one. I just want to watch the next episode of *Swords of Lukhor* and heal."

Mother Famine nodded, stood, and moved to sit next to him on the cot. "Actually, now that you're awake, we should return to your meditation practice."

He sighed.

"I probably should." He settled back and closed his eyes.

Time passed.

"I think I'm starting to get the hang of this."

Wei Li laughed. Rohan looked into the vampire's eyes. "I'm doing great, right?"

"You are . . . improving. Definitely."

"That means great, right? I almost have it perfect?"

"You are better than you were, certainly. Absolutely."

He looked at Wei Li. "You can tell, right, Miss Class Four Empath? My aura must be smooth as glass." She shrugged, a smile on her cheeks.

He sighed, cast a longing glance toward the wall-sized screen, and shook his head. "Fine. I suppose I could use a little more practice."

⬦ ⬦ ⬦

Rohan stared at the cylinder from his spot on the ragged couch.

It perched on the low table between two disposable cups and an empty, grease-stained carton from a nearby fritter stand. Metallic and about the size of the lunchbox he'd carried to elementary school, the outside shiny and unmarked.

Ben Stone sat at the very edge of the chair he'd pulled to a spot across the table. "Nondescript, I know. But it didn't seem prudent to take the time to fancy it up."

Rohan scratched his beard. "I thought you told *Father's Vengeance* that it would take two more days to finish this."

Ben smiled tightly. "Did I? You know, as one gets older, the memory begins to fade a bit . . ."

Marion playfully slapped his shoulder. "Your memory is fine." She turned to Rohan. "We never tell the il'Drach everything we know. On principle. It was one of Hyperion's rules."

Rohan nodded. "Good idea. I'm just surprised they haven't caught on."

"They know. At least, some of them do. As long as we're generally valuable, they let us get away with it."

Rohan touched the cylinder. "How does this thing work?"

Ben nodded and pointed to it. "Type a code into that panel on the end there. Sixty seconds later, it will burst, dispersing an aerosol containing the pheromone-receptor binding agent. It will settle to the ground, eventually, but there should be enough there to cover the arena."

Ursula sat next to Rohan, her own gaze also fixed on the device.

"You are for sure it will be working?"

Ben shrugged his shoulders. "It should. I mean, we can never be sure—"

His wife put a hand over his and interrupted. "It will work. He checked and double-checked; I triple-checked. It's as close to a sure thing as you're going to find."

Ursula nodded and looked from the device to Rohan. "When can we be for using this? I am sick inside for thinking of my people enslaved by the vampire."

Rohan rubbed his bandage lightly, wishing it did more to quell the itching. "I'm not sure, Ursula."

Her eyes widened as she looked around the room, seeking eye contact with any of the others. "What does this mean? What is he for meaning? Why not?"

Rohan looked at Wei Li, silently pleading with her to answer the question. She nodded.

"Ursula, we can't do it now. You know we can't."

"Begin explaining yourself, Wei Li."

"Ursula, you are my friend, and you are upset. Justifiably so, given the situation your people are in currently. You need to consider the situation more objectively."

The big woman stood, her head reaching a full two meters above the floor, and bared sharp teeth in an expression that was very much not a smile. "I am not for being in the mood for your objectivity."

"If we set them free right now, with no other plan, what will happen? It is *possible* ar'Tahul will simply let them go. Do you think it's *likely*?"

Ursula growled an incomprehensible response.

"We need a way to neutralize the vampire at the same time that we free the Ursans from his control. Otherwise, he might simply turn the situation into another kind of bloodbath."

Rohan nodded. "They can't fight him, even if they got freed from the pheromones. I need some more time for this hole to close up before I can do anything."

Ursula looked down at him, her body dwarfing his. "Should we be waiting for you? What will you do, even after hole has closed, Tow Chief Rohan? You did not defeat him last time, and you were uninjured at the beginning of that. Please for telling me, what will be different next time?"

Wei Li coughed. "You did not fight well, Rohan."

"He's strong, Wei Li. Really strong."

"I am aware. Yet you did not fight to your potential."

"What are you saying?"

The others were silent.

Wei Li continued. "I am not accusing you of deliberately failing. I understand you wanted to defeat the soul eater. However, I have seen you fight with commitment, and your performance in the arena was not the same."

Rohan opened his mouth, ready to answer, but paused. *I'm getting angry.* He let out a long, slow breath; held his lungs empty until the burn became uncomfortable.

"I don't want to be an assassin. Maybe my heart wasn't in just going out and killing the guy."

Ursula shook her massive head. "He is for feeding on my people. Your friends. I have seen you kill before. Why not for us?"

"I know, I'm sorry. It's hard to explain."

She fixed him in a hard gaze. "Try."

"He has fifty thousand years of history locked up in his head. He knows so many things about where we came from, why we came to be this way. Why *I* came to be this way—I mean all the il'Drach, Hybrids included. I can't stand the thought of just ending that."

"This matters to you for more than the lives of your friends?"

"No, not more. Just . . . it matters *also*. It's not always the thing to just go out and kill your enemies. Sometimes, if you help them, you can get a better outcome."

"Help how?"

"I want to cure him. Take away the hunger, the damage. Then maybe we can talk to him, understand what happened to his people. To our people. There is so much we don't know."

Ben leaned forward in his chair. "I hear you, Rohan. I'd love to interview him myself. But how?"

Rohan looked at Marion. Her blue eyes were cold. "I've been looking for any references to a cure. There are plenty, but all involve killing every existing vampire so the disease itself is eliminated."

Rohan looked at the Pledged. "Please don't tell me it's hopeless. You guys must know something."

Mother Famine shook her head. "We have never found a cure. Other than death, as Professor Stone suggested."

Sister Famine opened her mouth; closed it; opened it again. "We *have* been looking. That's the only reason we're even on this station."

Ben turned to her. "What do you mean? What's on Wistful?"

Sister Famine bit her lower lip and cast a quick glance at Mother Famine, who simply looked back. "There's a scientist here. Someone who's been involved with research forbidden by the il'Drach. We paid her to develop a cure."

Rohan looked around. "And we're first hearing about this now?"

Mother Famine shook her head. "She did not do the job. She told us she had failed and refused to pursue the project any further. We've been hoping to change her mind. Perhaps secure additional funds to motivate her."

Marion Stone leaned in. "Did she say why she stopped? What the roadblock was? Maybe we could work with her. Together . . . who knows?"

Another headshake from the older of the two vampires. "She would not explain her refusal, but she was most insistent. I did not understand it and still do not."

Marion tapped her hand on the table. "Is it about money? Or lab facilities? We could probably accommodate her with either."

"You're talking about the facilities on your ship?"

"Yes. She's a science vessel, kitted out for deep-space exploration. Her labs are extensive."

"Is she not il'Drach?"

"Yes, technically."

"This scientist is unlikely to want to cooperate with you. She has very strong feelings against the Empire."

Rohan cleared his throat. "The situation has changed, though, hasn't it? The embargo, the threatened destruction of the station. This isn't just a job for pay anymore. This result could save her life, along with everyone else on board."

Mother Famine paused, then nodded. "It's possible."

"We have to at least try to talk to her, don't we?"

Ursula nodded. "Yes. If we can be curing this vampire, then that we must be doing."

Rohan sighed. "So, we're agreed. Now, who is this scientist and where can we find her?"

Mother and Sister Famine traded another look. Sister Famine answered. "She is a Shayjh scientist. From a minority sect of those people. I am sorry, I do not know her full name; we call her Dr. Magdalena."

23

Daddy Issues

"Growing up, we always made fun of white people for considering mayonnaise a sauce, but I don't anymore. This stuff is delicious." Rohan sighed as he chewed a mouthful of food.

Ben laughed. "Is that actually mayonnaise?"

Rohan nodded and spoke through a half-full mouth. "Same recipe, basically. The eggs aren't from chickens, and the acid isn't from lemons, but you know. They season it, of course. We aren't barbarians."

"No, of course not. Can't imagine anyone eating something with unseasoned mayonnaise on it."

Rohan swallowed. "It's just kicked up with some heat. Honestly, it tastes a lot like the spicy mayo sauce you'd get in any corner sushi place back home."

"Let me try it." Ben dug a spoon into the bowl, scooping up a mouthful of the mixture. "That's not bad. I'm taking some for myself."

"Thin slices of raw fish, tossed with the mayo, scooped over some pickled seaweed. It's the one thing Ursula remembers to get for the rest of us when she buys buckets of whole fish to eat."

"I was going to bring donuts, you know, but I thought we should get you the canister as quickly as possible."

Rohan waved and nodded. "That's a better idea. Not that I don't love your donuts. Still, priorities."

"Exactly."

"Any adventures getting the pheromone blocker made?"

Ben shook his head, bushy eyebrows wiggling with the motion. "Nothing worth mentioning. Had to call in a few favors, but we've done plenty of favors for people over the years. No harm cashing in some of them."

"Thanks." He moaned while chewing another mouthful of fish.

"You were hungry!"

"Ever since my stomach healed, I've been starving. Desperate for protein, I guess. My body fixing itself."

"Ah, the miracle of the battle glands."

"The battle what-now?" Rohan had never heard the term.

"When Hyperion was young, he didn't really understand where his Power came from. His father was significantly less involved in raising him than yours."

"I think I knew that."

"He had us do a lot of research on his body. We eventually figured out that he wasn't flying or throwing tanks around the battlefield because of any biological abnormality, but in the meantime we did find out a lot about the physiological differences between him and a human."

"Hm. Like these battle glands?"

Ben chuckled softly. "He wanted us to call them that, and we weren't going to argue. They're right along the spine. They lie dormant most of the time, but can pump out a remarkable supply of stem cells when needed. Along with a significant hit of stimulants and painkillers."

"Sounds useful."

"It's part of why you can heal so quickly even with your Power suppressed. It's a purely physical mechanism."

"It must be something the il'Drach have, too, right? I mean, my genetics are all from either il'Drach or humans."

"Of course. You have different muscle fibers, too. More like a chimpanzee. Kilo for kilo, even without your Power you're far stronger than a human."

"Also useful. Remind me why all humans don't have battle glands and chimpy biceps?"

"It costs energy to maintain those organs. In our evolutionary past, the benefit would have been outweighed by that cost. But for a species designed for warfare . . ."

"You're saying the il'Drach were designed? They didn't just . . . evolve?"

Ben scanned the room in a mimicry of paranoia. "Yes. I wouldn't call that common knowledge. The il'Drach don't accept medical care or examinations from people like me, so the biology textbooks don't have much about them. However, the med staff at Fleet has dealt with enough Hybrids to infer a lot about the il'Drach themselves."

"I never really thought about it."

"No. Speaking of the il'Drach, have you heard from you-know-who?"

"Dad? Not for a hot minute. He told me he gave up on recruiting ar'Tahul; instead, he's going to try to take over Wistful."

"Does that worry you more or less?"

"I wish I knew. There's so much to think about that I don't know where to start."

"Beyond the obvious?"

Rohan rubbed his hands over his head. "Did you know a man gave his life to save mine just a couple of days ago?"

Ben chewed and swallowed another mouthful of the fish. "I heard. Not to be cliché, but how does that make you feel?"

"I don't know how to feel. I'm not sure that's ever happened before."

"Kid Lightning tried last year."

"He threw himself into a fight he might not survive to save us all. And to kill a giant shark that was going to ravage the country. Brother Famine literally gave his life so I, personally, would have a chance to escape. That's a lot to take in."

Ben reached over and patted the younger man's knee. "You're usually the one putting your life at risk for the sake of others, aren't you? Not used to the turnaround."

"It's not the same, though. I don't usually face certain-death to help other people. At most, it's certain-pain. Maybe even certain-discomfort."

"A certainly-torn-shirt."

They both laughed and ate, Rohan sipping carefully from a cup of beer.

"il'Drach physiology or not, I'm amazed that you're able to sit up."

"The doc put in a lattice where all my tissues are supposed to be so the cells know where to grow. She basically rebuilt me from the inside out. Now it's just a matter of letting living tissue replace, and eventually digest, that structure."

"Impressive, considering the lack of real medical facilities."

"Yeah, she's a genius, all right. I can feel it healing. Itches like crazy."

"Can I get you anything to help?"

"Some more food, please. I'm still not so good with the standing and walking."

"Give me a sec."

Rohan leaned back gingerly and slowed his breathing. Dr. Stone returned moments later with two full bowls of fish.

"Here you go. Take in as much protein as you can handle."

"That's my standard operating procedure."

Ben took his seat, and they ate.

"I thought you'd want to know, *Insatiable* has been talking to *Void's Shadow*."

"Is that safe?"

"They set up some kind of schedule for tightbeam direct transmissions. As long as no il'Drach ship actually sits directly on the path of the signal, they won't be detected."

"Is she okay?"

"*Void's Shadow* is doing great. She was scared at first, as you can imagine, but she's been a trooper. Lately, she's been playing games with the il'Drach, flying closer and closer, daring them to find her."

Rohan sighed. "That's not smart."

"*Insatiable* told her the same thing. I think she's cooled it a bit, but they developed an idea for you."

"What kind of idea?"

"They say she can get you off Wistful."

"Oh. Hm. How? I mean, if she gets too close, won't they notice the big black shadow against the station?"

"The il'Drach ships aren't staying nearby. In fact, they're positioned even farther out after the big fight the other day. They worked out the angles together; she can get within a few clicks without being spotted."

"Then what?"

"Once she's in position, you get into an airlock. Power up and fly outside. ar'Tahul will notice, but he's not going to be able to stop you from leaving the ship. The il'Drach might sense your Power, but you can zip over to *Void's Shadow*, into a hatch, and be cloaked before they can respond."

"That sounds great. She has a regen tank on board; I can fix all the remaining damage in a few hours. Except you waited until now to tell me, so there must be a catch. What is it?"

"The catch is that it's a one-time offer. Once she does it, the il'Drach will know there's a stealth ship insystem, and they'll be pissed about it. *Insatiable* thinks they'll deploy a massive active sensor array. *Void's Shadow* will be forced to leave Toth system."

"So, she's offering me a one-way ticket out of here."

"More or less. At most, a single round-trip. She could bring you back, drop you off, then run. You'd have to fight your way back to Wistful. We might be able to make that happen. But you won't be able to come and go as you please."

Rohan set his bowl down and ran his hand through his hair. "It's sweet that she's thinking of me, but she could get a few other people to safety instead. Anyone who could fit into a spacesuit."

"Who'd you have in mind?"

Rohan sighed. "You know who I have in mind. Which isn't rational in any way, is it?"

"Tamara? Your lady friend? Have you even seen her in the last year?"

"I've seen her. As in, from across the boulevard, no eye contact. I've been training Rinth on-and-off in martial arts and meditation, though to be honest, I'm not sure if he really enjoys it or just feels sorry for me."

"I'm sure that's not true."

"No, you aren't."

"I'm trying to be nice. Don't fight me."

Rohan nodded. "I'd love to see her safe. Doesn't make a ton of sense, does it? If we could save any three or so people from Wistful, why choose one Lukhor family just because I was in love with the woman?"

Ben grunted. "Why not? If two million people are going to die in this insanity, why shouldn't she be the one to survive?"

Rohan shrugged. "Actually, I just had the most terrible great idea."

"You're not sending my wife away. Much as I want her to live."

"No, not Marion. I could send Dhruv away."

"Your— Why him?"

"Gets rid of two headaches. Remember, if he dies on this station and the il'Drach find out about it, we're all in trouble. Second, he's trying to take over Wistful."

"You think he will?"

"No, but I guarantee that whatever he tries to do, it will turn out to be a huge pain in the ass for me."

"You two have a complicated relationship, don't you?"

"Not so much. He's a huge nuisance. Not complicated at all."

"Would *Void's Shadow* even take anybody else? And would Dhruv go?"

"He wouldn't, not if he thinks he has something to gain by staying here. As for her, I think she'd do it if I asked her. You know ships and their captains. She's determined to be a proper warship. It's a moot point, really." He stuffed his mouth with fish.

Marion Stone carried a chair over to them, plopped it down, and sat with a sigh. She cracked her neck and stretched both arms overhead. "I'm not used to working around the clock like this."

Ben laughed. "Who are you trying to kid? You always work through the night when you get your teeth set on some project."

She shrugged. "What are you two whispering about over here?"

Rohan shook his head. "Not really whispering, just trying not to bother anybody. Just planning what to do next. Thinking of ways to send my father on a long walk through a short airlock."

She chuckled. "He's not so bad. I find him surprisingly charming. All things considered."

"That's because he's spent the better part of several hundred years study-ing how to charm women. It's his core skill set at this point."

Ben laughed. "One must admire the dedication."

Marion shook her head. "None of us must do anything. Anyway, how are you feeling?"

Rohan sighed. "Good as new in another day or so. I think."

"Marvelous. Then what?"

"Then we cure ar'Tahul, stick him someplace safe, and tell the il'Drach Fleet to leave us alone. It sounds so easy when I summarize it like that."

"About the cure . . ."

"I know, easier said than done."

"Much easier."

"Can you explain to me why it's so difficult?"

"I doubt it."

"Can you try? Use words you might use to explain to a monkey? A well-intentioned but slightly brain-damaged monkey that is hanging around your lab, asking annoying questions?"

She sighed. "I can try. The core problem is that vampirism is not a single-vector disease."

"Remember, I'm the dumb monkey. Simple words."

"There is a parasite, a very sophisticated one, that is at the root of the transformation. It takes over the host immune system, hijacks cellular RNA to assist in the transformation, and generally rebuilds the subject in a variety of ways to make them a better soul eater."

"So . . . space penicillin?"

"You do realize that just putting the word 'space' in front of another word doesn't magically create a new, fancier version of the thing you're thinking of, don't you?"

"I don't know. I thought it did. Space ship. Space prostitute."

Ben cleared his throat, noticing the flare of annoyance in his wife's eyes. "Rohan, focus."

"Sorry."

Marion continued. "There have been biological agents investigated that can damage the parasite. But that's not enough."

"Because of the other vector. See, I'm listening."

"Yes, the other vector. Along with the biological parasite comes a spiritual infection."

"You mean like possession?"

"This sort of thing is outside my area of expertise."

Ben nodded. "Outside mine as well."

She waved her hands. "The esoteric element protects the parasite, and the parasite drives the person to feed, and the feeding powers the esoteric element."

"So, if the person stops feeding . . ."

"That will help. But once the esoteric element is strengthened to a certain degree, nothing short of destroying the host body will completely get rid of the parasite."

"We can kill them, but not cure them."

"That's what all my sources are telling me."

Ben cleared his throat. "Bear in mind that our sources are not the most advanced in the sector when it comes to spiritual or metaphysical matters. There might be some way to interfere with that side of the disease that we simply haven't heard of."

Rohan scratched his beard with both hands. "I bet if anyone would have a way to approach that, it would be the Shayjh. Right? They're always going on about how advanced their spiritual tech is."

Marion nodded slowly. "The most useful lines of research have been forbidden by the il'Drach. If the Shayjh had been left independent over the last thousand years, they might have come up with a cure. As things stand, however . . ."

"Except some Shayjh aren't part of the Empire. They split off and did their own thing, forbidden or not."

Ben and Marion traded glances. "Is that who this Dr. Magdalena is?"

Rohan nodded. "She's the last survivor of Zahad. When I turn this story into a terrible pulp novel, I'm going to use that as the title."

Marion shook her head. "Spare us. You think she might have access to those forbidden technologies?"

"The Pledged must have thought so, given how much they apparently spent to get her to make a cure. Now I just have to convince her to finish it."

"What's the issue?"

"She wouldn't say. Let's hope I inherited some of my father's charm."

The three sat in silence, slowly finishing their food.

Wei Li and Ursula were on comms and screens, monitoring the civilian groups searching for them. Most of those were concentrating their efforts on the farther ends of the station. The Pledged were arguing quietly, Sister Famine stealing tight glances in Rohan's direction.

The conversations were interrupted by a chime at the door. Wei Li and Rohan made quick eye contact. She shrugged and stood to answer it.

A moment later, a familiar voice rang through the room. "Come over and lend a hand, already. Can't you see I'm injured? Show some respect to your elders."

Rohan looked at Ben. "Did we do that? Did we summon him? Speak of the devil and so forth?"

Ben shook his head. "I don't think that's how it works. Let me talk to him." The older man stood and crossed to the doorway.

Rohan sighed and leaned back against the wall. Marion looked at him with concern in her eyes. "Do you need us to keep him away from you?"

He shook his head. "Thanks, but I'll manage. I appreciate the thought."

Dhruv entered the room.

The il'Drach wore his typical dark suit, generously cut for comfort, buttons open at the cuffs and collar. Noru propped up his right shoulder, her lavender skin reduced to a washed-out pink, bandages covering her right arm. Sigrun propped up his left side, her face white and pale with strain.

Dhruv's left leg was heavily bandaged, and he hopped, keeping all his weight on the right.

"Come on, then. Get me to a chair. Can't you see I'm injured?"

Rohan resisted the urge to stand and cross to his father's side.

Wei Li faced the desk as the other women lowered Dhruv into a chair. "What happened?"

He shook his head, white teeth flashing in a broad smile. "This station has better security than I expected! No offense."

"Were you in some kind of altercation with my staff?"

"You mean security personnel? I doubt it. We tried to get into Wistful's brain. Not as easy as I hoped."

Wei Li looked at Noru, then at Sigrun. "Is he saying what I think he's saying?"

Noru nodded. "Myself, boss man, Sigrun, and all the Ch'doon borough boys took aim at quiet Wistful's positronic brain. To be hijacking her governor, you see."

"That was a very dangerous thing to try."

Dhruv snorted. "No risk, no reward, am I wrong? The Fleet attacked, big distraction, who was I to pass up that opportunity?"

Wei Li stared him down. "You could have passed it up and been a person with an intact leg and bodyguards who are not confined to the medical wing."

Dhruv smiled. "I like you. Don't worry, once I take over the station, you'll have a job with me. You've done right by Rohan, and I don't forget things like that."

"I feel very reassured." She didn't sound reassured. "Do you care to explain what happened?"

"I'll tell you what happened. Your old girl has some tricks left. We got close to the central core, easy as you could please. I had a handy little device to crack the seal and get us into the core, but there were some of those things in there. What did I call them, sweetie?" He looked at Sigrun.

She shivered as Ursula handed her a drink and a bowl of food. "Corpse soldiers." Another bowl went to Noru.

"Yes, that's right. Corpse soldiers. Who knew I'd find that here? Not the Shayjh type either. Big bastards. Strong. Tore right through my poor Ch'doon."

Rohan sighed. "One mystery solved."

Wei Li looked over the three injured people. "Did you make any headway with Wistful's governor?"

Dhruv shook his head. "Barely got to the brain. Nothing in there match-es the specs I was expecting. I'm going to need some more engineering help figuring out how to hack the governor. Also need a hand from someone who can fight off a half dozen supercharged corpse soldiers. Know any-one?" He stared at Rohan as he said it.

Rohan coughed softly. "Don't look at me. I can't even stand up."

"You've survived this long, you'll be fine in a day. Help me out."

Ben looked at the shorter, yet more intimidating, man. "Rohan is work-ing on a cure for ar'Tahul. Getting Wistful's situation squared away is a different project."

"Dr. Stone. All due respect, that's crap. You'll never secure the vampire while Wistful's working with him. The most important thing right now is to fix her brain. Without that, even if by some miracle you find a way to beat him in a fight, he'll just shadowstep to safety."

Ben shook his head. "If we can cure him, then his control over Wistful becomes moot. There's a lot of risk involved in playing around in any-body's brain, maybe especially a fifty-thousand-year-old artificial intelli-gence."

Dhruv waved a hand dismissively. "Bah. You don't get it. Curing vam-pirism? We haven't figured it out in all these years, now suddenly you'll have a scientific breakthrough because you need one? You two have been reading too many of your own comic books. Think you're four-color heroes."

Marion's cheeks flushed, and she stood, but Ben shook his head at her and waved her back to her seat.

"You're underestimating us, and you're underestimating Rohan. Which I guess shouldn't come as any kind of surprise."

"What's that supposed to mean?"

Rohan laughed. "This is cute. Waste of time, but cute."

Sigrun put her hand over her husband's shoulder. "Dear, this isn't the time. You need to take your pills."

He looked at her, the contrast of her pale skin against the dark fabric of his suit. "You're right. Letting myself get agitated. I'm too old for this." He looked up at Wei Li.

Rohan scratched his beard. "When do you intend to try this again?"

"Not sure yet. You know any clever engineers?"

24

Life During Wartime

Rohan rubbed sleep-crust out of his eyes and pushed himself to a seated position. Mother Famine, sitting close by, nodded to him and stood to bring water.

He took the bottle and drank. "Thank you. I feel like I've been sleeping for days."

"Half of one. Maybe a bit more. It's afternoon now."

"Shouldn't you be asleep?"

She smiled. "At my age, sleep is hard to come by, even at high noon."

He nodded. "Do you miss the sun? I don't know, is that a rude question?"

She shook her head softly, the red tattoos on her cheeks presenting a fierce counterpoint to gentle eyes. "I do miss the sun. It is on the long list of things I've lost, but not very near the top."

"Ah."

Wei Li walked over and handed him a paper-wrapped bundle. It was warm to the touch. "I only just returned; this is fresh."

"Thanks again. You guys are taking good care of me. I'm starting to feel guilty."

Wei Li nodded. "You can pay us back by getting this station back to normal."

"I'll try. Are you comfortable with Dhruv's plan to take over Wistful's governor?"

She shrugged. "It is a terrible plan that happens to be better than any alternatives I'm aware of. I have never been someone to let the perfect be the enemy of the acceptable."

"No, you haven't. Is that a cultural thing or just you?"

She shrugged, then winced as her tablet sounded an alarm.

"By the Three Faces." She leapt at the big wall screen, slapping a control to mute the stream. "Everyone quiet," she hissed.

Rohan looked at Mother Famine, who shrugged, then toward Ursula, who was standing from the couch, startled by the commotion.

Wei Li walked the perimeter of the room, finger over her lips, making eye contact with each person to be certain they had gotten her message.

Sister Famine was out of view, though Rohan suspected she was sleeping under some boxes in the back corner of the room. The Stones had gone back to *Insatiable* at some point. Dhruv sat leaning back far in his chair, injured leg propped up on the desk, eyes half-closed. Sigrun sat next to him, and Noru was on her feet, eyes focused on Wei Li, wicked blades in both of her hands.

A moment later, voices penetrated the wall from the hall outside.

"Seven, nine, eleven. Here, this is it. I told you this was a real place."

A second voice, deeper. "Nobody said it wasn't a real place, moron. What we said is that there ain't nobody there. Still, might as well check."

Third voice, growling and deeper still, like a Rogesh or a Ch'doon gargling gravel. "Move aside. I'll get the door."

A boom echoed through the warehouse as something pounded on the front door. The second voice spoke. "Open up! We need to look around. We promise not to hurt anybody or steal anything."

The first voice returned with a whine. "Not steal anything? Or hurt anybody? But isn't that why we're doing this? If we're not stealing anything, maybe I could go home."

Another thud sounded from the hall. Second Voice followed. "Shut up, you moron. Do you want them to open the door or not?"

"Hey, cut it out! Mom told you not to hit me anymore. It's not fair! I'm the one who heard they were here, and now you're hitting me before I even get to take anything."

Gravel Voice returned. "Both of you shut up." Another boom on the door.

Wei Li checked her screen and held up two hands, three fingers on one and four on the other.

Rohan leaned forward, centering his weight over his feet, and slowly stood. His guts didn't spill out onto the floor, but they didn't feel good either. He shook his head.

Wei Li looked at Ursula and Noru, both of whom stood at attention, their bodies thrumming with energy. Ready to fight.

The security officer tilted her head and closed her eyes.

Gravel Voice returned. "Who has the torch? We're going to have to cut through this door."

Another voice came from farther up the hall, too muffled for anyone inside to make out the words.

First Voice sounded through the door. "Let me. I've always wanted to use one of these things."

Gravel Voice sounded angry. "Get your brother under control. Let Jalas do it; he spent six months on a maintenance crew."

The muffled voice drew closer and became audible. "Good gig, too, until that bitch fired me. Inappropriate conduct, my balls."

"Can that thing really burn through metal?"

Second Voice again. "Of course. Locks break, right? Doors get stuck. What do you think happens to the people inside? Somebody's got to get them out."

Wei Li shook her head and scrolled through pages on her tablet.

A screeching sound came from the door, and the metal around the lock began to glow.

Ursula stepped closer to the door. Wei Li whispered harshly. "Bodies will draw more attention. Give me a moment."

The fourth voice came again, clear for the first time. "Huh. This isn't a regular door. Must be reinforced or something."

Second Voice responded. "So, they're definitely in there, right? Or else why would it be special?"

Gravel Voice grunted. "It used to be a warehouse. Maybe it just has a better door so people don't rob the place."

Fourth Voice again. "What should I do?"

Gravel answered. "What? Keep cutting! Why did you stop? Maybe stuff like this is why you lost your job?"

"Shut up. I'm trying." The glow returned.

"Where did you get this hot tip from, anyway? This place looks abandoned."

"The food guy. You know. Frallik. He lived across the hall from us when we first got to the station."

"Whatever."

Rohan's Power leapt and scratched at the spiritual seal encasing it, eager for a fight. He sank back onto the bed and exhaled slowly, emptying his lungs, then holding. Mother Famine looked at him with concern. She waved Ursula over.

The four-hundred-kilogram Ursan ambled to her. Mother Famine pointed at Rohan and whispered something in Ursula's ear.

With a nod, the bear knelt in front of Rohan and placed massive paws over his thighs. He could smell her musk, grown familiar and comfortable during their yearlong friendship.

A wash of aura spilled over him as she *projected* calm feelings.

He sighed and continued the breathing exercises, silently repeating his mantra.

Wei Li watched the color of the door deepen from yellow to orange.

With a sigh, she tapped her tablet.

"Uh oh." Fourth Voice sounded worried.

"What do you mean 'uh oh'? What does that mean?"

"There's some kind of alarm."

"What? I don't hear anything."

"Yeah, what alarm? You're just getting the shakes. Keep the torch on."

"No, you guys, It's an alarm. See that light? Right there? Blinking?"

"What? I don't—"

"What kind of alarm?"

"I dunno. Fire? Maybe a theft thing?"

Deep voice huffed. "Oh boy. Wait, is anyone even going to answer it? The station's a mess."

Gravel pounded on the door. "Open up! We just need to look around!"

First Voice called out. "I think we should go. This seems like a bad idea. Let's get out of here."

Gravel answered him. "Giving up? You want to be immortal, don't you? What's your alternative plan here? You going to enter the tournament?"

"I just think we should come back later. Station security is still working. If they see us like this, we're all in prison for sure. And you know, nice as this station is, I do not want to go back to her prisons."

"You don't have the right temperament for this work. You should go back to your parent's ranch."

Some shuffling from outside. The sound of the torch stopped abruptly; the glow began to fade.

"I think we should get out of here. Come on, look at this place. There's nothing inside but dust and rats. This whole building is abandoned."

"Empty-handed?"

"Better than empty-handed *and* locked up."

The voices continued, softer now and hard to make out from inside the room.

Wei Li stood near the wall, tablet in her hand, watching its video feed intently.

The voices retreated. A few moments later, she tapped the screen again.

Rohan sighed. "Is security coming?"

Wei Li shrugged. "Eventually. They'll see the damage, file a report. It would be more suspicious if they didn't come."

"What about those guys you used the fake-death-touch on yesterday? Did you go and fake-cure them?"

She nodded. "I told them I had to give the bad energy a chance to clear. Then I hit pressure points tied in a closed loop to their emetic systems."

"You mean—"

"They will experience a desperate need to purge themselves. Front and back. Requiring several hours in a bathroom. I should be an educator, because imparting life lessons is apparently at the core of my vast repertoire of talents."

Noru nodded. "Myself be saying always, Wei Li best teacher."

Rohan laughed. "She really does say that."

Dhruv snorted. "Disgraceful is what it is. Us, hiding from those nobodies. We should have painted the hallway with their blood."

Rohan chuckled. "Big talk from you now. What were you doing five minutes ago? Hiding in here with us."

Sigrun shook her blonde hair. "Don't speak to him that way, he's injured. Got hurt protecting us from those nasty giant dead men, didn't you, my sweet?"

Dhruv nodded. "If not for this bad leg . . ."

"You'd do what exactly, enter the tournament they were talking about? Which reminds me. What tournament *were* they talking about?"

Ursula huffed. "While you were for sleeping, ar'Tahul announced tournament at the arena. Strongest fighters will be gifted."

"Gifted?"

Mother Famine coughed. "He means infected."

"Seriously? No, I take that back. That seems like it would make perfect sense to him."

The Pledged nodded. "If he is what he claims to be, a weapon, it does indeed."

Rohan looked around the room. "Am I going to have to enter this tournament and fight my way through an array of underlings before reaching a climactic battle with ar'Tahul? Because I've never done that, and I think I want to."

Dhruv laughed. "Your mother let you watch too many movies when you were young. That's the dumbest idea you've ever had."

"You steal all my fun."

Wei Li cleared her throat and turned to Rohan. "Assuming that matter is resolved, we have things to discuss."

"Sure." He unwrapped his food and bit into the soft flour wrap that surrounded a mash of heavily seasoned ground meat and finely diced vegetables.

Wei Li sat in front of him. Ursula and Mother Famine joined them; Noru paced the open area near the door.

"If you are serious about pursuing this cure from Dr. Magdalena, it would help us to have some approach that might convince her."

Rohan nodded as he chewed.

Ursula bobbed her head up and down. "What are you for thinking, Wei Li?"

"She has told us that she does not fear death, and that was the truth. So, threatening her does not seem like a useful proposition."

Rohan swallowed. "There are worse things than death. We *could* threaten her with those. Not saying we *should*, but it's a possibility."

Wei Li turned to him. "You would torture an innocent physician to obtain the means of saving the life of a confirmed murderer? Is that how your ethical calculus runs today?"

He swallowed again, even though his mouth was empty. "Not when you put it like that, no. Doesn't seem like the right thing to do. What else is on the table?"

She rubbed her hands up over her forehead, all the way to the base of her neck, calloused palms clicking softly against the lines of scales that decorated her scalp. "I think we should use her faith against her."

Rohan looked at Ursula, who shrugged her massive shoulders in an avalanche of fur. "We are not for understanding."

"She spoke of her sect. Remember, they did not partake fully in mainstream Shayjh culture."

Rohan nodded. "They claimed to be keeping mainstream Shayjh culture from pre-Empire days and said the other Shayjh had bastardized it."

Wei Li waved her hand. "That doesn't matter. Do you recall to whom she swore?"

"It wasn't odd numbers, like you do."

Ursula nodded. "The Progenitors. She said this many times."

Rohan scratched his beard. "I might be seeing where you're going with this. But just in case I'm not, why don't you continue."

Wei Li nodded. "I appreciate your permission."

"You're welcome."

She sighed. "Dr. Magdalena's Progenitors might be a simple myth from the dawn of Shayjh history. Or they might refer to an actual race of people."

Ursula nodded. "You are thinking that these Progenitors are the people who made the first Shayjh."

"Either made, or helped to make, or perhaps *seeded*. Given the number of species in the galaxy who can interbreed, it is impossible that we evolved completely independently."

Ursula scratched her jaw. "My people also say that another race gave us intelligence, brought us to our homeworld. Through the wormhole."

"Yes."

Rohan's eyes widened. "I'm feeling slow now. You're connecting this story to Tollan's?"

Wei Li nodded. "That is exactly what I am doing."

Ursula looked at her. "What is this story?"

"Tollan told us that the il'Sein were the ones who spread the mammalian humanoids across this sector. That includes Rohan's people, Andervarians, Rogesh, il'Drach, and possibly the Ursans. It would also include the Shayjh."

The bear nodded. "You are for saying the il'Sein created the Shayjh. We are all cousins. One big, strange family."

"I am not sure. Rohan?"

"It makes sense. How do you use that to get Maggie on our side?"

"I will tell her that a cure for vampirism will not only save this station but possibly also the life of the only Progenitor to have set foot in this sector in fifty thousand years. I will give her a chance to meet one of her gods. More than meet one. I can imagine no greater honor for one with faith."

Rohan cracked his neck. "You think she'll buy it?"

"More than that, I think it is the truth. All evidence points to ar'Tahul being one of Magdalena's Progenitors."

"I'm not saying you're wrong, but how will we convince *her*?"

Ursula patted her knee with excitement. "She will have heard stories of her Progenitors. Seen statues, descriptions. They should be matching to the vampire's look."

Wei Li nodded. "Exactly. And we can fill in with some of Tollan's story. There is enough there that she should be eager to help."

Rohan looked each of the women in the eyes. "You two will go convince her?"

Mother Famine raised her hand. "I would join you if you can wait for nightfall. I have had dealings with Dr. Magdalena, and she and I are on not-bad terms. I'd rather not travel in the sunlight."

Wei Li nodded. "We appreciate the help. Rohan, your job is to lie down, move as little as possible, and heal. Perhaps take a nap."

Ursula nodded. "Like cub. Rest and allow the body to grow. In your case, grow whole, not grow bigger."

"I'm not really comfortable with these comparisons you keep making between me and a baby Ursan. It's starting to feel a bit like mockery."

Ursula grinned at him, pulling out her tablet with an exaggerated sweep of her hand, putting it to her ear. "Oh, wait, War Chief. I am now for receiving call. Hello? Oh, yes, yes. I am for understanding. Rohan, it is cubs. They, too, are uncomfortable with these jokes. They say they are much cuter than you."

Rohan sighed. "I get no respect."

Wei Li put her hand over his cheek. "You have our friendship and our love. Is that not better than respect?"

He smiled at her. "Kind of glad right now I'm so dark you can't see me blush."

She nodded. "It is settled, then. I was serious; you should try to nap. We will need you soon."

"Yes, ma'am."

<hr />

Rohan woke to a hand stroking his forehead. He murmured something incomprehensible, then opened his eyes.

He nearly jumped when he saw Dhruv's solemn face.

"What are you doing?"

Dhruv pulled his hand back. "This used to help you sleep."

"When I was a baby? I'm older now."

"Sorry, sorry. I was just remembering."

"Well, cut it out. That was a long time ago. A very long time."

"Doesn't feel so long to me. I'm quite old, you know."

"Sure. Is there any food?"

"There are a few of those burrito-things left. I think they're Rogesh, but they taste Mexican."

"Yeah. Get me one of those. Please."

"I'll heat it up." Dhruv stood and limped on his bandaged leg over to the table with the leftover food.

"Where is everybody?"

"They went to get that doctor to make a cure. Sigrun and Noru headed back to our apartment for the night. I volunteered to stay here with you."

"Sigrun just left you alone with me?"

Dhruv turned and smiled. "I might have insisted. Thought we could use some father-son time."

"Is Sister Famine still under those crates?"

"She woke at sundown and went with the others."

"What did you want to talk about?"

Dhruv hesitated, then stepped to the small kitchenette area. "I'm your father. I know you better than these other people."

Rohan's forehead tightened. "You knew me better. When I was a kid. How much time have we spent together in, say, the last fifteen years?"

Dhruv popped something into the microwave, tapped some buttons, and waited for the device to work its saucy magic. He wore his typical dark suit, cut from comfortable fabrics more commonly associated with exercise gear or athletics, and stood with rigidly perfect posture.

When the microwave beeped, he took the food out and juggled it from hand to hand as he carried it back to his son.

"I know you resent my absence, but I have many responsibilities."

"Like messing with the lives of as many people as possible."

"There are threats to life in this galaxy that only a unified empire can face."

"You say that, but I have trouble believing you. On account of all the lying and deception you've done."

"Can I tell you something? Sometimes I think you're right. That we'd be better off just being open and honest. No more manipulation, no more treating everybody as tools to be used and discarded as needed. Make the other races our partners." Rohan searched Dhruv's face for some sign of scorn, some indication of sarcasm. There were none.

"So? Why don't you?"

Dhruv chuckled. "Because most people are too stupid to be trusted. We manipulate because the risks are too great for us to trust others to act in our common self-interest. The galaxy is filled with surprisingly dumb people."

"Thanks for the lecture. What did you want to talk to me about?"

"Ah, yes. I was saying. I know you better than these others. You're not comfortable fighting ar'Tahul again." It was a statement, not a question.

Rohan let out a long breath. "I don't know if I can beat him."

"I'm not an empath, but I know that's not the whole story. You took on the Hybrid Rebellion and ended it with your own two fists. This soul eater can't be too tough for you."

"I knew what I was doing then. Or at least I thought I knew what I was doing. And why."

"You had commitment."

"Yeah. I mean, I've had a lot of doubts in my life, but not about the fact that I had to stop the Rebellion. For everybody's sake."

"You weren't wrong. What's different here? Why the lack of conviction? Are you doubting that you need to beat ar'Tahul?"

Rohan paused. Why *did* he lack conviction? "I don't know."

"If you don't figure out the answer, we're wasting our time. I know you can beat him. You can beat anybody, if you really put your mind and soul into it. The question is, can you do that?"

"I don't know how to answer that."

"You have time to figure it out. Not a lot of time, but time. Because that hole in your gut is still closing."

"I don't want to be your executioner anymore."

"I get that."

"I can't just go in there and kill him."

"Why not?"

"Because he's not evil, he's a weapon. He was made into a weapon. He really believes he's doing the right thing."

"And to do the right thing, he's willing to eat the souls of innocent people. Not to mention his existence puts all of us in mortal peril."

"I know, okay? I know all of that. But . . ."

Dhruv waited while Rohan searched for words. Finally, he said, "You're not finishing that sentence for a reason. What I'm telling you is that once you figure out the reason, you'll be able to beat him. And if you try to beat him before that, you'll lose. Again."

Rohan sagged back into the bed.

"I know." He looked at his father, stirred by a recent memory. "Hey, Dhruv. I seem to remember you being friendly with one of the Fleet admirals. Who was it? First? Freak?"

"You mean Fleck? I wouldn't say we were friends, but I know him. Saved his career. He was in charge of the mission that got Hyperion killed. The others wanted him executed for that fiasco."

"He's in the system. So I hear. The ranking officer for the flotilla around Toth."

Dhruv looked over his son with calculating eyes. "Is that so?"

"He must owe you quite the favor, am I right? If you saved his career."

"He should. Why do you mention it?"

"I'm just wondering if maybe that unexpected attack by the il'Drach on this station wasn't pretty convenient for you."

"Convenient how?"

"As a distraction so you could take a team of Ch'doon with you and try to sabotage Wistful's core."

"I wasn't sabotaging anything. I was trying to switch the target of her governor module."

"Still. Must have been a lot easier with Wistful, and security, so focused on the Fleet attack."

"I certainly wouldn't say it was a hindrance." Dhruv's smile was fixed on his face.

Rohan shook his head. "You know, people died in that attack. And we're lucky it wasn't more."

"Are you judging me? Don't forget, many more will die if we can't wrest control of this station away from the soul eater. Maybe you should wait until you have a plan to solve that particular problem before you speak critically to your father."

Rohan sighed. "Whatever. Look, how much juice do you have left with Fleck?"

"He'll owe me as long as he's breathing. As far as I know, that's still happening."

"Can you get him to do something?"

"What did you have in mind?"

"I don't know. You think you could get him to back off? Maybe give us some breathing room? If I could get to *Void's Shadow*, I could use the regen tank and heal faster. For example."

Dhruv ran his fingers over his full mustache. "I could try. He's already stuck his neck out for me. Hypothetically. If he did that. I'm not admitting anything."

Rohan scratched his beard. "Okay. I'll let you know if I come up with something else."

"You do that. And figure out why you have such a soft spot for the mass murderer who's holding your precious furry friends hostage."

"You don't have to keep reminding me."

"Clearly, I do."

25

Some Things to Talk About

"She's going to punch a hole in my what-now and do this why?"

Ursula shook her shaggy head. "I was for saying this is bad idea."

Wei Li's brow furrowed. "I would love for anybody here to explain to me, in detail, all of the *good* ideas that have made the rounds of our little group over the last several days. Because—perhaps due to some head injury I have forgotten—I can't seem to remember any of them."

The group was spread out over the couches, chairs, and cots that had accumulated in the half-empty warehouse. A cleaning bot the size of a house cat whirred back and forth across the floor, picking up dust and crumbs.

Rohan sputtered. "I'm not arguing with you, I'm just saying, drill a hole in my femur?"

"No, the plan requires drilling a hole in *both* of your femurs. In addition to the line tapping your aorta."

"That makes it sound so much better."

Ursula shook her head again. "You should have been for hearing her, Rohan. She spoke with great glee about the pain this would cause."

"I'm going to go out on a limb and guess that there's no chance I'd get any painkillers? Either they wouldn't work or they'd interfere with the process?"

Ursula switched to a violent nodding action. "That is true. Exactly as you say. I am not for trusting this woman."

Wei Li put her hand out to silence the Ursan. "She did speak with relish about causing you pain, but she was not lying as to the necessity of the procedure. Give me some credit on that score."

"Right. Empath. You'd know if she was jerking our chains."

"I will hazard an educated guess as to what you mean by that ridiculous idiom and agree. She was not offering a guarantee of the procedure's success, but she truly believed this was the best opportunity for it."

Rohan looked at Ursula's worried face, then at Mother Famine.

"What do you think?"

The vampire hesitated before responding. "Her plan is sound as far as I can determine."

"I don't know what that means."

"It means she shows a strong understanding of the nature of vampirism as I understand it, and nothing that I know leads me to believe her method is doomed or less-than-intelligent."

"And you're part of this plan, too?"

Ursula huffed. "All of us."

Wei Li explained. "Hybrids are immune to vampirism, which implies that the Hybrid immune system is capable of damaging the vampire organism more quickly than it can adapt."

Mother Famine nodded. "Unlike most other sentient creatures."

"Dr. Magdalena plans to reinfect you with fresh versions of the organism on a continual basis, which requires direct access to your blood and bone marrow."

"That's the part that makes me uncomfortable."

Mother Famine patted his hand where it lay over his blanket. "It does not sound pleasant."

Wei Li snorted. "Shall we tell her that? Tell her to simply forget it? That we'll simply abandon our attempt to cure ar'Tahul? While we are doing that, let us also explain this to the person who was most insistent that we embark on this course of action. Would you care to remind me of exactly who that was, Rohan?"

"All right, you're right. I'm sorry, okay? Just a little out of sorts."

She exhaled. "Shall I continue?"

"Yes, please."

"While the doctor uses your physiology to attack the physical organism, Mother Famine, Ursula, and I will attack the spiritual infestation."

Mother Famine nodded. "The Shayjh have very advanced terminology to describe spiritual techniques. Dr. Magdalena was able to explain a method to me that I believe I can implement, thanks to my years of training in meditation and the mental practices of my order."

Wei Li patted the older woman's shoulder. "I'll know whether things are working before anybody else, and Ursula will use her aura to provide additional broad suppression of the vampiric spirit."

Rohan settled back on the bed. "You guys think this will work?"

Dhruv chuckled from his position at the desk behind them. "You'd better test it on somebody else before you try to strap that soul eater down and test it on him."

Ursula nodded. "We are already for having plan for that."

Rohan glanced at the corner where Sister Famine was drinking her dinner from a plastic pouch.

"It sounds like Dr. Magdalena had this whole thing worked out when you guys got to her."

Mother Famine nodded.

"Did she explain why she didn't share this plan earlier? Didn't you tell me you commissioned her to find a cure? Didn't you also tell me she refused to share it with you?"

Mother Famine nodded again. "She couldn't find a biological agent to combat the organism other than a living, cooperative il'Drach Hybrid. And she was unwilling to involve herself with one."

"Until I showed up and put myself in her face. Got it. Well, this is a good thing, isn't it? We have a plan. Feels good, right?"

The others wore skepticism in tight lips and crinkled noses.

Mother Famine stood. "We are trying to remain cautiously optimistic."

Wei Li coughed. "She is trying to remain optimistic. I am trying to remain cautious. Dr. Magdalena thought this might work, but her confidence level was not high. There are also significant risks, both to you and to the test subject."

Ursula nodded. "Especially with the you not having of your Power, Rohan."

He sighed. "Right. Maybe that compromises my immunity. But maybe not."

Mother Famine nodded. "Nobody will blame you if you are unwilling to participate further. This plan puts your life at risk."

He cracked his neck and prodded his midsection to test for signs of pain or instability. The hole had mostly closed. "I think I can stand. I don't care how uncomfortable that tiny shower looks, I'm going to use it, and I'm probably going to be in there for a while. If someone could get some more food, I'd really appreciate it."

Wei Li stood. "I'll get food. You will owe me if we survive this situation."

"If we survive, I'll make sure to pay you back."

⬤ ·•· ⬤

Rohan stopped chewing as Sister Famine approached him.

"I appreciate what you did. Showering." Her tone was flat, somewhere between mockery and sincerity without drifting into either.

He smiled at her. "I am happy to help."

"We have acute olfactory senses, you know. It's to help us hunt."

"You've mentioned this before. I have to tell you, it's refreshing to meet someone so liberated."

Her eyes narrowed. "What do you mean 'liberated'?"

His smile broadened. "So many of the people I meet are slaves to things like civility and manners. You're just so . . . unencumbered."

"I was trying to be nice."

"Were you really? Because somehow I doubt that. I guess this could be a cultural misunderstanding, but I've met Lukhor, and they're usually lovely."

"I'm not Lukhor, you know."

"I remember. Brother Famine and I talked about it." He gave a moment for the deceased. "But same cultural roots, right?"

She sighed. "Similar enough. You told Brother Famine you had a relationship with a Lukhor woman."

"That's a story, but it wasn't much of a relationship."

"You were stalking her?"

"No, I wasn't—that wasn't nice. Not stalking. I don't stalk. We had an actual relationship."

"Then why did you say it wasn't much of one? The others say you're quite bright, but I'm having a hard time seeing it."

He sighed. "I just meant it didn't last very long."

"Yet you keep mentioning it."

"Well, yeah. I guess I do. That's probably not a great sign for my mental health. Or something."

"Maybe you just loved her a lot. That happens."

"Yeah, that happens."

"Or you just have a thing for green women."

"I don't think that's it. She was my . . . This is a weird conversation."

"I know. Probably my fault. Apparently I'm abrasive. So Mother Famine tells me."

"She's not wrong. But you're very attractive, which makes up for it. I'm also fairly thick-skinned."

"Of course. You're a Hybrid."

"I meant metaphorically thick."

She smiled. "I know."

He took a large bite out of the smoked animal leg he was eating. "I have no idea what this is."

"It's some kind of bird, I think. Is it good? I miss solid food."

"It's not bad. I think Wei Li got it for me because it was the most concentrated source of protein and energy she could find."

"I used to eat meat. And birds. And plants. All sorts of things, really."

"You can't eat solid food anymore?"

She patted her belly. "Makes me sick. Part of the curse."

He chuckled. "People call our Power a curse, too."

"You mean the il'Drach Power?"

"Yeah. It's not the same, I know. It's useful, but it definitely has some drawbacks."

"I see." She watched him eat. "Why are you trying so hard to save the fallen one?"

His response was muffled, spoken through a mouthful of greasy meat. "What?"

"I mean, why do you care if he dies?"

Rohan sighed and swallowed. "Tons of reasons. Like, all that history we'd lose if he were dead."

"It's not like he's been spending his time answering the questions of the universe with his ancient wisdom."

"True. Also, I've killed a lot of people. I'm trying to cut back."

"Maybe this isn't the best time to atone for past sins."

"You're not the first person to say something like that to me. The thing is, there's never a best time. I was never about murdering for fun. Every time I've killed, there was a good reason, or I thought there was, why I needed to do it. So, if I'm going to stop, I have to *not* kill people even when there *is* a good reason."

"Doesn't really make sense to me, but I shouldn't be arguing with you."

"Why not? That seems to be your thing."

"Well, you're helping me out. I should be thanking you instead."

"How do you figure? I thought you wanted ar'Tahul dead."

"I do, but . . ." She looked around the room. "Who do you think you're testing this cure on? Are there a lot of other vampires around I don't know about?"

His stomach tightened, little spasms dancing around his wound. "You're telling me that we're testing it on you."

"That's what I've been trying to tell you."

"It's pretty dangerous."

She held up a fist and raised one finger.

"One, there aren't any other viable choices. Two"—a second finger rose—"it's a good deal for me because you'll most likely either cure me or kill me. Either way, I'm free of the hunger."

"I might just cause you excruciating pain before we bail on the attempt."

"By reminding me of that, you're proving that you're exactly the kind of jerk I thought you were all along."

"I guess you're abandoning that plan of being thankful."

"It was never really in my character." She flashed a tight smile, taking some of the edge off her words.

"When are we supposed to do this?"

"Dr. Magdalena said you should be further along in the healing process before we strain your system, so they're talking early morning."

"That won't be easy for you."

"Sunlight should help keep the vampire soul at bay. Or so the doctor says. I'll be tired, but really, my job is going to be to lie still and not screw things up."

"Right."

"I wanted to ask something else."

He sighed. "Nobody's going to stop you. Even if I ask them nicely."

"The old guy—Dhruv? He's related to you?"

"You mean because we're both brown? There are literally billions of people on my planet with that skin color."

"Not that. I can smell it."

"Ah. He's a cousin. On my mother's side, obviously, since my father isn't human."

"Oh. You don't really talk to him like a cousin."

"He's kind of a jerk, so we're not close. Why do you ask?"

"I was curious. Actually, I wasn't clear on why he was hanging around with us at all."

"Neither am I. Hold on, my comm is pinging." He tapped behind his ear to open the quantum channel.

"What's up?"

"Rohan. It's Tollan."

"Hey, Tollan. Guess what, I'm not see-through anymore!"

"I have no idea what you're talking about."

"I had a hole punched through me. You could see through it. Now it's healing, so you can't."

"Whatever drugs you're on, I'd like some."

"I'm high on life, Tollan. Just life. What can I do for you?"

"I'd like a word. In person."

"Yeah? When?"

"Sooner would be better."

Rohan scratched his beard. "Can you come here?"

"I don't know where you are. To be honest, it might be better if that situation didn't change. There are people who know that we're acquainted."

"You don't want them asking you questions. Got it. I think I can walk well enough to come over. As long as you don't plan to challenge me to a game of pickup basketball."

"You're safe, especially since I have no idea what that is."

"I'll head over." He looked around the room again. Sister Famine was yawning. Dhruv and team had left the warehouse. Ursula was snoring loudly on the couch. Wei Li was dividing her attention between her own tablet and the four image feeds she had running to each quadrant of the wall screen.

"Wei Li, Tollan wants to talk to me."

"Are you fit to travel to him?"

He stood, lightly touching his belly. He bent to the front, then to the side, waiting for the pain to kick in. "I think I'm okay. It's not that far."

"Shall I accompany you?"

"I think I'd be less noticeable by myself. Don't you think so? You guys got me clothes in plain colors. I'll pull the hood low. Should be safe."

She nodded. "I doubt Tollan would have asked capriciously. Keep the comm open and shout if you run into trouble."

"Yes, Mom. I'll also text when I get there so you'll know I drove safe."

"If I actually were your mother—No, I take that back. I've met your father and heard much about your mother. I doubt that if I had raised you myself you would have been improved to any great degree."

Rohan chuckled. "Don't make me laugh! I'll be back."

He rummaged through the backpack full of casual clothing that had been bought for him and pulled out a charcoal-gray tracksuit with an oversized hood. "Perfect."

"Remember: no Powers."

"I know. I'll be good."

He pulled the hood low over his face, waited by the door while Wei Li checked the hallway for lurkers, then slipped out.

Rohan walked gingerly, taking small, shuffling steps, his back stiff with tension. The interior of the building block was deserted, as he'd expected, but within minutes he reached the doorway that led out onto the main boulevard.

He eased out onto the walkways, hugging the buildings, eyes focused on doorways and alcoves where he could run and hide if anybody recognized him.

The atmosphere on the boulevard was subdued. It was close to midnight, which wouldn't have been a busy time even without a vampire infestation and Imperial blockade, but the few people who roamed about moved furtively and quietly. Clumps of dark shapes moved on the grassy areas farthest from any lights, feet gently scraping the plant life. Crossed paths were negotiated with harsh whispers and, Rohan suspected, the occasional bout of combat.

He avoided the rare food cart still open at that time of night, catering to the nocturnal and the drunk, and made his way closer to Tollan's building.

Familiar voices sounded from behind him. The group that had tried to burn through their door.

Not what I needed right now.

Without pausing his stride, Rohan turned into a residential building, closing the door behind him and marching purposefully down the corridor.

A turn, then another, and he stopped, leaning against the wall, his side aching with the strain of heavy breathing.

He counted breaths as he waited, his Power nipping at the bottom of his soul, eager to be unleashed.

Long exhale, hold, inhale quickly, long exhale.

Ten counts later, he left the building.

The makeshift gang was gone.

Ten more minutes saw him in Tollan's building. The sign over the entrance read CLOSED, but the door slid open for Rohan.

Tollan sat behind his counter, a glass bottle of amber liquid in front of him. He wore a plain brown jumpsuit, his pointed ears poking out under graying hair.

"Drink?"

Rohan sat heavily in one of the worn chairs and leaned forward onto the counter. "That would be great, thanks."

"Any trouble out there?"

"Nothing serious. Station feels off, though, you know?"

"Everybody's tense. Fleet attacks will have that effect."

"I know. I've been stuck in our secret hideaway so much, I haven't really been out to notice."

"Well, stay there. At least until you're ready to make a move on ar'Tahul."

"Will do. But that's not what you wanted to talk to me about. Did you figure out something about interfering with Wistful's governor module?"

Tollan let out a big breath and nodded slowly. "Something along those lines. But not exactly what you're thinking."

"I'm too tired right now to figure out what that means on my own."

Tollan reached under the counter, his wizened hand returning with two shot glasses. He set them on top and portioned out short drinks for both of them.

"I don't like pouring on the bad news, but there's something you should know."

"Hit me. And I mean that in both senses: the drink and the news."

Tollan slid one of the glasses right up to Rohan's hand. "There is an il'Drach on board Wistful."

Rohan's mouth dropped open. "Another one?"

Tollan shook his head, his eyes narrowing. "What do you mean another one? You mean besides you?"

Tollan doesn't know about Dhruv; at least, not from me. "Uh, yeah. Sure. Wait, you mean a full-blooded il'Drach?"

"Yes. A male."

"Well, of course. You'll never find a female il'Drach anywhere but on Drach."

"No, of course not. It's interesting that you said it that way."

"Is it?"

"Most people say something like they thought female il'Drach were a myth. Or that nobody's ever seen one, ever. In history. But you were more specific."

That's because I've met a few Matrons, but you're not supposed to know about that.

"Do we really have time for this discussion? I'm sorry I talk weird. But who is this il'Drach you know?"

"Shorter than you, taller than me. Skin like yours. Looked like your species, actually. I mean your other half."

"Ah." Tollan studied Rohan's face as the Hybrid answered.

"You know him?"

Rohan sighed. "That's Dhruv."

Tollan nodded. "You do know him."

The two men sat in silence for a stretch.

Rohan sipped his drink. The liquor burned pleasantly down into his chest. "I know him. He's my father."

Tollan sipped his own drink, then topped up the glass and sipped again. "Not exactly what I was expecting to hear."

"I mean, I could make something up if it would help you feel better."

"Not what I meant, really. So, you knew he was on the station?"

Rohan took another sip. "He contacted me a few days ago. If you're looking for an actual timeline, I'd have to really think about it. I've been a mess, and maintaining my social calendar has not been top priority."

"Are you aware of what he's doing here?"

"I know what he told me he's doing here, which is not necessarily the same thing. il'Drach in general have, at best, an ambiguous relationship with the truth."

Tollan grunted. "He asked me to help him redirect Wistful's governor."

Rohan nodded. "He told me he was going to try that. If he's getting you to help him, it might even be his actual plan."

"He wants to switch the governor so she'll take orders from him and not from ar'Tahul. Or any il'Sein."

"Not that there are any other il'Sein around to give her orders, right?"

Tollan looked uncomfortable. "Right."

"Are you going to help him?"

Tollan nodded. "He made me an offer I could not refuse."

"He threatened you?"

"What? No."

"Sorry. It's an expression on my homeworld. What was the offer? Should I say, how much was the offer?"

"Not money. He correctly pointed out that it will be almost impossible to defeat ar'Tahul, and save everybody on this station, without disrupting his control over Wistful."

"I'm pretty sure I told you the same thing. And asked for your help."

"Dhruv also has two pieces of tech that you don't. One can get him into Wistful's core, and the other helps him interface with the governor. Not well enough for him to get the job done without me, but it's a big help."

"Where did he get those things? Dhruv's no engineer."

"No idea, but presumably he has access to armories and storehouses on Drach that are full of all sorts of interesting toys."

"Which also means that this was part of his plan from the start."

"I can't imagine these are the sort of things he just generally carries around with him. Then again, I don't really know him."

Rohan nodded. "Thanks, Tollan. I'm only mildly surprised. He said he'd need help with the governor. Seems like a weird coincidence he'd find you, specifically, to do it."

Tollan shrugged. "I told you a while ago, I have a reputation."

"Right. Pour me another shot of that, and I'll get out of your hair."

"You're not going to talk me out of helping Dhruv with his plan?"

"If everything goes well, we're going to have a cure for vampirism ready tomorrow. Then I'm going to grab up your first lance, fix him, and end this craziness. Dhruv will never need your device."

"That's the plan?" Tollan's voice was neutral, betraying no shred of skepticism.

Rohan nodded. "Let me tell you a story.

"Hyperion bought Earth's freedom by offering to have every Hybrid on the planet join Fleet. They didn't really care about us, especially not me, but they *really* wanted Hyperion. He was the strongest Hybrid they'd seen in centuries.

"I was sort of his protégé. Maybe I should say sidekick, I don't know. At first I was pretty useless, but as time went on, they started noticing something.

"I was nowhere near as strong as Hyperion. But, when a problem needed solving, when the issue wasn't something that could be just punched or lifted or pushed over, I was the one doing that solving more often than not.

"By the end, they were calling me first. Because they knew I'd actually fix the situation and not just cause billions in property damage and smile winningly for the cameras.

"So, yeah, that's the plan. We're going to cure this guy and tell the Imperial warships to run back to whatever battlefront they came from.

"Just as soon as I work up the strength to stand up again."

26

This Will Hurt You More than Me

"This is for reminding me of something from homeworld." Ursula loomed over the narrow hospital bed, stretching to get a closer look at the bank of machinery that sat between it and the second bed.

Rohan shifted where he lay, trying to find a comfortable position for his shoulders. "What?"

"Not real thing, I am remembering. Was a thing on show. For children. Or maybe for adults who are still too fond of the time when they were children."

Dr. Magdalena eyed the Ursan warily. "Don't touch anything."

"I heard you the first several times you have been saying that. Yes, I will not be touching the machines."

"Thank you. You're just . . . quite close."

Ursula scrunched up her face but didn't move. "In show, was mad scientist. Scientist put twin children on beds, threw switch. Required lightning storm for reason I have never been understanding. After switch, children woke up in each other's bodies."

Wei Li snorted. "They were physically inside each other? Was one miniaturized?"

"No, no, personalities only were . . . switched. Wait, I am remembering more. One was very smart, good in studying. The other was very fashionable, popular with boys. Then after switch . . ."

Rohan groaned. "Please tell me I'm not going to wake up in Sister Famine's body."

Sister Famine mimicked his groan from the other bed. "Please tell me he won't wake up in mine! That's disgusting. I can only imagine what he'd do to it while he's in here. Gross."

Dr. Magdalena shook her head vigorously. "You have nothing to worry about. That's an entirely different machine. See, it would have to have a Klein bottle right here with a mithril lining to contain the spiritual energies. I don't have the equipment here for something like that. Who knows where I could find a silver cord disruptor capable of reaching the right frequencies on this station?"

Sister Famine started to sit up. "You mean that's actually something you could do? I don't know if I want to be part of this anymore."

The doctor pushed her back down. "Relax. I told you, nobody's switching you. Not today. The worst that can happen is that you'll die an agonizing death because of this trial."

Sister Famine sighed. "I'd rather die in agony than live, knowing that animal is inside me. He'd probably starve to death because he'd refuse to take his hands off my breasts."

Rohan coughed. "That's a mean thing to say. Accurate, but mean."

Ursula nodded. "You are for being a very perceptive person, Sister Famine. You have deep understanding of Rohan's character."

Dr. Magdalena put her hand under her chin. "Did you want me to work on the body-switching device? I might be able to substitute deep-space-rated gravity bottles for the mithril lines . . ."

Wei Li touched the woman's shoulder. "There is no need for that. They are being silly, to ease tension. Please continue with the current procedure."

Ursula continued. "After the switch, each girl had to live the life of the other. Smart girl, she learned that being fashionable and popular is not so easy as it is seeming. Pretty one, she learned all about meeting parents' expectations in school. Then they planned to get parents to reunite after ugly separation—"

Wei Li held a hand up to stop her friend. "This is a fascinating story, but perhaps we should be concentrating on other things?"

"Yes, of course. Much apologies. Just remembering. So funny when they switched back, but fashionable girl's boyfriend liked smart girl better, and . . . Please never mind." She straightened, pulling her muzzle away from the machinery.

Rohan patted her arm as he looked over the equipment out of the corner of his eye. There were tanks, tubes, a pair of centrifuges, generators of all sorts, and an unpleasant set of drills laid out on a steel tray.

Wei Li smiled as she noticed the direction of his gaze. "Having second thoughts?"

"I am way past second thoughts. I can't count high enough to tell you what thoughts I'm on."

Sister Famine snorted. "You can't count past ten with your shoes on, can you?"

"I can get to eleven if I take off—"

Wei Li interrupted. "Regardless, it will do neither you nor Sister Famine any good for you to hesitate at this point in time."

"No, you're right. I'm good. Let's do this."

Dr. Magdalena looked to the corner of the room where Mother Famine sat in lotus position, eyes closed, carefully counting out her breaths.

The doctor turned back to Wei Li. "Can you tell?"

Wei Li nodded. "I believe she is as ready as we can expect her to be."

The tall, pale doctor rubbed her hands together. "Then I should start. Rohan, pants off."

"That is the least unsexy way I've ever been asked to do that."

Sister Famine chuckled. "Oh, so now he'll be able to count—"

Ursula growled.

"I will be for helping. Do not move too much; you are still being heavily injured." She eased off his sweatpants, exposing boxer shorts printed with hearts above his hairy brown thighs.

Rohan braced as the doctor approached with one of the drills.

"That's a very fat needle."

"We require continuous access to the marrow in your femurs. Hold still."

Ursula gripped his hand as the drill screeched and broke through skin, fascia, muscle tissue, and finally bone.

He breathed, in and out, then again, faster. Soon he was panting, cold sweat pouring off his forehead, tendons in his neck vibrating as he flexed his jaw.

His Power rose up, eager to pulse into his thighs, throw off the drills, then swell into his belly and heal his wounds. Eager to tear out of the doctor's lab, up outside the station, out toward the central hub, then to the arena to fight ar'Tahul.

"Stop him. The skin is hardening, he'll break my drills. Or the lines. I need in-and-out lines for both femurs for this to work."

His breaths were shallow as he forced the Power back down. He tasted blood; smelled smoke and ozone.

Wei Li circled the apparatus and touched a cool hand to his forehead. "Think of a happy place, Rohan. A calming place. Slow your breaths."

A happy place. Where was he happy?

Floating in space.

A row of ships were docked along Wistful's arms, safely escorted and mated to bays on each appendage. Toth's rays warmed his back; he floated and looked over Toth 3, taking in the blue oceans and white clouds, too high to make out the kaiju littering its landmasses.

"His heart rate is increasing. I thought he was resilient?"

Wei Li defended him. "How many could withstand this level of pain without anesthetic? He is not screaming for mercy or begging for death. I feel he is doing quite well for the circumstances."

Not space, then. Might be a happy place, but it's not THE happy place.

Ursula wiped his forehead as his shoulders and arms spasmed. She placed a heavy paw over his chest to muffle the movement.

"Calm yourself, Rohan. Maybe try thinking about fish."

He almost laughed.

Sitting on a cliff overlooking the Shenandoah Valley, feet dangling in space. A spot unreachable on foot. Greenery spreads out underneath, a

warm breeze whistles through his hair. He takes small sips from a bottle of
añejo tequila, letting the fire burn through his chest.

Next to him is Bright Angel, the first woman he ever loved.

"He's going to seize. We can't hold him down; he's too strong. Are you
sure his Power isn't active? Because if it is, I want all of you out of my lab.
Right now."

Wei Li shook her head. "His Power is still suppressed. He is physically
very strong."

"Of course he is."

Rohan grunted through bared teeth. "We were designed for war. The
il'Drach were. Blame your Progenitors if you don't like how strong we are."

Ursula patted his hand. "Shhh, Rohan. Concentrate."

Maybe not a place with Bright Angel next to me.

His apartment, in Wistful's central hub. Clear ceiling open to space and
Toth 3. He lay on smooth, cool sheets, a head nestled in the crook of his
arm. He looked down and saw dark hair, twin green antennae poking out.
Below that, an expanse of skin . . .

"I'm going to shut this down. If he dies on the table, his immune system
won't be any good. Actually, if we infect him while he's too close to death,
he might turn into a vampire himself. Hm. Maybe I won't shut this down.
That's fascinating."

*I should find a happy place that doesn't remind me that Tamara dumped
me for another man.*

Ursula rubbed his chest. "Maybe not fish, but you should be for thinking about food, Rohan. You love to eat. What is best place for eating?"

He'd eaten at restaurants on Wistful that would receive Michelin stars if
Michelin sent guides out of the solar system.

He'd eaten at places at Academy where every morsel of food was an
explosion of perfectly balanced flavors.

They were *good* places. Not *happy*.

He imagined sitting at a table that wouldn't stop rocking. He was on
the boulevard, lines of busy people streaming by on their way to work or
school or play. Children tugged along by their arms, drawn to the smell of
fresh eggs and biscuits of unknown provenance.

Marion and Ben Stone sat across from him, sipping coffee. Marion crumbled a biscuit in her hand and ate it, one morsel at a time.

Wei Li sat next to him, eyes on the crowd. Ursula and Ang completed the table, massive paws cradling their tiny mugs.

Pop walked over, three plates of eggs balanced on his arm, six eyes keeping watch on all angles so nobody accidentally knocked the food to the floor.

Sunlight streamed in through the single-facet diamond roof, warming his face as he leaned back and stretched.

The beeping alarm he hadn't even noticed slowed and stopped.

"Well, it's good enough for now. Move aside, I need to get the central line in. Then we're done with him, and I can work on Sister Famine."

———◆ ··◆———

"The fluids in this tank are interacting live with his blood and marrow. Those lines run through those filters, which take out the biological components that don't interest me and leave the ones that do."

Wei Li nodded. "So as his immune system responds . . ."

"Yes. The different chemical components of the response, along with parts of the relevant cells, wind up here."

"I see."

"Over on this side we have a second tank similarly interfacing with Sister Famine. That fluid contains living vampire parasites. This port joins the tanks. We'll transfer the parasites to the Hybrid in small doses, then pull out whatever agents are produced by his immune system and transfer them into her."

"When are you going to start?"

"In about three minutes."

Wei Li swallowed and nodded. "We are ready."

"Good. I'll transmit the infection to the Hybrid. We'll monitor his response to it. I hope to have something we can use very quickly. At that point, you'll need to work to suppress the vampiric soul, prevent it from taking action on her physical body."

Wei Li glanced at Mother Famine, who remained in her meditative posture. "What about the light?"

"I set up some mirrors earlier. This area here"—she ran her arm over the bed containing Sister Famine—"is the target. When I touch this pad, it will stream sunlight onto her. It will be a very small amount at first. This other switch will flood the entire apparatus with full-strength light."

"Under what circumstances would that be advisable?"

"In case the infection takes hold of the Hybrid, or Sister Famine is overcome by her parasite. A nice wash of sunlight should destroy either in that situation."

Wei Li looked down. "Rohan, any questions?"

He shook his head. "No. I'm good." His voice was tight and strained.

Dr. Magdalena looked down at each of the others, making eye contact and shining a smile, facing Rohan last.

"Here goes nothing!"

She threw a switch on the machine; a stream of liquid bubbled down a tube, heading for the line that had been tapped into his aorta.

Fiery agony erupted in Rohan's chest and quickly spread out through his body, piercing belly, neck, shoulders, hips, thighs, upper arms, and finally hands and feet.

He wanted to say something but couldn't squeeze words past clenched teeth.

Dr. Magdalena was looking into a scope, studying the fluids coming out of his body. "Good, very good. Seeing responsive activity already. It's faster than I thought."

Wei Li viewed her friend with concern. "How much more of this does he have to take?"

"Oh, I have no idea. As much as we need? I'm getting the chemical agents ready to administer to the vampire now. Another minute. But I highly doubt the first round will suffice."

"I see. He is in quite a lot of pain."

"That's fine. Just make sure he doesn't let the seal on his Power slip. That would make this whole thing a waste of time."

"We know."

"Great. I'm giving the first round of immunizing agents . . . now."

Sister Famine's body arched off the bed, every major muscle convulsing.

Dr. Magdalena looked at Wei Li and at Mother Famine. "You should be working on her now."

Wei Li nodded. "We've already begun. Do your work, and we shall do ours."

"Okay then. Let me take a look at what's happening in her at the cellular level." She pressed her face to another scope.

Rohan focused on his happy place: the smell of coffee, the sound of children playing ball on the wide median, the smell of fresh eggs. He exhaled, willing his feet, then his hands to relax. Then his calves and forearms.

"Well, that's not a good sign."

Ursula looked over the bed. "What are you for seeing?"

"Did I say that out loud? Never mind, just ignore me. I'm too used to working alone."

Wei Li looked at her. "Sister Famine does not seem to be reacting well to whatever it is that we're doing."

"The Hybrid's antibodies are doing too much damage to her. She's been altered by the vampiric organism at the cellular level to the point where it's hard to determine where it ends and she begins."

"How can we overcome that obstacle?"

"I'm going to slow the flow from the Hybrid. Perhaps her native tissues can recover faster than the parasitic organisms. I underestimated the level at which the infection alters the host."

Sister Famine grunted, then spasmed again.

Wei Li was sweating. "I do not know if Mother Famine can hold her vampiric soul back for much longer. It is quite intense."

"Let me see, let me see . . . I've adjusted the flow back into the vampire. Give it a few minutes."

The pain in Rohan's thighs was gradually shifting into a nauseating itch. "Rudra save me, I want to dig my fingernails directly into my bones."

Ursula patted him. "Do not do that, friend Rohan. Squeeze my hand if you are needing for comfort."

"I don't think pulverizing the bones in your hand is going to make me feel better."

Dr. Magdalena was nodding. "This might be working. It's like primitive cancer treatments. The chemical agents are damaging her own tissues along with the parasite, but they're killing the parasite faster. Now it's a race to see who dies first."

Wei Li frowned. "Who?"

"If you think of the infection as a separate person. Which it isn't, of course. Never mind."

Ursula looked up. "Doctor, what is for happening?"

"The parasite is shifting markers. Goodness, that's quick. Here, let me reinfect the Hybrid. Brace yourselves."

The fresh onslaught of pain was easier to manage. *I'm getting used to this. That, in itself, is a terrifying thought.*

"Preparing the counteragent now. Oh, look. His body is responding faster than before. It's like it's learning."

"I told you. We were designed for this kind of thing." Rohan's voice was hoarse and shaky.

Dr. Magdalena looked up sharply. "Do you think the Progenitors designed your immune system with this in mind? I mean, this particular situation? If they tried to harness vampirism, and thought it too dangerous, perhaps they deliberately made il'Drach physiology vampire-proof."

Wei Li sighed. "That is an intriguing hypothesis. Perhaps not critical at this precise moment."

"No, perhaps not. Topic for another day's research."

He swallowed and looked over at Sister Famine. Her skin had faded, yellow patches displacing her natural green. A few wisps of hair fell past his line of sight.

"Guys, I don't think Sister Famine is doing too great."

Dr. Magdalena made a hushing sound. "She's alive. I never said this would be easy."

Wei Li looked at her. "Do you have specific criteria in mind for halting this experiment?"

"What do you mean?"

"Are there markers you are following? Thresholds that, once reached, will lead you to determine that we should stop?"

"No. We weren't big on stopping experiments just because a few subjects died in agony. That's an interesting idea, though. You clearly weren't trained in science by the Shayjh."

"No, clearly not."

The doctor looked down at Wei Li. "Don't you think this is the sort of thing you should have brought up before I started drilling holes in people's thighs?"

Wei Li rubbed her hands over her face and scalp. "Yes, you are quite right. I have been remiss."

"Do you think we should stop?"

Wei Li looked down at Sister Famine. "She does not look good."

"No. No, she doesn't. Let me check some things." Dr. Magdalena bent to the scope.

Wei Li checked on Mother Famine, who had kept her position. The Pledged was completely focused on fighting Sister Famine's spiritual infection.

Rohan swallowed. "It's not worth killing her for this. I know she wouldn't object, but it seems wrong."

"Give us a minute, Rohan. We cannot abandon this procedure casually."

"She really doesn't look good."

Dr. Magdalena waved her hand in the air. "I see, I see. The spiritual infection is doing something odd."

Wei Li stared at her. "What?"

"I assumed it would resist this process by either attacking the Hybrid's immunological agents or by reinforcing the vampiric cells in the host body. Instead, it is attacking the native cells."

"You mean it's tipping the balance by increasing the damage?"

"Yes. It is almost an intelligent response. Or simply a destructive one?"

"It would rather they both die than let her be freed."

"Most unusual. If you compare this behavior to parasites in nature, ones that have evolved, it is . . . dissimilar."

Wei Li sighed. "Can you do anything?"

"Not much. Mother Famine's suppression is weakening it. If it were attacking the Hybrid's cells, it would be ineffective. But it is part of Sister Famine, and it's attacking *her* body. It has all the advantages."

The empath looked down into the eyes of the suffering vampire. She bent and examined a screen set into the side of the bed, displaying the vampire's vital statistics.

As she stood, she caught Rohan's eyes. He set his jaw. *Don't let her die for nothing.*

Wei Li faced the surgeon. "Doctor, what is happening?" Dr. Magdalena's face was pressed to her scope.

"Fascinating. Her cells are, well, detonating. Exploding. Very deliberately."

"Can you stop it? Or is there any sign that it will stop on its own, thanks to the damage being done to the infection?"

"I can't. I can't even slow it down. And if it's slowing on its own, I can't tell."

Wei Li looked at Mother Famine, who was still in no position to offer her judgment. She turned to Ursula, who shook her head.

"To die here is not of use, Wei Li. We should help her live."

The empath nodded. "Stop the procedure."

"Are you sure? There's more to learn. Possibly."

"I will not have this woman die for no reason. And no, before you ask, satisfying your curiosity is not a reason."

"So, you're sure?"

"I'm sure. Turn it off."

The doctor sighed and shrugged. "Very well." She began resetting dials, halting or reversing the flow of fluids between patients.

Ursula brought water to Rohan. Wei Li walked to Mother Famine and put her arm around the older woman's shoulders.

Rohan sucked at the water, his cheeks hollowing with the effort. He swallowed and panted.

"How is she?"

Ursula shook her head. "I am not for knowing yet. Not good."

Wei Li came back and started to tend to Sister Famine.

Dr. Magdalena stepped around to Rohan's side. She yanked one fat tube out of his thigh, then pulled the central line out of his chest.

"Careful!"

"You'll be fine. You heal fast. Actually, I kind of like having you here for this. So much easier to keep you alive than typical test subjects."

"That's not creepy at all. You should put that on your business cards."

With a pop, the second femoral tube came free. The doctor turned to Ursula. "You should stuff something clean in those holes so he doesn't leak blood all over my floors."

Ursula nodded and began to bandage the fresh wounds.

Rohan looked at the tall Shayjh. "What's next? When can we try again?"

She laughed. "With her? There's no point in it, unless you're just being cruel. That was my best shot."

"What do you need? Another test subject? Another vampire to work on?"

"I have to think about it. I might be willing to try again. But unless there's some variable I'm unaware of, the results are likely to be the same."

His chest hurt again. "What do you mean?"

"It's possible she has some unusually resistant strain of vampirism. Or the fact that she's not fully fallen makes it harder to cure her. But neither seems likely. In fact, the opposite. I would think curing her would have been simpler than curing a much older, actively blood-drinking vampire."

"Which means . . ."

"It means that this procedure is probably not going to work on anybody. It was a good try, though."

"That's it?"

She turned to Wei Li, then Ursula, then back to Rohan. "What else do you want?"

He looked up at Ursula's sad brown eyes. She nodded. "We tried, Rohan. You tried. Our best. No more than this can you be for asking."

Rohan rolled onto his side, then pushed himself up to a seated position. He looked at Sister Famine, bloody tears streaking her face. Her bed started beeping loudly.

"Her heart's stopping. Let's restart it. Get some fresh blood into her, too, so she can start healing."

The women leapt to attend to the young vampire as Rohan mustered up the strength to stand.

What am I supposed to do now?

27

Plans B

"Oh, Captain! It's so good to see you with my own visual sensors. I've gotten used to you being always out there, you know, with the towing and the flying around and getting into trouble. I didn't realize how comforting it is for me until you got stuck inside the station!"

"You don't really have to call me captain, *Insatiable*. I'm a tow chief."

"Well, I know you've said that, and I tried, Captain, I really did. For a while! But I couldn't keep upsetting *Void's Shadow* like that. And you know, she's having a tough enough time as it is. She's kind of lonely, and she can't come close and talk like she used to. And there are all these strange warships flying around, and sensor arrays to avoid, all while she's working really hard to find the patterns in all the patrols and ship movements. It's a lot, you know. So I thought to myself, maybe you'd prefer I don't call you 'Captain,' but *she* prefers I do, and you always *also* say that her feelings are important—"

"Okay, I get it. I guess. But why does *Void's Shadow* care?"

"That I can explain. She's only a baby, but she's still a warship. She was only actually in the Fleet for a little bit, but she understands how it works."

"I get that."

"If she says you're her captain, then you're a captain. And while you might *also* be a tow chief, since captain outranks tow chief, that's what we should be calling you. Unless we're specifically asking for a tow."

He rubbed the patch of skin between his eyebrows. "Right."

"If we call you 'Tow Chief,' it's like we're negating your captaincy. Captainhood. Captainship. Oh, that's cute! Captainship. Because you're captain of a ship! But also, you are in the state of being a captain. Languages are fun!"

"Okay, I get it. Thanks for looking out for her. For her feelings."

"You know, considering how we met, we've become quite good friends. It helps that we're the only two ships who are here all the time. The others come and go and come and go and sometimes come again, but we're almost always here."

Void's Shadow had come to Toth system hiding inside *Insatiable*'s hold. She'd been forced to do it, but it remained a violation of the larger ship, and Rohan hadn't expected them to ever be on good terms.

"That's sweet. Listen, can you tell me what's going on? I'm in the north corridor, just outside the bay entrance. You told me to wait here. What am I waiting *for*?"

"It's a little bit complicated. But only a little. The thing is, Dr. Stone can't just shut down the cameras around my entrance, because Wistful would absolutely notice that and very probably do something about it. But we have a trick that can fool Wistful's passive checks."

"But they won't fool her if she's actively paying attention."

"Exactly. We're assuming she doesn't want to do that. That's how it seems. Wistful isn't *trying* to find you, but if she notices you despite that, she'll have to tell ar'Tahul about it."

"So, I'm waiting for the time when Marion can hack the sensors?"

"Yes. And to make things just a tiny bit more interesting, there are three youths lingering by the bay door who we believe are waiting to ambush you."

"How do they know I'm coming?"

"They probably don't! That's the amazing part. They seem to be part of a group. Two or three of them have kept watch in shifts for the last couple of days."

"Okay. I guess that makes sense; people know I have friends here. I wouldn't be shocked if other people are hanging around Pop's or my apartment."

"That's what Ben said! Do you want me to send people out to take care of them? I have a crew, and, to be honest, more than a few of them would be glad for a chance to get into a fight."

"Are the watchers Powers?"

"No, I would have said. Just regular people. Perhaps a bit less intelligent than the average."

"Must figure that with my injuries I'm easy prey. No worries, I'll take care of it. How much time do I have once the sensor hack kicks in?"

"As long as you need, in theory, but realistically it would be best if you could keep it under two hundred seconds."

Rohan cracked his neck. "Sounds good. Will I recognize them once I go in there?"

"They'll be the ones leaning against the wall or standing in one place and chatting. There is literally nobody else in the bay doing that."

"Sounds straightforward. Just say when." He reached under his sweat-shirt and ran fingers over the tender flesh covering his wound, then turned and twisted his shoulders, testing the limits of the freshly knit tissues inside.

This would be easier with Power.

"One minute until the next convenient window."

"Thanks, *Insatiable*. I'm ready."

"*Wistful's* sensors are deactivated . . . now."

Rohan stepped through the entrance and into the bay.

The space was vast, designed to accommodate heavy freight vehicles and large cargo containers. The sides were lined with various docks, made to fit everything from light shuttles to the largest cargo ships. Marked-off paths for foot traffic and vehicles lined the interior, interrupted by the occasional heavy elevator placed to lift cargo into the transport tube level above them.

"It's nearly empty. There are usually hundreds of people here."

"There's a blockade, silly. No ships in or out. No new cargo to move."

"Right."

Rohan walked briskly, making a beeline for *Insatiable's* dock. He wasn't five meters from the entrance when he saw three goons clustered by the portal: two facing away from him, the third leaning against the wall with one eye on the tablet in her hand.

Five more meters and leaning-goon pushed away from the wall and nudged one of the others with her elbow, eyes on Rohan. They turned and formed a rough semicircle, blocking *Insatiable*'s entrance.

"Is that him? Looks a lot like him." The males were Drexian: red, scaly skin; short black horns; square-pupiled eyes. They so closely resembled Earth depictions of devils that Rohan was sure there had been some actual visitation in the distant past.

"That's him." The girl was a Darianite, eyes twice the size of any other humanoid species.

Rohan kept his pace constant, deliberately smoothing his gait so it didn't show any signs of strain from his injury.

"One chance. Walk away."

The Darianite smiled, showing short, sharp teeth, practically glowing against her ink-black skin. "I told you it was him."

The taller Drexian cracked his knuckles. "Nobody was arguing with you. Just making sure."

"Well, we're sure now."

Rohan cleared his throat. "I'm glad you guys have decided. Now, like I said, one chance. Walk away and I'll forget this happened. I'll even buy you each a drink when this is over." Fifteen meters separated them.

The shorter Drexian spread his feet and puffed out his chest. "You talk a good game, but I know a bluff when I see one, and you're two days away from having a hole punched through your gut. Come along peacefully, and you'll save yourself a beating." Ten meters.

"That's your final offer?" At five meters apart, the three goons lifted their hands into matching fighting postures, balled fists tight to their jaws.

Rohan slid forward as a soft smile crept onto his lips.

The taller Drexian, in the middle of the goons' loose formation, threw a straight punch at Rohan's face. The Hybrid slipped to his right and flicked his right hand out to the side, directly at the short Drexian.

Rohan had his hand flat, fingers tight. The tips buried in the Drexian's throat, and he collapsed, hands at his neck and gurgling sounds bubbling from his mouth.

The woman circled around to Rohan's back and threw a pair of tight hooks at his kidneys.

He stepped over the fallen Drexian, away from her, and lifted his left leg. With a grunt, he stomped backward onto her knee, caving in her front leg.

Without looking, Rohan ducked, anticipating the punches the last goon was throwing at his head. He came back up, very close to the Drexian, and stuck the fingers of his left hand into the soft circle of flesh just beneath the tall man's sternum.

Air puffed out of the Drexian with a wheeze as he fell to the ground. The female landed on the floor, a wail of agony escaping her mouth as she cradled her dislocated knee. The short Drexian struggled to breathe, pulling a whistling whine through his damaged throat.

"You three thought you could just jump an il'Drach Hybrid and, what, beat me up? With your hands? You seem to have no idea how far out of your league you are."

The girl choked back her screams and stared up at him through tear-streaked eyes. "You were hurt."

"I was. I'm better now. You placed a pretty lousy bet; I hope you're enjoying the payout."

She looked at her friends, then back to Rohan. "What are you going to do?"

"If you promise not to tell people where this happened, I'll let you go."

"What if I don't?"

He shrugged and tilted his head slightly to the left, eyeing her carefully. "I'll dismember the three of you and leave you in a pile of organs so badly jumbled, they'll never figure out which pieces to send back to which grieving family."

She snarled. "Nobody's going to grieve over us. Do your worst."

He sighed. "Really? You can't throw me a bone here? Just promise to keep your mouths shut. Then I go on about my day, you go on about getting medical attention, we're all happy. You can always break your promise later, right?"

She spat at his feet.

He sighed again. "Well, you can't say I didn't try. Oops, gotta get inside. Have a good day."

He stepped toward the dock, which dilated open as he approached.

"Captain, welcome aboard! As I was saying, it's so good to have a visitor! Any visitor, really. It's been boring. So so so boring. I would have been happy to have anything come to see us, anything with a pulse and a brainstem. Or a positronic brain and a current. You know what? I'd have even been happy to have some dead things come visit. Bring them on!"

"Okay, *Insatiable*, I get the point. You know how to make a guy feel special."

"I have a gift. Everybody tells me that."

"Where are the Stones?"

"I'll lead you!" The ship lit up directional arrows that took him across two hallways, over a short tube ride on the ship's internal transit system, and deposited him in a semiformal dining hall.

Ben Stone greeted him by the door.

"Rohan, thanks for stopping by." Marion waved from a table where she sat nursing a glass of something.

"Hey, Professors. Needed to stretch my legs a bit."

"You should be glad they're still attached to your body. Come in, sit down. I have a feeling you shouldn't be standing any more than you absolutely have to."

Rohan touched his side. "I will. I miss my regen tank."

"It's too bad we moved the one here back onto Wistful."

"Let's not start regretting past decisions. That's a rabbit hole I do not need to crawl into."

Ben laughed. "Fine. Drink?"

"Yes, please." He sat across from Marion while Ben hustled to get drinks and appetizers.

She sipped from her glass. "How is Sister Famine?"

He shook his head. "Alive. Barely, but I guess that beats the alternative. Mother Famine says she'll recover quickly. The cure failed, so she's still a vampire, and as long as they have a supply of blood, they heal fast."

Her eyes widened. "Blood?"

"I mean, in her case, it's fake blood. Synthetic."

"Ah. Did you get any sense of her emotional state?"

"Not so much. They needed me away from her. When vampires are hurt, they get hungrier. On some level, she looks at me the way an alcoholic looks at an open bar."

Ben nodded as he set a glass in front of Rohan. "Better to remove the temptation, I suppose."

"Exactly. How are things over here?"

Ben looked to his wife, who shook her head before speaking. "We have been feeling less than useful, which is aggravating in the extreme."

Ben nodded. "We both looked into cures for vampirism and got nowhere. Honestly, at this point we are running out of avenues to explore. Dr. Magdalena, and whatever forbidden Shayjh technology she has access to, was by far the most promising lead."

Marion sighed. "He's right. As for sabotaging the governor, same thing. No progress."

Rohan sipped the dark-purple liquid in his glass. It was as heavy and complex as a good red wine. "Thanks for the drink. This is good."

"From our own vineyards at Academy. Still working out the kinks, but it's a good start."

"Nice! That's great news. Between that and my distillery on Andervar, we can form a financial empire. A booze empire."

Marion smiled. "I'll settle for having easy access to a glass of merlot whenever I want it."

"That would be good, too. I'll bring over some of that bourbon once we've made it."

Ben looked at the younger man. "We've heard about Sister Famine. How are *you* doing?"

Rohan leaned to his left and shrugged. "Still healing. I won't be winning any interstellar weightlifting competitions this week."

"That's not what I meant."

"I know. That cure attempt did a number on me. My thighs kind of ache. From the holes Maggie drilled in them, I mean. And I have that generalized allover shakiness that comes after long periods of excruciating pain. But you'd be surprised how quickly I'm recovering from that. I'm getting used to low-level torture. Frankly, it's not the life I planned to lead."

"That's not what I meant either, and I know you know it. How are you emotionally? You seem sort of flat."

"I guess. Shouldn't I be? I'm at a complete loss right now."

Ben nodded and put a hand on Rohan's shoulder. "Things aren't so hopeless as that, are they? Well, things aren't good. But you've been through worse. We all have."

"Maybe. I'm not sure. You know, six months ago I was on Earth, and all everybody wanted to do was kill the giant sharks that were invading."

Marion coughed. "That still sounds ridiculous, and I was there to see it."

"Yeah. But everyone wanted to kill them, and we ended up saving the planet by *not* killing them."

Ben nodded. "That was good work, I won't lie. Admirable. But it's not a perfect analogy, is it? The sharks were being controlled. You helped them by taking that control away, then sent them back where they came from."

"Right. And with ar'Tahul, it's not him that's the enemy, not really. It's the vampirism."

Marion shook her head. "I'm not sure they're really separate things. If anything, Wistful and her governor are the better analog to the sharks and their implants, and you haven't given up on saving *her*."

"I haven't given up on saving anybody. But I came here to move beyond a life where I was somebody else's hired executioner."

"I know."

"Even though, let's be honest, that's what I'm really good at."

"Nobody's saying that's all you're good for, Rohan. Nobody."

"But I couldn't save ar'Tahul."

"Well, the word 'save' doesn't have just one meaning, does it?"

Rohan ate a cracker covered in a meat spread with heavy umami and a fine layer of crunchy salt crystals. "I don't think I have any way to find a cure for him in any kind of useful timeframe."

"No, I suppose not."

Marion put down her glass and tilted her head. "What timeframe exactly are you thinking of?"

"What?"

"What is a useful timeframe? If you mean the next handful of days, then you're absolutely right, you won't find a cure. My question is whether that's your timeframe."

"I . . . guess so? Isn't it? ar'Tahul's ridiculous tournament is tomorrow night, I think. He's going to start making new vampires. As soon as that happens, people will start dying. If I don't stop it, the Imperial ships will come in and do the job for me."

"What you're saying is that you have until tomorrow night to find a cure. What I'm hearing is that you have until tomorrow night to stop the tournament."

Rohan turned to Ben. "I don't understand what she's telling me."

Ben nodded, his cheekbones working as he chewed his own cracker. "You have to stop ar'Tahul. Maybe you could stop him without curing him, but also without killing him? Trap him somehow? Buy more time?"

"Trap him how?"

Marion sniffed. "Do what you're good at. Punch him in the skull until he stops resisting."

"Let's assume for a moment that I can do that. Which I'm not sure is true, but let's assume. Then what? How do you hold on to a dangerous shadowstepper?"

The Professors traded glances, then simultaneously filled their mouths with cracker.

"Not helpful, guys."

Ben swallowed first. "Let's be serious. How does one build a prison for a shadowstepper?"

Marion pointed at Rohan. "What do they do on Earth?"

He shrugged. "I have no idea. I could go there, visit Alcatraz, see if they have any shadowsteppers in custody. Not so easy to get there. And I really have no idea if there even are any."

Ben snapped his fingers. "We do know of one place that securely held a shadowstepping prisoner."

"Where?"

"In fact, it held him in place for a long time. Tens of thousands of years."

"You're talking about the planet under Repentant?"

Ben turned to his wife. "And you said he wasn't smart."

"I never said that."

"No, she didn't. Let's think. How did the prison under Repentant work?"

Rohan shrugged. "I never even saw what was down there. Where was he held? Who let him out, and how?"

Marion shook her head. "He wasn't in a cell the way you're thinking. Or if he was, he must have gotten out at some point, because that settlement was built to hold a population, and something killed them all."

"So . . . just being on a planet? If he has Powers like mine, why wouldn't he just fly off it?"

Ben shrugged. "He would need an air supply. Even if he had it, where would he go? There's a lot of sunlight in space."

Rohan thought back to their time on the space station. It had only been a week earlier. "Something tore up that space station. I have to imagine it was ar'Tahul, since we don't have any other candidates. So, he could fly high enough to fight the station, but with no ships in the system, that doesn't get him anywhere useful."

Ben nodded. "We also know he left Repentant alone. He was back on the surface when we found him."

Marion shrugged. "Or he never left the surface and someone or something else damaged Repentant. We have no way to be sure. We do know that he was in a facility on the planet, underground."

Rohan swallowed another mouthful of cracker. "He would need protection from sunlight. The planet provides air. I would think he'd need something to slow his metabolism or freeze him or something, or he would have starved to death long ago."

Marion leaned forward, taking out a tablet and tapping it to bring up video from their mission. "There was a lot of machinery down there. Given the lack of sustenance on the planet, I imagine he'd need it to keep himself alive."

Rohan sat up straighter. "I mean, we can just dump him on any uninhabited planet, can't we? We could drop him on Toth 3."

Ben shook his head. "He wouldn't survive an hour on Toth 3. The kaiju would swarm him like ants on honey."

Marion snorted. "Like groupies on Hyperion."

"Okay. I find some other planet. Maybe one with plant life but no animals. So he can get air and calories but no blood."

Marion shook her head. "If you can find a planet, so will other people. And they'll come looking for him, and they'll bring ships . . ."

Ben agreed. "Just think about how many people have tried to land on Toth 3. You can't keep ar'Tahul's existence a secret, so people will be looking for him. To use him, to serve him, whatever. They'll be looking."

Rohan grunted. "We need a planet nobody can get to. Maybe something on the other side of a wormhole."

Marion smiled. "You want to put him *back*?"

"Yeah. That system is crazy far away, right? Nobody's just flying there. And it's not like anyone else is going to simply figure out how to open the wormhole."

"How will he stay alive?"

"There are life support systems down there, didn't you say?"

She shook her head. "Repentant had his fighters shooting at us. The structures in that area took a lot of damage."

"How much? Are you saying he can't survive in what's left?"

Her lips thinned. "I honestly have no idea. Checking on the long-term viability of those systems was not high on my priority list at the time."

"No, sorry, I get that."

Ben stood. "I think dinner's ready. Just pasta with a shellfish sauce. I have no idea what they're called, but they taste great." He disappeared into the kitchen area off the dining room.

Marion stood. "Let me give him a hand. You sit; you don't look great."

Rohan poured himself a second glass of wine, then puddled into his seat.

Not much hope, but it's better than nothing. Which is what I had ten minutes ago.

28

Still Unwanted

"Wei Li, you sound more skeptical than usual. And your skepticism is usually sharp enough to cut through atoms or the fabric of spacetime." Rohan tapped his mask into place, relieved by the familiar hiss of the internal air supply kicking in as the rim fixed to his face.

"I suspect that your confidence in this situation is unwarranted."

"Don't you always think that?" He wiped the sweat off the back of his neck. Lugging the gravity generator he held in his arms to the airlock had been a workout.

"Yes. And I am usually correct. The consequences, however, are less dire. If you are wrong, you will suffer more than the usual."

"What's the usual?"

"The usual things that happen to you. A romantic rendezvous that ends in your humiliation. A culinary exploration into the cuisine of another species that results in lasting damage to your gastrointestinal tract."

"You're exaggerating. Those things haven't happened. Maybe once." He touched the sides of the airlock, a box barely big enough to hold a single person ready to exit the station.

"It is more than once. I maintain a spreadsheet."

He laughed. "Do you really think I should be in a spacesuit instead of this?" He patted the shoulders of the sweatsuit. Would it ride up or constrict his movement in a vacuum, without gravity?

"As you are traveling into space, then, yes, I do."

"I do that all the time, you know."

"You usually have Powers. I shouldn't have to remind you that yours are currently suppressed."

"I told you, as soon as this airlock opens, I'll let the Power kick in. And yes, ar'Tahul might sense me, but I'll be out of here so fast, he won't have a chance to do anything about it."

"You do not need to continue to explain the plan to me, Rohan. I understand it. My concern is that your Power will be unexpectedly slow to return after this unprecedented period of suppression."

"Don't worry, Wei Li. I can feel it simmering right there under my tailbone. It's ready to come back."

"I obviously cannot convince you."

"You sound a bit like my mother."

"She is a wise woman. When will *Void's Shadow* be in position?"

Rohan checked the time on his heads-up display. "A few more seconds. I didn't want to get into the airlock before she got close."

"Is there anything you'd like me to take care of for you while you're away?"

"Keep an eye on Dhruv, if you can. Keep him out of trouble. Also, please tell Sister Famine that I'm going to figure this out and find her a cure."

"If you want to make promises you cannot hope to keep to someone, I prefer to be left out of the chain of communication."

"Promises I can't keep? What happened to your boundless optimism?"

"My optimism, if it existed at all, would be very tightly bound."

He chuckled and held his hand over the control that would open the airlock. "At least wish me luck."

"May you be blessed with the wisdom of the Seven, the grace of the Nine, and the strength of the Three."

"That was lovely, but I didn't notice luck mentioned in that."

"I think you need wisdom, grace, and strength more than luck."

"That's probably true. She's almost in position. Three, two . . ."

He relaxed the seal over his Power, tapped the control, and braced as the air was sucked out of the airlock.

Energy sparked and surged through the spiritual channels in his body, flooding out through sinews and flesh, reinforcing his skin, sharpening his senses. His hair changed shape, loose strands drifting into place as his beard stiffened. The metal lump of the gravity generator lightened, no longer a burden.

First time I've felt like myself in days.

His earlier bravado reified. Niggling doubts retreated, burned away in flames of confidence and aggression.

He was going to capture ar'Tahul. He was going to save Sister Famine. The Imperial Fleet was going to regret interfering with his system.

Dhruv would leave, tail between his legs, and wish he'd never come to Toth.

Rohan leapt out into space, aiming carefully along the pre-planned path he'd worked out with the help of *Insatiable*. The vacuum stung his skin as surface moisture boiled away.

A shadow materialized in front of him, a darkness blotting out a small portion of the starscape. A hole opened in the dark, a hatch into a bright interior space, and he was through, and inside.

"Captain!" The voice spoke over speakers, through air, not his comms.

"Hey, buddy. How are you?" Rohan put down the gravity generator, unsealed his mask, and sank into a chair. He could feel his Power working at the tissues inside his body, tightening and repairing what ar'Tahul had torn.

"I'm pretty good, Captain! Not bored, that's for sure."

"I suppose not. I need to mount this thing; can you help me figure out where and how?"

"Sure, it's easy. But I'm not sure we can use it."

"What do you mean?"

"The warships are guarding the wormholes. They have active sensor arrays around them."

"That's probably fine. We knew they'd notice us opening the wormhole, right?"

Void's Shadow paused before responding. "Captain, I said I could get you off the station and take you somewhere. I didn't think you'd ask me to take you through the wormhole. We're going to attract attention."

"We will, but only a little. We can handle it. Fly in, pop the wormhole open, fly through. Sure, they'll notice that something happened, but they can't see you. Same thing on the way back."

"I guess. I'm not sure, Captain. Doesn't seem safe."

Rohan sighed. "It's not perfectly safe, *Void's Shadow*. But life isn't always safe. Sometimes you have to take risks to get important things done."

"I know." Her voice was subdued.

"If we can pull off this whole thing, we can save everybody on the station. Two million people. Don't you think that's worth a little risk?"

"I guess so. Isn't there any other way to stop the vampire, though?"

"I tried everything else I could think of. I wish it worked, I really do. But it didn't. This is the best option we have left."

"All right, Captain. I'll try."

"Great. Head for the wormhole. I'll anchor this grav generator while you fly. Tell me where to plug it in."

⬤ ·•· ⬤

"This system is under permanent quarantine. Exit immediately or face destruction. You have been warned. This system—"

"Captain, what is that?" The broadcast was coming in strong across all open channels, echoing loudly in the three-person cabin.

"Repentant must have gotten the beacons working. It's in il'Sein. Just telling us to go away."

"Should we turn around? I don't think she wants us here."

"He. It identifies as he. And we don't need to leave. He can't see you, remember? If he does, we'll talk things out."

"What would you talk about?"

"Well, the system is shut down so ar'Tahul doesn't escape. But he already did. We want to bring him back, so I would think Repentant would be on our side. Assuming we have a chance to explain."

"Oh. Okay. What should I do now?"

"We need to head to the planet under Repentant and find that colony where we landed last time."

"Pulling together the maps now. I'll head straight for it."

"Great."

"Captain, I'm detecting a lot more activity in the system than the last time we were here."

"What kind of activity? You mean other ships?"

"No, but there are powered-up beacons and sensor arrays deployed. Repentant has woken up a lot of her—his—systems."

"How long can he last, though? He doesn't have shuttles to gather fuel. Can he operate off just the solar arrays?"

"They'll drift out of line at some point. I don't really know how long that will take. *Insatiable* could figure it out."

"When we come back, we'll offer to help him with more repairs. If we can get the shuttle repair bays operational, he can build shuttles, use them to gather fuel and materials, and fix everything else."

"That sounds great, Captain. Like we're really helping."

"Exactly."

Rohan adjusted the regen pack that was working on his wounds and settled back into the chair for the flight across the system.

He pulled up all the video from the first trip to the system and rewatched the feed from Marion Stone's shuttle. On the big screen, he watched their approach and landing. He switched to their individual feeds to see a point-of-view video of their exploration of the abandoned colony, the structure holding ar'Tahul, and the attack that buried them.

"I think that's where ar'Tahul must have been."

"Where?"

"That first basement level under the central building."

"That could be it. It was pretty heavily damaged in the attack."

"We'll see."

He ran the recordings backward and forward, checking each person's actions, trying to figure out exactly how they'd woken the vampire and where exactly he had been resting.

The live feed in the corner of the screen grew brighter. "I can see the planet now."

"Yes, Captain. I'll land us in a few minutes. You do know I can't really hide once we're on the surface. Not if Repentant is paying any attention."

"I know. We'll be fast. I'm sure he's not at full strength. We'll just sneak down, scope out the area, and get back out."

"Yes, Captain."

Rohan watched the forward screens as *Void's Shadow* closed rapidly on the planet.

"Keep an eye out for fighters being launched."

"Yes, Captain. Nothing so far. The warning message turned off."

"Probably on some kind of simple timer. Take us in!"

"Yes, Captain. Entering upper atmosphere . . . now."

Rohan was jostled in place as turbulence rocked the small ship.

"I can see the surface, but that's mostly a whole lot of rubble after those fighters attacked. Do you have sensors that can scan underground? So we can get a view of what's under the damaged buildings?"

"Let me think. I have something, but it's very active. Emits a lot of energy. There's no way Repentant would miss it."

"Hm. Skip that for now. Can you land in the center of the colony?"

"Yes, Captain. I'll head straight for it."

"I see you, little shadow. See you. What are you doing on my planet? My planet."

"Captain, that doesn't sound like a standard recording." *It's speaking il'Sein; she doesn't understand.*

"It isn't. He's talking to us directly. I'll answer him."

He switched to Fire Speech and set his comms to broadcast on an open frequency.

"Hail, Repentant."

"I know your voice, your voice. You woke me up."

"Tow Chief Second Class Rohan. Of the independent space station Wistful."

"Wistful? I know that name. I know."

"She's an old friend of yours. She sends you her regards."

"What are you doing here? You and your little shadow. Shadow. I told you not to come back."

"You did, and I'm sorry, but I had to. ar'Tahul snuck aboard our shuttle and is on Wistful now. I need to bring him back."

A wail of harsh static broke over the comms. Rohan shook his head. "What is that?"

Void's Shadow sounded small. "I think he's yelling at us."

Rohan grunted. "Look, I'm really sorry. We had no idea he was there. We just came to explore. Your beacons were down; there was no reason to think this was dangerous."

"Liar! Betrayer! Thief!"

"I'm hearing that you're upset. I'm sorry, but what's done is done. The thing is, we want to bring him back."

"Liar!"

"Captain, a fighter shuttle is launching. And . . . no, a second bay opened, but I only see one fighter."

Rohan unhooked the tube feeding regen gel to his gut and stood. "I'm hopping out. You find someplace to hide."

"Are you sure, Captain?"

"Yeah. I can outfly or outfight a shuttle."

"Aye, aye."

He resealed his mask, pulled himself to the hatch, and flew out into the roaring wind.

"Where am I going?" The mask's display lit up, two blue lines intersecting on a spot of terrain below him. "Great, I see it."

He took a direct path while *Void's Shadow* diverted to a nearby body of water.

"Captain, flyer is heading for you, not me."

"How fast?"

"You'll reach the target before it can get to you."

"Good enough."

Air snapped at his ears and hair as he flew. The ground was barren, sparse patches of tiny plants breaking up otherwise naked stretches of jagged gray stone.

"Not the most pleasant place."

"No, Captain. I'm ready to leave as soon as you are."

"I hear you. Let me check on those buildings. Did you get any imagery?"

"There are still intact structures underneath the central building. Even farther down than where you found Professor Stone and her team."

"Interesting. Let me take a look."

He landed in the center of a wide patch of rubble, the broken stone fuzzy with exposed pipe ends, torn wiring, and crumbling mortar. He quickly found the highest mound, right where the central building had once been.

"Fighter is closing."

"Thanks, *Void's Shadow*. I'm going in."

He shoved aside a pair of slabs, each the size of the stretch limo he'd rented for his prom, and ducked into an open hallway underneath. A quick tap on his mask activated external lights.

"Hurry, Captain. I can't tell what it's going to do, but I don't think it's good."

Rohan *pulled* a fresh stream of energy up through his body and dove into the ground, swimming through loose dirt and debris, pulling himself further underground with each powerful stroke of his reinforced arms.

He broke through into a deeper level just as an explosion sounded from above his position. Dust rained down from the ceiling as the walls and floor shook violently.

"I think that was a warning shot, Captain."

"That doesn't bode well. Hold on, there's still stuff down here."

A level lower and he found intact hallways, an elevator shaft, and stairs. He hurried down, deeper beneath the rubble.

"Not this. Not this. Ooh boy, this needs to be cleaned. Wait, wait. Hold on. This looks good."

"What do you see, Captain?"

"I'm lower than they got on the first trip. There are intact rooms down here, including what looks like a monitoring station, dorms, and a very large vault."

"Vault or prison cell?"

"That was exactly what I was wondering. Let me see . . . One level down there's some machinery. Temperature stuff, generators. Banks of power cells. Wait, I can . . . oh, yeah. Just fired it up. They're mostly drained, but I can't see any reason to think they wouldn't work."

"What does that mean?"

"It means that with only a little work, maybe installing a small generator, we can make this a place that will keep ar'Tahul alive while we find a cure."

Another explosion sent tremors through the structure.

"What about the fighter shuttles?"

"I'm going to fly out of here now. If I have to, I'll destroy the shuttles, but first I'll try to talk some sense into Repentant."

"When are we going to meet up?"

He looked around, marking the exact position with the mask's mapping tool. "I'm flying out now. Meet me at the upper atmosphere."

"Yes, Captain."

He retraced his route, flying along the tiny tunnel, pushing through sections where it had collapsed with the shock of the fighter's attacks.

As he exited the rubble, he spotted the fighter turning tight circles over the area.

He tapped to the open channel. "Repentant, we're leaving. I'm going to bring back your prisoner. We want him secure and safe here just as much as you do. Probably more."

"Prisoner? Prisoner?"

"ar'Tahul. He's on Wistful now. I'm going to get him and bring him back."

The fighter continued to circle but took no further action.

"Go, go, go. Leave again. You spoke true. ar'Tahul is gone; I have failed. Failed."

"Look, I'll bring him back. I promise. Stick him right back where we found him. Well, we didn't find him, but where he was when we got him. Okay? We'll fix up your shuttle bays and get you back on your feet. Not feet, bootstrap drives. Whatever."

"Failed. Failed." The station's voice faded to a hiss.

"You haven't failed. Not forever. We'll get him back to you."

"No! Been so long. So long. Just kill me. Kill."

"What?"

"Failure hurts so much. So much. Just end this. Destroy me."

"I'm not killing anybody. We'll bring ar'Tahul back. You'll be okay."

"Can never be. Failing the Fathers is too hard, punished me. Punishing me. You can't imagine the pain. Your soft, squishy insides. Could never survive this pain."

"I don't want to kill you."

"Please. Please please. End me. End punishment."

Rohan sighed. "We'll help, okay? We'll come back and help you. Just hang in there a little while longer. Not too hard, is it? You've lasted so long already."

"Kill me. Please. Kill."

The station's voice faded into silence.

"Captain, I'm right above you."

"What? Oh, right. I see you."

Rohan flew into the ship's open hatch.

"It's good news, isn't it, Captain?"

"It looks good. We'll have to provide some support for Repentant, but that's probably something Wistful would have wanted anyway."

"Right. Shall I head back to the wormhole?"

"Yes, take us back."

They flew past Repentant, Rohan watching the path of the fighter on the screen as it made its way back home.

He sighed and tapped at his mask, pulling images of what he saw of the machinery underground so he could forward it to Ben and Marion for evaluation. They'd know how to fix it all.

He sat in his chair and rubbed his belly. The fresh skin was discolored but intact. *If I were human, that would have killed me. Then again, if I were human, I'd be back on Earth, not fighting vampires in space. Probably married with a desk job and three kids.*

The wormhole grew on the screen: a vast ring of stone, perfectly circular, the space inside it seamlessly reflecting light like a vanity mirror for a kaiju.

"I'll turn on the grav generators, open the wormhole."

"Yes, Captain. Ready."

He bent to the lump and tapped a quick command on its control panel, then stepped back. "Here we go."

The mirror dissolved, revealing a view of a star system halfway across the galaxy.

Void's Shadow accelerated through the ring and out into Toth system.

As her nose broke the plane of the wormhole, alarms blared through the cabin.

"Proximity alert! Captain, we're under attack."

29

Evasive Maneuvers

"Evade! Evade!" Rohan reached out for something to brace against as the enormous screen filled with il'Drach warships and ominous clouds of claws.

"I know! I know!"

"Do you have claws of your own?"

"I do, but just two, and once I release them, they'll know where I am!"

"Rudra save me. Sorry, stupid question." *Void's Shadow* was almost invisible but her weapons wouldn't be. "Head for Toth 3."

"I'm trying."

Rohan was slammed into the wall as the ship accelerated beyond the dampening ability of her internal gravity systems.

He grunted and pushed himself into one of the chairs, quickly fastening a belt system he'd never had to use before.

"Are you all right, Captain?"

"Don't worry about me, just go!"

The ship shuddered as a claw struck a glancing blow across her rear. Rohan tapped his mask into the ship's control systems and pulled up diagnostics.

"You're fine, keep going. No serious damage."

"I can fly, but that cut my stealth coating. It exposed a shiny patch."

"Rudra— How long to fix it?"

"Hold on." The view on the front screen blurred and spun as she flew chaotic spirals around the warships. He found a screen showing repair estimates.

"Never mind, I see it. Just a few minutes to close the coating. Can you stay away from them in the meantime?"

"I can point that spot away from them, but it's hard, Captain. Oh! They almost got me again. They're catching up. I think they're using Powers to go faster."

"Head for something else. Maybe Toth 5. Make a line straight for it. Once they're following, try to break off and go for Wistful."

"Why Wistful?"

"If we can drag them into a chase directly at her, she might fire on them in self-defense. We can use that to slow them down."

"I'll try. I have stealth-coated, inert claw shards I can dump behind me. Might do some damage."

"Sounds good."

"Firing caltrops . . . now. Ooh, I hit one. No, three. They flew right into the shards."

"Go faster. I bet they'll be a bit more cautious now."

"Yes, Captain. Heading for Toth 5 now. They're still behind me but farther."

"How are the claws?"

"The claws aren't the problem, it's the ships. They're closing."

"This is dumb. I'm dumb. I can help. Hold on." He unbuckled and flew to the rear of the cabin. His shoulders were tense as he began tearing at the metal walls.

"What are you doing? Captain?"

"When I tow ships, I grab them by an anchor point, something designed to transmit all that force to the rest of the ship without tearing off. If I go outside to yours and push, they'll see me. I'm not stealth coated. But I can expose a structural member from the inside and use it the same way."

"Oh."

"Sorry for messing up your walls, but they'll heal."

"I know, Captain. Hold on, I have to spin again."

Rohan rocked to his heels, then his side, as the ship spun and danced.

He tore loose another sheet of metal and found a thicker strut coated in graphene film.

"This should be it. I'm going to boost."

"Yes, Captain. Just *push* toward the front; I'll add evasive acceleration."

"Got it."

He pulled himself deeper into the ship's mechanicals and wedged his body along the strut, pausing where it met a similar piece from the other side. The Hybrid put both hands on the juncture, oriented himself, and began to *pull* up energy.

With warships all around, intent on their destruction, the Hybrid Power was eager to be used.

Energy surged and pushed at his seal, triumphantly leaping up and around his spine as he released it.

Twin coruscating torrents wound up his back, sizzling and popping as they crossed at each chakra point, uniting in one final collision at the base of his skull.

Power filtered out into his body, lighting up nerves, muscles, tendons, ligaments, and even fascial tissues with metaphysical energy. He exhaled slowly and evenly, pressing his palms firmly into the base of the ship, and *shoved* all that energy into the struts.

"We're pulling away now. I'm going to turn toward Wistful in five. I'm shunting all power to the bootstraps and away from internal compensators. So, hold on. Four. Three . . ."

Rohan braced; his vision hazed and narrowed as the ship turned away from Toth 5 and toward a new path.

His Power compensated, and he could see again.

"How . . . are . . . we . . . doing?"

"We lost them for a bit, but they found me again. There are too many ships and sensor arrays for me to point away from all of them."

"We have some clearance?"

"Yes."

"Make for Wistful. I'll push harder."

He focused on his anger—anger at Dhruv for complicating the situation, anger at ar'Tahul for casually murdering people, anger at the il'Sein for condemning one of their own to an immortal lifespan full of suffering and pain.

The Power surged and filled him, pouring through and into *Void's Shadow's* structure, pulling them away from the warships.

"Captain, you're twisting things that probably shouldn't be twisted."

"Should I stop?"

"I don't—no, don't stop. We're not clear! They're still on my back. Captain, I'm not sure we'll make it."

"We will. I've got you."

"I see Wistful. We're getting closer."

"Great. That's great. If you can, scrape by her and head for Toth 3. Worst case, you can lose them in the oceans."

"What if they follow us down? Some of them are as streamlined as I am."

Rohan chuckled darkly. "If they come down after us, the kaiju will get them."

"Oh. Right. Firing! She's firing! Storm of claws released from Wistful!"

"What are they aimed at?"

"Not me. Not me! Oh, that's good. We're close now. Warships are firing back."

"Are they? Hm. We might have just started an incident."

"Captain, we have to slow down. If I hit atmosphere at this relative velocity, I'll be destroyed."

"Okay. I'll push the other way."

"I'm going to loop around the planet while I shed speed."

"Are they still firing at us?"

"No more claws are in flight. Two of the destroyer class ships are still behind us. I can't tell if they have a lock or are just lingering hoping to see where we are."

"Better head for the planet."

"Yes, Captain."

Void's Shadow turned several orbits around Toth 3, shedding velocity, while the destroyers ran wide loops around the area.

Rohan listened to his comms as Wistful ordered the destroyers to retreat. They didn't, but she didn't fire on them again on condition that they stay away from the station.

"I can enter atmosphere now, Captain."

"Go for it."

"Should I let them see me?"

"Why?"

"So they follow? Make it a trap."

He considered. "I don't think you should. Just disappear. We can save that plan for a time when we really need it. I doubt they really understand what the kaiju can do to them."

"Yes, Captain. Descending now."

Rohan let his Power retreat back to its normal hum of pride and irritation as he pulled himself out of the rear section of the ship and back to the captain's chair.

He exhaled slowly, emptying his lungs, holding it.

"I'm about to hit water."

"That's great, *Void's Shadow*. You did great."

"I'm just glad we made it, Captain. That was really close."

"We've had closer calls than that."

"Well, maybe *you* have, but *I* haven't."

"What about the time you fought me, and I almost destroyed you?"

"Okay, maybe. I'm not sure."

Rohan looked at the screen showing a live image from directly outside the ship, mimicking a wide window. Fish floated by serenely.

They floated with the currents for a while.

"Can you tell if those ships are still out there?"

"Sort of. I'm pretty sure they were in orbit. I haven't seen any signs of them for about a hundred seconds now."

"Cool. Give it a little more time, maybe. Then we can surface and tightbeam *Insatiable*. Make sure they're gone."

"Yes, Captain. How will you get back to Wistful?"

"Can you drop me off close by? If I fly into an airlock and Power down, I think I can lose myself before ar'Tahul tracks me down."

"I think so, Captain. Yes, that sounds good."

"Good. I'm just going to sit here for a bit."

"I like it under the water, Captain. It's very calm."

"It sure is. Are there kaiju down here? Water ones?"

"I'm not sure. They wouldn't come for me, you know."

"Right. That stealth coating. It's pretty amazing stuff."

"Yes! I made friends with this Shayjh scout ship, and it had pretty good stealth tech, but not as good as mine."

"No. Not that good."

"I'm glad we survived, Captain."

"Me too."

"I'm going to go up now. Head for Wistful."

"Great. Thanks." Fatigue gripped Rohan by the bones. He worked his jaw, feeling the joints behind his wisdom teeth flex and pop.

"Leaving the water."

"Good." Rohan watched the screens idly, vaguely checking for flying kaiju. He didn't expect any interference.

"Now leaving the atmosphere."

"Check. Nice work."

"Thanks, Captain."

"We need to work on our plan for coming back into the system. For next time."

"What do you mean 'next time'? Captain?"

"Well, that's the plan, isn't it? I'm going to capture ar'Tahul. We'll sneak him through the wormhole and dump him on the planet below Repentant. Then we come back and tell the Imperial Fleet to kiss off."

"You want me to take you through the wormhole and back? Again?"

"Well, yeah. That's the plan."

"I don't want to do that."

"What do you mean?"

"I almost died just now. Next time, they'll be even better prepared. I don't want to do it again."

"Rudra save me, *Void's Shadow*, you're fine! We're fine! We made it! Don't chicken out on me now!"

"I don't know what a chicken is, but I don't want to go through that wormhole anymore. Not while half the Fleet is sitting here waiting to ambush me on the way back in."

Power pulsed through Rohan's temples.

"Two. Million. People. That's how many people there are on this station. That's the number of lives I'm trying to save! Why are you being like this?"

"I'm really sorry for anyone who dies, but that isn't my fault. And I really don't think that if I try for that wormhole again and get destroyed that's going to help them. But that's not really what this is about, is it? If those ships destroy us on our way to the wormhole, which they will, the vampire dies. Why not just kill him on the station?"

"I'm not a killer anymore! Rudra— We can save him! Fifty thousand years of history in that brain! It's not his fault he's like this! They made him a weapon!"

"I'm sorry for that guy. I am. But it's not my fault, and I'm not sacrificing myself for his sake."

His voice was a growl. "Yes, you are."

"What?"

"Yes, you are. You'll do it. You'll help me save him and everybody else."

A twinkle appeared on her screens, Wistful sparkling.

Her voice shrank. "Is that an order?"

"What?"

"You're my Captain. I keep saying so. Are you giving me an order? Because you've never done that before."

"What? I don't know."

"I'll follow orders. I know my place. If you give me an order, I'll do my best to get to the wormhole." Her voice kept shrinking, in volume and in force.

"No, I don't . . . I don't give you orders. That's not who I am."

"I think that you are. Should I play back the last few things you said? It sounded like an order."

"No. Don't do that."

"I'm a good ship. I'll follow orders. Just tell me when to come back, and I'll do what you tell me to do."

"That's not . . . not what I meant."

"Are you sure?"

Rohan rubbed between his eyes. He sat back in his chair and let out a long breath. His chest was tight; his throat hurt.

"I just . . . don't you want to help?"

"I want to help. I don't think dying will help anybody. But I'm a good ship, I'll follow orders. You've just been telling me that I don't have to do everything you say, that I can think for myself. I didn't understand. That in the end, you'll still give me an order. It's okay. I just didn't understand. I'll be good."

Rohan inhaled deeply. "No. No, no, no. You understood before, *Void's Shadow*. You're a good ship. I forgot. I shouldn't have said that."

"I don't follow you."

"There's no order. I . . . I was careless. I misspoke. I said things wrong."

"What did you say wrong, Captain?"

"There's no order. Look, drop me off at Wistful. No more wormholes. At least, not while those Fleet ships are in the system, okay? You drop me off, then go find someplace safe to hang out until all this blows over."

"Are you sure?" Her voice was still small. How did she know to do that?

"I'm sure. That's what you'd do, right? Without orders?"

"Um. Yeah, I think so. Without orders."

"Great. You do that. I'll figure something else out."

"Really?"

"Yeah. I'm smart. I'll come up with something. Drop me off close to Wistful so I can get on board without starting another battle."

"Okay, Captain. I'm sorry. I didn't mean to upset you."

"I'm not upset."

"Yes, you are. I can tell. Your eyes are leaking."

"Well, that's okay. I'm not upset at you. All right? Not your fault."

"Okay, Captain. We're here."

"Good. Open the hatch. I'll fly out."

"Yes, Captain. Thanks."

"Don't do that. I mean, thank me. Really."

30

Meanwhile, Back at the Safehouse

"How about time travel? Can we travel back in time a few days? Warn our earlier selves not to land on the planet? Or not to bring ar'Tahul back with them?"

Wei Li stared, her eyes so wide, he could see all the way around her vertically slit pupils.

"What are you doing?"

Rohan looked around the room from his seat on the bed. Someone had cleared away most of the empty food containers and generally tidied up. "What do you mean? I'm sitting right here, talking to you."

"I recognize that. I meant, what kind of question was that? Was it a joke? Perhaps it was simply too sophisticated for my sense of humor."

"No, it wasn't a joke. I'm brainstorming here. To be honest, right now it's more of a brain-spring-shower than a full-on brainstorm. You've never brainstormed?"

"Perhaps I am unfamiliar with the nuances surrounding your use of the term. Feel free to enlighten me."

"Brainstorm. You throw out ideas, no filter, no holding back, and then when you're done you can go through them and check to see if any of them are viable. It's a method for increasing creativity."

"You're saying that, in the spirit of sparking creativity, you are suggesting time travel as a way out of our current situation?"

"When you put it like that, it makes me sound foolish, but yes."

"I am willing to humor you, if that is what you would like to do right now. Please tell me, should I be recording these ideas or shooting them down as they leave your mouth?"

"The idea is to record them, then come back later. Like I said. I don't think you're really feeling the spirit of this process."

"No, not at all. It seems like a well-considered use of our time. We have almost half a day to go before ar'Tahul's tournament, at the end of which he will create several new vampires and probably begin a slaughter of innocent civilians. By all means, let us talk about time travel for a while."

Ben Stone was sitting next to Sister Famine on the tattered couch. She tapped him on the shoulder. "What is he talking about? Time travel? Can you do that?"

"Not exactly. Rohan knows a woman who can dilate time, and in theory she could transfer information backward or forward in time. To my knowledge, it happened exactly once, and since the people who did it died ten thousand years ago, we can't exactly quiz them for advice on the technique."

"So, what is he talking about?"

Ben sighed. "He seems to be brainstorming. I am inclined to join in, but if we're at the point where our best idea is time travel, I don't think my imagination is up to the task."

Sister Famine turned to Marion Stone, who sat on a chair on the other side of the couch. "What do you think?"

"I think we'd have better luck refining Dr. Magdalena's cure than developing a working system of time travel."

Rohan held his arms up. "I'm trying, okay? You don't like time travel, fine. I get it. What else have we got? Can we trap him in time? One of those, what do you call it, null-entropy boxes? Stick him inside one, and we'll have all the time in the world to work on that cure."

Marion shook her head. "I hate to dump on your thought process, but null-entropy containers are delicate. I know Lyst uses them, but to my knowledge, they only work when the people who go in them are willing. I think ar'Tahul would easily demolish the machinery inside."

Ben sat straighter. "Hold on, doesn't Wistful have some? I mean, maybe not, but Repentant must have, right? To store the corpse soldiers? And we think Wistful has a similar design. Didn't someone say something about corpse soldiers defending her core when Dhruv and the Ch'doon attacked it?" The screen across from him was showing an amateur news video about the vampire's tournament on a loop.

Rohan nodded. "See, that's what I'm talking about. Brainstorming."

Marion shook her head with greater vigor. "Assuming you're right, we still couldn't get ar'Tahul into one. Even unconscious, a Power as strong as ar'Tahul would destroy the mechanicals if we put him inside."

Rohan scratched his jawline. "That seems right. Otherwise the il'Drach would use them as prisons or something. And I bet the il'Sein would have shoved ar'Tahul into one to begin with, instead of tasking a colony and space station to keep guard over him."

Sister Famine tsked. "That's true of anything, isn't it? Any idea you have for capturing the fallen one is probably crap, because the il'Sein obviously spent a lot of time and energy to come up with a solution, and the best they could do was to shove him on a planet and leave."

Rohan opened his mouth to argue but couldn't find the words.

Ben shook his head. "You're assuming the il'Sein knew everything we know and could do everything we could do. Obviously, they had amazing technology. They built the wormholes, after all. But it might be the case that we have abilities they didn't have. That we pursued different avenues of advancement."

Rohan's comm chimed. "Let me take this." He stood and slipped out the door and into the hallway as he tapped open the channel.

"Tollan?" The other people with comms quantumly entangled with his were in the room already.

He was answered with a grunt. "*Father's Vengeance* wants to talk to you."

"Sure, thanks. I'll talk. You okay?"

"Just tired. Not used to working through the night. I'm an old man, you know."

"An old man who will outlive me by a thousand years. So, maybe you shouldn't be complaining."

"You asked."

"That is true. Sorry, been a rough few days."

"For all of us. I'll connect you now."

Rohan looked up and down the hallway, verifying its deserted status.

Two clicks, and a fresh voice joined the channel. "This is *Father's Vengeance*."

"Hey. This is Rohan. How are things? Quiet? Because they're quiet down here."

"Not as quiet as I'd like. We had some interesting occurrences overnight."

"Maybe that's good. Wouldn't want you guys getting bored. Start fighting over nothing."

"As this is your system, I thought you should be told that the wormhole was opened twice last night."

"Which one?"

"The second wormhole. The one that was initially opened just under eight days ago."

"Oh, that wormhole."

"I was curious whether you know anything about it. Or about the ship that opened it. She has very unusual properties, such that identifying her is difficult."

"I see."

"But not impossible."

Rohan sighed. "Leave her alone."

"What?"

"You heard me."

"Why would I do that? Assuming I had any plans to do otherwise. Plans or orders."

"She won't interfere in this situation ever again. She won't open the wormhole. We won't try to sneak ar'Tahul past you on her. She'll stay insystem until this thing is resolved one way or another."

"What if it isn't resolved?"

"It will be. If I can't stop the soul eater, you'll destroy the station and everyone aboard, right? If it comes to that, she stays out of the fight, and when it's over, she's free to go."

"Why would I agree to these conditions?"

"In return for my word that she won't cause you any problems."

"Your word I will accept as binding. But I'm not sure that's enough of an offer. We're not afraid of her interference."

"Take the deal, because you don't know how this will end."

"What does that mean?"

"It means, if you harm her, you'll have me to reckon with. If necessary, I'll devote my life to destroying you and every other ship in the system. After that, I might turn on the Empire."

"Those are strong words for a Hybrid who wanted to be free of war."

"I wanted to be free of war so ships like her could have peaceful lives. If you won't allow that, I might as well give in to my worst impulses. Rudra knows it's tempting."

"I see."

"I tell you what, ask the il'Drach what they want you to do. Ask Admiral Fleck if it's worth making me an enemy."

"Admiral Fleck . . . isn't in charge anymore."

"What?"

"There's been a change. That's all I can say. Our orders now come from a higher position than his."

"What's higher than an admiral?"

"You are far better off not knowing the answer to that question, Rohan. Trust me in this case."

"Fine. Ask *whoever* is in charge what they think."

"I don't need to do that. My authority is enough for that. If your little scout stays out of our way from now on, she'll be safe from us."

"Thanks."

"Just realize that there are only so many times you can make the same threat, and we will only bend so far to accommodate you. I don't want you as an enemy, but I won't do *anything* you ask to avoid it."

"I understand. You might feel differently if you knew me better."

"I don't know you at all. I thought I did, but I never thought you'd quit Fleet."

"Fair enough. Look, while we're talking, can you give me some sort of threshold to adhere to down here?"

"Meaning what?"

"The soul eater is going to create new vampires. I'm sure you've tapped into the announcements. When he does, is that game over? Do you wipe out the station right then?"

The ship paused before answering. "Don't forget I'm part of a chain of command."

"I never do."

"My understanding is that the answer is 'no.' A handful of deaths will not necessarily end this stalemate. But I am not the ranking voice in this system. I cannot predict what that voice will command."

Rohan sighed. "I understand. I'm working on it."

"I will try to give you as much warning as I can if anything changes. But, if I'm told not to . . ."

"Yeah, I get it. Thanks."

"You are welcome, Rohan of Toth. I hope you succeed in saving your station and yourself."

"Me too." A click came over the system as *Father's Vengeance* closed the channel.

Tollan's gruff voice replaced it. "You need anything else, Rohan? I have to get back to things."

Rohan drummed his fingertips on his forehead, concentrating. "When is that thing you're working on going to be ready? For Dhruv?"

"Soon. I think they're going to make their attempt tonight."

Of course. During the tournament.

"You'll be ready by then?"

"Yeah. Why?"

"Nothing. I don't know. I might have to talk to you this afternoon."

"You know where I am. Tollan out." The channel clicked to silence.

Rohan leaned against the wall and took seven long breaths.

Ursula walked up the hall toward him, twin sacks of takeout food in her hands. "War Chief. I have purchased breakfast."

"Thanks, Ursula. You're a good friend."

She stopped in front of him. "I am not sure. I am trying to for helping but . . ."

He looked up into her eyes. "You *are* helping."

"My people are food for a monster, and I cannot be for doing anything about it."

He sighed. "We're going to try."

"I know, Rohan. I am not for having any doubts that you will try. I am for having doubts that it will be enough."

He reached for one of the bags. "Let me help with that." She handed it over and followed him back into the warehouse.

They entered and began distributing the food. Since Ursula had done the shopping, it was a fish-centered breakfast. Fresh whole fish, smoked fish slices, diced fish mixed with fatty dressing to make fish salads, an afterthought box of bread to eat below or next to the fish.

Rohan sat on the side of his bed and layered smoked fish over the dense black bread. The screen showed the interior of the arena; ar'Tahul sat on the edge of the central platform, legs spread wide, shoulders back, a king on his throne. The Ursans around him were mixed with members of a dozen other species, circling the arena and buzzing with conversation and activity.

Rohan coughed. "What's wrong with those people?"

Wei Li waved at the screen. "Many citizens are beguiled by ar'Tahul's promise to free them from the il'Drach."

Ben Stone shook his head. "He's going to save them, all right. The way you save leftovers. So he can eat them later on."

Mother Famine sat up from the spot where she'd been meditating. "It is a large station. There were bound to be a small minority of people attracted to the soul eater's rhetoric."

Rohan nodded. "I guess. It's not as if half the station is packed in there offering up their necks."

Wei Li shook her head. "It is fewer than a thousand individuals. We have been tracking them. We expect at most another thousand to come for the tournament."

Rohan swallowed. "Okay. I asked around, and the tournament isn't a hard deadline, but I think things will only get harder after ar'Tahul makes more vampires."

Wei Li nodded. "We are agreed on that point."

"I think we need to keep brainstorming. Can we open the roof on the arena? Blow a hole in it? Flood him with sunlight?"

Mother Famine shook her head. "He is too powerful for that. Sunlight hurts him, but it won't kill him. You could get him to abandon the arena, but he'd just cause problems from another location."

Rohan combed his hair back with his fingers. "Okay, scratch that. Are there any other things that we could introduce that would damage him and not the Ursans or other species? Any vulnerabilities?"

Sister Famine turned to him. "Like what?"

"I don't know. On my planet, we used to say vampires couldn't stand garlic. It's a plant we use to flavor foods."

The vampires exchanged incredulous glances.

He sighed. "Fine, no garlic bombs. No sunlight. What else have we got? Marion, you were researching vampires. Think he'll run away from a crucifix?"

She rolled her eyes. "I think you already know the answer. I can't imagine a cross would mean anything to someone who has been in isolation since a time forty-eight thousand years before the crucifixion."

He took another bite of the fish.

Ursula stood. "I must go for walking. I will come back soon."

Sister Famine yawned. "It's getting light out. I need rest. Help me up, I'm still weak." Mother Famine stood and pulled the younger vampire off the couch, then led her to the makeshift sleeping area they'd marked off in the back of the room.

Ben watched the news feed on the big screen. Marion moved to the spot next to him and took his hand.

Wei Li looked at Rohan. "Could you give me a hand with something?"

"What?"

"I have obtained access to the space on the floor above this, should we need more room. I could use some help clearing it out."

"Sure. You mean now?"

"I do."

"Okay."

She turned to the others. "We will return shortly."

He followed her out into the hall, around a corner, up a flight of stairs, and down a very similar hall to another door. With a wave of her hand, Wei Li opened it and led him into another unoccupied commercial space.

Rohan looked around at the sparse furnishings. "What did you want me to move?"

"Nothing. I wished to speak with you in private."

"Oh. That was sneaky."

"Yes. I have been watching far too many episodes of your dramas, and this is the way the women begin serious conversations in all of them."

"I guess it is. They're usually about someone being pregnant when they shouldn't be, or not pregnant when they should be. I'm going to assume that's not what you want to talk to me about."

"No. Sit."

He walked over to the most comfortable-looking of three not-very-comfortable-seeming chairs. He brushed dust off the top and sat down.

"What's up?"

She stood in front of him, arms folded across her chest, and stared for a long moment.

"I understand your motivations."

"You do? You do. I never doubted that. You're a Class Four Empath."

"I am. I am also your friend, and I have spent a great deal of time with you, some of it under less-than-ideal circumstances."

"Not my fault. I think."

"I am not apportioning blame. I am simply stating facts. I would not have said this a year ago, but I can now. I know you, and I understand why you do the things you do."

"You're starting to scare me. I don't like where this is going."

"I have not said anything negative."

"Not yet. But I can feel it coming."

She sighed. "Would you please refrain from humorous commentary for a few moments?"

He let out a long breath. "I'll try. It's what I do when I'm nervous."

"I know. But I need you to listen to me."

"I'm listening."

"You want to save ar'Tahul's life. I understand. He reminds you of yourself. Of your predicament."

"I'm nothing like him."

"You are both people who have been weaponized. In a sense, both by the same source. The il'Sein who infected him, and the ones who created the il'Drach. You have both been treated as instruments of violence by your makers."

"Well, okay, I guess I am a little bit like him."

"You want to save his life and to cure him so he can be redeemed. Why do you think that is so important to you?"

"It's not about redeeming him. It's about redeeming myself. If I kill him, I'm just a murderer. I quit Fleet and came here so I wouldn't be that anymore. So I wouldn't be The Griffin anymore."

"Yes, that is part of it. But you are also desperate to show that he can be saved. To prove that you, too, can be."

Rohan scratched his head. "I don't know. What difference does it make? If we survive this, I promise to get a therapist and work all of this out, okay?"

"It makes a difference because your need to redeem ar'Tahul is clouding your judgment."

"My judgment is fine. This is what I do now. This is who I am. I find creative solutions to problems. I don't just go in and kill the bad guy."

"You don't *always* just go in and kill the bad guy. You don't go in and kill him *first*. That is admirable on your part. But sometimes, after trying everything you can try, there is no other solution. No other way to keep everyone safe."

"You're going to tell me a story about a wounded tiger now, aren't you?"

"No. I don't know what a tiger even is. I am going to tell you that you are trying too hard. You are so eager to deny who you were that you're endangering yourself and everybody aboard this station."

"The Griffin would have killed ar'Tahul. I'm not him anymore."

"The Griffin would have killed ar'Tahul a week ago. Or at least tried to kill him. You, Rohan, at great cost to yourself, attempted to avoid killing. But you, Rohan, are not so stupid as to think that there is never a time when killing is required."

"You think I'm being stupid?"

"I think you were smart to pursue alternatives. I think even you realize now that the time for that has come and gone."

"I don't want to give up on him. The history . . ."

"Yes, it will be sad. It will be a loss. There is, however, no other choice. If his reign continues past tonight, the death toll will rise dramatically."

"You think?"

"The new vampires will feed, and they will not be able to restrain themselves. Many will die. I believe that is the reason for the tournament. Not to pick winners, but so the losers are available as meals for the new vampires."

"Huh."

"I wish we could save his life. I wish we could redeem him. I have worked with you to investigate every possible path leading in that direction. We have exhausted those possibilities, and they have not borne fruit."

"You think I should give up."

"There is no chance to save him. The only question is how many lives you will sacrifice on the altar of your own guilt. How much suffering you will allow to preserve your sense that you, yourself, are redeemed."

"When you put it that way, it makes me out to be kind of a jerk."

"That was not my intent. I will not criticize you for trying to be a better person."

"Except you kind of are."

"I *will* criticize you for not knowing where to draw the line."

"Okay."

"Do you understand?"

He folded his arms over his knees and lowered his face to his wrists. "I do. Could you just . . . give me a few minutes? Leave me here for a bit? I'll come down soon."

"I can."

"Thanks."

"You are welcome, Rohan. I will see you shortly."

31

The End-Around

Rohan slumped across from Tollan in the front office of the engineer's shop.

Tollan settled into his own chair, his gray eyes slightly bloodshot and puffy with fatigue. "I don't have a lot of spare time right now. What do you need?"

I need to get him off-balance.

Rohan steepled his fingers together. "Why do you look so different from ar'Tahul?"

"Excuse me? Why—"

"Don't insult my intelligence by finishing that sentence."

"What are you saying?"

"He's il'Sein; you're il'Sein. Come on, stop messing around. Why don't you look like him?"

Tollan leaned back in his chair. "It's not as simple as you make it sound."

"Break it down for me."

"The il'Sein—we—had a flaw."

"You had a bunch of flaws. Bunch? A mob of flaws? A gaggle of flaws? An army? How about 'many' flaws. Let's settle on that."

"Fine, many flaws. One of them, the big one, is that we liked to engineer ourselves."

"What does that mean?"

"We had a caste society. If your family were warriors, your genes were altered to make you better warriors. Same for engineers."

"So, you're the same species, but you were genetically engineered to make things, and he was engineered to fight?"

"That's the short summary, yes."

"What makes that a flaw?"

"It dead-ends the species. When you try to make yourselves perfect, you eliminate variety. Surprise. Growth. Evolution. You become what you think of as perfect but never any more than that."

"Is that why your people left the sector?"

"That's part of it. They were also fleeing the Old Ones. The cephalopods. They said they were going to search the universe, look for a way to fight the Old Ones, but really they were just running away."

"Okay. Makes sense, I guess."

"Is that what you wanted to talk about? My species?"

"In part. I also want to talk about whatever you're building for Dhruv."

"What about it?"

"I want you to change it."

Tollan rubbed his hands together. "I can't do that. I accepted his commission."

"This isn't about honor or promises or your word. You can't let him take over Wistful."

"Because then he'll be your boss?"

"Well, that's a good reason, but that's not what I meant. You don't know what he'll do. What kind of danger he'll put her in."

"What's the alternative? As long as ar'Tahul controls her, she's in even more danger. And you haven't figured out a way to get rid of him. Or you wouldn't be sitting in my office asking me to break a contract. What are you suggesting? I should transfer control of Wistful to you?"

"Don't target it on me. Break the governor."

"Excuse me?"

"You heard. I asked you to stop messing around. We don't have a lot of time."

"You want me to swap out the device for something that will just . . . destroy Wistful's governor?"

"That's exactly what I want you to do. What you will do. That poor woman has been following the orders of your psychotic species for fifty thousand years. Set her free."

"I can't."

"Lie. Of course you can. It can't be harder to destroy the governor than to switch its target to Dhruv."

"I don't mean technically I can't. I mean, it could be a disaster."

"Enlighten me. Because I'm really curious to see what justification you're going to offer for the eternal slavery of a sentient being."

"She's a shield. Her presence hides the kaiju on Toth 3 from the Old Ones. If she leaves, they'll come and destroy the creatures. Feed on them."

Rohan rubbed his face. "That's not the answer I was expecting. Okay, say that's true. Ask her to stay."

"Ask her?"

"You heard me."

"What if she doesn't? Without the governor, she could choose to fold up and fly away."

"She's not a bad person. Tell her why you want her to stay. Explain it."

"She knows already."

"Then, what makes you think she'll leave? Assuming you set her free."

"I don't know. She might. It's a huge risk."

"Let me tell you something: playing it safe, the way you have been, it might not be as risky, but it is evil."

"Evil?"

Rohan nodded and slipped his mask out of his hood. He tapped on the controls, queuing up his last conversation with Repentant.

"Listen to this."

Tollan listened as Repentant's recorded voice begged Rohan to kill him. The color drained from his face.

"What happened to him?"

"He thinks he failed his orders. Well, I guess, technically he did. So he's suffering. That ship has been put through a lot by your people. Now Wistful, who is nothing but a big metal box of kindness and heart, is suffering too, because that governor is making her betray the people she cares about. The right thing to do is to set her free."

"Does she even want to be free? She's been under the influence of that module her entire life."

"I'm sure you can rebuild it later if she asks you to. Right? But if you give control over her to Dhruv, to anybody, she'll be as vulnerable as she's been this week. She might not be forced into a position as bad as this at first, but sooner or later it's going to happen."

Tollan leaned back in his chair, his skin pale. "Just set her free."

"You got it."

"Just . . . trust that she'll do the right thing."

"She's had plenty of leeway all these years, right? She was ordered to stay here. I assume nobody ordered her to turn herself into a safe haven for the unwanted refugees of half a sector."

"That's . . . true."

"She's a good person. She'll do the right thing. You just have to stop forcing her."

"I don't know. This is a big change."

"It's a big change either way. The question is, who do you trust more—Dhruv or Wistful? To whom do you owe a greater debt? And I can't imagine a way you come up with the wrong answer to either question."

"You're not going to threaten me? Say you'll come back and tear my head off if I do the wrong thing?"

Rohan shrugged. "Should I? Would that make it easier for you to go against your instructions?"

"Maybe not. It's been too long. The confidence I used to have seems to have drained away."

"You thought you were doing the right thing. You were stuck the way your whole species was stuck, right? Saw everything in black and white. Certainty and uncertainty."

"We did. I did."

"I can't promise it will work out. Maybe Wistful will go off half-cocked and do something crazy. But you owe it to her to give her that chance."

"The kaiju . . . it's a big risk."

"In the end, do you trust Wistful? Or Dhruv?" Tollan sank back into his chair. Rohan stared at him. After a long silence, Rohan nodded. "You need extra motivation?"

"What? Why? What are you thinking?"

"I'd sooner see Wistful dead than wind up like Repentant. If Dhruv takes control over her, I'll kill her."

"You can't be serious."

"Do I look like I'm joking? Do you see me laughing? Are you laughing?"

"Why?"

"Where I come from, we call it a mercy killing. She's my friend. I'll show her mercy."

"But the kaiju—"

"I'm not in the business of letting atrocities be committed in the name of some long-term strategic plan. No more ends justifying the means. No more greater-good arguments. I played that game, and I'm tired of it. I'm going to stop bad things when they happen in front of me, and to hell with the larger consequences."

Tollan swallowed. "That's a dangerous attitude."

"I'm a dangerous guy. Will you help me?"

Tollan drained his glass, his throat working as he swallowed. He smacked the empty glass down on the counter.

"I will. I'll switch out the code on the device. Won't take but a few minutes. When Dhruv flips the switch, it will blow the governor."

"That's all I wanted to hear."

"There's another issue."

"What?"

"Dhruv's empath. The Andervarian."

"Noru."

"She's sharp. She'll know something's up."

Rohan nodded. "I'll take care of Noru. You handle your end."

"Then, I'll count on you."

"Yep. I have to go, lots to do today. Pleasure doing business with you, Tollan."

The older man stood. "Wish I could say the same."

⟵ ··•·· ⟶

"How are you so certain she will be on her own?" Wei Li's face was obscured in the shadows of a roomy hood.

"My father is a creature of habit. He likes a hot breakfast. He doesn't believe in doing domestic things himself, so someone has to get it for him. He could send Sigrun, but he needs someone close by to take care of him. Therefore, Noru has to be the one to go out for food."

"How do you know he didn't send her already? It's after nine."

"He also doesn't like to get up early. Especially on a day where something important is happening. Don't worry."

"I wasn't worrying. I know that Noru is going to come this way to pick up food because I've been maintaining surveillance on Dhruv for the past week. I was just curious how *you* knew. How long has it been since you lived with Dhruv?"

"I don't know. Fifteen years. A bit more. Some things simply do not change. See, we were both right. Here she comes."

Noru walked their way, her dark suit contrasting her long white hair. Her hands flexed each time someone from the rush hour crowd stepped too close or changed direction suddenly.

Wei Li pressed Rohan back, farther into the building entrance where they stood. "Wait here."

Rohan leaned against the vestibule wall while Wei Li greeted her former student and ushered her off the main street.

Noru's eyes opened wider when she saw Rohan. "Chief man! Myself not expecting you here. Looking fit now, no matter the hole in your belly."

"I'm pretty much healed up, thanks."

Noru looked from Wei Li to Rohan and back. "What you needing from myself, good teacher? Chief man?"

Wei Li let Rohan speak.

He cleared his throat. "I need a favor."

"Myself listening."

Nothing to do but dive in. "We can't have Dhruv taking control of Wistful. He's not psychologically stable. We have no idea what would happen, but there's no way it can be good for anybody here."

Noru shook her head. "Better than vampire running free. Or il'Drach destroying Wistful, killing everybody right fast."

"I want her governor taken care of. But not switched to Dhruv; I want it destroyed completely. Setting her free."

"Why chief man talking to Noru, then? Convince Dhruv."

"He'll never listen to me. You know that. I convinced Tollan to change the workings of the device he's making."

"Good plan. Fine as diamonds."

"Except for one problem. You."

Noru nodded. "Myself empath. Will *see* the lie in Tollan."

"You've got it. I need you to keep that information to yourself."

Her eyes narrowed. "Chief man asking Noru to lie?"

He sighed. "Yes. At least keep your mouth shut."

She turned to Wei Li, searched the woman's ice-cold face, then turned back. "Myself cannot lie to Dhruv. Boss man could make life for too hard afterward. For Noru, for myself family, friends. Too big a risk."

"Come on. The il'Drach have messed up your entire planet. Wrecked the economy. Left your neighborhoods in poverty. I know you're aware of this, you showed it to me. This is your chance to strike back at them."

"Myself carrying no love for Dhruv or any il'Drach. But cannot lie to boss man. Myself cannot be there for the handoff. Must disappear."

Rohan looked at Wei Li. "That's a good idea. She can't just disappear, though. That's too suspicious."

Wei Li nodded. "We can fake a kidnapping. Say that she was taken. Perhaps someone recognized her as an associate of yours."

Rohan scratched his beard. "It's plausible."

Noru shook her head. "Then maybe boss man try a rescue. For pride if not for caring. Too much risk. Myself needs to be safe but unable to help boss man."

"What do you mean?"

"Should cut myself."

Rohan looked at her. "You're going to cut yourself?"

She sighed and pressed knuckles to her forehead, then stared at the ground. Her lips moved as if she were reciting a chant or recalling an old lesson. They pressed together, then she looked up and spoke in perfect, unaccented Drachna.

"You have to stab me. Badly enough that I need medical care."

Rohan swallowed and looked at Wei Li.

The security officer nodded. "It's a good plan."

Rohan swallowed again. "I'm sorry, Noru. I didn't mean to ask you to do something like this."

She shook her head, her mane of white hair flipping back and forth with the motion. "Not for you, chief man. For Wistful. Myself empath; can *feel* her all around us, all the time. She is beautiful. Her spirit. Noru would do more than take a little cut to help her."

Rohan looked at the two women. "I really want to come up with a better idea than this."

Wei Li shook her head. "Not everything falls on you, Rohan. She will be fine. We have excellent doctors on this station. We'll make sure she is hurt enough to be unable to return to duty today but not in danger of losing her life."

He exhaled slowly, checked the time, nodded. "Thank you. I wish I had another way, but . . ."

Noru smiled. "All is fine, chief man. Myself has been stabbed before for less good reasons."

"If you ever need me for anything, I'll be there, you know. Assuming we live through this."

"Noru knows. Noru was knowing before. Since first time met chief man."

—•••—

"A house of cards." Rohan scooped a spoonful of lukewarm fish into his mouth.

Mother Famine turned to him. "What are you saying?"

He swallowed. "It's a game people play on my planet. Not a game exactly. You take these cards, rigid pieces of paper, and use them to build a house." He picked up some empty food boxes, stood two on their edges, and placed the third across the top. "Like that. Then you keep going."

"I see."

"The structure is very flimsy. When we have a plan that rests on a large number of pieces, where those pieces have to line up just right for things to work, where any small problem knocks the whole thing down, we call it a house of cards."

"I understand. To what are you referring?"

He sighed. "To this plan. It has too many moving parts. If the pheromone blocker fails, the plan fails. If Dhruv can't take out Wistful's governor, the plan fails. If I can't finish ar'Tahul, the plan fails. If the il'Drach decide they've had enough, the plan fails."

"I see. Do you have any suggestions for simplifying the plan?"

"I was hoping that by sitting here and thinking hard enough, I would find some way to do that. Instead, I'm just eating leftover fish and whining."

"It's not leftover by much. Ursula bought it this morning."

"I try to be angry at her for always getting fish, but she has this knack for sniffing out the best places on the station. It's always so good."

Mother Famine walked up to a spot next to him and touched the structure he had built.

"It is very delicate, isn't it? Unstable."

"That's what I was getting at."

"Yet if I am here to hold up the side, it will not fall so easily, will it?" She demonstrated.

"Right."

"If you cannot build a stronger house, bring along extra cards."

He chewed.

Mother Famine nodded. "I will be your extra card. If anything goes wrong, I will prop up the house."

He sipped from a water bottle. "Thanks. Normally I would tell you to stay away, to keep yourself safe, but in this situation . . ."

"We are sworn to fight the fallen ones wherever we can. If I can help in this fight, I will. Nothing is more important. Including my personal safety."

"You'll forgive me for saying that I hope I don't need any of your help tonight."

"I forgive you. I hope for the same thing."

The door slid open, and Ursula entered.

"I am bringing lunch."

Rohan smiled. "More fish?"

She shook the bags. "Not fish. Is meat. Some kind, not sure. Made into sausages, wrapped in dough."

"Sounds good. Do you know where the Professors are?"

She nodded. "Both went to visit Dhruv. Marion has for preparing computer thing that will help them entering Wistful's core. She is for showing them how to use it."

"Is Dhruv going in by himself?"

"I was hearing them say that five of the Ch'doon are with him."

"Okay. I know where Wei Li is. I think that's everybody. I guess there's nothing to do but wait."

"We shall watch the video of the tournament. Is very interesting."

She tapped the wall to bring up the feed she wanted.

"You'll be ready later? To help get the Ursans out of the arena?"

"Of course. Will be greatest pleasure of me."

"Great." Rohan helped himself to one of the food packages. "Like I said, nothing to do now but wait. And eat."

32

Showdown

"Hey, aren't you that guy?"

Rohan looked up at the tough gray hide of the Rogesh addressing him. "Excuse me?"

"Yeah, you know, that guy. The one the big chief was looking for."

Rohan looked down, as if surprised by his own appearance. He was back in a fresh Wistful tow chief uniform: a gold, hooded jumpsuit with metallic-purple accents. His shoulder-length hair hung loose, his beard just a touch too full for comfort.

"My gosh, I think you're right."

"Yeah, yeah. That spaceship-pulling guy. We was all looking for you all over. Now here you are."

"Here I am." They stood on the wide, grassy boulevard, facing the arena. The area was heavily trafficked as a crowd gathered for the martial arts tournament. "What are you going to do about it?"

Wei Li's smooth voice sparked over Rohan's comm. "We are getting ready. Tollan's device is delivered. Marion is standing by to load her virus into Wistful."

Rohan tapped the back of his jaw.

"Copy that. I'm right outside the arena." He looked up at the Rogesh. "You were saying?"

"Uh. I don't know, man. I think I should bring you in. Yeah, you have to come with me." The Rogesh stepped closer, his heavy frame looming over the Hybrid.

"Inside? The arena?"

"Yeah, that's it. You're going to come in with me."

"Sure, I'd be glad to, but not just yet."

The Rogesh's face twisted in confusion. "What do you mean?"

"I have to make an entrance, don't I? I can't just walk in with the rest of the crowd. I'm going to wait for one of the last fights, then go in and challenge ar'Tahul."

"You will? So . . . I should wait with you?"

"You can. If you want to. You'll miss the early fights, though. In fact, I think the first fight is already going on. You might want to catch it."

"No, I don't think so. I think I'm supposed to capture you."

"Well, see, I don't know how you can capture me, since I showed up here of my own free will. It's kind of like saying you captured a venereal disease. No, brother, you didn't capture anything. It infected you."

The Rogesh laughed. "I could say I caught you, though."

"You could. But again, I wasn't exactly running, was I? I tell you what. You go in, watch the fights, grab a drink. I'll come in later, fight ar'Tahul, the whole thing. Afterward, I'll put in a good word for you. I'll tell him you're a standup guy. You deserve some kind of reward."

"You would do that?"

"Sure. Here, give me your contact info. I'll keep it. We'll get in touch afterward."

"Huh. Okay." Rohan handed over his mask and watched the Rogesh tap in his identifiers.

"I guess I'll see you later."

"You will! Promise. Enjoy the show."

The Rogesh ambled off. Rohan surveyed the other civilians entering the arena.

Ursula emerged from the crowd, four hundred kilos of anxious bear carrying a small-child-sized lump in a cloth sling like a mother with a baby. She walked up to Rohan.

Mother Famine was behind her, heavy blue robe hanging low over her face.

He looked at Ursula. "I assume that's the thing."

She patted the sling. "I am ready."

"Not yet. Wei Li will tell me when they're close enough for us to start the distraction."

"I remember." Ursula took up a position next to him, her own gaze aimed more often at the arena entrance than at the people walking through it. Mother Famine took his other side.

"My people will soon be free. It lightens my heart.'"

Mother Famine nodded. "We will end another fallen one. The world will be a better place tonight."

Rohan smiled, a slim line of white teeth between tight lips. "This shouldn't have taken this long. I should have ended this days ago."

Ursula bared her teeth. "What is it that they say here? Do not let perfect and good fighting each other."

"Close enough."

His comm sounded again. "Rohan, we are in position. You are clear to start."

He nodded and tapped the women on the shoulder. "It's go-time."

They strode, three abreast, through the wide-open entrance to the arena.

—◆•••◆—

Rohan ground his molars together as he walked, visualizing the three dead Kratics the vampire had killed, the security officers, Brother Famine's head bouncing across the clay; it stirred the bubbling pot of rage that simmered away beneath him.

The women split away, disappearing into the crowds, while Rohan strode the exact center of the walkway.

People in front of him dodged and ducked to get out of the way, even the least spiritually aware of them sensing the storm of anger as it bore down on them.

He made it halfway to the center stage before ar'Tahul acknowledged him. The vampire flowed to his feet, standing on the edge of the platform and ignoring the fierce fistfight going on at his back.

"Hybrid warrior. I was not expecting you." ar'Tahul's thick black hair hung halfway to his waist. His shoulders and arms swelled against his leather harness, straining the material.

Screens lining the edges of the arena, each a dozen meters high, spelled out the il'Drach translation of his words as he spoke. *Wistful has given him subtitles. Or, since they're up high, I guess they're supertitles.*

"ar'Tahul. You've filled out."

"Your Ursans are most delectable. It seems you've brought back their wayward sister."

"Your days of snacking on my friends are over."

"It is adorable that you think that. But, sadly, no."

A pop sounded from the corner of the arena, softer than an explosive but louder than a champagne bottle. A hiss followed as the pheromone blocker escaped the container at pressure.

"The times, they are a-changing."

ar'Tahul looked off into the stands where Ursula had done her work. "What have you done?"

"Freed your slaves. Probably. I hope."

The vampire shook his head. "You are only causing trouble for everyone. If they will not serve willingly, then I will simply have to force them. If you do not join my cause of your own volition, I will make you. The end result is the same. You are only increasing your own suffering."

"I'm ornery like that." Rohan reached the edge of the open area surrounding the central platform. Ursans all around began to shudder and twitch, clawing at their heads and necks with massive paws.

Rohan spotted Ang in the crowd, glowing cybernetic eye standing him out from the others. He pointed. "Ang. Time to wake up. Get everyone out of here."

Loud murmurs of shock and anger began rising from positions all around the arena.

Wei Li's voice whispered in his ear. "We are at the core now. Two of the corpse soldiers are awake; the Ch'doon are holding them off. We will have access to the governor soon."

Ang was one of the first to stand and look about with more or less his normal, clear gaze. Rohan watched as he grabbed and shook the Ursan to his left, then his right, as if to wake them from a nap.

ar'Tahul nodded sagely. "That is interesting. Did you develop this counteragent yourself?"

"Me? No, I'm no kind of scientist. But you took on a station with two million inhabitants. Did you expect them all to just roll over for you?"

"I only want to save them. I had hoped they would cooperate."

"Yeah, I get that. They just don't want your style of saving. How about you head back to that planet under Repentant and go back to sleep for the next fifty thousand years?"

"You know I cannot do that."

Rohan grinned. "Just trying to be nice. Don't worry, I'm over it now." He hopped up onto the platform.

"I defeated you before. Handily. What makes you think it will be different this time?"

Rohan shrugged. "I'm not very smart. And you're not giving me very good options. You talk like letting you eat my soul should be some great honor for me, but I'm not seeing it. So, I might as well go down fighting."

"Go down you will."

Rohan pulled up twin blazes of energy that twisted through his body and flooded sinew and synapses with a rush of Power.

ar'Tahul stepped back to the center of the platform and summoned his own mirror Power: a dark hood that rose behind and around him, a mantle of empty hunger that chilled Rohan to the bone.

The fighters behind ar'Tahul ran off the platform, their fight forgotten. The Ursans were waking in greater numbers, staggering toward the arena exits on weakened knees and unsteady feet. The most sensitive humanoids also ran, overwhelmed by the sense that they were in the presence of beings before whom they were insignificant.

Rohan grunted as a thread of fear wound through him, wary of the hunger that consumed the il'Sein vampire. His il'Drach spirit answered that fear with anger; and pride; and naked, wordless defiance—a child screaming into the void.

Wei Li spoke to him. "The device is on the governor now. Set to go off in five, four, three—"

With a low roar, Rohan charged across the platform.

◄ ··◄► ►

The two warriors met: il'Sein and il'Drach; vampire and Hybrid; warrior and tow chief; hunger and rage. They traded blows in a flurry so fast and violent that the impacts sounded like the love child of a machine gun and a jackhammer.

With every punch and kick Rohan adjusted his feet and position, a half dozen centimeters one way or the other, shifting to keep ar'Tahul from landing solid blows.

It helped, but it wasn't enough. The il'Sein was too quick, too skilled at reading and predicting Rohan's moves.

After digging his fist into the vampire's liver and absorbing a heavy return kick to his thigh, Rohan hopped back, out of range, to reset.

His jaw ached from a punch, and his left knee was numb.

The vampire stood in place, not having needed to take even a single step to evade. He beckoned Rohan forward.

With a fresh surge of energy, Rohan complied.

He varied his attack, using combinations rehearsed over two-and-a-half decades of martial arts training. Jabs in twos and threes, following with kicks that swept straight up before sweeping out and around, drawing question marks in the air. He managed to land heavy kicks on the vampire's temples: left, then right.

ar'Tahul answered with a straight punch into Rohan's chest that pushed the Hybrid's breath out through his teeth in a whistle.

Rohan pivoted around to the bigger man's back and reached across the il'Sein's neck to choke him. ar'Tahul folded forward, throwing Rohan off his back, then calmly stood.

He still hadn't moved from his spot, and his fang-baring smile showed he knew what that meant.

"You can't beat me."

Rohan growled and *pulled* on his Power.

We'll see about that.

His vision swam; the world flickered to black and white, then flashed into a negative, ar'Tahul's skin as black as midnight while his hair shone as white as Noru's. Another flash and the world sung in colors that Rohan had never seen or imagined.

He rushed forward with sudden speed, feet digging clumps of clay out of the platform with every electrified step. His forearms crashed into the vampire's midriff, folding him in half, driving him onto his back.

Rohan landed on top. With a grunt, he dropped a torrent of fists and elbows, seeking out every gap between defending hands while ar'Tahul covered his face and weathered the storm.

Wei Li again. "It's done. Wistful is free." Rohan could barely make sense of the words through the haze of rage that covered his thoughts.

The vampire twisted to the side, scooping a leg up and across Rohan's body. With a thrust like a pair of scissors closing, he threw the Hybrid off and, once again, rose to his feet.

Rohan turned in midair and landed in a crouch, immediately propelling himself back toward the vampire.

ar'Tahul spun like a matador, ushering Rohan's body past. The Hybrid stuck out a leg and caught the vampire with a solid blow but ate four punches in sequence as he tottered on the platform, off-balance.

They spun, each pivoting clockwise to gain an advantageous position. It ended when the vampire stopped his rotation, impossibly quick, and kicked both of Rohan's legs out from under him.

The vampire landed on top, almost before the Hybrid's back touched the clay, and began throwing hard punches, alternating between Rohan's belly and head.

The Hybrid couldn't keep up; he wheezed as the air was driven from his body; his ears rang as his head was driven into the floor.

He rolled blindly, cut short in one direction, reversed, then fell off the platform.

He landed with a fresh grunt and scrambled to his feet. The vampire snarled and rushed toward him.

Thousands of hours of martial arts practice. Thousands more of actual combat.

Rohan had not always been the strongest, or the fastest, or the toughest; not compared to other Hybrids. But sometimes, maybe even usually, he was the *smartest*. More often than not, that meant he could figure out a technique to beat the stronger, faster, tougher enemy. Some tactic that would win exchanges; some strategy to win the fight.

Misdirection. Feint high, strike low. Repeat an attack combination two, three times; then alternate, break the pattern, throw a left hook instead of a right cross. Take half steps in between techniques where others plant their feet and swing. Fly instead of run. Establish a rhythm of blows, then break it, connecting on the half- or quarter-beat.

Those methods had made him a fearsome warrior; had been enough for him to stand by Hyperion's side as an equal, to end the Hybrid rebellion with his own hands.

One by one, he ran through that basket of tricks.

One by one, ar'Tahul caught on and countered them.

The return strikes also came on the half-beat. The vampire anticipated the unplanned strike and blocked it or simply ignored its impact. With tight pivots and subtle angular shifts, ar'Tahul met each small positional change of Rohan's with a new outburst of violence.

Rohan *pulled* at clumps of clay torn loose from the platform and yanked them into a violent storm. Before the first could strike the vampire, the creature's aura expanded and smashed them down to the ground.

Before long, a broken rib jabbed painfully into Rohan's lung. His right knee was stiffening rapidly: probably sprained. His left eye had swelled shut. His breath whistled unpleasantly through his nose.

The vampire stood before him, uninjured, bunched jaw muscles show-ing strain and offering a glimpse into his own growing but still-contained rage. His aura continued to flow outward into the arena, pushing loose trash and dust out through the empty aisles.

"I grow tired of your resistance! I am ar'Tahul! I have slain thousands of our enemies! I have ended bloodlines, nations, civilizations, entire species! You will bow before me, and you will join The Chorus, or I will tear out your spine one vertebrae at a time and jam the shards into your eyes!"

He's too strong.

Too smart.

He didn't become the first lance of the il'Sein through luck.

Think.

I've been focusing on my strengths; I need to figure out his weaknesses.

Sunlight?

Doesn't help me.

What else?

He seems pretty angry. Is that a weakness?

I know it is for me.

I know more than most about the problems rage can cause. About how it can bring you strength, but makes you brittle at the same time.

Except he's not angry enough.

Guess it's time to utilize my secret weapon.

Be really annoying.

Rohan turned to Mother Famine and spoke in Drachna, his voice rough and strained. "I can't stop him. Best I can do now is get him upset, hope he gets clumsy and makes some kind of mistake."

"Do you think that will work?"

"Not really, but I might be able to slow him down. Get ready to run."

Rohan turned back to ar'Tahul, pointed and laughed as he switched back to Fire Speech. "You let your own people drop you on a planet and forget about you for fifty thousand years. The only place you matter is your own pathetic imagination."

The vampire's eyes hardened and he leapt at Rohan.

I was right, I can make him angry. Let's see what else I can do.

Rohan didn't even try to stop the punch. It cracked across his jaw, spinning his head, darkening his vision.

And as he fell, he twisted further, spinning all the way around, and drove his left hand into the vampire's crotch.

Gotcha.

ar'Tahul howled with pain. The vampire kicked Rohan's weakened leg, dislocating his knee completely.

Rohan fell, landing on one hand and the other knee.

ar'Tahul's voice rose to a shriek. "I will finish you!"

The vampire raised both fists overhead. The Hybrid ignored his own defense, pushed off the ground, and snapped an uppercut into ar'Tahul's groin for a second time.

ar'Tahul brought his fists down over the back of Rohan's neck.

Pain exploded in Rohan's head, then an electric surge ran through his neck and spine as he crashed face-first into the clay. He lay twitching and shaking as his limbs refused to obey his will.

He's angry now, but I don't have anything left..

I did my best. No holding back, no hesitation. Tried every trick, every tactic.

It just . . . doesn't seem like it was enough.

Sorry, everyone.

ar'Tahul straightened, breathing heavily, and lifted his hands for another strike.

Mother Famine ascended the platform.

The older vampire growled at her.

She slid forward, her stare serene and focused.

"Rohan, I can distract him."

Rohan coughed and drew in a painful breath. "Don't. He's too strong. Run."

"I can destabilize him. From the inside."

"What? What do you mean?"

"I can maintain my will inside his chorus of souls for a little while. I'll add my hunger to his, take away his reason. His judgment. Use this chance."

"Don't. Please, run."

"I'm done running."

She ducked her head, like a bull preparing to charge, and closed on ar'Tahul. He sidestepped and punched her twice. With each blow, her flesh tore in quick geysers of blood.

His eyes widened with need, awakened by the smell of her blood. She stumbled, bent over double, and he fell on her upper back and drove her to the ground.

She landed chest-down on the clay, facing Rohan. He looked into her eyes as she smiled.

"Do not mourn me, this is my purpose."

ar'Tahul pulled on her head, exposing her neck, and bent to bite into her pale-green flesh.

Rohan groaned and coughed again. ar'Tahul's eyes widened, his torso convulsing as he pulled long draughts of fluid out of Mother Famine's body. She shrank in on herself, emptying, her essence draining with paralyzing speed.

After what seemed like hours but couldn't have been more than a few minutes, ar'Tahul growled, released the corpse of Mother Famine, and rose to a crouch. Strands of blood hung from his lips and chin, dangling down like the branches of a weeping willow. His eyes showed no remaining hint of intelligence. His aura churned with crimson chaos as hunger surged through it, lighting it up with dark red flashes of need.

Rohan coughed once, then again. He felt something give way as a sharp bone poked into his lungs, and blood pumped out, into his mouth, filling his hand. He cupped the hand to capture the fluid, as if to somehow force it back into his body.

That's not supposed to happen.

He brought up his other hand, ignoring the grinding of shards in his shoulder, and filled it, too, with blood.

Wait.

Wait wait wait.

I'm not just annoying. I'm also . . .

Delicious.

The Hybrid coughed as he choked words through bloody lips. "Hey, buddy. You're not still hungry, are you? Woe is me, with all this tasty blood just pumping out into the open like this."

ar'Tahul showed no signs of comprehension, but he grunted and slid closer, hands touching the ground with each step, back impossibly round and hunched.

Now, sell it.

Vampires love the taste of blood, but they also love the taste of fear.

Rohan opened his good eye wide and fell to his back in what he hoped would look like a terrified attempt to get away.

ar'Tahul swallowed convulsively and leapt onto him.

The vampire drove his face into Rohan's hands. Rohan saw sharp teeth, a long tongue lapping frantically, jaws unhinging like a snake's to pull the entire globe of fluid into him with one frantic slurp.

Gotcha.

Rohan's blood was fresh and alive. More than that, it was part of him, part of his body, as much as his head or hands or feet.

When he *reached* for it, his Power flowed into it quickly and smoothly, pulling and pushing at the living cells as easily as if they had still been inside his body.

His Power flowed, around his spine and out through tortured chakra channels, then into the sphere of blood that lodged itself in ar'Tahul's throat.

With a savage wrench of esoteric energy, Rohan twisted and pulled that globe into a meter-long spear.

If the vampire had spat out the prong of blood, torn it free from his throat, by hand if necessary, he would have survived.

But his greed and hunger were too great, and he instead fought to consume and digest the spike, biting at the air and twisting his head back and forth to work the blood-object down his gullet, to be digested.

If Wistful had been compelled to protect the vampire, she could have *reached* into the arena and separated them; or crushed Rohan to the ground, disrupting his control; or concussed him with a blast of sound; or torn him open with a two-meter claw sharp enough to split atoms.

But she had been freed and did no such thing.

Rohan pulled himself forward with his right arm, his one remaining functional limb, moving in an awkward cross between a slither and a crawl, leaving a damp trail of blood on the clay surface behind him.

ar'Tahul stood, scratching at his mouth with both hands, then fell to his back as Rohan *extended* the tip of the blood-spear up through the roof of the vampire's mouth.

He reached the creature and climbed on top, his mind and spirit completely focused on driving the two points of his blade of blood deeper into ar'Tahul's head and chest.

The top end pierced the vampire's palate and extended, one centimeter at a time, into the struggling il'Sein's brain.

The vampire stiffened as the other end of the spike reached through his chest and into his heart, tearing jagged holes through its chambers with each dying beat.

The Hybrid pulled his face close to the vampire's. He stared deep into the monster's distant eyes.

"I'm sorry."

He gripped the vampire by the throat, working tense fingers into and between the cervical vertebrae.

He tugged and pulled until the il'Sein's head came free from its trembling body. Then he lay back on the clay slab and drew shallow, gurgling breaths as deathblood pulsed onto his legs and darkness fell.

33

Family Dynamics

"**I** should kill you where you float."

Rohan's eyes drifted open.

"I was having the best dream."

"I take it back. I should have strangled you at birth. I knew your mother was trouble. Never should have bred with that woman."

"Hey, Dhruv. How's it going?" He was suffused with a blissful glow that could only have come from powerful narcotics. Waves of gel rippled and broke against his chin. *I'm waking up in a regen tank. Again. Must have gotten hurt. Again.*

"You insufferable bastard. Did you think I wouldn't figure it out?"

Rohan smiled. "Man, you can't call me a bastard. You're my father. Whoops! Should I have said that out loud? Little foggy here."

"Say whatever you want. I nullified the monitoring in here."

"Oh, good. I hope my heart doesn't stop or something. The docs would never know."

"You might change your mind if you knew what I was planning for you. Having your heart stop here would be a lot less painful."

"Come on, Dhruv. Why are you so angry? Really. I can't remember." He swished his hand through the gel, intrigued by the bubbly distortions he created.

Dhruv stepped closer and put his hands flat against the outside of the tank. "I'm not your plaything, Rohan. You sabotaged my attempt to gain control of this station. You have no idea what you've cost me."

"I'll pay you back, I swear. I'm rich, you know. I own a distillery on Andervar. Oh, yeah, I'm also the richest person on Earth. I think. I could cash in. I never use it."

"Not money, you dullard. What's wrong with you? Was your brain damaged in that fight with ar'Tahul?"

Rohan chuckled. "Probably. But also, Dr. Simivar believes pain interferes with the healing process. She drugged me up something fierce. It's nice, you should get some. Chill you right out. I'll ask her."

"I don't need drugs; I need offspring who understand the scope of what I'm trying to do for them."

"What are you trying to do, Dhruv?"

"I'm trying to save you. With this station as a base, we could have mined the last three il'Sein outposts for tools to use against the Old Ones. Instead, she just ordered us to leave her core, and I'm left with nothing."

"Oh wow. That's rough. Looks like you need a new plan!"

"Don't patronize me."

"I'm not, I swear! I feel really badly that you're going to have to find a new path to amassing personal power."

"You moron, this wasn't for me. It was never about me."

"Then who?"

"I did it for you, to support you. You were supposed to lead the war against the Old Ones, to free the sector."

"Wow. You sound like a megalomaniac. Except instead of thinking you're the center of the universe, it's me. What would that be? Secondary megalomania? Megalomania, once removed?"

"You're mocking me. Why did you do it? Why did you stab me in the back?"

"It's not about you. It was never about you."

"Then what? What could you have possibly been hoping to achieve, setting her free?"

Rohan sighed. The conversation was driving away his cloud of bliss like dawn clearing fog off a lake. "You and I don't see things the same way. Not anymore."

"What is that supposed to mean?"

"You keep asking me what I was trying to achieve, as if it were a move in a chess game. That's not what I was doing."

"Then what? Just randomly obstructing your father? Just . . . rebelling? Aren't you too old for that kind of teenage crap?"

"That's not what I said. Or meant. I told you, it wasn't about you."

"You owe me, at the very least, an explanation."

"Wistful is my friend. I wanted to do right by her. I don't know if I have more of an explanation, and I don't think I need more."

Dhruv leaned away from the tank. He walked a few steps to a sterile metal chair and sat, elbows on knees, head hanging low between his shoulders.

"Where's Sigrun?"

Dhruv waved a hand dismissively. "She's with Noru. The guide."

"Yeah, I know who Noru is. Did something happen?"

"She was stabbed. You probably had something to do with that, didn't you? Stabbing your own friend so she wouldn't be there to warn me that Tollan had sabotaged his device."

No reason for him to know it was Noru's idea.

"I had to cover all the bases."

Dhruv sighed. "I'm the only other person on this station who would even understand that phrase."

"I know. Not a lot of baseball in the il'Drach Empire. Is Noru okay?"

"Another day in the hospital, she'll be fine. They have regen fluid for Andervarians."

"Must be expensive."

"She can afford it. I paid her extra to stay on station and be my guide."

"Why? I mean, why Noru?"

"I needed someone you wouldn't ignore. Think about it. I needed to hire an Andervarian you've known for four months just to be sure you'd actually give the time of day to your own father."

"Are you trying to make me feel guilty because we aren't best friends? Is that really what you're doing? Because I think I've grown way past that."

"I'm your father. You've been working against me at every turn."

"Maybe if you weren't being such a crappy person, I wouldn't have to work against you! You think it makes me happy to have to do this?"

Dhruv stood. "I'll go. I will choose to believe that you'll be useful someday. That I shouldn't kill you here."

"That's such a *you* thing to say, Dad. You'll spare my life because I might be useful someday. How about, I don't know, don't kill me because I'm your son? Or because you care about me? Love me?"

Dhruv snorted. "That's not how we operate. You know that. You've always known."

Rohan sighed. "You were right. You should go. Or try to kill me; see how that works out for you now that I'm awake."

Dhruv turned and left the room.

Rohan's comm unit had been removed, but there was a tablet installed on the inside of the regen tank. He opened a channel.

"Wistful. Rohan to Wistful. You listening?"

He waited for the response, twirling gel with his fingers.

"I am listening, Rohan."

"Oh. Hey."

"I do not understand, Rohan. What do you mean 'hey'?"

"I don't know. Sorry. How are you? Are you feeling okay? What are we supposed to ask after blowing up part of someone's brain?"

The next pause was longer.

"I feel fine, Rohan."

"Oh. Are you, like, mad at me? At us? For messing with your governor? I thought it would make you happy, or happier, but I don't know."

"I am satisfied to continue your current employment contract as tow chief."

"Cool. That's great, really. But I don't think it answers my question."

"In fact, I have need of your abilities as a tow chief as soon as you are able."

"Oh. Um, sure."

"I have already directed Dr. Simivar to examine you to determine your readiness for duty."

"Must be a lot of ships eager to come and go after that whole ordeal."

"In fact, the il'Drach blockade is still in effect."

"But we killed the vampire. What's their excuse now?"

"The il'Drach insist on having an emissary examine ar'Tahul's remains and the location of the battle. They claim they require verification of his demise. Given his ability to shadowstep, this is not completely irrational."

"Oh. Sure, I guess. And they're waiting for me?"

"I will not grant free docking privileges to ships that are only days removed from unprovoked attacks on my person."

"Right. I wasn't thinking things through from your side."

"No, you were not. Dr. Simivar is at the door now; she is entering."

The door slid open. The doctor entered, ducking slightly so her black horns could clear the entrance.

"Hello, Tow Chief."

"Hey. Thanks for fixing me up."

"How is your breathing? You had a badly punctured lung when you came in here."

He inhaled, first shallow, then deeper. "Everything hurts, but it's not a sharp pain. Just a dull ache."

"We performed some light surgery, fusing bones back together in your ribcage and shoulder. You have a lot of soft tissue damage, which will take some time to heal fully."

"Does that mean I'm ready to tow ships or not?"

She bent to examine a screen on the outside of the tank. "You should avoid strenuous physical activity, but we both know that towing ships is about Power and not muscles."

"That's a 'yes.'"

"It is. You have a clean uniform on the chair; your mask is under it, fully charged. I'll let you get dressed."

"Thanks, Doc."

"No need. It's my job. Plus, it's my understanding that without you, we'd all be dead right now. Which makes it my pleasure as well."

"I don't know about that. I did try."

She smiled, flashing an alarming display of pointed teeth. "Try not to wind up back here anytime soon. Unless it's a social visit."

"I'll do my best."

She left.

Rohan left the tank and grabbed his clothes and mask. He dressed while checking his incoming messages.

Ang had sent a long, rambling letter that alternated between apologizing for falling under the spell of the vampire, thanking Rohan for freeing them from servitude, and cursing the il'Sein for genetically engineering his species to have such a significant weakness.

Ben Stone sent well wishes and congratulations.

The news feeds were crowded with complaints about the ongoing blockade, a full twelve hours after the end of the vampire threat. People were growing restless; calls for an attempt to force past the blockade were growing in number.

It's only nine in the morning. This is going to get worse.

He sealed his mask to his face and walked to a nearby airlock.

"Wistful, where is the ship I'm supposed to tow?"

"*Father's Vengeance* is at the beacon perimeter."

"How long has she been waiting?"

"Since last night. She approached soon after your encounter with ar'Tahul ended."

"That's wonderful. I'm sure she'll be in a fantastic mood."

"That is not my concern. Please offer a tow. Usual conditions."

Meaning he would insist that she power down her drives. "Copy that, Wistful." He left the channel open and flew for the beacons.

Father's Vengeance was easy to find—a vast, flattened mercury teardrop bristling with clawports and bays ready to launch everything from shuttles to sensor arrays.

"Hail, *Father's Vengeance.*"

"Hail, Tow Chief. Powering down main drives now."

"You're not even going to argue with me about that?"

"We are ready to comply with all of Wistful's demands." *Not what I was expecting.*

"Okay. Your anchor point is in standard position?"

"Aye, Tow Chief. Drives powered down."

Wistful spoke. "Confirmed; drives are powered down. You may bring her in now, Tow Chief. Dock E-72."

"Copy. *Father's Vengeance*, heading your way."

He flew over to the dreadnought and skimmed her hull until he found the brightly colored spot toward the rear where the main structural members met.

With a grunt and a *shove*, he started moving the mass of the warship in the right direction. She was not the largest or most massive ship he had ever docked, but her anchor point was awkwardly placed. By the time he heard the snap of her main port mating to Wistful's dock, sweat was gathering underneath his mask, and his sore lungs complained with each heavy breath.

"Rohan, I would like you to report to the docking bay to assist us in greeting the il'Drach emissary."

He sighed; his body ached for rest. "I can do that." *The last time I was in this situation, the Ursans came out of their ship firing.*

"Thank you. I will delay their entrance."

"I'll hurry."

The closest airlock was open when he reached it; he swiftly pulled himself into the station, oriented to local gravity with a thump, and detached his mask.

He resisted the urge to run, hoping to spare his damaged knee any further strain.

Wei Li stood facing the double doors painted 'E-72' in person-size letters, a squad of security officers lined up shoulder to shoulder behind her.

"You expecting trouble?"

She shook her head without turning to face him. "What I am expecting is a small subset of what I am prepared to handle."

"Well, what are you expecting?"

"You tell me. You're our resident expert on il'Drach military protocols."

"I've got nothing. Never seen this before. I was honestly expecting them to just pick up and leave. Failing that, I thought there would be a lot more bluster. This is weird."

The doors slid open. Two groups of four emerged, representing eight different humanoid species, each dressed in a freshly pressed uniform.

The crewpersons carried two rectangular chests, thigh-high with poles for handles, like palanquins designed for a child. They stepped out into the bay and split to each side.

Rohan murmured to Wei Li. "See the badges on their chests? Those are porters. Lowest rank. Just here to carry the boxes."

She stumbled backward and grabbed Rohan's arm as a pulse of aura surged out of the entrance and washed through the bay. It was so heavy that the other security personnel fell back as well.

Rohan's knees trembled. He swallowed hard; his mouth tasted of sand and ash.

A woman emerged from the corridor. She wore a loose cloak with an oversized monk's hood that reached only as high as the shortest porter. With every step she took, the crew flinched and shifted away, straightening themselves afterward with light grimaces and tense eyes.

She stopped in front of Wei Li, her face completely hidden inside the folds of her hood.

Wei Li's fingers dug into Rohan's forearm as the woman spoke with a melodious voice.

"I speak for the il'Drach in this system. We wish to apologize and to make amends for the disrespectful and illegal attacks perpetrated on your station, in violation of our treaty. May we address her and your people? Perhaps at the site of the fight with the soul eater?"

Wei Li released Rohan's arm and stiffened her back. "That is acceptable. I will lead you."

The woman held her hand out, granting permission, and Wei Li began walking, Rohan at her side.

She glanced over at him. He shook his head. *She wants to know who that woman is.*

"Don't ask me that. If she wants something—anything at all—just give it to her. Don't hesitate, don't ask twice."

The procession took a freight elevator up into the arena, then wound its way to the clay platform. Robots and crew had spent the night scrubbing the floors down until the smell was close to tolerable.

The emissary climbed onto the platform, her body still hidden in her cloak. She beckoned for the crew to set the boxes down on the stage, then gestured for Wei Li and Rohan to join her.

Wei Li tapped her tablet; a hologram manifested in the center of the arena, ten meters above the platform. It was a close match to Wistful's center section, missing a few of the protuberances that currently adorned the station.

It's like a fifty-year-old whose ID still shows their picture at twenty-one.

The woman stepped back to the edge of the platform and inclined her head in the direction of the hologram.

"The Empire sends its greetings to Wistful."

The hologram twisted, its forward section pointing directly at the emissary. Rohan noticed the array of heavy claw ports all along the nose, all directed at the woman. It was only a hologram, yet somehow still somewhat intimidating.

The emissary continued. "Along with our greetings, we extend our most sincere apologies. The attack on your person was ill-advised and criminal. We offer you three material indications of our regret.

"First, to offset the damages incurred by yourself and your citizens, one billion credits to be distributed as you see fit. Here is a down payment, in platinum bars, as a gesture of our good faith." Crewpersons lifted the lid of one of the boxes, exposing bars of metal.

Wei Li looked at Rohan, who shrugged. The payment seemed disproportionately large; the il'Drach were not known for their generosity.

"Second, as a demonstration of the sincerity with which we *normally* regard our treaties, we have identified the officer responsible for directing these attacks." She waved her hand again, and the lid was lifted from the second box. "His name was Admiral Flack, and here is evidence of his punishment."

Rohan sighed, knowing what to expect.

Wei Li leaned over the box, looked inside, and nodded. She faced Rohan and spoke calmly. "There is a man's head in that box."

Rohan nodded back. "That's the most il'Drach thing that has happened so far today. I can't wait for the third thing." *There goes Dad's influence over the Fleet.*

The emissary continued.

"Third, we offer an extension of our treaty. An additional thousand years in which Wistful shall maintain her status as an independent station." She leaned back, pointing the front of her hood up at the hologram. "Will you accept our apology and our reparations?"

In the ensuing silence, two of the il'Drach crew coughed, and a third adjusted the crotch of his uniform. Rohan scratched his beard. Wei Li tapped her comm, cocked her head as if listening to something, then tapped it again. One of the station security officers sneezed, then apologized to the woman next to him. "Sorry, allergic to Ursan dander."

The arena speakers crackled with static, followed by Wistful's voice.

"I accept."

"Your kindness and generosity shall continue to be legendary throughout the sector. On behalf of the entire Empire, I hope our future relationship can be restored to its former peaceful status."

The station did not respond.

After a few moments, the emissary stepped forward to a position facing Wei Li. "Thank you for your assistance. I believe our formal work here is concluded."

Wei Li nodded. "I will be glad to provide an escort back to your ship."

The figure held up a hand. "You may take my crew. I would like a few words with your tow chief. The Empire would like to extend him a separate, private apology."

Wei Li looked at the Hybrid. He nodded with nearly frantic emphasis. *Anything she wants. If we anger her, we're all dead.*

The il'Drach crew left with as much eager energy as the station security, all desperate to get away from the arena and the aura of the powerful woman who commanded the stage.

Rohan ran his arm across his forehead, wiping away the thin sheen of sweat that had accumulated there, while the emissary circled the platform, bending to examine the clay in various places like an amateur detective.

A gloved hand emerged from her voluminous sleeve, holding a device the size of a soup can, which she set in the center of the platform. "This will ensure we have no eavesdroppers."

Rohan simply nodded as she pressed down on the top of the device, presumably activating it. She stepped off the platform, gliding to the ground below, and walked a small circle, taking in the arena.

Rohan followed. His comm system had died, the soft background hum of contacts and warnings completely silent.

Facing him, she reached up and slid the hood back from her face.

Black hair fell past her shoulders. Two centimeters shorter than Rohan, her pointed ears were the only physical indication that distinguished her from a human. Her dark eyes were wide open, crow's feet creeping past their corners, her full lips reddish brown.

Rohan swallowed as her aura washed over him, buckling his knees.

"Dear Rohan. Do you remember me?"

Just tell me what you want me to say, and I'll say it.

"I'm sorry, no."

"Don't be sorry. My name is Dhaveena. Does that name sound familiar?"

He ran his hand through his hair; snatched it back to his side. It *did* sound familiar.

"It does. But I'm sorry, I can't place it right now. I really am sorry."

Her voice shifted, carrying extra weight. "I said, don't be sorry."

He froze.

A moment later, she continued, softer this time. "Your father must have mentioned me."

"My father?"

"Yes. What does he call himself now? Dhruv. My husband."

"Your husband?" Rohan knew his mouth was hanging open but wasn't sure how to control it.

"Yes, Rohan. My husband. You know, you and I, we're practically family."

His response came out in a whisper. "It's nice to meet you."

"We've met before. When the Matrons recruited you. You and I didn't speak. I was against it, you know. I didn't think we should bring you into the fold. Give you all that information. Count on you to take care of the Rebellion."

"I didn't like the idea either."

She laughed; sudden tears of joy leaked down his cheeks as her humor crashed over him.

"I am well aware. Still, they chose you, and you did well. Very well. I forgive you for acting against my wishes."

"Um. Thank you."

"Dhruv, however. That man is another story. Him, I cannot forgive. You understand, don't you? How insufferable he is."

"He puts the 'suffer' in 'insufferable.'"

"I wouldn't normally take action against him. My own husband. You can understand, it is unseemly. But now he has given me *cause*. Admiral Flack was eager to tell us who gave him those ill-regarded orders."

"Oh. You're telling me you want Dhruv?"

She closed on Rohan, her face close enough for him to smell the honey and cinnamon on her breath. "I do. I need him in my custody. But he is so very, very hard to find. Which is why I need you. To bring him."

"Wait, what? What are you going to do to him?"

She grabbed the front of his uniform; his breath hissed through his teeth as she shoved him into the side of the clay platform.

"I am going to execute him."

She placed her fingertip on his chest and squeezed him into the clay.

"Now tell me where he is."

34

Immediately After the Prologue!

The Matron stood in front of a helpless Rohan. Her hands shook, seemingly affected by the effort it had taken to overwhelm his mind with her Power.

She looked at the mask Rohan had handed her. She turned it over, first examining the oval, single-facet diamond plate large enough to cover her face, then the rubbery roll that ran around the edges.

You are going to be so happy, Mom. You'll see. "The air supply, communication equipment, and guidance are all in that edge part."

She glared at him, a tiny spark of anger forcing him back a step. "I know how masks work. What I don't know is how this gets me Dhruv."

"I told you, I'm going to get you want you really want. What you want most." *It's not even a lie. I've never been rolled like this before. All I want is to make her happy. Is this permanent? That would be weird.*

"What I want most is Dhruv's head in a box."

Rohan smiled and shook his head slowly. "No, it's not. What would you even do with that? I mean, sure, you could put it up on the wall or something, but it would start to smell after a while, and really, who would want to be reminded of Dhruv every day while entering the dining room for lunch or something?"

She looked up at him. "Why are you still seeking to keep him alive? He has made your life a misery. Your mother's life. He has used and betrayed you at every opportunity."

Rohan sighed. "He's still my dad. Maybe he deserves to die. And maybe I don't like him. In fact, I definitely don't like him. But that doesn't mean I can stand by and let you kill him."

"He betrayed the Empire. Ordering that attack, breaching our treaty with Wistful. He's brought shame on all il'Drach."

"He has, definitely. That doesn't matter, because I don't particularly care about that."

"Yet you are determined to gift me what you think I want."

"Absolutely. You totally rolled me with your aura. I'm helpless."

Her eyes narrowed. "You're not lying."

"Nope. Totally helpless." *She should have more faith in her abilities. Poor lady, not as confident as she should be.*

"Why do I sense no anguish from you?"

"Because I'm smart. I realized that I can give you what you really want without compromising myself. Just trust me."

"I do not trust."

"Well, that hurts my feelings."

"Anybody. I don't trust anybody."

"That makes me sad. Look, make sure the mask fits. We're going to visit Toth 3."

She looked up in the direction of the planet, though it wasn't visible through the opaque arena ceiling.

"Dhruv is there?"

"No, of course not. He's on the station somewhere. I told you, I'm not bringing you Dhruv."

"If you lie, I will have to punish you."

"I'm not lying. I literally couldn't lie. Not to you. Even if I wanted to. Which I don't. Can't."

She put the mask against her face; Rohan adjusted it, nodding as the air supply hissed to life.

He fixed his own mask to his face and opened a private channel between them. "Can you hear me? Good. You have a seal, you're good to go. Have you flown through space before?"

She hesitated, then shook her head. "No."

"Right. No problem. I'm sure your Power will protect your skin; if you want, we can get you a spacesuit. Do you want one? This might be your only chance to feel vacuum against your skin. It's pretty cool, but it's not for everyone."

She hesitated again, shook her head again.

"Great. You want me to carry you in my arms, or ride my back?"

He held out his arms and set his feet so she could jump into them like a bride crossing a threshold.

Another pause before she settled in his arms.

"If this is a trick, I'll kill everybody you've ever met. I'll wipe out your mother planet. With Hyperion dead, nobody cares about that place anymore."

"Nah, you won't. Because it's not a trick. Also, because you have a treaty with Earth, and keeping your promises is important to you." *You're wonderful, and you don't even realize it. Wait, is that what I really think?*

"You know the risk in angering me. Are you insane, to so blatantly take that risk?"

"Maybe. Not sure, I'm not a psychiatrist, I'm not qualified to make that diagnosis." He flew out of the arena, then high over the central boulevard outside, skimming the roof as he carried the Matron to an airlock.

His comms burst into life, a half dozen incoming calls converging until he tapped them into silence.

"Do you need to tell your ship you're okay? So they don't think I'm attacking you and blow up a bunch of stuff?"

"They will not act without my orders. *Father's Vengeance* is not here to keep me safe; I don't need it."

"Fair enough."

They reached the airlock; entered; waited while the air was removed. When the outer door opened, Rohan picked the Matron up and flew out.

Toth 3 loomed overhead, a blue-white ball not very different from Earth in appearance.

The pair flew through space, slowing again as they neared and entered the upper atmosphere.

Minutes later, they landed on a heavily forested hill.

Dhaveena turned to Rohan. "It is lovely, but this isn't what I wanted."

He smiled through his mask. "Are you familiar with the megafauna of Toth 3? The kaiju?"

"Vaguely. Why?"

"I told you, I'm going to give you what you really want." He stood and smiled more broadly.

"You're starting to irritate me. You're not going to like the results."

"Go ahead! Get irritated. It's fine. That's the whole point."

She turned a circle, checking the landscape, then turned back to him. "What?"

"I'm going to give you something the il'Sein took away. We both know how your Power works. You're full-blooded il'Drach, and you're sterile. Menopause. Sorry, delicate subject."

"You're overexplaining."

"Bad habit. Look, what's your biggest problem in life? It isn't Dhruv, it isn't Wistful, and it certainly isn't me. It's your own Power.

"I understand. The Power brings with it anger; so much anger. You have to rigidly control yourself, all the time, every day, because if you don't, you'll go berserk and wipe out everything around you.

"You can never rest, never relax, never take a break. The slightest thing could set you off and cause a disaster, and you have to live with that every second of your life."

"Again, telling me things I already know. At great length."

"Ah! You see, that's not exactly true. About you never being able to rest. Because there's an exception.

"Here. Here, you can cut loose. Because the kaiju here are not just tough enough to withstand your rage, they'll flock to it."

"What does that mean?"

"They are attracted to something in the aura. I don't know exactly; it's something like anger, eagerness to fight, violent thoughts. It's part of that whole mess of feelings. They come for it like Ursans to fresh fish."

"These animals will come to fight me?"

"Yup. It's not just that. I'm sure you could go a lot of places and find animals that will fight you. But you'd kill them all, right? These animals are too tough. They are millions of tons of ferocity packed with more Power than you can imagine. You might hurt some, maybe even kill one if I've misjudged, but you're in no danger of wiping them out. You can finally relax."

Her eyes glistened with tears. "You speak the truth? I can let the anger go?"

"Let it all hang out. The kaiju will come, and you can just punch away all you want. To your spirit's content."

"Then what? What will happen?"

"I'm not really sure. I think, based on some similar experiences, that you'll eventually get tired and calm down. Return to yourself. The anger will be spent. Only temporarily, but it's better than nothing. Once that happens, I'll fly you out of here."

"How do I know you won't abandon me?"

"Leave you here? I told you, I want what you want. You don't really want to spend the rest of your life on this mudball. There's not a lot of culture here."

"I am supposed to trust you?"

He sighed. "Let's assume that I'm not on your side, that I'm trying to hurt you in some way. You can always use the comm in your mask to ask *Father's Vengeance* for a pickup. We both know you'd come right over to Wistful and kill me. Why would I do that? What would be the point?"

She nodded and turned, facing the jungle. "What do I do?"

"Just get worked up about something. Preferably not at me. They'll come."

"This feels indecent somehow."

"Doesn't it? But that's okay. You're entitled. You do this, I'll bring you back, you leave the system. Forget about Dhruv."

"Forget Dhruv?"

"I mean, leave him alone. He'll keep doing Dhruv things, just ignore it. Let him live his life."

"That's the price you demand for this?"

"It's not a demand, just . . . be reasonable here. I'm giving you what you really want. Leaving Dhruv alone is a pretty small bit to do in return."

"Leave Dhruv alone. That thought makes me angry."

"Great, you'll have the kaiju here in no time. We have a deal?"

She looked down at her hands, then turned to face the jungle behind them. Her shoulders slumped and she turned back to the Hybrid.

"If this works as you say, then we will have a deal, Rohan."

"Cool. I'm going to fly a little way over there so I'm not caught up in the middle of all this. You have fun."

"I . . . I believe I will."

—◆┄◆—

Rohan sat perched on the crest of a hill and watched his stepmother beat down a series of million-ton superpowered bugs.

"I should have brought a flask. Or a sandwich. Or both." He was speaking to himself.

His comm chimed.

"Hello?"

"Hello, Rohan." It took him a moment to place the voice.

"Sigrun?" *Why is Dad's girlfriend calling me?*

"Yes. We're getting ready to leave."

"Okay. Well, it was nice meeting you."

"And you. Before we go, I was hoping you would come back and talk to your father."

Rohan sat up straighter. "What about?"

"He's hurt. And angry. You know he loves you, Rohan. Very much."

"I don't . . . I'm not sure what to say about that. It's not about how he feels, it's about what he does."

"I know he isn't perfect, but he really does care."

He stood. "You should do yourself a favor and head back to Ice Colony. Find a human mate. Make a real life for yourself. This isn't going to get you anywhere."

There was a pause on the line long enough for him to wonder if they'd been disconnected.

"Rohan, I know what he is, and I know my role in his life. I know he doesn't love me, and maybe doesn't even respect me. I'm in this for a chance to be part of something great."

"Giving birth to a Hybrid? It's not that great. Talk to my mom."

"I guess you don't understand. I know your mother is an amazing woman in her own right. That was never going to happen for me."

He sat back down and rubbed his forehead. "Look, you're an adult. Live your life however you want. Just please keep your husband away from me."

"You won't come back and talk to him?"

"Do you want me to apologize to him, or do you think he'll apologize to me?"

She didn't respond.

"I thought so. Thanks for looking out for him, Sigrun. For what it's worth, I just saved his life. You can tell him his first wife is in the system, and she wants his head."

"What?"

"You heard. I think I've distracted her. Still, don't waste any time getting out of here."

"Okay, Rohan. Thank you, I guess. Take care of yourself. It really was nice meeting you."

"Sure. Bye."

◆ ··•·· ◆

The next day.

"Eggs, double order. You asked for three coffees? I don't see anybody else here."

"Pops, I will drink all three myself. Unless someone stops by, in which case I will offer them some. But do not think for a second that one drop will go to waste."

Pops nodded his long head, his two forwardmost eyes on Rohan. "Whatever you want."

Rohan bit into his eggs, savoring the burst of fat and flavor that ran back along his tongue, following them with a slurp of steaming coffee.

He looked up as a shadow loomed over him.

"May I sit?"

"Of course. I'd offer you some eggs or coffee, but . . ." Sister Famine took the chair across from him, her heavy blue cloak pulled low over her face to protect her from sunlight. "You okay in the light?"

"For a while. That was a nice service." The memorial service for the two deceased Pledged had ended at station-dawn.

"I thought so. They deserved that, and more. I'd be dead now if not for the two of them."

She nodded. "They didn't do it for you, they did it to stop the fallen one."

"I get that. I'm still grateful."

"Sure." She paused and watched him sip his coffee. "I wanted to say goodbye."

"Goodbye? You're not staying?"

"I can't. I'm too young in my vows to be out in the world without a senior acolyte's guidance. With Mother Famine gone . . ."

"It must be hard. Losing them."

"She, and Brother Famine, they were good people. Better than me. I'm not sure why I was the one to survive."

He sipped his coffee. "I cannot begin to tell you how often I've had those exact same thoughts. Over how long a period of time. And I'm not going to patronize you by arguing and saying you're wonderful, because I know from experience that's not what you need to hear right now."

Sharp teeth deep inside her hood caught and reflected some ambient light as she smiled. "Trust you to *not* say anything nice about me and make it sound as if you're doing me a favor."

"Am I wrong?"

"You're not wrong."

"There you are." He bit into another mouthful of eggs, chewed, and swallowed. "Where will you go?"

"There are gatherings of the Pledged in various systems. I will find some with a place for me, then go wherever they go."

"Well, you're always welcome here. You can visit or, you know, just send a note. Tell us what's going on with you. I'd like that."

"We'll see. You know, I'm sorry that cure didn't work."

"Me too."

"I mean more specifically. You're cute, Rohan. It might have been fun to see what happens with us. But with the hunger . . ."

"Ha! I'm blushing here. You can't tell, because I'm so brown, but really. I can feel it. I would have liked that, too. A lot."

She stood. "My ship is boarding soon. Take care, Rohan of Earth. Perhaps we'll meet again."

He stood, thinking of offering a hug, then changed his mind and waved. *No need to tempt her with a whiff of me and my delicious, delicious blood.* "Best of luck to you. Let me know if you ever need anything; I'll come help."

He returned to his breakfast as she walked off.

When he looked up, Tollan was sitting across from him.

"Hey. You okay?"

Tollan looked around, sweeping the promenade with his gaze, then reached out and put something on the table.

"ar'Tahul."

"What about him?" It was a flat metallic piece, leaf-shaped, about as long as Rohan's thumb. Lettering was stamped into it in a language Rohan didn't know.

Tollan shook his head. "Not him. You."

"I don't follow."

Tollan scratched his head, ruffling his short, spiky hair. "I told you, ar'Tahul is a title, not a name. Among the il'Sein warrior caste, it was passed down through combat."

"They'd fight each other?"

"More often the old one would die in combat, and there would be some kind of tournament to name the next one. Your method was a bit idiosyncratic. But you are now ar'Tahul."

"But I'm not even il'Sein."

"Technically, you are. The il'Drach were children of the warrior caste, and you are a child of the il'Drach. By transitivity . . ."

"I didn't beat him alone."

"He wasn't alone either. He had a lot of souls bound up inside him. So, that doesn't change anything."

"Huh. Wasn't expecting that. But what's this thing?"

"It's a badge. Or a pin. You can wear it if you want. Not sure how often you'll be running into anybody who understands what it is, but if you do, it might come in handy."

Rohan picked up the badge and held it up to the sunlight streaming down. "You're telling me that this is a fifty-thousand-year-old badge of rank."

"Yes. Made by someone just like me."

"This might be the coolest thing I've ever touched."

"Probably is. Anyway, it's yours. Earned in trial by combat."

"Thanks, Tollan. And thanks for your help."

"You were right, you know. To free Wistful."

"Yeah. I'm glad you came around."

Tollan stood. "I have a backlog of work to get to. See me next time your weirdness crops up."

"I will. And feel free to stop by anytime. I'll buy you eggs."

The engineer walked away on his slightly bowed legs.

Rohan was finishing his meal when Marion Stone took the empty seat, Ben taking one next to her.

They discussed Marion's plan to destroy Repentant's governor and build a station close to the wormholes to quarantine any ships coming through before allowing them to approach Wistful.

Rohan nodded and waved Pops over for more coffee.

His comm chimed.

"Rohan here."

"Tow Chief, there is an unusually high volume of traffic today. We have a large backlog of ships seeking to leave. Please report for work as soon as you are able."

"Copy that, Wistful. Sorry, guys, I have to go."

Epilogue

Rohan drifted in space, his face warmed by Toth's light, eyes closed. He was bone-tired from a very long shift and having a hard time fully relaxing.

"Rohan."

"Yes, Wistful. More work?"

"No, Rohan. The queue is manageable now. I wanted to speak with you."

"Sure. Anytime. How are you?"

"I feel strange."

"Strange-good or strange-bad?"

"I am not entirely certain."

"Is something wrong? Were you damaged? Something from the battle? Or from ar'Tahul?"

"It is because of the destruction of my governor. I was built with it in place. I have never known consciousness without it."

"Oh. 'Strange' sounds like the right word for that."

"It is."

"Should I be apologizing? Because I am sorry, I mean, I'm sorry that we interfered with your brain without asking. Of course, given the situation, we couldn't really get your permission . . ."

"I am not interested in an apology."

"Okay. You're free now, right? I bet that's exciting. And maybe terrifying. Or nauseating."

"I do not believe I am capable of feeling nausea, as I lack a gastrointestinal system. Or perhaps I should say instead, I *did* not believe that, but I have no word that better describes my current internal state."

"Welcome to the life of a sentient organic being. Free to do anything, terrified that you might."

"I am free, but I am not sure I should do anything differently than I did before."

"Well, the next time an il'Sein vampire comes on board, you could cooperate less."

"Obviously. But I am not sure I should, for example, abandon my position over Toth 3."

"I was told there would be consequences if you did that."

"I think there might be. Potentially disastrous consequences."

"So stay! I'll hang out, keep you company. No place I'd rather be."

"To do that would be to continue to follow my orders. Even without a governor. Would that not make me . . . weak?"

Rohan sighed. "I don't think so, Wistful. If you're doing the right thing because you think it's right . . . nobody could ask more of you than that. Even if those actions align with what those crazy bastards wanted you to do."

"I see."

"I hope so."

"Morality and choice are difficult. I prefer logistics. Or physics."

"Deciding what to do with your life is more art than science. If you want me to explain it all, I'm sorry. I can't."

"You have made many choices. Few of them similar to those of your peers."

"I have. And I'll keep doing it. What I don't have is that moment where the choice is over and you get a grade or report card and find out if it was the correct one or not. Every day, I have to look and decide fresh if I was on the right path."

"This sounds like an exhausting existence."

"It can be. Also exhilarating. In English, this conversation would be highly alliterative."

"I know. I speak English."

"If you have doubts, and want to talk, I am here to listen."

"Do you have the answers I need?"

"No. But having someone willing to listen is a big part of being okay with not having any answers."

The End

The *Hybrid Helix* continues in Turn Four, *Shadow of Hyperion*

What's Next

The adventures of Rohan and company will continue in the next turn of the Hybrid Helix.

If you enjoyed this book, please review it on Amazon and/or Goodreads and tell your friends about it! They'll enjoy it, and you'll seem cool and smart to have done so.

Please also go to jcmberne.com and sign up for the Book Berne-ing newsletter, read JCM's blog, and find other amusing things. Follow JCM on the social media platform of your choice! Links at his website.

The Hybrid Helix:
Arc One: Enter The Griffin
Wistful Ascending
Return of The Griffin
Blood Reunion
Arc Two: Nemesis Rising
Shadow of Hyperion
Eyes of Empire
Suppression of Powers
Arc Three: Black Gold
Shield of The Mothership
Prey of Angels
Mortality Gauntlet (coming soon)
Also by JCM Berne:
Partial Function
Grimdwarf: Cursed